Become our fan on Facebook **facebook.com/idwpublishing**
Follow us on Twitter **@idwpublishing**
Subscribe to us on YouTube **youtube.com/idwpublishing**
See what's new on Tumblr **tumblr.idwpublishing.com**
Check us out on Instagram **instagram.com/idwpublishing**

ISBN: 978-1-63140-750-5   19 18 17 16   1 2 3 4

COVER BY
MICHAEL STRIBLING

EDITED BY
JUSTIN EISINGER

EDITORIAL ASSISTANCE BY
LESLIE MANES AND
ALONZO SIMON

COLLECTION DESIGN BY
**RICHARD SHEINAUS/
GOTHAM**

PUBLISHED BY
TED ADAMS

Ted Adams, CEO & Publisher
Greg Goldstein, President & COO
Robbie Robbins, EVP/Sr. Graphic Artist
Chris Ryall, Chief Creative Officer/Editor-in-Chief
Laurie Windrow, SVP of Sales and Marketing
Matthew Ruzicka, CPA, Chief Financial Officer
Dirk Wood, VP of Marketing
Lorelei Bunjes, VP of Digital Services
Jeff Weber, VP of Licensing, Digital and Subsidiary Rights
Jerry Bennington, VP of New Product Development

For international rights, please contact licensing@idwpublishing.com

The X-Files created by Chris Carter.

FILES

ARCHIVES VOL. 3

GOBLINS page 1
by Charles Grant

GROUND ZERO page 161
by Kevin J. Anderson

based on the characters created by
Chris Carter

GOBLINS

By Charles Grant

ONE

The tavern was filled with ghosts that night.

Grady Pierce could feel them, but he didn't much care as long as the bartender kept pouring the drinks.

They were ghosts of the old days, when recruits, mostly draftees, were bused almost daily into Fort Dix for basic training, scared or strutting, and hustled out of their seats by drill instructors with hard faces and hard eyes who never spoke in less than a yell. The scared became terrified, and the strutters soon lost that smug look they wore—it was apparent from the moment they were shorn of their hair that this wasn't going to be a Technicolor, wide-screen John Wayne movie.

This was real.

This was the real Army.

And there was a damn good chance they were going someplace to die.

Grady ought to know; he had trained enough of them himself.

But that was the old days.

This was now, and what the hell—if the ghosts of the boys who never came back wanted to stand behind him and demand he teach them again and this time do it right, well, hell, that was what they did, no skin off his nose.

What he did these days was drink, and damned good at it he was.

He sat on his stool, bony shoulders hunched, hands clasped on the bar before him as if he were saying grace before taking up the glass. His face under the mostly gray brush cut was all angles, sharp and dark with shadows; he wore worn and stained fatigues loose at the waist, a too-large field jacket torn at one shoulder, scuffed hiking boots so thin he could feel pebbles beneath the soles.

From where he sat at the bar's far end, he could see the dozen scarred dark-wood tables, the half-dozen dark booths along the side wall, the twenty or so customers bent over their drinks. Usually the place was close to bedlam with top-of-the-voice, not always good-natured arguments about the Giants, the Phillies, the 76ers, the government. Waylon would be howling on the jukebox, a game on the TV hanging on the wall, and beneath it all the comforting clatter of balls over at the pool table, floating green in the light of the single lamp above it. There might even be a few working girls hanging out, joining in, not always looking for business.

Good thing, too, he thought with a quick grin; most of the gals these days were a little long in the tooth and short in the looks.

Tonight, however, was pretty damn miserable.

Rain all day, changing to a hard mist at sundown. The temperature had risen, too, slipping pockets of shifting fog into the alleys and gutters.

It was April, nearly May, but it felt a whole lot like November.

He glanced at his watch—just a few minutes past midnight—and rubbed his eyes with bony knuckles. Time he was having one for the road, then getting on that road while he could still find it.

He reached for the glass, one ice cube and Jack Daniel's halfway to the rim. He frowned and pulled his hand back. He could have sworn that that glass had been full a second ago.

Man, I'm worse than I thought.

He reached for it again.

"You sure about that?" Aaron Noel, who was more muscle than any man had a right to own and still be able to move, flipped a drying towel over his shoulder and leaned back against the shelf fronting the smoke-fogged mirror. His white T-shirt was tight, the sleeves cut off to give his upper arms some room. He was a younger man who looked as if he had lived one lifetime too many. "Not that I'm complaining, Grady, but I ain't taking you home tonight again, no offense."

Grady grinned. "You my old lady now?"

"Nope. But the weather sucks, right? And every time the weather sucks, you get the miseries, drink too much and pass out, and then I gotta lug your sorry ass to that sorry hole you call a house." He shook his head. "No way. Not tonight." He waggled his eyebrows. "Got a meeting when I'm done."

Grady glanced at the window by the exit. Past the neon he could see the mist, the dark street, the empty storefronts on the other side.

"So?" the bartender said, nodding toward the unfinished glass.

Grady straightened, yanked on an earlobe and pinched his cheeks. It was an old trick to see if he was numb enough yet to go home and sleep without having those damn dreams. He wasn't, but he wasn't drunk enough to defy a man who could break his back with his pinky, either.

If the truth be known, Noel was good for him. More than once over the past fifteen years, he had stopped Grady from getting into fights that would have easily turned him into one of his own ghosts. He didn't know why the guy cared; it had just turned out that way.

He considered the glass carefully, grimaced at the way his stomach lurched with acid, and said with a resigned sigh, "Ah, the hell with it."

Aaron approved.

Grady slipped off the stool and held onto the bar with his left hand while he waited for his balance to get it right. When he figured he could walk without looking like he was on a steamer in a hurricane, he saluted the bartender and dropped a bill beside the glass. "Catch you around," he said.

"Whatever," the bartender said. "Just get the hell home and get some sleep."

Grady reached into his hip pocket and pulled out a Yankees cap, snapped it open and jammed it onto his head, and made his way toward the door.

When he checked over his shoulder, Aaron was already talking with another guy at the bar.

"Good night, gentlemen," he said loudly, and stepped outside, laughing at the way some of them snapped their heads up, eyes wide, as if he'd just shaken them out of a nap.

As soon as the door closed behind him, the laughter twisted into a spasm of coughing, forcing him to lean against the brick wall until it passed.

"Jesus," he muttered, wiping his mouth with the back of a hand. "Quit drinking, quit smoking, you old fart, before they find you in the damn gutter."

He paused at the curb, then crossed over and moved on up the street, keeping close to the closed shops, the empty shops with plywood for windows, and decided as he did it that he'd finally had it with this burg. As the government kept chipping away at Dix's assignments, folks up and left, and nobody came in to take their place.

Hell, if he was going to drink himself to death, he might as well do it somewhere pretty, Florida or something, where at least it stays warm most of the damn year.

He hiccuped, spat on the sidewalk, and belched loudly.

On the other hand, he decided the same thing every damn night, and hadn't moved yet.

Goddamn Army.

Too old, pal, we don't need you anymore. Take your pension and split, you old fart.

He belched again, spat again, and seriously considered going back to Barney's, to have a farewell drink. That would shake them up, no question about it.

Half a block later he stopped, scowling at himself, and squinted down the street. The tarmac was a black mirror, streetlight and neon twisted and shimmering in the puddles. Nothing there but small shops and offices, a distant traffic light winking amber.

He looked behind him.

The street was deserted there, too.

Nothing moved but small patches of fog.

You're spooking yourself, bud; knock it off.

He rolled his shoulders, straightened his spine, and crossed to the other side. Two more blocks, a left, a right, and he'd be at the worn-down apartment complex where he had spent most of the years since his discharge.

He could find the damn thing blindfolded.

He glanced back again, thinking someone from the bar was following him.

The end of the block, and he turned around.

Damnit, there was someone back there. It wasn't so much the sound of footsteps as it was a presence. A feeling. The certainty that he wasn't alone. He knew that feeling well—it had almost driven him around the bend, over there in the jungle, knowing they were in the trees, watching, waiting, fingers on triggers.

"Hey!" he called, glad for the sound of his voice, wishing it didn't echo so much.

Nothing there.

Yes, there was.

Screw it, he thought, turning with a disgusted wave of his hand; I don't need the aggravation.

If it was another drunk, he didn't care; if it was some kid looking for a quick mugging, he didn't care about that either because he didn't have anything worth taking.

But by the end of the block he couldn't help it; he had to look.

Nothing.

Nothing at all.

A sudden breeze made him narrow his eyes as it sifted mist against his face, and when he did, he saw something move at the mouth of a narrow alley about thirty feet back.

"Hey, damnit!"

No one answered.

And that pissed him off.

Bad enough the Army had fucked him over, and bad enough he hadn't been able to leave this damn place and leave the ghosts behind, but he was not about to let some goddamn punk mess with his head.

He pulled his hands out of his pockets and marched back, breathing slowly, deeply, letting his anger build by degrees instead of exploding.

"Hey, you son of a bitch!"

No one answered.

Nothing moved.

By the time he reached the alley, he was in full-bore fighting mode, and he stood at the mouth, feet slightly apart, fists on his hips.

"You want to come outta there, buddy?"

A sigh; maybe the breeze, maybe not.

He couldn't see more than five feet in—three stories of brick on either side, a pair of dented trash cans on the left, scraps of paper on the ground, fluttering weakly as the breeze blew again.

He wasn't sure, but he thought the alley was a dead end, which meant the sucker wasn't going anywhere as long as he stood here. The question was, how far was he going to push this thing? How drunk was he?

He took one step in, and heard the breathing.

Slow, measured; someone was trying very hard not to be heard.

This didn't make sense. If whoever it was had hidden himself back there, Grady would have heard him moving around. Had to. There was too much crap on the ground, too much water. His own single step had sounded like a gunshot.

And the breathing sounded close.

"I ain't got time for this," he muttered, and turned.

And saw the arm reach out of the brick wall on his right.

The arm, and the hand with the blade.

He knew what it was; God knows he had used it himself dozens of times.

He also knew how sharp it was.

He almost didn't feel it sweep across his throat.

And he almost managed to make it to the street before his knees gave out and he fell against the wall, staring at the arm, at the hand, at the bayonet as he slid down, legs stretched out before him.

"Goddamn ghost," he whispered.

"Not quite," someone answered. "Not quite, old man."

That's when Grady felt the fire around his neck, and the warmth flowing over his chest, and the garbage beneath him, and the fog settling on his face.

That's when he saw the face of the thing that had killed him.

TWO

The afternoon was pleasantly warm, the sky a sharp and cloudless blue. The sounds of Thursday traffic were muted by the trees carrying their new leaves, although the cherry trees hadn't yet sprung all their blossoms. The tourists were few at the Jefferson Memorial, mostly older people with cameras around their necks or camcorders in their hands, moving slowly, taking their time. A handful of joggers followed the Tidal Basin rim; two paddle boats glided over the water, seemingly in a clumsy, not very earnest race.

That's why Fox Mulder preferred this place over the others when he wanted time to think. He could sit undisturbed on the steps, off to one side, without having to listen to terminally bored tour guides chattering like robots, or schoolkids laughing and horsing around, or any of the rest of the circus that Old Abe or the Washington Monument managed to attract.

His dark blue suit jacket was folded on the marble step beside him. His tie was pulled down and his collar unbuttoned. He looked much younger than his years, his face as yet unlined, his brown hair unruly in the light breeze that slipped over the water. Those who bothered to look in his direction figured, he supposed, that he was some kind of academic.

That was all right with him.

His sandwich was almost done, a plastic cup of soda just about empty, when he saw a tall man in a dark brown suit moving around the edge of the Basin, staring at those he passed as if expecting to discover someone he knew. Mulder looked quickly from side to side, but there was no way he could duck around the building or into the trees without being seen.

"Hey!" the man called, catching sight of him and waving.

Mulder smiled politely, but he didn't stand.

This was not what he needed on a great day like this. What he needed was his sandwich, his soda—although he'd prefer a cold beer in a bottle, preferably sitting in a booth at Ripley's, in Alexandria—and maybe that short brunette over there, taking slow tight circles on a pair of in-line skates, earphones attached to a Walkman at her waist. He supposed maintaining balance was a lot like being on ice skates; it seemed to be the same principle. Not that he was all that good when roller skates had wheels at the corners, spending, as he had done, more time on his rump than attaining great speeds.

The skater shifted suddenly, and he blinked, realizing for the first time how tan she was, and how snug her red satin shorts and red T-shirt were.

Then a shadow blocked his view.

It was the redhead.

"Mulder," the man said, standing two steps below him, grinning like an idiot, "where the hell have you been?"

"Right here, Hank."

Special Agent Hank Webber stared over Mulder's head at the daylit figure of Thomas Jefferson standing tall beneath the dome. A puzzled frown came and went. "Never did see this place, you know what I mean?" He shook his head, scratched through his dark red hair. "What do you want to come to a place like this for?"

Mulder shrugged. "It's nice. It's quiet." He deepened his voice. "It's not the office."

Webber didn't take the hint. "So, did you hear what came in?"

Mulder just looked at him.

"Oh." The younger man grinned sheepishly. "Sorry. Of course you wouldn't hear. You were here."

"Hank, your powers of deduction have never failed to give me a shiver." He smiled when the younger man sputtered, telling him with a gesture that it was only a stupid joke. Hank was a good man, but there were times when Mulder thought him dense as a post. "Hear what?"

"Helevito."

He sat up slowly, lunch momentarily forgotten. "What about him?"

"They got him."

He didn't know whether to laugh, cheer, shock the kid with a victory dance, or play it the Bureau way by simply nodding, as if the outcome of a three-month manhunt for a kidnapper had never been in doubt, especially since the kidnapped child had already been recovered safely. What he decided to do was take another bite of his sandwich.

Webber hooked a thumb in his belt. "Yep. Not two hours ago. You figured it right, Mulder. They staked out his cousin's place in Biloxi, and sure enough, he comes strolling in this morning all by his lonesome. Spent most of the night on one of those new riverboats, pissing away half the ransom money at roulette. Most of the rest evidently went to some blonde." He laughed and shook his head. "I heard the first thing he said was, 'I knew I should've played thirty-six and red.'"

He nodded.

Mulder took another bite, another sip, and waited.

"So." Webber squinted as he checked out the memorial again.

A quartet of nuns chattered past, smiling at him, smiling at Mulder.

The skater left, not even a glance in their direction.

Webber sniffed, and fussed with his tie. "So."

"Hank, I am eating my lunch. I am enjoying the fresh air, the sunshine… and I am especially enjoying the peace and quiet that comes with not being at the Bureau for a while. I'm not sure what you want me to say."

The younger man seemed bewildered. "But… but if it hadn't been for you, they never would've gotten him, right? I mean, nobody else figured out his gambling problem, right? Nobody else knew about that cousin. So…" He spread his hands. "So aren't you glad?"

"Overjoyed," he answered flatly.

And instantly regretted it when Webber's expression sagged into youthful disappointment. He knew the kid believed that every bust was righteous, every arrest an occasion for celebration, every crook large or small put behind bars a reason to dance. What he hadn't figured on was, between the first bust and the fourth and the fiftieth and the millionth, the exhilaration was always there. Always. And the feeling that finally one of the bad guys lost.

But the good agents, the best ones, never forgot that on the far side of that exhilaration there was always someone else waiting in line.

It never ended.

It just never ended.

That fact alone sometimes turned a perfectly good agent into a cynic who made mistakes. And it sometimes got him killed.

Mulder didn't want that to happen to him.

He had too much to do.

He had too much yet left undone.

On the other hand, he also hadn't finished his lunch, and there were still five other folders waiting on his desk in varying stages of investigation. He wasn't the primary agent on any of them, but he had been asked to take a look, to see if he could spot something the others had missed.

It was what he was good at; very good, if you paid attention to some of the talk around the office. Although he really didn't see it that way. It was, simply, what he did, and he had never really bothered to analyze it.

When the younger man finally looked as if he were either going to cry or scream, Mulder swallowed, touched his chin with a finger, and pointed. "If I remember, Hank, you were the one who came up with the Biloxi connection. We all missed it. You got it."

Webber blushed.

He couldn't believe it—the kid actually blushed, ducked his head, scuffed his shoe on the step. Mulder decided that if he said, "Aw, shucks," he would have to be killed.

"Thanks," he said instead, fighting hard not to grin. "That... well, that means a lot." He gestured vaguely. "I didn't mean to interrupt but..." He gestured again. "I thought you'd want to know."

"I did. Honestly. Thanks."

"So." Webber backed away, and almost toppled off the step. He laughed self-consciously, his right arm flapping. "So, I guess I'll get back, okay?"

"Sure."

"You'll be—"

Mulder held up what was left of the sandwich.

"Right. Sure." He waved, reached into his jacket pocket, pulled out a pair of sunglasses, and slipped them on.

Suddenly he wasn't a kid named Hank Webber anymore.

Suddenly he was a man in a suit too dark for the weather, wearing sunglasses too dark for the sun. Suddenly he wasn't a part of the scene anymore. If he had painted a sign on his back, he couldn't have said FBI any better.

Mulder smiled to himself as Webber walked off, practically marching, and washed the last of his lunch down with the soda. Then he glanced around, not really seeing anything, before hooking his jacket with a forefinger, draping it over his shoulder, and moving into the memorial itself.

He liked it in here, especially now, when there was no one else around. It didn't feel like a cathedral, the way Old Abe's place did, yet he was in awe just the same of the man who rose above him. Jefferson wasn't a god. He had his faults. But those faults only made his accomplishments all the more remarkable.

This was where he liked to work puzzles out, following crooked mental paths to see where they led, maybe hoping some of the third president's genius would rub off on him.

In here he couldn't hear the traffic, the tourists, nothing but the sound of his shoes on the polished marble floor.

What he had to consider today was a case in Louisiana that involved at least one brutal murder, one daylight robbery of $25,000, and witnesses who swore on every Bible handed to them that the person who had done it had vanished into thin air. In the middle of a circus tent. While wearing the costume of a hobo clown.

His instincts were usually pretty reliable. This time they suggested this had nothing to do with an X-File, those cases he specialized in, that had about them an air of the bizarre, the inexplicable.

The paranormal.

The kind of cases the Bureau officially frowned upon, but couldn't always ignore.

Which was why he had been shown this one. This kind of thing, whether the upper echelon liked it or not—and they usually didn't—was his specialty.

Louisiana just didn't have that X-File scent.

Still, there was always a chance he was wrong. It wouldn't be the first time. His usual partner, Dana Scully, had told him that so often, he had finally suggested she print up cards: *Mulder, this is an ordinary case, only with weird stuff; aliens, monsters, and UFOs need not apply.* Whenever he began to think that X the unknown was actually something they should look into, she was supposed to hand him a card, or staple it to his forehead, and get on with it.

She hadn't thought that very funny.

Except for the stapling part.

Still, he had been right often enough in the past, even if she was too stubborn to admit it.

What he was afraid of now, what always kept him alert, was that every case with supposed "weird stuff" in it would make him jump before he thought, and thus bring down the wrath of his superiors, forcing the X-File Section closed.

It had already happened once.

He didn't want it to happen again.

Especially when he had been so close to final proof that the Earth wasn't alone... so close....

Too close for some.

Others would call that paranoia; he called it simply watching his back. Not for the knife. For the razor.

The fact that he tended to elaborate on or improvise on the Bureau's standard operating procedures also hadn't made him many friends in high places.

That the Section had been reinstated was a stroke of good fortune, but he never gloated.

He did his job.

Looking.

Always looking.

Following the crooked path.

He wandered around to the back of the statue, tracing his fingers along the marble base.

What he wanted to do now was make sure that this Louisiana thing was weird stuff, nothing more.

He had to be sure that he wasn't so desperate that he saw only what he wanted to see, not what was really there.

Not so easy to do these days, when he had been so close.

So damn close.

He stepped back as he slipped into his jacket and looked up at the president, dark bronze and gleaming, towering above him.

"So what do you think?" he said quietly. "You bought the stupid place, is there anything out there?"

A hand gripped his shoulder.

When he tried to turn, the grip tightened, ordering him to stay where he was.

His throat dried instantly, but he did as he was bidden. He wasn't afraid, just wary. He lowered his head slowly to keep his neck from cramping.

The hand didn't move, nor did it relax its grip.

"Well?" he asked mildly.

Mint; he smelled an aftershave or cologne with a faint touch of mint, and the warmth of the sun on someone's clothes, as if he'd walked a long way to reach him. The hand was strong, but he couldn't see it without turning his head.

"Mr. Mulder." A smooth voice, not very deep.

He nodded. He was patient. Not often, however; both his temper and his temperament never had liked short leashes. He tried to adjust his shoulder, but the fingers wouldn't let him.

"Louisiana," the voice said, fading slightly, telling him the man had turned his head. "It's not what you hope, but you shouldn't ignore it."

"Mind if I ask who you are?" Still mild, still calm.

"Yes."

"Mind if I ask if—"

"Yes."

The grip tightened, pinching a nerve that made Mulder's eyes close briefly. He nodded, once. He understood—*keep your mouth shut, ask no questions, pay attention.*

Voices approached outside—children, for a change sounding respectful, not rowdy.

A car's horn blared.

"The fact, Mr. Mulder, that your Section has been reactivated does not mean there still aren't those who would like to make sure you stay out of their way.

Permanently." A shift of cloth, and the voice was closer, a harsh whisper in his left ear. "You're still not protected, Mr. Mulder, but you're not in chains, either. Remember that. You'll have to."

The grip tightened again, abruptly, just as the voices entered the memorial and turned to echoes. His eyes instantly filled with tears, and his knees buckled as he cried out softly. A lunge with his arm couldn't prevent his forehead from slamming against the pedestal as he went down. By the time his vision cleared, no more than a few seconds, he was kneeling, head down, and when he looked to his right, grimacing, the only person he saw was a little girl with an ice cream cone, braids, and a vivid blue jumper.

"Are you okay, Mister?" she asked, licking at the cone.

He touched his shoulder gingerly, swallowed a curse, and managed a nod while taking several deep breaths.

A woman appeared behind the girl, gently easing her away. "Sir, do you need help?"

He looked up at her and smiled. "Just felt a little dizzy, that's all." Bracing one hand against the pedestal got him to his feet. The woman and the girl, and about a dozen others, backed away warily as he moved. "Thanks," he said to the woman.

She nodded politely.

He stepped outside.

The breeze attacked his forelock, and he swiped at it absently. His shoulder stung, but he barely noticed it. What he did notice was the breath of ice across the back of his neck.

Whoever the man was, there had been no threats, but there had been no promises either.

And for the first time in a long time, he felt that tiny rush of excitement that told him the hunt was on again.

Not the hunt for the bad guys.

The hunt for the truth.

THREE

Corporal Frank Ulman was tired of lying in bed. His back was sore, his ass was sore, his legs were sore. The only thing that wasn't sore was his head, and he figured that would fall off if he had to count the holes in the ceiling one more time.

It was, no question about it, a lousy way to spend a Saturday night.

What made it worse was the fact that he was here because he had been stupid. Really stupid. All he had wanted last night was a quiet drink, pick up someone for the evening because his regular girl had to work, and wake up the next day without a hangover. No big deal. So he had wrangled a pass from the sarge, no sweat, put on his civies, and hitched a ride into Marville with a couple of half-bald Warrant Officers who spent the whole time bitching about the way the DoD couldn't make up its mind whether to close Dix down or not.

They had dropped him off at Barney's Tavern.

He went in and had his drink, passed a few words with the muscle-bound bartender, watched a couple of innings of Phillies baseball on the TV, and listened while the curiously noisy crowd gabbed about old Grady getting his throat slashed the weekend before.

It was a shame. He had kind of liked the old fart, had bought him a drink now and then, and enjoyed listening to his stories. Grady had called him "Sal," because, he said, Frankie looked like some old actor or something named Sal Mineo. After the first couple of times, Frankie hadn't bothered to correct him. If the old guy thought he looked like a movie star, it was no skin off his nose.

Now that Grady was dead, so was Sal.

Too bad.

Another drink, another inning, and he made his first mistake: He tried to pick up a woman sitting by herself at a table near the back. Not bad looking in the tavern's twilight, but he wasn't about to be fussy. Angie wasn't here, and he was. Just like always. It was a mistake because the bitch didn't want to be picked up, said so loudly when he persisted, and finally suggested that he perform a certain number of mind-boggling, and definitely unnatural, sexual acts upon himself on his way home to his momma.

His second mistake was dropping a twenty on the table in front of her and telling her to either put up or shut up, and don't forget the change.

His third mistake was not listening to that muscle-bound bartender, who told him to get his sorry ass out of his bar before the roof fell in.

Corporal Ulman, with too many boilermakers and a hell of an attitude under his belt, called the bartender a fag.

The next thing he knew he was in Walson, the Air Force hospital on post, getting stitched under the chin, getting a cast on his left arm, and getting a face-full of the sarge, who had been waiting for him when the cops brought him in.

Bed rest was the order, take these pills, stay out of trouble, don't come back.

All day he stared at the barracks ceiling, his left arm throbbing in a sling, his face a road map of yellow and purple bruises.

Nobody felt sorry for him.

The sarge had told him that when he got up the next day, he was going to be busted. Again.

So he figured he didn't have a whole hell of a lot to lose when he swung his legs over the side of the bed and waited for the dizziness to pass. He had to get out. Walk around a little. Get some fresh air. Maybe find a card game and tell a few stories of his own. Anything but count those damn holes again.

Clumsily he dressed in boots and fatigues, made it as far as the door before he felt the first ache, deep in his jawbone. It almost sent him back, but now it was a matter of pride. A busted arm, a few bruises, what kind of a soldier would he be if he let something like that keep him on his back?

He checked the second floor corridor and saw no one, heard nothing. Why should he? Everyone else was having a good time, bumping around Marville, Browns Mills, drinking themselves blind, getting laid, catching a flick.

The thought made him angry.

One goddamn lucky punch, one lousy mistake, and here he was, practically a cripple. And he wouldn't put it past one of the guys to call Angie and tell her everything.

Son of a bitch.

What he needed, he decided then, wasn't a card game, it was a drink. Something to calm him down, something to ease the pain.

He knew just where to get it.

Five minutes later, after slipping a cheap and slim flashlight into his hip pocket and dry-swallowing one of the pain pills the doc had given him, he was in and out of Howie Jacker's room, two pints of Southern Comfort tucked into his shirt. The jerk never learned to lock his locker, his loss, Frankie's gain.

Five minutes after that he was outside. Behind the brick barracks the woods began, and he slipped into them quickly, making his way along a well-worn path toward a clearing half a mile in. He'd been invited there last summer, a place reserved for those who wanted to drink, or whatever, alone, without the hassle of officially leaving the post.

Actually, the clearing was beyond the post's boundary, which meant that its users were technically AWOL.

Not that anybody cared.

One part of these damn woods was the same as another.

He took the first sip almost before the barracks lights were blocked by the trees, gasping at the hundred-proof sweetness, smacking his lips as the throbbing began to fade. This was a great idea, and beat counting holes all to hell and gone. He took another drink, tucked the pint into the sling, and pulled out the flash. The beam was narrow, but he only needed it to warn him of pine boughs and oak branches. The trail itself had been used so often, it was practically a ditch.

He moved quickly, glancing up now and then in hopes of seeing the stars or the moon. It wasn't that he was afraid of the woods. Not really. For a city boy, he had learned to take them or leave them.

What he didn't like was the voice the trees had.

When the breeze blew, there were whispers, like old men talking about him behind their hands; when the air was still, the leaves still moved, nudged by night things who stayed just out of reach of the narrow white beam.

He drank again.

The woods talked to him.

He stopped once and checked behind him, slashing the beam up the trail, seeing nothing but grey trunks and colorless underbrush.

He drank, walked, and cursed when he realized the first pint was already empty. He tossed the bottle aside angrily, took out the second one, and slipped it into the sling. Later; that one was for later.

The breeze kicked into a gust of strong wind, damp and cool.

The branches danced and whispered.

Okay, he thought, so maybe not such a hot idea after all. Maybe he should just go back, lay down, drink himself into a stupor and let the sarge do his worst in the morning.

His head ached, his arm ached, his jaw ached.

"Jesus," he muttered.

Another gust shoved him off the trail, the beam blurring across the ground, sparkling as it passed through pockets of mist.

Something moved, out there in the dark.

Something large.

Frankie swayed, wishing he hadn't drunk so much, wishing he hadn't taken those pills first.

His stomach felt on fire, and sweat had broken out across his brow and down his spine.

It wasn't warm at all.

The wind had turned cold.

He heard it again, something moving toward him, not bothering to mask its approach.

His first thought was *Jersey Devil*, and he giggled. Right. A real live monster in the middle of New Jersey. Right. Tell me another.

His stomach lurched.

He swallowed hard and hurried on, swerving around a bush whose thorns clawed at his legs. His broken arm burned now, too, and he cradled it with his free hand, sending the beam sideways, poking at the black without pushing it away.

When he collided with a sapling that threw him to the ground, he cried out, cursed, kicked himself awkwardly to his feet and demanded to know who the hell was out there, he was a sick man, he was lost, goddamnit, and he didn't need this shit.

The wind tugged at his hair, plucked at his shirt.

A drop of rain splattered on the tip of nose.

"Oh great," he muttered. "That's just fucking great."

Something in the trees overhead. Something in the dark just behind. He wiped his face with a forearm, used the flashlight like a lance as he found a clear path and broke into a slow trot. It wasn't the right trail, but it had to lead somewhere, and right now somewhere other than here was exactly where he wanted to be.

Stupid; he was stupid.

The sarge was going to kill him, Angie was going to kill him, and Howie would definitely kill him when he found his stash gone.

Something behind.

Something above.

Light rain slipped between the leaves, between the branches.

God, he thought, get me outta here.

He swerved easily around a gnarled oak, dodged the grasp of a cage of white birch. He couldn't hear anything but his own breathing now, and the wind, and the patter of the rain, but he couldn't stop running. Every step exploded in his arm, but he couldn't stop running, following the sweep and dart of the beam until he rounded a thicket and the ground was gone.

He yelled as he tumbled into a ditch, screamed when he landed on his arm, and blacked out until the pain brought him back.

Rain on his face, like the touch of spider legs.

He rolled onto his knees and hand, and threw up until his throat burned. Then he rocked back on his heels, amazed that the flashlight was still in his grip. He used it to check the ditch, saw it was barely three feet deep.

And there was a road.

"All right!"

Dizzy, swallowing rapidly, he staggered to his feet and looked back at the woods.

No way. No way. He would hike until someone found him, or he found a way back to the post. If it was an MP patrol, who cared? Anything was better than this. Even the sarge.

He slipped—crawled up the other side and onto the tarmac, took a deep breath, and began walking.

The ditch ended a few yards later, the trees closing in, not even leaving a shoulder.

It didn't take long before the pain finally reasserted itself and he had to stop, lean against a dead pine whose branches had been stripped off all the way to the top. There were several of them here, and he figured it was lightning, a quick fire; there was a lot of patches like this here in the Barrens.

"Okay," he said. "Okay, move your butt."

Maybe a drink.

One drink.

The rain was cold and the wind was cold and he was too cold for a spring night like this. He reached into the sling, and laughed when he pulled out the second pint, intact.

He unscrewed the cap and lifted the bottle in a toast to the sky.

He drank and licked his lips.

He lowered his head and saw the outline of a covered Jeep not fifty yards ahead, parked on the left.

He grinned, waved the flashlight, and started up the road, every few feet bracing himself against one of the trees. It wasn't the MPs, thank God. Probably somebody out to get a little with a townie. He laughed. A Jeep, while it was possible, was hardly the best way in the world.

He drank and waved the flashlight again.

The passenger door swung open, and he saw a woman's face. "Hey!" he called. Hiccuped. "Give a guy a lift?"

The woman's face disappeared.

He drank and grinned, stumbled, and reached out to catch himself on a trunk.

The wood was soft.

Too soft.

He yelped and jumped back, the bottle dropping from his hand.

He aimed the flashlight unsteadily, and saw the arm reach out of the bark.

He saw the blade.

He heard himself scream.

But he could only scream once.

FOUR

Mulder freely admitted to anyone who asked that his office, such as it was, seldom complied, strictly or otherwise, with regulations. While he knew where everything was, usually, it wasn't always where Bureau Section Heads decreed it ought to be. Controlled tornado was how one of his friends had put it; a hell of a mess was how he described it. Usually with a shrug. Always without apology. Nevertheless, despite the fact that it was in the basement of the J. Edgar Hoover Building, it served its purpose; and the fact that he still had it after all the waves he had made over previous X-File cases was, to more than a few, a minor miracle.

He sat there now, chair tilted back as he wadded up blank sheets of paper and tossed them toward a metal wastebasket set in front of a pair of brown metal file cabinets. "Toward" was the right word. "Into" would have been nicer, but that rarely happened.

Like visiting with Jefferson, it helped him think.

Today, it also helped him kill time while waiting to be summoned to his appointment with his new immediate superior, Arlen Douglas. The word on the floor was, the man, even though he was only in the slot temporarily, wasn't pleased with the success rate of his agents, and he was hunting for scalps.

Which was why the floor in front of his filing cabinets looked like a snowfield when Carl Barelli walked in, visitor's pass clipped to his sports jacket's breast pocket.

Mulder tossed, missed, swiveled his chair around and said, "Michael Jordan is safe for another season."

"Jordan retired last year."

Mulder rolled his eyes. "That's the trouble with you, Carl. You pay too much attention to details. It's the big picture you have to consider."

To his surprise, his old friend didn't respond. Instead, he wandered around the room, fingers drifting but touching nothing, glancing at without really seeing the charts and Most Wanted sheets, the notes and NASA posters taped and tacked to the wall.

He was a swarthy man with thick black hair and a classic Italian profile dented and scarred just enough to prevent him from being pretty. He was also a former semi-pro footballer who had all the heart and few of the major skills to make it in the NFL or Canada. Luckily, he had recognized the shortcomings before it was too late; now he wrote about the sport for the revitalized *New Jersey Chronicle*, and once every six weeks or so came down to Washington to check out the Redskins, or to see what Congress was up to with a recent flurry of sports safety legislation. While he was here, he always dropped in, looking for a free meal, or a long night of pub-crawling.

Mulder never asked how his friend always managed to get a pass without calling ahead; he had a feeling he didn't need to know the answer.

"So," Barelli said, finally lighting on a chair, kicking aside the paper balls as he stretched out his legs. He glanced through the doorway to the quiet flow of agents outside, then back at the walls.

"So," Mulder echoed.

"So where's Scully?"

"She took some time off. She went West someplace, to see friends, I think. She's too cheap to send me a postcard." A shrug with his eyebrows. "Today's Wednesday, the fifth, right? She'll be back on Monday."

"Too bad. I could've saved her."

Mulder smiled, but it wasn't wide, merely polite. Carl had been trying to get Scully out of the Bureau and into his love life, not necessarily in that order, ever since he had met her just over a year ago. Scully, although she claimed to be flattered by the attention, didn't think this was the guy who would, as she put it, light up her life.

Neither did Mulder.

While he liked Carl a lot, and they had good times together, the man was incorrigible and unrepentant when it came to chasing women. As far as Mulder was concerned, Scully was permanently out of bounds.

Barelli folded his hands over his stomach, pursed his lips, licked them, blew out a silent whistle.

"What?" Mulder was puzzled. No handshake, no raucous invitation to debauchery, no futile attempt to show him exactly how to shoot a basket. The established routine had been abandoned, and he didn't care for the way the man refused to meet his gaze.

The reporter shook himself elaborately, forced a smile, crossed his legs. "Sorry, pal. To be honest, I've had a pretty shitty week, all in all, and it sure ain't getting any better sitting in this place. When the hell are you going to get a room with a view?"

"I like it here. It's quiet."

"It's like a tomb is what it is."

Mulder didn't take the bait. "What's the problem, Carl?"

The man hesitated before clearing his throat. "You remember Frank Ulman?" Mulder wadded up another sheet. "No, I don't think so. Should I?"

"He was at my sister's a couple of Christmases ago. Skinny kid? Regular Army? He kept hitting on my cousin Angie, she kept shooting him down, and you decided to show him how to do it right."

Suddenly, as he threw the paper ball, he remembered the night, and the memory brought a smile. The kid, and he wasn't much more than that, had paraded around the Barellis' suburban North Jersey house in his dress uniform, desperately trying to find a woman who would be impressed by his bearing and ribbons. He was so eager, he was laughable, and Mulder had finally taken pity on him. Unfortunately, the heart-to-heart they had had in the rec room didn't take. Barelli's cousin's brother had had to be physically restrained from punching the guy into the new year.

"Yeah," he said, nodding. "Yeah."

The ball went in.

"Well, a couple, three months ago, he and Angie got together. Kind of serious, actually. I heard they were talking marriage and stuff."

Mulder's eyes widened. "Your cousin and that guy? Really? Why didn't her brother kill him?"

Barelli winced and looked away.

Oh shit, Mulder thought; open mouth, insert foot.

He abandoned his slouch for a posture more attentive. "Tell me."

"He was killed last weekend."

"Damn. Hey, I'm sorry, Carl. I didn't mean—"

Barelli waved him silent. "It's okay, don't sweat it, you couldn't have known." His smile was bitter. "Not exactly national news, you know?" Then he inhaled slowly. "The thing is, Mulder, he was stationed at Fort Dix, some kind of pissant clerical job, even though he thought he should have been something else. You know, glamorous? Green Berets, something like that. Anyway, he got himself into a fight at a bar in a nearby town, they call it Marville—"

"Over a woman, I'll bet."

"Yeah. Something like that. Anyway, he ended up at the base hospital Friday night, busted up some, and was supposed to stay in bed until Sunday. Frankie didn't want to stay in bed, apparently. He was found on a road just south of the post, on Sunday morning."

"How?"

Barelli swiped at something invisible on his shirtfront. "Somebody cut his throat."

Mulder closed his eyes briefly, both in sympathy and at the image. "Have they caught the one who did it?"

"No."

"Witnesses?"

The man snorted. "Oh yeah, right. In the middle of the night out in the middle of nowhere? Jesus, Mulder, gimme a break." Then he shrugged. "Yeah. Actually, there was one. A woman." He leaned forward, bracing his arms on his legs. "But Jesus, Mulder, she was hysterical and drunk and maybe doped up. You know what she said? She said the damn tree grew an arm and killed him."

\\\\\\\\\\\\\\\\\\\\\

Arlen Douglas could have been anywhere from his early forties to early six-ties. His perpetually tanned face was finely lined, his hair an aristocratic mix of brown and silver, and his figure one of someone who was in close to perfect shape. He sat behind his desk and took a single swipe at his tie before closing the manila folder that lay before him on the leather-trim blotter.

It hadn't taken him long to make the office his—framed photographs of his family on the desk, framed photographs of him and three presidents, a handful of movie stars, and a dozen senators on the walls. An American flag in a brass stand to the right. Behind him, a large window whose view of the city was cut off by pale beige blinds.

When his intercom buzzed, he touched a button, said, "Send him in, Miss Cort," and checked his tie again.

Special Agent Webber opened the door hesitantly, smiled, and stepped across the threshold. Another hesitation before he closed the door and marched to the desk.

Douglas prayed that the kid wouldn't salute him.

"You sent for me, sir?"

"Indeed I did, Hank." He tapped the folder. "A fine job your team did on that Helevito case. A very nice job indeed."

Webber beamed. "Thank you, sir. But it wasn't really my team, it was Agent Mulder's."

Douglas smiled without showing any teeth. "Of course. But it seems you came up with a vital piece of the puzzle, and exhibited some very fine inves-tigative techniques."

He waited while the young man did his best to contain his pleasure. This, he thought, was going to be a piece of cake.

"Tell me something, Hank, how did you like working with Fox Mulder?"

"Oh, boy," Webber said enthusiastically. "It was great. I mean, they teach you all that stuff at Quantico, but it doesn't really have anything to do with…" He stopped himself and frowned briefly. "What I mean, sir, isn't that Quantico doesn't do its job. Not at all. I mean—"

"I know what you mean," Douglas said, still smiling, hands now flat on the folder. "It doesn't come alive, does it, until you actually see it all in action."

"Yes, sir. Exactly."

Well, of course, it doesn't, you idiot, he thought. Someone was going to owe him big time for this. Real big time.

"And you found working with Mulder instructive?"

"Absolutely."

"By the book, everything in its place, nothing for anyone to be ashamed of?"

He knew the young man would falter, and he did, torn between his liking for Mulder and his loyalty to the Bureau. Douglas was well aware that Mulder used the book when he had to, and his own, rather unique experience when necessary. The problem was, that experience. Half the time, it seemed like nothing but hunches; the other half consisted of such wild speculation that Douglas was amazed the man had any arrest record at all.

He waved a dismissive hand. "Never mind, Hank. It's not really important." He slid his hands off the folder. "As I said, this is fine work. Thanks to you, we should have no trouble in court putting Helevito away for most of the rest of his life." The smile faded to an expression that was both an invitation to the inner circle and a warning against betrayed confidences. "But before you decide to make Mulder your hero, there's something you should know."

Webber frowned his puzzlement.

"And something I'd like you to do for me." The smile returned, this time with teeth. "A personal favor. One, I think, which will not hinder your advancement in the Bureau one iota."

\\\\\\\\\\\\\\\\\\\

Mulder wasn't sure what he was supposed to say next. He had already explained to Barelli as carefully as he could that he couldn't take on the case without authorization, or without a request from the local law enforcement agency, but the reporter refused to accept it. He kept insisting this was Mulder's kind of thing, right up his alley.

Weird stuff, Mulder thought sourly; famous throughout the whole damn world for weird stuff.

"It doesn't matter," he said, making sure Carl heard and saw the regret. "You said yourself the woman had been drinking. And was hysterical. As anyone very well might be who had witnessed something sudden and gruesome like that. Which is why, believe it or not, eyewitnesses aren't always the best way to pursue a case. Get three people at the scene of a violent crime like this, and I'll guarantee three different versions of what happened."

"Look, Fox, I know—"

Mulder held up a palm. "What I'm saying is, Carl, that this woman was obviously severely shaken up. Like I said, anyone would be, and—"

"Speak for yourself," a dry voice said from the doorway.

Barelli instantly leapt to his feet, a great, wolfish smile cracking his solemnity. "Dana! Darlin'!"

Mulder merely looked to the door. "You're back early."

Dana Scully made a face, tossed her purse at him and shrugged out of her light topcoat. "I got back last night. I got tired of looking at interstates. After a few days they're all the same—boring. And very exhausting."

She didn't look exhausted to him. Her light auburn hair was in place, her slightly rounded face clear of any hint of weariness, and her clothes—a ruffled blouse and wine-colored jacket with matching skirt—were impeccable.

As practically always.

"You look perfect," Barelli said, crossed the room and engulfed her in a hug.

"Hi, Carl." She accepted the hug for only a few seconds, then slipped out of it so deftly Mulder wanted to applaud.

He nodded toward his friend instead. "Carl has a problem, but I'm afraid we can't help him."

"Bullshit." Barelli laughed heartily. "You just need some convincing, that's all. And this is just the little lady who can do it."

Scully avoided another hug by catching the purse Mulder tossed back to her and, at the same time, preempting the other chair.

"So how was the trip?"

She took her time answering. "Nice. Very relaxing."

"You should have stayed the whole time."

"What, are you kidding?" Barelli folded his arms and leaned against the jamb. "You don't know that little lady very well, Mulder. Can't keep her mind off business for more than two hours at a time." His smile was seductive, he knew it, and he used it. "Which makes me glad to see you, Dana. Maybe you can talk this guy into giving a friend a hand."

Scully quickly glared at Mulder, who had already raised his hands to offer mock applause. Instead the right hand shot to scratch at the back of his head, while the left answered the perfectly timed ringing phone beside him.

He listened.

He watched Dana watching him.

He hung up and said, "Carl, I'm sorry, but I have to see the boss" as he rose and reached for his suit jacket. "Let Dana know where you're staying and I'll call you later."

"Mulder?" Dana frowned.

"No, don't worry, I'm not in trouble." He paused at the door. "I don't think I'm in trouble." He stepped over the threshold and looked over his shoulder. "How can I be in trouble? We just closed a big case."

FIVE

Diamond Street was barely wide enough for two lanes of traffic on its easy downward slope toward the Potomac River. Richly crowned hickory and maple lined the worn curbs, hiding for most of its length old and small, brick and clapboard homes with front lawns scarcely large enough for the name. At the top of the slope were a handful of businesses, spillovers from South Washington Street. On the west side was Ripley's, flanked on the left by a corner grocery, and on the right by a narrow three-story Victorian converted to a dress shop on the ground floor, law offices above. The bar's simple brick facade was deliberately no advertisement; all there was was a dark green padded door over which hung a scripted sign in red. No window large or small. It was a neighborhood bar, no outsiders or the outside need apply.

Mulder stepped in and immediately stripped off his coat, sighing a little, pushing a weary hand through his hair. To his left were a half-dozen small tables, already taken; to his right, a wall covered above dark wood wainscoting with film and old radio show posters framed in polished wood. As soon as his vision adjusted to the dim lighting, all except for the bar itself from short candles in amber chimneys on the tables and sconces on the walls, he moved slowly toward the back, down a narrow aisle created where the mahogany bar began. That was filled too, but the noise level was low.

Conversation, quiet laughter, a few nods and smiles in his direction.

When the bar ended, the room opened up into a large square, with more tables, and high-backed booths settled against the walls. There was no TV, no jukebox; the background music piped through hidden speakers was barely loud enough to register. Sometimes it was country, sometimes jazz, sometimes themes from films and Broadway shows. It all depended on the mood Stuff Felstead was in when he opened for lunch.

It didn't take Mulder long to recognize the soundtrack from *Alien*. Stuff had apparently seen him coming.

With a grin he swung left and dropped into the booth nearest the end of the bar, shifted, and sat with his back against the wall, one leg stretched out on the padded seat, his topcoat dumped on the other seat. Within seconds, a tall woman stood in front of him, in loose black slacks, puff-sleeved white blouse. Black Irish from head to toe—hair, eyes, fair skin, a faint suggestion of freckles across her upturned nose.

"Are you dead or drinking?"

He rolled his eyes and groaned. "Both, I think."

"Beer?"

He nodded.

She winked and drifted away.

He covered his eyes with his left hand, elbow propped on the table, and wondered if maybe he had slipped into some alternate time zone, some parallel universe.

All the signs were there: Arlen Douglas hadn't kept him waiting, but had personally ushered him into his office. Congratulations on the Helevito case were suspiciously effusive, as was praise for taking such good care of Hank Webber. Mulder hadn't had a chance to say a word save a murmur of thanks before the Section Head asked him what he thought about the disappearing clown.

"A trick, obviously."

"What makes you think so?"

"He's not the Invisible Man, sir. Nobody can snap his fingers and vanish."

"Intriguing, though, don't you think?"

He heard the warning bells immediately and did his best to avoid what he feared was coming, pointing out suspect witnesses, the very backdrop of the circus, incomplete preliminary reports from the local sheriff...

It didn't work.

He had one day to finish the Helevito paperwork, and then he was off to Louisiana over the weekend.

"Just up your alley, wouldn't you say, Agent Mulder?"

Mulder had wanted to say, "Up your alley, too. Sir." But a sudden attack of restraint kept him silent as he was handed a blue-tabbed case folder and ushered back out before he had a chance to continue his objections.

It wasn't until he'd returned to his empty office and flipped through the pages that he realized Scully wouldn't be going with him. Hank Webber would.

This wasn't right. Not that he didn't mind shepherding the younger man through the minefields of Bureau investigations; that was the least of his problems, and Webber was a personable, if somewhat overenthusiastic man.

What wasn't right was the smell of it. Right up his alley, the man had said. Weird stuff. But this wasn't weird at all; it was just nuts, and he wondered exactly who had asked for the FBI to join in what looked to be an obvious local matter.

Plus, let's not forget the man at the Memorial. Invisible as well, and all too real.

Not protected, but not chained.

Alice was right—curiouser and curiouser.

Parallel universe; it had to be.

"If it's that bad, maybe I'll bring hemlock for a chaser."

He opened his eyes and kept his expression bland as the waitress set a bottle of beer on the table, along with a plate filled with french fries. He pointed. "I didn't order those, Trudy."

"You haven't eaten."

Their aroma made his stomach growl, and she laughed silently when he reached for one and popped it into his mouth, hissing as it burned his tongue. Reluctantly, stiffly, he swung his leg back under the table and saw that a thick, all-the-trimmings hamburger had been buried beneath the fries. He looked at her sideways, and she winked again before heading across the room at a customer's call.

He didn't hide his interest. She was an attractive woman, a law student now at Georgetown, and they had dated a couple of times, nothing fancy, nothing hot. He enjoyed her and her company, although he couldn't always take her mothering. Tonight, however, it was right on target, and he ate as if he hadn't done so in a week, ordering a second burger before he'd finished the first. Taking his time. No hurry at all.

Because it was the middle of the week, the room didn't fill. The booths were taken first, and a handful of tables changed occupants once or twice as he watched them. Mostly younger people back here; the old-timers stuck to the stools where they were closer to what mattered.

A couple of times women seated close by would glance at him, glance away, glance back, but he didn't acknowledge them and so lost their interest. Two men in golf caps and cardigans argued quietly at a table with someone in a booth he couldn't see. A married couple dressed more for the theater than Ripley's fussed unhappily with kaiser roll sandwiches. A quartet of college kids tried to pick Trudy and the other two waitresses up.

A normal night.

In a parallel universe.

Oh, brother, he thought; maybe it's time I took a vacation.

\\\\\\\\\\\\\\\\\

A room whose walls weren't all the same color, mostly shadow now, mostly dark.

On the right-hand wall a dark-framed print, Gainesborough's *The Blue Boy*, fronted with non-reflective glass.

Against the left-hand wall, a bunk with a thin mattress, blanket and sheet drawn taut and folded in the military style. A footlocker at the head, closed, chipped and scarred.

A metal desk set perpendicular to the rear wall. On it two piles of paperback books, a stackable stereo system, a handful of compact discs. A yellow legal pad, with a ballpoint pen just off-center. A green-shaded lamp, softly lit. A swivel chair whose seat and back were comfortably padded.

In the far corner a club chair, with a standing brass lamp behind it, an end table beside it with a seashell ashtray.

The floor was concrete, uncarpeted save for a remnant throw in front of the chair.

A man in a long lab coat wandered around the room, poking at the books, the COs, scowling at the legal pad whose top sheet was blank, picking up the pen, stabbing the page lightly before dropping it again. Although he was only in his mid-forties, he had more scalp than hair, his face sharp angles without seeming harsh. When he straightened, he was tall, broad at the shoulders and chest, and broad at his stomach. He glanced around, his nose wrinkling at the faint stench of cigarette smoke and mildew, sweat and blood, and finally, with a satisfied nod, strode to a padded door in the wall. He opened it without hesitation and stepped up into a corridor whose ceiling lighting was contrast enough to force a squint as he checked through the round judas window before turning right and stepping up into the next room, itself dimly lighted.

"Ready?" A woman in white sat at a wall-long shelf on which was a series of monitors and keyboards, space for notebooks and pads, and two styrofoam cups of steaming coffee.

The shelf was set just beneath a window that looked through the ghost of the Blue Boy, down into the other room.

"Leonard, I asked if you were ready." Long blond hair pulled back and held back by a rubber band, feathered bangs on a high forehead.

Leonard Tymons, when he had first met her, thought Rosemary Elkhart quite attractive in a hard sort of way. After four years he hadn't changed his mind, but he had changed his plans for seduction and a brief affair. She indeed did have fair hair and fair skin, pale lips and pale blue eyes, but when he was alone he called her a black widow.

"Leonard, damnit."

He dropped into a wheeled chair beside her. "You saw."

She nodded toward a microphone attached to one of the computers. "For the record, okay? Let's remember the record."

He nodded. "For the record, everything is fine. Nothing has changed since last time. Jesus, can't we get anyone to clean that place right? It smells like a… a…" He shook his head in disgust. "Just get someone to scrub it down before next time."

"I will."

There was silence then as they worked at their keyboards, setting programs in motion, for the moment paying little attention to the diagrams and numbers that flashed across the screens.

Then Tymons reached out and flicked off the mike.

Rosemary looked at him oddly.

"We blew it, didn't we," he said matter-of-factly. A tilt of his head toward the glass. "We're not going to bring it off, are we?"

Her face hardened as if she were about to lose her temper, and for several seconds she refused to answer.

"Rosemary."

She sagged, and whispered, "Damn."

The soft hum of fans, the creak of his chair's wheels as he pushed away from the shelf desk and rubbed his face with both hands.

"Maybe," she said, "there's a way."

"Maybe," he answered, "there's a Santa Claus."

Her face hardened again, and she gestured him back to his position. "Santa Claus or not," she told him, "we will find a way." She glanced at him sideways. "If not, we'll just get another."

\\\\\\\\\\\\\\\\\

The music had changed to the muted soundtrack from *Damn Yankees* when Trudy Gaines slipped into the seat opposite Mulder, lit a cigarette, and brushed a strand of damp hair from her brow as she blew smoke at the ceiling. "One day, he's going to find everyone in here puddled on his precious floor."

Mulder raised an eyebrow. "You're warm?" He hadn't noticed.

She nodded, and even in the gloom he could see the lines, the shadows, that made her more her age. "I think I'm getting the flu or something."

He finished the last burger, picked up his second beer. "So take a day off."

"You pay my rent?"

"You give me that autographed *Thing From Another World* poster?"

"In your dreams, G-man. In your dreams."

The Golf Caps' argument grew louder. "Jesus," she muttered.

"What's up?" The person in the booth was still in shadow; all he could see was one arm, in a tweed, elbow-patched sleeve.

"The Redskins," she said in disgust.

He couldn't help a laugh. "What? May's just started, for God's sake."

She looked at him with one eye open. "It's always autumn when you're a Redskins fan, Mulder, don't you know that?"

One of the Golf Caps stood, his chair scraping back. Before anyone could move, a man in shirtsleeves, a white apron tied around his waist, appeared by the table. He was, Mulder thought, the perfect walking cadaver. Only the badly arthritic hands spoiled the image. Evidently the Golf Cap didn't think Stuff Felstead could do anything but glower. He was wrong. Ripley's owner said something so low only the other man could hear. It was enough. He sputtered, gestured placatingly, and by his expression suggested to his companion that they leave.

It was over in less than ten seconds.

"Magic," Trudy said, catching him staring.

"Probably. After all this time, I still don't see how he does it."

"Keep it that way," she advised him. "Believe me, you don't want to know." She set her palms flat on the table. "Well, break's over. Gotta finish up."

"Nice visiting with you, too," he said, sweeping up the last of the ketchup with the last french fry. "So what's the problem?"

She froze halfway out of the booth, avoiding his gaze, staring at the seatback behind him.

He waited.

Finally, she slumped back and shook her head. "It's silly."

"Probably."

"I feel like a jerk."

He reached out his hand and waggled it until she handed him his coat. "You're off in ten minutes, you've had another fight with your boyfriend, you have a tort quiz tomorrow, and you want a walk home in case he tries to hassle you."

She didn't blink. "You know, Mulder, sometimes you're damn weird."

He shrugged. "So they tell me."

"Fifteen minutes?"

"Sure. No problem."

A quick smile was her thanks as she returned to work, and fifteen minutes later she was back, heavy sweater over her arm. He paid at the register at the end of the bar and followed her to the street. His own apartment was a couple of blocks past King Street, closer to the Potomac; she lived the same distance in the opposite direction. He didn't mind. It was a nice night, a comfortable breeze, and Trudy spent most of the time complaining about her landlady in a way that, at one point, had him laughing so hard he tripped over a raised section of sidewalk.

He didn't fall. A quick, exaggerated turn kept his balance.

But not so quick that he didn't see the man in the tweed jacket strolling behind them a block away.

It didn't register at first because they had already reached her place, a renovated colonial divided into a half-dozen apartments, hidden beneath a clutch of oaks. She kissed his cheek quickly for thanks and hurried up the walk, fussing in her purse for the keys.

He didn't leave until the front door was open and she was inside.

Then he turned around and headed back the way they had come, hands in his pockets, whistling softly. His footsteps were loud. Traffic didn't exist. A dog raced silently across a sloped lawn to check him out, tail wagging, fangs bared. Mulder gave the animal a smile and walked on.

Checking the shadows for a shadow that didn't belong.

By the time he had crossed King Street again, he had begun to scold himself. After all, people had to live someplace, some of them actually lived in the same area he did, and the Tweed Man was probably one of them.

His own building was on a quiet residential street. Well-kept dark brick with a slight arch over the recessed entrance. Hedges that made the tiny lawn seem even smaller. As he slipped his keys out of his pocket, he began making a list of things he'd have to do in the morning, not the least of which would be to try to change Douglas's mind.

A disappearing murderous clown was not his idea of a good reason to see Louisiana.

By the time he reached the door he was already in bed; all he had to do was get his body settled in the same place.

He turned the lock and absently glanced over his shoulder.

The Tweed Man strolled by on the other side of the street, cigarette in one hand tracing orange in the dark, face hidden by a felt hat pulled low.

Weariness slowed Mulder's reaction. In the few seconds it took to convince himself he wasn't imagining it, the man was gone, lost in the shifting shadows between widely spaced streetlamps.

SIX

Dana Scully stood amid the clutter of Mulder's office and flapped her arms hopelessly. There were times when she admired the way he could find needles in haystacks and times like this, when she wanted nothing more than to put a match to it and force him to start from scratch. Which, she knew, wouldn't change a thing. Two days later it would look just the same.

Hefting her briefcase in one hand, she turned with a resigned sigh to the woman standing in the doorway and said, "Sorry, Bette, but I don't think it's here."

"Sure it is," the secretary said brightly. She crossed the room to a waist-high shelf built out of the wall, shoved a pile of papers aside and held up a blue-tagged folder. "I can smell 'em a mile away."

A cheery smile, and she was gone, leaving Scully openmouthed and slightly annoyed. She didn't mind cases being targeted to other teams; that was part of the game, and part of the procedure. And that particular case was, by FBI standards, so perfectly ordinary she was surprised Mulder hadn't pushed it on himself. What she did mind was the new Section Head's near-imperious refusal to give his reasons. If he wasn't happy with the way things were going, he simply changed teams. Fresh minds and fresh bodies was his only explanation.

"Hey."

Mulder came through the door, dropped his coat onto the back of his chair. "Listen, I've been thinking about that Louisiana thing."

Dana shook her head. "Mulder—"

He dropped into his chair, swiveled it around to face her, and tented his fingers beneath his chin. "Not that I think it's really going to be as bizarre as the mighty Douglas thinks it is, but I've been looking through the folder, see…" He reached over to the shelf without looking. "I think what they've got there is a—"

"Mulder—"

He frowned, kicked the chair around, and began slapping papers aside. "Damn, I swore I left it here last night. Maybe Webber took it. That guy's so gung-ho, he makes me nervous."

Dana closed her eyes briefly to summon patience, then tapped him on the shoulder. Hard. "Mulder, pay attention."

"What? What?" He didn't look around. "Maybe I filed it." He shuddered. "God, what a thought."

"It doesn't matter."

"Of course it matters. Do you think I'd actually…" He fell silent and slowly turned to look at her. "You have news."

With a look to the ceiling, she thought thank you before pushing a hand absently at her hair. "In the first place, I do not appreciate your leaving me alone with that human octopus. I swear to God he has hands growing out of his ears."

At least he had the grace to look contrite. "Sorry. Douglas had the appointment already set up. I had no choice."

When she heard what the Section Head had to say, she told him she had already been briefed. The man had caught her in the hall on the way to Mulder's office.

"But that doesn't make any difference right now."

He was startled. "What do you mean?"

"Table that for a minute. What I want from you now is your word that you'll never, ever leave me alone with that reporter again." She shuddered to prove her point. "I am a doctor, Mulder. I know secret doctor things. If I'm forced to, if he lays one more paw on me, I swear I'm going to make sure he never touches another woman again."

Mulder held up a hand. "Okay, okay. I didn't think he'd be that bad. Honest." He frowned. "I guess this thing about his cousin's boyfriend shook him up more than I thought."

Angrily she told him that was no excuse. It was perhaps understandable, but it was still no excuse. When he apologized again, she allowed herself a moment to calm down, then took the other chair and hauled her briefcase onto her lap.

"What's the other news?" he wanted to know, eyeing the case suspiciously.

"Good news and bad news, actually."

He stared at her for so long, she thought he hadn't heard. Then he slumped a little in resignation and gave her his full attention.

"The good news is, you don't have to go to Louisiana. You can't find the file because Bette took it back just a few minutes ago."

He barely reacted, little more than a blink.

"The other good news is, you're still stuck with me."

A lopsided smile flared and vanished. "The bad news is," he said dryly, "we're going to North Dakota, no bathrooms, and we have to live in a tent."

"Not quite." If it wasn't so infuriating, this whole thing would have been laughable. "Actually, it's New Jersey."

"What?"

She looked up without raising her head. "New Jersey."

He frowned his puzzlement. "Why New Jersey? What—" His eyes widened in dismay. "Oh, God, Scully, please, not the Invisible Man."

She unsnapped the briefcase flaps and pulled out a folder marked with a red tab, set the case on the floor and the folder on her lap. She flipped it open and picked up the top sheet. Only then did she nod, and waited patiently until he had stopped muttering to himself and grunted for her to continue.

"The—"

"Hold it," he said. "Wait a minute. What changed the mighty Douglas's mind? Yesterday it was disappearing clowns, today it's Claude Rains. I don't get it. Does he really think this is an X-File?"

Scully smiled. "I don't know. But it seems your friend has a friend."

"Carl? The sports reporter Carl?" He didn't believe it. "Carl Barelli has friends in high places?" He shook his head slowly; wonders never ceased.

"Not quite," she admitted. "Angie Tonero, his cousin, has a brother. The one who tried to dismember her soon-to-be boyfriend, remember? The brother's name is Major Joseph Tonero. Air Force. Temporarily attached to Medical. You'll never guess where he's currently stationed."

Mulder didn't bother. His expression was enough; he knew that McGuire Air Force Base was adjacent to Fort Dix. "And Major Tonero is… ?"

"Apparently, a very good, dear, close personal friend of the Garden State's junior United States senator, John Carmen."

Mulder clearly couldn't decide whether to be amused or angry, and at the moment she wasn't inclined to give him a hand. She only nodded when he said, "Whose office just happened to call the Director, right? Probably in the middle of the night. Probably causing the Director to be not all that happy, which means that when he called the mighty Douglas, our supposedly temporary Section Head lost a lot of sleep. Which, I suppose, means he's really pissed off."

"To put it mildly." She fussed with her skirt, her hair again. "Now, granted, we're not supposed to be at the beck and call of individual members of Congress, but there are budgets and there are appropriations. And the senator is a ranking member of a couple of pretty important committees."

"I love this town," Mulder groused.

She handed over the paper. "This is the report on Frank Ulman."

He took it; he didn't look at it until she stared him into it. When he was finished, no more than a cursory glance at best, she handed him the second one.

"So what's this?" he asked, barely giving it a glance as well. "A second opinion or something?"

"No. And if you'd just look instead of griping…"

He did as he was told as he gave her his best martyr's sigh, and she only just managed not to laugh when he sat up so quickly he nearly slid off the chair. "Scully..." He read the papers carefully, one hand pushing through his hair.

"Right," she said. "Two killings. One week apart. Saturday night, early Sunday morning. Each victim with a slashed throat, no other injuries, no indication of robbery or sexual assault. That wouldn't necessarily make them connected, except for the fact that now it seems there was a witness to the first murder too."

Mulder's lips moved as he read the second sheet more carefully. "Another Invisible Man?"

"Could be."

"Or the same one."

"Could be."

"This first guy"—he checked the report— "Pierce, he was drunk. So was the witness."

"No question."

He compared the reports again. "And the second witness, to Frank's murder, she was drunk, too. And... drugs?"

"That's right. Heroin."

She saw the look, saw the slight quickening of his movements.

"So..." He closed one eye, and his lips twitched into a faint smile. "So... maybe."

"Could be."

"Scully," he said, "I give up, all right? You've made your point about Barelli. Several times, in fact." He reached for the folder.

She shook her head. "Not yet."

The frown returned. "What is this? I'm being tortured because I wouldn't look at the slides of your trip? You want me to personally break Carl's arms?"

"No. It's just that there's... well... a tad more bad news."

"Tad?" He leaned forward. "You just said tad?"

"Hank, actually."

It took him a moment to figure it out, and dismiss it with a *no big deal, we can live with it* wave.

"And company," she added.

Someone knocked on the doorframe.

"What the hell does that mean, 'and company'?" he snapped. "Scully, what's going on, huh?"

She stood, pointed to the door, and said, "Fox Mulder, meet the company."

"Hi," said the tall blonde entering the office as Mulder stumbled to his feet. "I'm Licia Andrews. I'm really glad to meet you, Agent Mulder. Hank's told me so much about you."

"Hank?" Mulder echoed dumbly as he shook her hand.

Licia glanced at Dana. "Why, yes. Hank Webber. Didn't he tell you? We're partners. Sort of. We're going to New Jersey with you. Right, Agent Scully?"

"Oh, yes," Dana said, enjoying herself immensely, and not the least bit ashamed of it. "Absolutely."

\\\\\\\\\\\\\\\\\\

The view from the apex of the Delaware Memorial Bridge was probably spectacular—the Delaware Bay below, wooded shoreline upriver, the ocean to the right, the factories and plants that lined the banks on both sides. It probably was, but Barelli never saw it. He hated the height, hated the seagulls gloating at him from eye level, and his knuckles bled white every time he crossed it. Still, it was better than flying by a factor of ten.

And once on the north side, he aimed his battered yellow Taurus straight for the Turnpike, not wasting any time. Despite the call he had made even before he had seen Mulder, and despite the senator's reassurances that the family matter would be expedited, he didn't quite believe it.

Especially after what Dana had said.

After refusing, again, to succumb to his charms, she had coldly walked him to the hushed, vast lobby and had, for God's sake, patted his goddamn arm as if he were a kid.

"Stick to sports, Carl," she'd said. "I'm sorry about the corporal, but use your head, okay?"

He'd been so mad, he'd barely been able to kiss and hug her goodbye.

Stick to sports.

Who the hell did she think she was, Sherlock Holmes in a skirt?

Besides, he was not a sports reporter. He was a reporter whose interests happened to lie in sports. There was a difference, and he was going to prove it.

Fifteen minutes later he was speeding north on the Turnpike, through a speckled twilight rapidly slipping into dusk, ignoring the press of the forest on either side, or the late-hunting hawks that drifted patiently above the dense scrub oak and twisted pine that made up the Pine Barrens. He ignored the speed limit as well, keeping to the left of the two lanes, pushing seventy. The Yankees on the radio. Wind from the open passenger window stirring scraps of paper and crumpled tissues on the back seat and floor. A cigarette in his left hand.

Goddamn bitch. He wondered why he wasted his time, and smiled mirthlessly at the all too obvious answer—she wouldn't give in. He admired that. Hell, he admired her. And one of these days she would learn to admire him.

Soon.

It would be soon.

Although he wasn't exactly a national figure, his byline in this state carried with it no little recognition. He figured he could trade on that once he reached Marville, wherever the hell that was. It sounded like, and most likely was, a two-bit town that leeched off Fort Dix and McGuire. A celebrity like him should find loose tongues easily. A few drinks, a few questions, a few slaps on the back and a couple of knowing winks, and effing Fox Mulder could kiss this reporter's ass.

Besides which, Ulman had practically been family. The last time he had seen Angie, her eyes had been so puffed from crying she could barely see.

Nobody, but nobody, did that to his people.

In fact, with a little luck, he might catch the creep alone, the one who did Frankie in.

He smiled again as he switched on his head-lamps.

The smile didn't last.

He couldn't hold it.

All he could hold was the steering wheel, and the idea that Carl Barelli wasn't going to be deterred by some freak with a knife. He knew others saw him as soft, too long at the desk. Too often for them, those others found out different.

Don't worry, Angie, he promised to the early night; *you hang in there, kid, Cousin Carl is on the job.*

\\\\\\\\\\\\\\\\\

Dana had never liked the way moonlight and headlight bleached the land of its color. There was never any real white, only black and shades of grey, and the things that moved between them.

Graveyard time.

She reached for her left ear and pinched the lobe, just sharply enough to hurt and wake her up. She had thought, had hoped, she would be done with long-distance driving for a while, but Mulder had insisted there was no sense waiting until tomorrow. They might as well get their act together and the show on the road so they'd be ready to work first thing Friday morning.

That wasn't so bad, actually. He had volunteered to do all the driving, brought the coffee and some sandwiches, and had somehow convinced Webber that he ought to drive on alone with Andrews, get to know her, let her get to know him. Partners, he had lectured solemnly and truthfully, had to be able to predict each other's reactions so backs could be guarded and missteps minimized when the action got hot. What he had failed to tell them was that the action hardly ever got hot, except in the movies.

Unless, of course, the partner was Fox Mulder.

Licia hadn't minded; Webber, to Scully's amazement, had actually seemed flustered .

Now she figured them to be fifteen minutes ahead, their first assignment to book rooms in a motel called the Royal Baron, a recommendation Mulder had picked up from a visiting agent stationed in Philadelphia.

There was no question it would be as horrid as it sounded. Mulder was an expert at picking such places. He called it a knack; she knew it was a curse.

"You okay?" He glanced over. "You can sleep if you want."

"Mulder, it isn't even nine. If I sleep now, I'll be awake at dawn." She watched him for a moment, then reached over and turned down the heater. The night was chilly, but it wasn't that cold. "What's the matter?"

He shrugged. "Nothing."

"This breaking into pairs isn't your style."

"Maybe, but four agents driving into a place called Marville would be like a parade, don't you think?"

"And two cars with agents isn't?"

He said nothing.

A mile passed, black and grey, before she repeated her earlier question. "And don't jive me, Mulder, I'm not in the mood."

He laughed silently. "Good lord. First 'tad,' now 'jive.' What the hell did you do on that vacation?"

"I didn't change the subject every time I was asked a question."

He drove on, thumb tapping lightly on the wheel. "I had a visitor the other day."

She listened as he told her about the man at the Jefferson Memorial, not saying a word. At one point she pulled her coat closer across her neck; when he had finished she had folded her arms across her stomach. She didn't doubt that the meeting had occurred, but she had never been able to fully accept his absolute belief in extraterrestrial life, or his notion that there were those in the government, and those seemingly beyond the government's reach, who were just as convinced, and were as dangerous to him as any murderer they had ever sought.

Add to that the equally bizarre idea that among those Shadow People, as he called them, there were also a handful who were actually on his side, and in any other human being she would see a full-blown case of whatever lay beyond extreme paranoia.

In Mulder, however, it almost seemed plausible.

All right, she admitted; maybe more than "almost."

The Tweed Man, on the other hand, was more likely a coincidence, nothing more, and when she said so, he only grunted. Not entirely convinced, but with no solid reason to think otherwise.

"So what does this case mean to… whoever?" she said, staring out at the dark by her shoulder. "And what does it have to do with Louisiana?"

"Beats me. I'm not a psychic."

She shifted. "Mulder, weird stuff, remember?"

He tapped his forehead. "Got it stapled right here."

She caught the grin and held her silence until the silence made her sleepy. Then: "So what does it mean to you?"

"I don't know. Well, yes, I do. It means we have two people dead, and there'll probably be more." A glance, a quick smile. "That's all, Scully, that's all."

She nodded her approval, even though she knew there was no question he was lying.

SEVEN

The Royal Baron Motel was a long, white and red, two-story stucco building facing the two-lane county road that led into Marville. On the west side was the office, whose spotlighted top was supposedly a bejeweled gold crown; on the east was a restaurant; between them were two dozen rooms, twelve up and twelve down, with a red iron stairway in the center and at each end.

Behind it, and across the road, there was nothing but dense forest.

The restaurant—booths along the windows, round tables at the far end, and a long counter—was called the Queen's Inn.

Exhausted, Mulder slumped by the window in a red leatherette booth, still feeling as if he were on something that moved and had no intention of stopping. His head throbbed, his vision blurred now and then, and all he really wanted was to crawl into bed and forget the world existed for a while. Webber and Andrews, however, had been waiting in the office, rooms already booked, just as he and Scully had pulled up. Despite his protestations, he was dragged off for something to eat.

They were the only customers in the room; the young waitress spent her time dusting gleaming tables and whispering to the cook through the serving gap in the back wall.

He didn't order anything—the very thought of food made his stomach lurch—but when the orders arrived, he had to admit that the plate of silver dollar pancakes Webber had in front of him actually smelled pretty good.

"That bacon's going to kill you," Scully said dryly, nodding to the double side order beside Webber's plate.

"My guilty pleasure," Webber told her with a boyish grin, and poured what Mulder figured was at least a gallon of syrup over the heavily buttered stack.

Scully watched in amazement. "Never mind."

Andrews had contented herself with a cup of soup, her lean face etched with weariness, her topcoat buttoned all the way to her chin.

Outside the window, a breeze danced with a handful of dead leaves, guiding them onto the road where they were scattered by a passing car.

"So are we going to check it out tonight?" Webber wanted to know.

Mulder looked at him blankly. "What?"

The agent pointed over Mulder's shoulder with his loaded fork, then yanked it back when syrup began to drip on the table. "Marville. Are we going to check it out tonight?"

He shook his head. "Not until morning. Then the first thing we have to do is introduce ourselves to the local chief, let him know we're here."

Webber nodded. "Hawks."

Mulder blinked.

"Hawks," Webber repeated. "Todd Hawks. The Chief of Police. That's who he is."

"Ah."

Webber glanced at his partner, but her attention was on the empty road, and stifling a fierce yawn with her hand. "Didn't you read the file? I mean, it's all in there. About him. Hawks, I mean."

A gust shimmered the window.

Andrews shivered, but she didn't look away.

"Fox?"

"Mulder." He pushed a hand back through his hair. "Don't call me Fox. Mulder is fine."

Webber nodded once, correction noted and filed, it won't happen again.

This kid, Mulder thought wearily, is going to drive me up the wall.

And since he knows the drill full well, he must either be too excited, too eager, or he's scared. That wouldn't be surprising. So far, the young man's field work had been primarily confined to the immediate DC area. Now he was out here, no convenient home office to run to, working with a guy supposed to be more than a little off-center.

That almost, but not quite, made him feel better.

Andrews finished her soup, yawned, and stretched her arms stiffly over her head, clasping her hands and popping her knuckles. "God," she said huskily. "God." The topcoat did nothing to mask her figure.

Mulder felt Scully's shoe poke his ankle, so he figured he must have been staring, even though nothing had registered. That more than anything convinced him it was time to stop being sociable and make his good nights. What he hadn't counted on, however, was Webber trying to save the Bureau a buck by booking only two rooms, one for the ladies, one for the men.

As he unlocked the door and staggered in, tossing his small suitcase on the nearest bed, he said, "If you snore, Hank, I'm going to have to shoot you."

Webber laughed nervously, swore he slept like a baby, and laughed again while he unpacked, toiletries neatly arranged in the bathroom, fresh suit hung on the clothesrack by the bathroom door, the rest put away in the second drawer of a low dresser that stretched halfway along the left-hand wall.

Mulder was too tired to watch the ritual; he'd take care of his own things in the morning. He washed, he undressed, he was in bed and sleeping within ten minutes, ignoring the soft voice of the news on the TV.

He dreamed.

of a room not quite fully dark, outlines of bedroom furniture, outline of a window where the moon crept around the curtains;

a cool night and all the voices that go with it, from soft whispering leaves to the call of tree frogs and crickets;

a faint rumbling, but he knew he didn't live near the tracks, knew it wasn't a train;

louder, and the light around the curtains brightened to a glare, spearing suddenly into the room, shifting, slants and darts stabbing across the walls, the bed and the figure that lay on it, the ceiling, as if its source was spinning slowly outside the window;

frightened

he was frightened, standing by the door, slowly dropping into a crouch;

too frightened to move when the light became too bright and the rumbling too loud and the figure on the bed rose and tossed the coverlet aside, her young face colorless, her young eyes wide not with fear but with intent;

he wanted to stop her, but he couldn't stop dropping, couldn't stop himself from trying to push backward through the wall to get away from the light that exploded into the room, making him scream as the girl child was taken and swallowed by the white.

making him scream.

Making him gasp and sit up, crushing his pillow against his chest, blinking sweat from his eyes, sheet and blanket kicked away from his legs.

When he thought he could move without falling over, he sat on the edge of the mattress and put the pillow against the headboard. A forced shudder, a hard swallow, and he pushed himself to his feet, padding around a cheap table beneath its hanging lamp to the thin drapes on the room's only window. He parted them and looked out, and saw nothing but the road and the trees ranged beyond.

He couldn't see the stars, but he knew they were there.

Behind him, Webber snored lightly.

Oh, boy, he thought; oh, brother.

He wiped his face with a forearm and moved quietly into the bathroom, closed the door, but didn't turn on the light. He knew what he could see—a man forever haunted by the disappearance of his sister, Samantha, when both of them had been children. The dream tried to tell him how. Maybe it was true, maybe it wasn't. It didn't make any difference.

Dream or not, it was what kept him going.

He splashed water on his face to sluice away the tears he hadn't noticed, before, dried himself, and returned to bed.

He didn't look at his watch, but he didn't think it was much beyond midnight. A truck rumbled by.

When he slept this time, he didn't think he dreamed.

\\\\\\\\\\\\\\\\\

"Dana?"

Scully grunted to tell Licia she was awake, and to tell her she was also trying her best to get to sleep, whatever it was, it could wait until morning.

"Is there something... is there something wrong with Mulder I should know about?"

The voice out of the dark was naturally husky, almost masculine; she had already seen its effect on Webber and Mulder, and wondered how well Licia knew how to use it. It could be a devastating weapon, no question about it. She smiled at the ceiling—*when used for Good, not Evil.*

"Dana?"

She sighed loudly and rolled onto her side. "No. He's fine."

"He sure seemed out of it."

"It's the beginning."

"The what?"

Scully wasn't sure how to explain; after all this time, she barely understood it herself.

"At the start of every case that really catches his attention, he gets... hyper. Charged up." To say the least, she added silently. "Then, unfortunately, he has to get where the case is. He doesn't like that, the traveling. In fact, he hates it. It's valuable time wasted when he... we could be doing our job. So whenever he gets there, all that initial energy has been expended on the trip. So he crashes."

Silence for a moment before: "Will he be all right in the morning?"

She frowned her puzzlement. Concern was understandable for someone who hadn't worked with Mulder before, but she thought she detected something more in the woman's voice. Her eyes closed, half in a prayer that Andrews wasn't going to screw things up by developing a crush.

"He'll be fine," she answered at last.

"Good."

She said nothing.

The woman's voice faded as she rolled over. "I'd hate to have my first real case screwed all to hell."

Scully almost sat up to demand an explanation and, in the process, an apology. It was natural for someone like Andrews to want to shine first time out. God knows, she had prayed for it herself a hundred times before that first one. In fact, it had made her a nervous wreck. But not only didn't Andrews seem nervous, she seemed almost too calm, too ready. And that could be just as bad.

Or, she thought, I could be overreacting because I'm so damn tired.

A truck growled by.

She yawned, and tucked the covers up under her chin.

"Dana?"

This time Licia's voice sounded very small, very young.

"I'm listening."

"Do you think I'll have to use my gun?"

The corner of her mouth pulled back. "Hardly ever, Licia, believe me."

"Really?"

"Yes." She paused. "The government's too cheap to buy us all that ammunition."

Silence again, while she thought, dear Lord, I'm starting to sound like Mulder.

Then Andrews giggled, laughed, and said, "I guess I've been watching too many movies." The rustle of sheets was followed by, "Good night. And thanks."

"You're welcome, and good night."

Another truck drove by, this one in the opposite direction. Scully listened to the engine until she couldn't hear it anymore, using the fading grumble to pull her into sleep.

Her last thought was of Mulder.

She hoped he wasn't dreaming.

EIGHT

The blue of the previous day turned to thickening overcast shortly after Friday's dawn. By the time Mulder and his team were on the road, Webber driving, a chill easterly wind had begun to coast down the road, sweeping leaves and brown pine needles in front of the car.

Mulder didn't like it; it looked too much like late autumn.

Marville itself began a quarter of a mile from the motel, with a handful of houses squatting in clearings hacked out of the Barrens on either side of the road. Sandy, pebbled soil served as shoulders, and showed as bare spots on lawns looking as tired as the houses themselves.

He sensed right away the little town was dying.

The commercial district was five short blocks long, some of the businesses spilling around the corners. None of the buildings were more than three stories tall, mostly wood, a few with weather-stained stone or brick facades. He counted six that were for rent, and far too many whose display windows had been boarded up with plywood or painted a dead white. A narrow banner sagged over Main Street, announcing the community's 150th anniversary, which made him wonder, as he often did, what had caused this place to attract settlers in the beginning. There was no river, the trees weren't lumber quality, and Fort Dix hadn't been established until 1917, neighboring McGuire Air Force Base some time later.

Webber snapped his fingers, and jerked a thumb to his left. "Barney's Tavern."

Mulder spotted the corner bar, one of several still operating on the street, and supposed that, whatever the reason for Marville's founding, its eventual life support must have been traffic from the post and Air Force base. And solid support as well, from the looks of things. He could see, behind the faded paint and needed repairs, a town that had done quite well for the time that it had had, especially considering what must have been the fierce competition from other towns around it.

A stolid granite bank anchored the next corner, on the left. The shops here were still very much in business, or as much as they were going to get with the economy the way it was, and the Army post drastically cut back over the past several years.

"This is depressing," Andrews said from the back seat. "How could anyone live here?"

"Cheap housing, for one thing," Webber supposed, slowing to allow a trio of old women to make their way across the street. "It's not near very much. I remember the map, but I don't think you can commute all the way to Philadelphia from here easily. Not and make any money."

Inertia, Mulder suspected, was the rest of the answer. No place to go when you can barely afford to live here. Anyone asked would probably give a different answer, but it no doubt boiled down to, "Why bother?"

"There," Scully said, the first time she'd spoken since breakfast.

A single-story, long white clapboard building took a third of the block on the right. A new, gold-lettered sign in front marked it as the police station; an American flag drooped from a flagpole next to the double-door entrance.

Webber pulled into a space in front, rubbed his hands eagerly, and fairly leapt from the car, hustling around to open the rear door for Andrews.

Mulder moved more deliberately, waiting until Scully joined him. They didn't speak, just exchanged quick are you ready glances and started up the concrete walk. Andrews wanted to know why they had to start here since the senator's connections were with Fort Dix and the Air Force.

Scully averted her face from a mild gust. "Let's just say it's usually a little easier dealing with civilians."

"Their loss," said Webber brightly.

Mulder looked at him, looked at Scully, and pulled open the door, allowing the others to precede him into an open room that took up the entire front third of the building. A waist-high wood rail stretched from wall to wall, and just left of its center gate a uniformed dispatcher sat at her radio, scribbling in a logbook; behind her were three metal desks, none of which were occupied.

To the gate's right a fourth, much larger desk faced the entrance. Behind it was a policeman whose uniform, Mulder reckoned, had been tailored for him ten years and twenty pounds ago. His face belonged to a man who spent most of his time outdoors, and a lot of that time drinking. His hair was brush-cut, and at one time had been red.

Mulder took out his wallet and held up his ID. "FBI, Sergeant, good morning." He spoke politely, with well-practiced due deference. He introduced the others quickly. "We're here to see Chief Hawks."

Sergeant Nilssen wasn't visibly impressed. He said nothing, just pushed away from his work and took his time walking to an unmarked door in the rear wall. Mulder saw the puzzlement in Webber's expression, the outrage in Andrews's. "It's their turf," he reminded them quietly. "They didn't ask for us, remember?"

"Still," Webber answered.

Mulder had neither the time nor the inclination for a quick lesson on the politics of competing law enforcement agencies. He kept his attention on the sergeant, who stood in the open doorway, one hand on a cocked hip, the other trying to scratch the small of his back, then his nape. Beefy, maybe, but not very soft. A glance at the dispatcher, who stared back at him without apology. She was in her late twenties, evidently enamored of heavy makeup and the way her wavy brown hair puffed down to her shoulders.

When she finally nodded a greeting, he nodded politely back.

"Slow day?" Scully asked her, looking around the empty room.

She shrugged—her name tag read Vincent—and waved one hand. "Guys are on the road." A faint smile. "Rush hour, you know?"

Scully chuckled as the woman coughed lightly into a fist.

"Poison ivy?" Mulder said, nodding at the blotches of white lotion on the back of her hand. "I hate that stuff."

Vincent made a face in agreement. "Yeah, I got it—"

"Hey."

The sergeant beckoned with a crooked finger.

Webber stiffened, but Scully touched his arm as Mulder led the way through the gate, smiling, always smiling, thanking the sergeant as he stepped aside to let the others precede him.

Nilssen didn't smile back. After an expressionless, just shy of openly rude once-over, he returned to his desk, leaving Mulder to make the introductions again, this time to Todd Hawks.

\\\\\\\\\\\\\\\\\\

The Marville chief was younger than Mulder expected, not much older than his mid-forties, thick black hair brushed straight back from a widow's peak that pointed at where his heavy eyebrows nearly met across the bridge of a slightly hooked nose. He did not wear a uniform, nor did he wear a tie. White shirt and black trousers, their matching jacket on an antler coat rack in the corner.

His desk was battleship gray, just like the others, the only personal touch a silver-frame triptych Mulder noted held pictures of what must be his wife and three children.

Hawks rose and shook their hands, waving Scully and Andrews to the only other chairs in the room. Webber chose to lean against the wall near the door, arms folded casually across his chest.

The chief picked up a sheet of paper, glanced at it, and frowned. "I have to tell you, Agent Mulder, this fax your man Webber sent kind of took me by surprise. I wasn't expecting any feds to get involved." He let the paper drop, glanced at the closed door, and fingered a pen in his breast pocket. "To tell you the truth, though, I think I'm glad to see you. This shit's a little deep for me and my people, and those—" He stopped, lowered himself back into his chair and picked up a pencil he rapped on the desktop. "The gentlemen from Dix aren't really much on letting us hick boys in on much of anything, even though the corporal wasn't killed on post." He used the eraser to scratch at his temple. "Technically, the Ulman murder is ours. Try to tell them that, though."

Mulder gave him the perfect *us against them* smile. "That's what we're here for, Chief. We're going to need all the assistance we can get, and we'd definitely appreciate all you can tell us."

"No problem." Hawks, like his sergeant, wasn't awed, but not for the same reasons. "You just let me know what you need, I'll do what I can." The pencil tapped as his expression darkened. "The thing is, I didn't know that corporal at all. Grady Pierce, though, he was a royal pain in the ass, but I could think of a couple dozen guys I'd rather see take it the way he did. The poor son of a bitch."

"Friend of yours?" Webber asked from the back of the room.

Hawks looked around Mulder at him, shaking his head. "Not really, no. Just known him a long time. Retired drill instructor, wife left him right after the service forced him out." He looked back at Mulder. "He had no skills to speak of except bending his elbow, and AC."

Andrews, who had been sitting stiffly in her chair, distaste clear in the set of her lips, said, "AC?"

"Atlantic City, Agent Andrews," the man explained.

"Oh." Distaste became disdain. "Gambling."

Hawks didn't blink; he only nodded.

"So you think it was a gambling debt or something?" Webber asked, dropping his arms, eagerness creeping into his voice. "Pierce, I mean?"

"Not hardly. When he went, he mostly won." He grinned. "Nicely supplemented his retirement pay, which wasn't a hell of a lot." He opened the center drawer and pulled out a folder. "This is pretty much what we've got on both men, Agent Mulder." He handed it over. "You can see it isn't much, even after two weeks with Grady." He shook his head and shrugged. "The trail's probably dead, if you'll excuse the expression. You're welcome to it, though."

Mulder nodded his thanks and handed it to Scully, who flipped through it and frowned. "I don't see any body diagrams in this autopsy report. Just photographs, and not much commentary."

Hawks scowled. "You'll have to ask them on the post about that. It seems they cared as much about old Grady as we did."

Well, well, Mulder thought. No love lost between Marville and Fort Dix. He wondered if that extended to the merchants as well.

Scully held a sheet of paper closer to her eyes, frowning in confusion. "What's this say here in the margins? Gablin? Goblin?"

Mulder looked at her quickly. "Goblin?"

"Go see Sam Junis," the chief suggested as she slapped the folder shut. "He's the local doc, did the work on both men. He scribbles a lot, half the time nobody can read it but him. He lives in the first house west of where you're staying. He knows you'll be dropping in."

"How did you know where we were staying?" Andrews demanded. Mulder didn't turn, but he hoped the chief wouldn't take offense.

"Miss," Hawks answered with a lazy smile, "you maybe have noticed we're not exactly the metropolitan Washington area around here. And this time of year, Babs out there at the motel doesn't get hardly any business except on weekends, and not much even then. Hell, if you want, I'll even tell you what you had for breakfast."

"What?" Webber asked, as if the chief were a magician about to reveal an ancient secret.

Hawks looked at Mulder—Is this one for real?—and stood. "You're the redhead, so you had more pancakes than you ought to, gonna need a new notch on that belt, son, before long. Agent Scully had toast and coffee, bran cereal, orange juice. Agent Andrews had tea, toast, corn flakes. And you,

Agent Mulder, had toast, bacon, two eggs over medium, coffee, orange juice, and blueberry jam."

Mulder grinned his appreciation as the chief came around the desk and ushered them to the door.

"And I suppose you know what side of the bed I slept on?" Andrews asked coldly.

"Beats the shit out of me, Miss," he said. "Damn drapes were closed too tight."

Mulder couldn't help it; he turned away and laughed as the chief asked them to wait outside while he cleared a couple of things up before taking them down to the first crime scene. Although it looked as if Andrews was about to object, Mulder agreed immediately and shook the man's hand, thanking him again for his cooperation. Then he herded the team into the outer office, nodded to the sergeant—the dispatcher was gone, replaced by a man who stared at them, bewildered—and didn't stop again until he was on the front walk, but unfortunately, not before Andrews made a deliberately loud comment to Hank about the "insufferable hicks in this damn burg." Mulder, hands in his open topcoat pockets, looked up the street, seeking patience and inspiration, and a way to heed Scully's silent warning not to lose his temper.

"Look," he finally told them, "we have to work with these people, you understand? We need them on our side so we can do our job and get back to Washington as quickly as we can. I don't care what you think of them personally," he said to Licia, "but you keep your comments to yourself from now on, understood?"

She hesitated before nodding, and he made a note to have Scully Dutch uncle her later.

Webber, chastened even though he hadn't been the one scolded, cleared his throat. "Uh, Mulder? Who's Babs?"

Mulder nodded toward the far end of town. "Babs Radnor. She's the owner of the motel."

Webber frowned. "How did you know that?"

Without looking at Scully, he said, "Spooky, Hank. I'm just damn spooky," turned and pointed to a brick-faced diner across the street. 'We'll meet there about one for lunch, okay?" He told Hank and Andrews to canvass the area around Barney's, talk to everyone they could find about the dead men, the bar's reputation, the night of the murder, anything at all that might yield them information the reports hadn't told them.

Webber almost saluted as he led his partner off, leaning close, whispering urgently.

"Hello," Mulder said quietly as Scully came up beside him. "My name is Agent Webber, FBI. Tell me all you know or I'll smile you to death."

She slapped his arm lightly. "Give him a break, Mulder, okay? He's not all that bad."

He agreed. "But it's not him I'm worried about."

He looked at the sky, at the lowering clouds, and smelled the first hint of rain as the wind strengthened, snapping the tired banner, scattering debris in the gutters. At that moment, nothing moved on the street.

No pedestrians, no cars, not even a stray dog or cat.

"Ghost town," Scully said.

"Graveyard," he answered.

NINE

They walked east along Main Street, Mulder on the outside. The deserted moment had passed, and shoppers, not many, drifted in and out of stores, while automobiles and pickups made their way between the traffic lights. Few bothered to look at him and Scully, and those who did smiled faintly and moved on.

A breeze drifted down the sidewalk, picking up strength, flapping his open topcoat against his legs, slipping an unpleasant chill inside his suit.

Scully followed the meandering progress of a mongrel along the curb. "Did you notice how he changed? Hawks, I mean?"

He nodded. "Cop for us, hick for Licia. The man's no dope. I'm actually a little surprised he didn't ask for help right away. As far as I can tell, when they need a detective, he's it. And what's with Andrews, anyway?"

She shrugged. "First case jitters?"

He supposed it could be, but he didn't like it. Like the assignment of this case, it just didn't feel right. He didn't doubt she was competent; she wouldn't have gotten this far otherwise. Something, however, would have to be done about that superior attitude she had taken in the station. Behavior like that would shut Hawks up faster than a judge's order.

As Barney's slipped by them on the far side, he glanced over and saw, as before, nothing special. A tired bar in a tired town. Pick it up and put it down in Michigan or Oregon, it wouldn't change. And immediately he thought it, he realized he had probably made a big mistake, letting her go with Webber. The man had a knack for getting people to talk to him. That face, that grin, that shock of red hair was disarming. He hoped it would be enough to offset Licia Andrews.

The morning light dimmed.

The scent of rain grew stronger.

From the corner of his vision he watched Scully tracing the probable path Grady Pierce had taken, leaving the bar, making his way at some point across the street, maybe weaving, maybe not. An empty street. Light rain.

"He didn't see anybody," he said as they approached the alley. It was set between a pair of three-story brick buildings, clothing stores on the ground floor in both, what looked to be apartments above.

Scully didn't question him. "Or he didn't notice."

"That late, in this town? On a Saturday night? It may not be very healthy, but it isn't dead yet. He would have noticed. Especially if it was raining."

Again Scully didn't argue. She only said, "Unless he knew him."

A sideways glance: "Sexist comment, Scully. I am offended."

"Impersonal pronoun, Mulder. I am unbiased. So far."

Just as they reached their destination, a gleaming white patrol car pulled in at the curb, facing in the wrong direction. Chief Hawks slid out, jacket and tie in place, hair barely touched by the breeze now a wind. As he came around the trunk, he was greeted by several pedestrians, and he responded in kind, calling each by name. He slipped a hand into a pocket as he joined them, pushing the suit jacket behind his arm.

Mulder saw the shoulder holster.

The chief shivered, rolling his shoulders against the damp. "Are you sure about this?"

"I know it's old," Mulder answered, "but it's always better than reading about it in a report."

"Visualization," Scully added.

Hawks nodded understanding. "So…?"

The alley was a few inches wider than six feet, extending another twenty yards to a twelve-foot-high, weather-stained stockade fence. Although there were no garbage cans or a Dumpster, there were small fluttering islands of wind-deposited trash against the base of the walls. There were no windows.

There were no fire escapes. The yellow crime scene ribbon had long since been taken down.

They stood on the sidewalk, forcing what foot traffic there was to walk behind them.

The stores on either side had SALE signs in their windows, but the one on the right was dark, nothing on display. Above, the windows were all curtained or blind with shades.

Somebody died here, Mulder thought; some poor guy bled to death here.

It was time to walk the crooked path.

Hawks pointed: "Grady was found there, a couple of feet in, sitting against the wall. Even with the rain, it looked like he took a shower in his own blood."

Mulder took a single step in and hunkered down, looking at the spot, looking over and up at the wall. He saw no evidence of the dying, but he could sense it here just the same.

Scully stood behind him. "He was killed where?"

Hawks walked around them and stood about a yard from Mulder. "The way the blood trail was—and again, remember it was raining—it looked like he was cut here, took a step or two, maybe trying to get to the street, and ended up there, where Agent Mulder is." He moved aside when Scully took his place. "The thing is, those streetlights don't reach in very far. A couple of feet at most, and I'll bet he wasn't seeing all that clearly."

"Mulder?"

He rose slowly, watching her turn until her back was against the right-hand wall.

"The killer was standing about here."

Hawks frowned. "How do you know that?"

"The autopsy report," she said, gaze constantly shifting, examining the ground, the opposite wall, the ground again. "If your Doc Junis is right, he'd have to be. Can I borrow your pen?"

The chief, looking for and not getting a reaction from Mulder, handed her a ballpoint, which she held in her right hand as if it were a knife, not for stabbing but for cutting.

"The photographs weren't all that clear," she continued, almost as though she were talking to herself. "But look ..." She gestured until Hawks stood with his back to the street, then stood in front of him and, before he could move, whipped the pen through the air at his throat.

He jumped.

Her apology was a sardonic smile. "No blood on the walls. It was a single slash, very strong, cutting jugular and carotid. There wouldn't have been a gusher, so to speak, but some significant blood would have hit the walls if he'd been facing in or out." She handed the pen back. "There was none." She pointed in. "And there wasn't any back there, either."

"Rain," the chief reminded her. "And it was at least an hour before he was found."

She nodded. "But the trail, even after all that time, seemed pretty clear, at least from the pictures." She looked up, squinting, using her chin to show the chief the opposing roofs' slight overhang, bulging with sagging copper gutters; it may have been raining, but only a downpour and strong wind would have made the alley as soaked as the street. Then she looked at Mulder. "He was facing the wall."

And that, Mulder knew, was a hell of a thing.

If Scully was right, Grady Pierce would have had to have been damn near blind not to see his attacker.

Unless the attacker was invisible.

"No," she said to the look on his face. "There's another explanation, Mulder."

He didn't respond. He walked carefully, slowly, to the back and poked a finger at the fence. The wood was spongy with rot, and there were no marks on or in it to indicate anyone had climbed over. Or had tried to.

So the killer had left the way he had come in.

"Pierce must have known him," Scully said as he rejoined them.

Hawks agreed. "The way it looks, there's no other reasonable explanation." He sniffed, laughed, hitched at his belt. "Unless you believe Elly."

"The witness," Mulder said.

"If you want to call her that. I wouldn't bet my life on it, though." He led them back to the sidewalk. "See, Elly is what we call in our small town, scientific jargon, a fruitcake." He laughed again, shaking his head. "She's a dear, Elly Lang is, but she has this theory."

"Which is?"

"Oh, no. I'm not going to spoil it. This is something you have to hear firsthand."

\\\\\\\\\\\\\\\\

The first floor apartment was nearly as dark as the approaching storm.

A single lamp with a saffron chimney on a tilted end table lit only that part of the love seat where Elly Lang sat. Hawks stood in the living room entrance, his back to the tiny foyer; he leaned casually against the wall, hands loose in his pockets. Scully sat in a Queen Ann wingback that smelled of must and mildew. Mulder was on a padded footstool, leaning forward, hands clasped on his knees.

A small room, a Pullman kitchenette at the end of a short hall, a bathroom, a bedroom barely large enough for the single bed and a dresser missing two of its five drawers. Framed prints on the papered walls; a false fireplace with no logs; a jumbled collection of plastic and ceramic horses on the mantel; a fringed carpet worn through in places, only the ghosts of its original colors left behind. The bay window was covered with yellowed flocked curtains tattered along the edges and at the bottom. No television; only a small, portable clock radio on the end table beneath the lamp.

Elly Lang wore discolored, thick-soled nurse's shoes, argyle socks rolled down to mid-shin, and a simple brown dress without a belt or trim. There was no telling how old she was. In the lamplight she could have been ancient—no lower teeth, collapsed cheeks, strings of dirty white hair untrapped by a hair net. No makeup at all. She kept her hands primly folded in her lap, no rings or watch.

But Mulder watched her eyes. They weren't old at all, and of an odd pale grey that made them appear almost transparent.

"Goblin," she said with a sharp nod, and a *don't you dare contradict me* glare at the chief.

Mulder nodded. "Okay."

She closed one eye partway as she regarded him suspiciously. "I said goblin."

He nodded again.

"Okay."

"They live in the woods, you know." Her voice was low, harsh, the rasp of a childhood Halloween witch. "Came when the army did, back in '16, '17, I don't remember, just before I was born." She straightened her spine, and she faded, leaving only the shine of her eyes, the bloodless line of her lips. "Things happen sometimes, and they don't like it."

"What things?" he asked patiently.

"I wouldn't know. I ain't a goblin."

He smiled, just barely, and just barely, she smiled back.

"Miss Lang—"

"Ms.," she instructed. "I ain't blind. I read the papers."

"I'm sorry. Ms. Lang. What my partner and I need to know is what you saw that night. The night Grady Pierce died."

"Profanity," she answered without hesitation.

He waited, head tilted, watching her eyes, watching her lips.

"A profane man was Grady Pierce. Every other word out of his mouth a profanity! Especially when he was drinking. Which"—her lips pursed in disapproval— "he was most of the time. Always going on about his ghosts, his stupid ghosts. Like he was the only one in the world who saw them." A slow disapproving shake of her head. "He never listened to me, you know. I told him once, I told him a hundred times to stay home when the goblins were out, but he never listened. Never."

Quietly, respectfully: "You were out?"

"Of course. My obligations, you know."

Mulder questioned her with a look.

"I mark them," she explained. "The goblins. When I see them, I mark them, so this so-called policeman can lock them away until they burn up in the sun. But he never does, you know." The head turned, and Mulder sensed another glare.

"He could have saved that old coot's life if he had picked up the marked ones."

"I have a feeling that will change, Ms. Lang," Scully said.

"Damn right it will," the old woman snapped.

"What you saw," Mulder prompted softly.

She shifted, pushing back into the love seat. Her fingers began an endless weaving.

"I was heading home."

"From?"

"The Company G."

Mulder kept his expression neutral. "And that's... a bar?"

"A cocktail lounge and restaurant, young man, use the brains God gave you. I do not go to bars. Never have, never will."

"Sorry. Of course."

"It's east of that hideous place Grady always went to, whores and old men, that's all that's there. Around the corner, on Marchant Street. A very nice establishment." The lips smiled. "I know the owner personally."

He heard the chief shift impatiently, heard a faint rustle as Scully shifted in her chair.

Elly cleared her throat to recapture his attention. "I saw Grady up ahead, going into that alley between McConnell's and The Orion Shop. The Orion Shop is closed, you know. They cheated on your change. And the clothes they sold weren't fit for a cow. The goblins drove them away. They do that sometimes, drive the robbers away."

The fingers weaving.

The patter of light rain against the windows.

"I didn't care, of course. About Grady, I mean. He called me names all the time, drunk and sober, so I didn't care at all when he went into the alley. I kept on walking, didn't dare stop, it isn't safe for a woman on the streets at night these days, you know." She looked over to Scully, who nodded her agreement. "I heard a voice."

"From across the street?"

"He was yelling, young man. Grady Pierce always yelled. The army did that to him, made him deaf, I think, so he was always yelling even when he wasn't, if you know what I mean."

Mulder looked at the carpet. "Did you hear what he said?"

She sniffed. "I don't pay attention to things that don't concern me. He was yelling, that's all. I just kept walking."

Fingers weaving, then abruptly still.

He watched her left heel rise and fall, silently tapping. "I looked over. Natural curiosity, to see what a drunk was yelling at in an alley."

He watched her hands clasp, in a grip so tight he thought the bones might snap. He wanted to cover them, calm them, but he didn't dare move.

"I couldn't see him, except one leg kind of sticking into the light. I saw the goblin, though."

"You did."

The heel stopped; the fingers unwound.

"You don't have to humor me, Mr. Mulder. I don't like being humored. The goblin stepped out of the wall, kicked that old man's leg, and ran up the street."

"Did you call the police?"

She snorted. "Of course not. I knew what they would say. Don't need to be locked up again, not at my age. I'm going to die right here in this house, not in any damn cell."

He gave her that smile again. "But you did call later, didn't you?"

She leaned farther back, all her face now in shadow. "Yes. Yes, I did. Damn conscience wouldn't leave me be until I did, even though I knew they wouldn't do anything about the goblin."

"Ms. Lang?" It was Scully.

Mulder sat up carefully.

"Ms. Lang, what did the goblin look like?"

"It was black, child," Elly said.

"You mean—"

"No, not a Negro, that's not what I mean. I mean just what I said. It was black. All black. It had no color at all."

\\\\\\\\\\\\\\\\\\\'

They stood on the sidewalk outside the building. A handful of children played noisy baseball in a small park diagonally across the street. The brief rain had stopped, leaving behind the clouds, and the smell of wet tarmac.

Hawks seemed embarrassed. "She drinks," he said quietly. "Like a fish. That's all she does when she's not marking her goblins." The laugh he uttered was partly embarrassment, partly mirth. "Orange spray paint, if you can believe it. Most of the time she sits over there in the park, watches the kids play ball. That bench there on the grass by the third base line, that's hers. But every so often she goes off on a tear, I have no idea what triggers it. She starts walking around town, zapping people with orange spray paint. Then she comes to the station and tells me to lock the goblins up."

He waited until they were in the patrol car before he jammed a toothpick into his mouth and pulled away from the curb. "Just about everyone knows her, see, so we don't arrest her or anything. We pay for the clothes or whatever she wrecks, and that's usually the end of it. No real harm done." He grinned around the toothpick. "What you might call local color."

"So you don't think she saw anything?" Mulder asked from the back seat.

"I wish I knew, I really do. We looked, of course, but we didn't find a thing. Myself, I think she saw shadows, that's all. It was raining, there was wind… that's all."

No one spoke as he headed back to the station. "But what," Scully asked, "if she did see something?"

The toothpick flipped from one corner of his mouth to the other. "A black goblin, Agent Scully? What the hell am I supposed to do with that?" He didn't wait for an answer. "Like I said, she was drunk, like always, and it was shadows."

Maybe, Mulder thought; but wherever there's a shadow, there's always something to make it.

Then Scully said, "Is she the only one, Chief?"

Mulder saw him twitch. "Only one what?"

"Is she the only one who's seen the goblin?" They passed another small park where a pickup baseball game had drawn a small crowd.

"No," he admitted quietly. "No, damnit, there've been others."

TEN

Major Joseph Tonero loved his sister, even if she did have appalling taste in men. With their father gone and their mother an invalid, he had automatically assumed the role of head of the family. He didn't mind at all. It was not unlike his role in the service, mediating crises between people who were grown up enough to know better, issuing orders carefully couched as strong suggestion, and laying plans for the time when he could trade his uniform for a well-tailored suit that would fit right in on Capital Hill.

So he wasn't all that concerned with the fit Rosemary Elkhart threw in his office in Walson Hospital. He simply sat back, folded his hands in his lap, and let her rant, pacing the oak-paneled room until she finally dropped into an armchair. Her lab coat fell away when she crossed her legs, and he made no effort not to stare.

It wasn't as if he hadn't seen those thighs before.

"So what you're saying," he told her mildly, "is that you're annoyed."

She glowered, but couldn't hold it, finally laughing and shaking her head. "You amaze me, Joseph. You absolutely amaze me."

"Why?"

She sputtered, blinked, slapped in frustration at her bangs. "All that's at stake, and you, of all people, actually call in the FBI. Leonard's thinking about running to Brazil."

The smile he gave her carried no artifice. It wasn't necessary here; she knew all the tricks of his trade, and had taught him a few new ones herself. "I didn't exactly call them personally."

Close enough, her expression told him.

He waved her objection away. "I'm not worried about the feds, Rosie, and neither should you be. They come in, they read the reports, they look at a crime scene that's been cold for a week—"

"And what about Kuyser? She's a witness."

"Oh, really?"

Rosemary shrugged a minor concession. "Okay, not much of one, granted." She toyed with the edge of her coat, just above the knee. "But what about Leonard?"

His expression hardened. "We need him. I don't like it, you don't like it, but the Project needs him." He rose and walked around the desk, stood behind her and stared blindly at the wall while he massaged her shoulders. "Once this little problem—"

She barked a laugh.

"—is settled, once you're back in the groove, then we'll see about Dr. Tymons."

She tilted her head and kissed his hand. "I can do it, you know, Joseph. It's not hopeless."

"I have every faith in you, Rosie."

"A small adjustment, that's all."

"As I knew it would be." She turned to look up at him. "A week, perhaps two."

His gaze shifted to her face, that back of his left hand to her cheek, gliding down across her chin. "And… confinement?"

She leaned into the hand, eyes partly closed. If she had been a cat, he thought, she'd be purring.

"None."

The hand stopped. "We can't, Joseph," she said, easing out of the chair. "We have to trust Leonard's judgment on this."

"We already have. Twice."

"If we confine, we lose."

He sighed without a sound. He knew that, yet it was so untidy, so uncontrolled. But if the Project was to work, if the Department of Defense was to be convinced, it wouldn't do to have a psychotic subject. He had little choice. Tymons would continue to be the control until perfection was achieved.

Unless...

He took her hand and led her to the door. "Rosie, if there's another failure, I don't think I'll be able to protect him."

Her smile was genuine as well, and he suppressed a shudder when he saw it. "You won't have to, Joseph."

She kissed him quickly and left, the smell of her, the taste of her, lingering in the office. He savored it for a few seconds before striding back to his desk. The problem with Tymons and the Project was the least of his worries right now. He didn't much care if the subject wiped out half the goddamn state; with the right slant, a well-chosen word, it would only prove the Project's ultimate worth. And he had been telling Rosie the truth—his concern over the FBI was minimal as well.

The real problem was that asshole Carl Barelli. The idiot had already called him twice this morning, demanding an appointment, and the major knew well that kind of man—if no appointment was forthcoming, he'd show up on the post anyway and make enough noise to wake the dead.

Not to mention alerting those whose need to know did not, by any stretch of the regulations or imagination, extend to the Tymons Project.

You don't turn on a spotlight when you're working in the dark.

That was the problem with goddamn reporters these days—they thought they owned the goddamn Constitution. Barelli would have to be mollified. Having the FBI around would help. So would assurances that he himself was personally monitoring the situation, maintaining constant contact with the CID and the civil authorities. He'd do that anyway; he wasn't a fool. The fact that he had thought Ulman was a class-A jerk shouldn't deter him from extending what comfort he could to his sister.

Still, if Angie took up with a serviceman again, he would personally see to it the jerk was transferred to South Korea.

He took his chair and reached for the telephone, his free hand drumming thoughtfully on the desk. He would get hold of Carl, meet him for a late lunch, take him on the two-bit tour, pat him on the back, shed a tear with him for the loss of Angie's love, and get the sonofabitch the hell off his post. Let him go back to writing about hockey or basketball or whatever the hell it was he wrote about in April.

Hell's bells, he was only a cousin, for Christ's sake.

It wasn't like he was real family.

\\\\\\\\\\\\\\\\\\

Goblins, Elly thought nervously; the goblins are back. She stood in the kitchenette, squinting myopically at a calendar hanging on the refrigerator door. She knew those government people hadn't believed her, nobody did, but tomorrow was Saturday again, and the goblins would be back.

She was tired of being the only one who saw them.

That young man, though, he might be persuaded. He had the look about him. The believing look. The wanting look. All she had to do was mark one and show it to him.

That's all it would take.

Once he knew, the others would come around.

She licked her lips and turned to the cupboard under a rust-stained sink. From it she pulled a brand new can of marking magic, shook it, took off the rounded top, and tested it in the sink.

It worked.

She cackled.

Her pale eyes hardened to steel gray.

\\\\\\\\\\\\\\\\\\

"So when he took off for California," said Babs Radnor, a distinct Tennessee drawl in her voice, "I got a lawyer, emptied the bank account, took over the motel, and have become, as you can see, a lady of leisure."

She sat in her king-size four-poster, two pillows fluffed behind her back. She bordered on the painfully thin, with short black hair brushed behind her ears, hard black eyes, and a voice that husked with too much liquor, too many cigarettes. Her right hand held a floral sheet modestly over her breasts, while her left hand held a tumbler of bourbon and ice.

"I am not a lush, though," she insisted, waving the glass from side to side. "Like the French, I always have a little something with every meal. It's supposed to be good for the heart and circulation."

Carl stood at the low, twelve-drawer dresser and watched his reflection try-ing to make sense of his tie. "That's wine, Babs. Wine."

She shrugged. "Who gives a damn. It's working, right? So who cares?"

He didn't argue. Not even twenty-four hours, and he already knew she did not take lightly to contradiction or correction. Nor did she exaggerate when she had suggested without being coy or cute that he would have a much more pleasant evening in her company than the company of a TV, even if it did have free HBO.

It beat all to hell paying for a room.

It also afforded him a way to keep tabs on Mulder and his team. Babs, as she had already proven, knew everything about every blessed person who stayed in her motel. And if she didn't know, she found out. There wasn't, she had confessed, a whole lot else to do around here.

"So anyway, I'm figuring one more year, maybe two, sell out and get my buns to someplace like Phoenix, Tucson, someplace like that. Have you ever been to Arizona, sugar?"

He shook his head, damned his tie and yanked it off. He didn't figure the major would take him anyplace fancy anyway. There was, as the saying goes, no love lost between them, and it didn't bother him a bit. Tonero was an am-bitious little toad, and Carl's skin crawled each time they met. He didn't know how Angie could be from the same mother. Still, the guy had been sincere enough when they finally connected, and this lunch thing would give him a chance to see where Frankie had died.

Once he had done that, gotten the lay of the land, he could take the next step.

Whatever that might be.

"On the other hand, San Diego is supposed to have perfect weather, you know?" She laughed hoarsely. "The trouble is, it's in California. They hate it when you drink, smoke, and eat a decent meal, a steak and all. I don't know if I could stand it. I'm not too thrilled about those earthquakes, either."

He turned and spread his arms. "So? Do I look good enough to see a major?"

She waggled her heavy eyebrows. "Good enough to eat, if you ask me."

He laughed and sat on the edge of the bed, taking the hand that held the sheet in both of his. The sheet began to slide. "When I'm done, how about I take you out to dinner?"

"Yeah, right."

"Really, Babs, I'd like to. Is there a place around here, someplace nice?"

She looked at him carefully. The sheet made it to her waist.

"If you don't mind driving a little… ?"

His eyes widened comically, showing her his struggle not to look at her chest. "A little?"

"An hour?"

"What's an hour?"

"Atlantic City. There's some really nice places at Resorts and the Taj." Then she stuck her tongue out and laughed, pulled his hands to her breast, and stuck her tongue out again. "Just so you don't forget."

He kissed her then, long and soft. "Like I would," he whispered.

"Liar."

"Maybe." He slipped away and stood. "But I'm damn cute, right?"

She didn't laugh, didn't smile.

He leaned over and kissed her again, quickly but just as earnestly. "See you later."

"I'll be here, sugar. Noplace else to go."

He blew her a kiss from the door, closed it behind him, and hurried down the long gold and royal blue corridor. Her apartment was above the office, tucked behind the crown facade, and he used the outside back stairs to get to his car, hastily parked there when he had spotted that redheaded agent pull up not long after he himself had arrived. He figured he would run into Mulder sooner or later, but right now he preferred it to be later. The way he figured it, the agents wouldn't be here more than a couple of days, not on a case that was as cold as this one, and they'd probably eat at least one meal at the Inn.

They would talk while they ate.

Whatever they said, he would know less than an hour after they were done.

It was so perfect, he crossed his fingers to ward off the feeling that it just might be too perfect.

But he wasn't going to run from it, either. Hell, he got a free room, a free woman, and a chance to sneak up on Dana again. What the hell more could he ask for?

The killer, he answered as he pulled slowly around the side of the building; I want the killer, that's what I want.

He had another feeling, and he leaned forward, looked up, and saw her standing at her bedroom window. He gave her the smile, and the wave, and when she waved back he blew her a kiss before speeding out onto the road.

What a day this was going to be. Lunch with a uniformed toad who thinks his cousin is a jerk, a little investigative work around town, dinner in Atlantic City, a roll in the hay in a bed so big he could build a house on it.

Life, he decided, just doesn't get any better.

\\\\\\\\\\\\\\\\\\\`

Leonard stood at the end of the basement corridor, listening.

He didn't know what he expected to hear. There was never any noise save for the faint grumble of the machines that gave the building its power.

Nevertheless he listened, and wished there were more lights.

A single bulb over the entrance, one down at the far end. Nothing more. No need for more. He and Rosemary were the only ones who used it; Major Tonero was the only one who visited.

Still, he couldn't help thinking there should be some sound other than the rasp of his breathing.

You're making yourself jumpy, he scolded as he started toward the Project office. Not that he shouldn't be. So much had gone right, and so much had gone wrong, that half the time he didn't know whether he should shout or cry. Rosemary didn't help either, nagging at him constantly, pushing him, reminding him unnecessarily that this had to be the right one or all support would vanish as if it had never been.

And, he feared, him with it.

Ten yards down he reached the first of three doors on the right—there were none on the left at all.

The first was his private office. No markings, just dull steel. The second door was the same, the Project center within. He glanced through the wire-mesh window and saw that it was empty. Rosemary must still be at lunch.

The third door was closed.

He glanced at it nervously, checked back toward the exit, and decided he had to know.

With one hand in his pocket to stop his keys from jangling, he hurried to it and looked through the reinforced glass judas window.

No one sat in the armchair, or at the desk now stripped of everything but the pen and legal pad. He couldn't see the bed.

He flipped a switch by the jamb and rapped lightly on the window with a knuckle, and jumped back with a stifled cry when a face suddenly grinned at him from the other side.

"Jesus," he said, eyes closing briefly. "You scared me to death."

Above the door was a microphone embedded in the concrete, a speaker grille beside it.

"Sorry." The voice was distorted, asexual. "I'm on break. I thought I'd drop in. Sorry."

It wasn't sorry at all.

"How do you feel?" He approached the door again, warily, as if the face belonged to a superhuman monster that could, at the slightest provocation, smash through the steel. The stupid thing was, the door wasn't locked. He could walk right in if he wanted to. If he had the nerve.

"How do you think I feel?"

Tymons refused the bait, the invitation to guilt. That sort of emotion had died the first time he had skinned a subject capuchin alive. He hadn't liked it, of course, but there had been no other way.

Guilt, for the Project, was too damn expensive.

"When do I get to see the results?" It wasn't a plea, it was barely a question.

"Later," he promised. Below the level of the window, he crossed his fingers. Just in case.

"I feel pretty good."

"You're looking good."

He returned the smile.

"I've almost got it, too."

Tymons nodded. He heard that every week, every month. "You'd better. They're…" He couldn't help a grin. "They're a little annoyed."

"It wasn't my fault. You're the doctor."

He had heard that one, too. Every week. Every month.

"But I'll take care of it."

Tymons glared and pointed. "You'll do no such thing, you understand? You let me handle everything."

The face didn't change expression, but Tymons looked away from the contempt.

"I'd like my books back, please."

He shook his head. "That didn't work, and you know it. The books, the music, the TV. Too many distractions. You need to concentrate on your concentration." He chuckled. "As it were."

"I can concentrate, damnit. I concentrate so much my brain is falling out." ~

Tymons nodded sympathetically. "I know, I know, and I'll talk to you about it later. Right now I have work to do."

Even through the distortion, the sarcasm was clear: "Another little adjustment?"

Tymons didn't answer. He switched off the communication unit, waved vaguely, and hurried to his office. Once inside, he locked the door behind him and dropped behind his desk, switched on his computer, leaned back and closed his eyes.

This was wrong.

Things weren't getting better, and no goddamn adjustments were ever going to work.

He sighed and checked his watch—he had almost two hours before Rosemary arrived. Plenty of time to complete copying his files. Plenty of time to take the Army-issue .45 Tonero had given him and go back next door. And use it.

Plenty of time to vanish.

After all, he thought with a hollow laugh, he was the expert at things like that.

Then he glanced through *The Blue Boy*, and started.

The room was empty.

"Damn." He flicked a switch beneath the shelf, activating the lights embedded in the room's ceiling. All color vanished, all shadows.

Still empty.

The bastard had already left. Like a ghost, he thought, glancing nervously at the door; the damn thing moves like a ghost. After all this time, he couldn't bring himself to think of it as human.

ELEVEN

The overcast thickened, splotches of shifting cloud from grey to black bulging and spreading, using the wind to warn that the rain that had fallen before would be nothing like the rain to come.

Dana stood uneasily in the middle of a narrow paved road, not at all caring for the way the woodland pressed around her, not liking the faint hint of ozone that promised lightning when the storm broke again.

They had eaten in the diner as planned, but neither she nor Mulder had been either surprised or pleased with what they had heard: Webber and Andrews had learned nothing that hadn't been recorded or implied in the reports already. No one had seen anything, no one had heard anything; many of the shopkeepers knew Grady, most of them not kindly; a couple recognized Ulman's picture, but there was nothing more than that. He was from the post. Big deal.

No miracles.

No one had mentioned goblins, either.

Hawks had explained that, over the past couple of months, some kids and a couple of adults had reported seeing... something drifting around the town. They called it a goblin because everyone knew of Elly Lang's obsession.

"But it doesn't mean anything," he had insisted calmly. "A story like that, it kind of feeds on itself."

By two, the afternoon light had worsened, shifting closer to false twilight. Mulder decided to check the site of the corporal's murder before the storm broke. Andrews, on a hunch, volunteered to return to the motel to interview the owner; it was possible, she said, Ulman had used the out-of-the-way place for weekend escapes. Maybe he had provoked the wrath of someone's husband. Chief Hawks quickly volunteered to drive and introduce her.

"And keep her out of trouble," Mulder had said later, in the car.

Scully hadn't liked the idea then, and she didn't like it now. Webber, on the trip out, had already told them that Andrews, her attitude unchanged, had made the interviews, brief as they were, "kind of difficult." Except, predictably, when the subjects were men.

Webber stood now some fifty yards up the road, hands in his pockets, playing the part of the Jeep the Ulman witness had been in. He looked miserable as the wind slapped his hair and coat around; about as miserable as she felt.

Mulder was on his third circle of the tree from which the arm and weapon had allegedly appeared. It had been easy to find—there was still a ragged piece of yellow crime scene ribbon wrapped around its thick trunk.

She glanced up; the sky was lower.

Nothing moved in the woods but leaves and bare branches. And the slow-strengthening wind.

Behind her, their car shuddered when a gust slammed it broadside.

She turned in a slow circle, shaking her head. The corporal had been drinking; he had, for some reason, come out of the woods down there by the ditch, staggered up here... and had been killed.

Mulder joined her, waving Webber to them. "You see it?" he asked.

The road was a flattened loop that left the county highway just west of Marville, skirted the post boundary here, and met the highway again a mile farther on. While it was possible Grady had been a random victim, there was no way she would believe Ulman had simply been in the wrong place at the wrong time.

The killer had followed him through the woods.

"He was meant to die," she said.

He nodded. "I think so, yes."

Webber trotted up. "So is it hollow or what?"

She frowned. "What? The tree?"

"Sure. That woman saw—"

Scully took his arm gently and turned him around, pointing to the place he'd just left. "There are no lights, there was no moon, and all she saw, from way back there, was whatever the corporal's flashlight showed her."

She waited.

"Okay." He nodded. "Okay. But what was she doing out here?"

Mulder didn't answer. He grunted, and headed back for the tree.

"Well," she said, watching Mulder circle the tree again, squeezing between it and the caged white birch on either side, "she could be an accomplice. She could have been waiting for the killer."

Webber disagreed, as she knew he would. "That would mean they both knew Ulman would be here, at that time. And they didn't, right?"

"Right."

"So it was what? Her bad luck?"

"That's about the size of it," she said. She also reminded them that the so-called witness, Fran Kuyser, had been drinking, and taking heroin. Not exactly the most reliable observer they could hope for.

"When are we going to see her?"

Scully hunched her shoulders briefly. "Later, or tomorrow. From what the chief said, the condition she's in, she won't be able to tell us anything anyway."

"A hell of thing," Webber said. He shifted uneasily. "Can you tell me something?"

She nodded.

"Are the cases you work on... I mean, are they always this screwy? Messed up, I mean." He shook his head once, violently. "I mean—"

She laughed in spite of herself. "Yes. Sometimes."

"Brother," he said.

"Tell me about it."

Mulder rapped the trunk with a knuckle, then pried at the overlapping bark. Scully knew, however, that he saw more than just the tree. That was only the center; his focus touched it all.

"That old lady you told me about," Webber said, for some reason keeping his voice low.

Scully didn't look at him. "Ms. Lang. What about her?"

"She said... I mean, she was talking about goblins."

She did look then, sharply. "There are no goblins, Hank."

But she knew what he was thinking: She and Mulder were the X-Files, and that meant this case contained something well out of the ordinary. It didn't matter that the so-called paranormal had perfectly reasonable explanations, once you bothered to examine such incidents more closely. It didn't matter that the extraordinary was only the ordinary with curious trappings. They were here, goblins were mentioned, and now she wasn't sure Hank didn't believe it a little himself.

Mulder snagged his coat on a bush, yanked it free angrily, and took it off.

A hoarse cry overhead made her look up—a pair of crows flew lazily across the road, ignoring the wind.

"This place is kind of spooky," Hank said, rolling his shoulders against the damp chill.

She had no argument there. They could see barely a hundred feet into the trees now. If it was twilight out here, it was near midnight in there.

Slipping her hands into her pockets, she called Mulder's name. They would find nothing here; the trail was, for now, too cold.

He didn't hear her.

Goblins, she thought; please, Mulder, don't.

"I'll get him," Hank offered, and was off before she could respond.

He hadn't taken three steps before the first shot was fired.

\\\\\\\\\\\\\\\\\\

Immediately, Scully yelled a warning, threw herself around the car and pressed herself hard against the rear fender, gun in hand before she even realized she'd drawn it.

A second shot chipped the tarmac at Hank's foot, and he cried out, moving backward so rapidly he fell.

Scully eased herself up, squinting into the wind, trying to pinpoint the location of the shooter, knowing only that he was hidden somewhere in the woods east of them. She fired off a quick, blind shot, was answered by a barrage that peppered the road, forcing her back down just as Hank scrambled around the hood and squatted beside her, panting.

"You okay?" she asked.

He nodded, winced, and nodded again.

There was blood on his shoe.

He saw her look and shrugged. "Just a chip from the road on my ankle, that's all." He grinned. "I'll live."

She could see it, he was scared, but she could see the adrenaline, too.

Another barrage, this time at Mulder's position, and she rose again and fired as Hank fired over her head.

Nothing.

She could see nothing.

There was no question it was an automatic weapon, its bark suggesting something less than an Uzi. M-16, maybe. Not that it made much difference now. Bullets slammed into the trunk, walking up to and shattering the rear window.

"Mulder!" she called into the silence that followed.

No answer.

Hank tugged at her sleeve when the firing paused. "Gas tank," he warned, and on a count of three, they slipped back toward the hood. When the next round was aimed at Mulder, she took the opportunity to dart low across the pebbled verge and into the trees, pressing her shoulder against the trunk of a fat black oak. Webber found a position to her right and deeper into the woods.

"There!" he called, and fired at a point just beyond the far end of the ditch on the other side of the road.

She couldn't see anything, and then—she rubbed a hand quickly across her eyes. In the twisting leaves, a shadow. Or a figure all in black. It didn't move until Hank fired again, and then it vanished.

She looked to her left, and caught her breath.

"He's down!" she called to Webber. "Mulder's down!"

\\\\\\\\\\\\\\\\\\\\\

Mulder froze in shocked surprise at the first shot, dropped to the ground at the second, his own weapon out as he heard Scully and Hank return fire. But he couldn't see where the shooter was. The oak, the birch, the underbrush, all blinded him. Quickly, keeping low, he moved to his left, and dropped again when leaves and twigs were shredded above him, peppering his skull, stinging his cheeks.

He covered his head with one arm and waited, moving again when the firing concentrated again on the road, letting instinct take him deeper into the woods, tree to tree, searching for a muzzle flash, firing once, and once again, in hopes of diverting the shooter's attention away from Scully and Webber.

He heard glass shatter.

He heard Scully's voice.

A pine gave him cover, but he flinched anyway when the attack resumed on his original position.

It was luck, then, that the shooter hadn't seen him maneuvering deeper and around, and he used the time to search again, grunting softly when he saw the flash, and a dark figure pressed against the dark trunk of a lightning-blasted tree. He couldn't tell from this distance who it was; the figure had dressed in black from ski mask to shoes.

It didn't look like any goblin to him.

The wind quickened.

He angled inward again, and east, hoping the coming storm's thrashing branches and spinning leaves would make enough noise and present enough distraction that he'd be able to get close enough for a decent shot.

Scully's voice, and Hank's answer; he couldn't tell what they said, but the fear was there.

The black figure backed away, firing.

Mulder cursed and moved more quickly, keeping as low as he could without losing his balance. There were too many shadows now, too much movement.

He had to get there before the shooter disappeared.

At the south edge of a small clearing, he braced himself against a trunk, took several deep breaths to calm down and clear his head, and waited until the firing stopped.

There was no silence.

The wind and the woodland husked and shrieked at each other, pinwheeling debris across the clearing.

He would have to go across it; to go around would waste time.

He inhaled, blew out, and spun away from the tree in a crouch. He was halfway across, aiming, finger already squeezing the trigger, before he realized the shooter was gone.

Damn, he thought, and slowly straightened, not trusting his vision, gun still out and ready, squinting into the wind and throwing up one hand in disgust.

Something moved behind him.

He had only half-turned before something hard slammed off his temple, a glancing blow that drove him to his knees. His gun whipped out of his grip. His right arm lashed out automatically and struck something soft, but he couldn't see clearly; there were too many flares of blinding, painful light.

But he saw something, and it made him hesitate.

Then a blow to his spine almost toppled him, and he lashed out again, losing his balance as he did, landing on his shoulder before he was pinned on his chest.

A giggle in his ear, hoarse and inhuman.

Then a voice: "Mulder, watch your back," just before a foot caught him under his ribs.

TWELVE

He couldn't breathe.

"Mulder!"

Eyes watering, he tried to push himself to his hands, but he couldn't breathe.

"Mulder!"

Forget it, he told his arms, and rolled over instead, blinking furiously to clear his vision, spitting when a shard of leaf caught on his lips.

But he still couldn't breathe.

Voices, normal voices anxious and searching, until his name was called again, and he saw, or thought he saw, Scully kneeling beside him on his left, someone else on his right.

"I don't see any blood," Webber said.

"Mulder?"

He tried to smile reassurance, but it was too much trouble, and he let himself black out, to rest in the dark for a while.

By the time he regained full consciousness, there were sirens and shouts, the distant crackle of a radio. The wind had died, but the afternoon was still night. Scully was gone; Webber hovered nearby, and Mulder groaned to signal him and bring him over.

"Up," he said, stretching out an arm when the younger man leaned down.

"I don't know. Scully said—"

"Up," he insisted, and Webber brought him to his feet.

It was a mistake.

His head swelled to accommodate the fire inside, and he swayed and didn't argue when Webber eased him to a stump at the clearing's north end and made him sit. Bile burned the back of his throat; his stomach surged without delivering. He spat, and spat again, bracing an arm on his leg and resting his forehead on his palm.

"Jesus," he whispered.

Webber hunkered down beside him, concern adding too many years to his face. Mulder glanced over and smiled briefly.

"I'll live."

Webber didn't look as if he believed it. But he told him that an MP patrol, alerted by the gunfire, had arrived only moments after the shooting had stopped. Within minutes, other patrols had arrived, and Scully was advising them and their captain on a search of the woods. When Mulder looked up, he saw silver beams slashing and darting among the trees. Voices called softly. Through the trees he could see half a dozen MP Jeeps and cruisers parked on the road, and a single civilian patrol car, its roof lights still whirling.

"Chief Hawks," Webber confirmed.

Mulder nodded, and wished he hadn't—the fire rose, and fell, and his finger gingerly traced what would be a hell of a lump by nightfall. There was no blood. Then he pushed aside his jacket, opened his shirt, and tried to have a look at his ribs.

"Damn," Webber said. "What'd he use, a brick?"

"It sure felt like it." He winced as he probed the area. He knew nothing was broken, however. How a broken rib felt was something you never forgot.

"Button up, Mulder, you'll catch pneumonia."

He smiled at Scully hurrying toward him. She seemed more annoyed at the wind slapping hair into her eyes than at him.

"You gonna examine me or what?"

"Please," she said. "I've had a bad enough day."

"What happened?" He nodded toward the search party.

"The shooter's gone. No surprise. They found a crushed area back around the bend where he probably stashed his car. No tire tracks, nothing but this." She dug into her pocket and pulled out a casing. "M-16."

"Army?"

"Maybe not," Webber said. "They're not all that hard to get outside the service anymore. Cops, bad guys, collectors." He shrugged. "Even guys leaving the service have smuggled them home."

Mulder muttered about having it easy once in a while. "Well, maybe we should check. How many can there—"

Webber groaned in anticipation. "Mulder, no kidding, it's the weekend. That means there's about eight, nine thousand reservists running all over this place. And you want to find one rifle that's been fired recently?"

"Hank, you amaze me. How did you know that?"

Webber shrugged again. "The interviews, remember? I'll bet the people in town know as much about what's going on on post as anyone who works there."

"Not quite," he muttered. He straightened slowly, hissing at the too-slow lessening pain.

"What I don't get," Scully said, "is how the shooter got to you before we did." Her expression turned sheepish. "I saw your coat on the ground, I thought it was you."

"It wasn't."

"So I see. I don't know what he hit you with, but he knew what he was doing. He could've cracked your skull wide open." She frowned. "What I don't get is how he managed to change positions so quickly. You were a good—"

"No. I mean, it wasn't the shooter."

She was startled. "What?"

"It wasn't the shooter, Scully. I saw him, the shooter, just before I got hit." He winced as he touched his head again. "From the side, Scully. I was hit from the side, right over there. The shooter was still in front of me."

Doubt was evident in her expression as she put the casing back into her pocket. "The goblin, right?"

"You got it. I just got a glimpse, but believe me, it was enough."

Webber almost laughed, but caught himself when she shook her head in exasperation. "Mulder, you'd just been clobbered, remember? Anything you saw, or thought you saw, would be suspect, you know that."

With Webber's reluctant help, he stood, looking at but not seeing the MPs' shifting lights. "It was a hand, and part of the forearm. The skin looked like bark."

Scully opened her mouth to say something, changed her mind and waited.

"I heard it, too."

She leaned away, an eyebrow cocked. "He left you a message?"

"It was like no voice I've ever heard." He closed his eyes again, to try to sharpen the memory, felt Webber's fingers lightly on his arm for balance. "I don't know. It was hoarse, whispering, as if it had a hard time saying the words." When he looked, she was scowling, arms folded across her chest. "Honest."

"I don't doubt you heard something. But I—"

"This is a joke, right?" Webber asked nervously. He looked from one to the other. "Some kind of private joke, right?"

Mulder shook his head. "Sorry, Hank, no."

"Oh, man," Webber said, almost in a moan. "Wait 'til Licia hears this one."

\\\\\\\\\\\\\\\\\\

Carl Barelli was furious as he sped back through the woods toward Marville.

First, that sanctimonious toad, Tonero, tried to pass off the glop in the Officer's Mess as some kind of fancy food, instead of taking him to a decent restaurant; then tried to hand out some pious bullshit about family unity and Angie's peace of mind being more important than interfering with official investigations; and then he had the nerve to march Carl out to his car and tell him, with a smile, to go on back home and write about baseball or something.

He had fumed behind the wheel, debating the chances of his landing in jail if he went back inside and popped the toad one on the point of his spongy jaw.

Then an MP ran up, intercepted Tonero, and the two were hustled into a car. The next thing Carl knew there were sirens and men with rifles boiling out of the Provost Marshal's office, and, after a suitable interval, he followed them.

To the goddamn woods.

Where another goddamn MP suggested with drawn .45 that the reporter find something else to report on, this area was sealed off to civilians.

"Bastards," he muttered, and muttered it often until suddenly he grinned.

He had seen a town cruiser at the scene, which meant the locals were involved, which meant...

He laughed aloud, and by the time he pulled up in front of the police station, his mood had lightened considerably. A quick check of his hair in the rearview mirror, an adjustment of his tie and jacket, and he was inside, smiling at the two men at desks near the back of the room, and the front desk sergeant, who couldn't have looked more bored if he were dead.

"I'd like to see the chief," Carl said, as politely as his excitement would allow.

Sergeant Nilssen told him gruffly the chief was out, and there was no sense hanging around. He had work to do, half his people had some kind of lousy flu, and those who were around had police business to attend to.

A dispatch radio muttered static to itself while a gawky young officer flipped through a logbook.

Carl's smile didn't waver. "Then perhaps you can help me, Sergeant. I work for the *Jersey Chronicle*. My name is Carl Barelli, and I'm—"

Nilssen's boredom vanished. "Barelli? The sports guy in the paper?"

Amazing, Carl thought smugly; *absolutely amazing.*

"That's right, Sergeant. But today I'm looking into the death of a friend of mine. Corporal Frank Ulman."

"Man, yeah," the sergeant said, grinning. "So you want to hear about the goblins, right?"

The smile still didn't waver. "That's right. Can you help me?"

The policeman leaned back in his chair, hooked his thumbs into his belt. "Anything you want to know, Mr. Barelli. All you have to do is ask."

Tonero remained in the back seat of his staff car, watching as the MPs began to make their way slowly and methodically back toward the road. His driver was gone, ordered to sniff around to see what unofficial word he could pick up. It was better than talking to the captain in charge. Tonero knew the man well, and knew that the MP wouldn't give away a thing.

The car rocked a little when the wind slapped it.

He glanced warily out at what sky he could see, hoping he'd be able to get out of here before the storm broke.

This was not turning out to be one of his best days. Tymons was jumpy, and Rosemary was getting pushy; and he knew without doubt that Barelli wasn't going to leave until he had gotten some kind of crumb to fill his meager reporter's plate.

He sighed for all the injustices dropped on him since waking, and sighed again when the front passenger door opened and Tymons slipped in at the same time that Rosemary slipped into the back, beside him.

"We heard," Tymons said, agitation making his voice too high.

"What's going on?" Rosemary asked more calmly.

"I'm not sure. Someone tried to take care of the FBI, as near as I could tell." Tymons groaned.

"It wasn't us," Rosemary snapped at him. "Jesus, Leonard, use your head."

"We should abort," was the answer. "We don't have any more control. We have no choice, we have to abort." He twisted around to look at the major. "Joseph, the FBI isn't going away now, you know that. No more just having a look around and running back to D.C. They're going to dig. And they're going to find something."

Tonero gripped Rosemary's leg briefly to keep her silent. "Leonard, I want you to pay attention."

"Joseph, we—"

"These people," and he indicated the MPs, "are looking for a shooter, okay? Not us and ours. There is no connection, and no connections can be made. Use your head, Doctor, use your head."

Tymons jumped as if slapped. "I don't know. They're going to ask questions."

"Well, that's no problem," Rosemary answered. "We'll just make sure there isn't anyone around to answer."

Tonero looked at her in astonishment.

She shrugged. "We may not have complete control, but we still have some." Her smile was cold. "Simple suggestions ought to do it."

"Jesus!" Tymons shoved his door open. "You're crazy, Rosemary. And as Project Director, I forbid it." He slammed the door and stalked away.

Tonero didn't look, didn't care where he was going. What he cared about was this new woman beside him. Something had changed since a few hours ago. Something drastic. He wasn't sure, but he thought he liked it.

"You better leave," he said quietly.

"And the problem?"

He gave her his best smile. "In for a penny, Rosie. In for a penny." He patted her knee. "Use your best judgment. Just be sure, all right? Whatever you do, just be sure." Then he grunted and took her arm to stop her. Ahead, he saw a man and woman helping a second, somewhat disheveled man out of the woods. *Shit*, he thought.

"Rosie, I think you'd better stick around a minute."

\\\\\\\\\\\\\\\\\

"You are not dead, Mulder," Scully complained. "Don't lean so hard."

She couldn't help a smile, though, at his melodramatic sigh. He might be different, but he was still a man, not above playing sick and injured to the hilt.

Someone called to them, and they stopped on the road.

"Well," Mulder whispered. "Well, well."

A man in uniform fairly marched toward them, and, when he was close enough, quietly demanded a report on Mulder's condition. When Scully balked, he ducked his head in apology. "Sorry. Major Joseph Tonero, Agent Scully. Air Force Special Projects." His smile turned to Mulder. "This incident happened on my watch, so to speak, and I apologize for being slow getting here. A late lunch with an old friend. But I don't have to tell you how concerned I am. Is everyone all right?" Before she could answer, he rubbed his hands together. "Good, good. I'd hate to think what would happen if we lost an FBI."

His smile was intended to be warm, but Scully didn't buy it. The man was less a career soldier than a politician, she decided as she briefed him; his medical knowledge doesn't go much farther than using a bandage.

As soon as she was finished, two others came up behind him—a tall, balding civilian, and too nervous for her peace of mind, and a striking, hard-edged blonde whose bearing was military, but she too was civilian. Neither spoke much save for a perfunctory mumbling of sympathies.

The major introduced them as part of his team, offering their services should the need arise. Scully assured him matters were well in hand, but thanked the officer for his concern.

"As a matter of fact," she added, "we were going to see you this afternoon, when we were done."

Mulder opened his mouth, closed it when she stepped in front of him and put a heel down on his foot to keep him silent.

"Corporal Ulman worked for you, isn't that right?"

The major grew solemn. "Yes, he did, Agent Scully. A tragic loss. He was a good man. And I've been working closely with the Provost—"

"He was going to marry your sister," Mulder said over her shoulder.

Tonero didn't miss a beat: "There was talk, yes. But just between you and me, I don't think it was going to happen." He sighed. "However, I certainly owe it to her to assist you in any way possible."

Neither made any mention of the phone call to Senator Carmen.

"Who attacked you?" Dr. Elkhart asked suddenly, sharply.

"There were two," Mulder answered before Scully could stop him.

"Really?" the major said, grabbing his hat against a gust. "I had no idea."

Scully was relieved when Mulder didn't elaborate; she watched instead as Dr. Tymons whispered something to Elkhart and hurried back down the road, one hand massaging the back of his neck.

"Major," she said, "I'm not sure, it's too soon, but if Agent Mulder here needs more assistance than I can—"

"Walson is mostly shut down," the major interrupted stiffly. "We function primarily as an outpatient clinic now, with only a few long-term patients. Cutbacks." He shrugged a *you know how it is* before the smile returned as he clapped his hands once. "However, the important thing is that you're all right, Agent Mulder." He turned to Scully. "He is all right, isn't he?"

She nodded. "But he could use some rest now, Major, so if you and Dr. Elkhart don't mind, I'd like to get him back to his room."

The major nodded, shook hands all around, and ushered Elkhart away, pausing only to have a brief animated conversation with the MP captain in charge of the search.

"What do you think?" Mulder asked when they were alone.

"I think," she said without turning around, "that there's a shooting incident, and the major brings scientists along instead of doctors."

She checked the car they'd ridden out in, the shattered glass and punctures, at the one shredded, flat tire.

"Hank," she said quietly, "get us a ride to the motel."

Then she looked at Mulder, and instantly knew what he was thinking: *you're not protected*, Mr. Mulder, *you' re still not protected.*

THIRTEEN

It took a while before Webber was finally able to get them back to the Royal Baron. Once there, as a doctor, not a partner, Scully ordered Mulder to bed with an ice pack and aspirin until she returned from a visit with Sam Junis. He didn't protest. Just a crooked smile and a phony sigh, and she knew he wouldn't sleep; he'd be too busy trying to squeeze the obvious so it ended up looking like a goblin.

Licia she found in their room, transcribing her notes from the Radnor interview. "Shorthand," the agent said apologetically. "Can't keep up otherwise, and I hate recorders." As she slipped the papers into a briefcase, Scully asked her what, if anything, she'd found out.

"It was like she didn't care," Licia complained, the insult to justice clear in her tone. "And even though she has exercise stuff—says she uses it when she remembers—in that downstairs room off the office, she still drinks like a fish." Then she smiled. "She knew the corporal, though."

"How?"

The smile became a smug grin. "It seems the engaged to the major's sister corporal enjoyed an occasional R&R. Like, nearly every weekend."

"Did she say who he was with?"

"No name, and she only got a glimpse. The corporal, it seems, was very careful. I don't know if that has anything to do with anything, though."

Scully agreed before hustling Andrews into her coat and outside. Webber would watch Mulder in case the shooter tried again, or Mulder decided to have an adventure on his own.

They took the second car, and on the way, she filled Andrews in, ignoring the comments and the outrage.

It also helped her think.

It was evident they were dealing with two different suspects. Aside from the fact that Mulder had been attacked by someone other than the shooter, she was certain the murderer of Ulman and Pierce hadn't suddenly decided to switch to a rifle as his weapon of choice. He was too good with the knife. And a knife was more personal, requiring close range; a rifle was too remote, dispassionate, requiring little or no victim contact at all.

When she had proposed this on the way back, both Mulder and Webber had agreed, but neither could find a reasonable explanation of why, suddenly, they were faced with two opponents.

"Maybe somebody's protecting the goblin," Andrews suggested.

"It's not a goblin," Scully snapped. "Please, don't you start, too. Mulder's already got Hank thinking that way."

"So what do I do? Call him Bill?"

"I don't care. Just don't call him a goblin!"

Andrews laughed and shook her head. "Boy," she said, "he really gets on your nerves, doesn't he?"

Scully didn't answer.

\\\\\\\\\\\\\\\\\\\

The doctor's bungalow was in only marginally better condition than those of his neighbors, its saving grace a large front garden whose arrangement and vivid blossoms signaled a great deal of time taken and care bestowed. The doctor himself was on the tiny front porch, sitting on the railing, smoking a cigarette. He seemed to be in his early fifties, his greying hair plastered straight back from his forehead; and despite the wind and the chill, he was in shirtsleeves and jeans. Most of him was lean, but his arms were hugely muscled, all out of proportion to the rest of him.

"Popeye," Andrews muttered as they took the narrow slate walk toward him.

Scully almost laughed aloud. She was right; all the man needed was a corncob pipe and a sailor's cap to complete the image.

"Been having a time of it, haven't you," he said by way of greeting. Then he nodded to a police scanner on a small table behind him. "It's either that or Oprah." He grinned.

Scully liked him immediately, and wasted no time getting into his reports. He took no offense at her questions, and asked no questions about the way Andrews barely took her gaze from the surrounding woodland.

The interview didn't last long—Junis agreed with her reconstruction of Pierce's murder, and actually apologized for not getting better photos. He also suggested that the knife used wasn't ordinary. "Sharp as hell, sure," he said, "but the cut of it, I think it might have been heavier than you'd find in your average kitchen."

"Like what?" Scully asked.

"I don't know. I've been thinking about it, but I still don't know."

She knew then she had to ask the next question, and for once, she was glad Mulder wasn't with her. "You had some notes in the margin."

He laughed as he flicked his cigarette onto the lawn. "Yeah. Goblin, right?"

"What does that have to do with anything? As far as your examinations went, I mean."

"Not much." He pulled another cigarette from his pocket and stuck it between his lips. He didn't light it. "Nothing. I'd just been to see Elly Lang, had to calm her down a little with a mild sedative, and that's all she talked about." A sideways glance. "You heard about it, huh?"

"We talked to her, yes."

Junis followed the wake of a pickup heading west. "Don't think she's crazy, Agent Scully. Don't write her off. I don't know who she saw, but she's no fool."

"She was drunk, Dr. Junis."

He laughed abruptly, loudly, until his eyes began to water and his face reddened alarmingly. "Sorry." He laughed again and wiped his eyes with a sleeve. "God, I'm sorry." He gripped the railing with both hands. "Drunk? Elly? You've been listening to Todd Hawks. Nope, never. She goes to that bar for the company, that's all. She's outlived her family, has no real friends to speak of. She has one drink, a Bloody Mary, that she nurses until she's ready to go home, and that's about it. That woman has never been drunk a day in her life."

"Then what about the spray paint?"

Junis watched another truck pass. "Because she believes it, Agent Scully. She believes it as sure as you believe there ain't no such thing. That doesn't mean she's certifiable."

Scully wasn't so sure about that, but she didn't know enough to pursue it. Instead she asked about the other witness.

"Fran?" Junis lowered his gaze to the garden. "I can take you to her, if you want, but she won't do you a whole lot of good."

"Why not?"

His expression hardened. "The heroin she took that night was damn close to an overdose. I brought her to a facility up near Princeton." He paused. "A mental rehab, by the way, we don't have anything like that around here. She was pretty far gone." He lit another cigarette and blew smoke into the wind. "She'll recover from the overdose most likely, but as for the other… she isn't going to be released for a long, long time."

Swell, she thought; just what I need—an addict who probably can't even recognize her own reflection. Interviewing Fran Kuyser quickly dropped toward the bottom of her list.

"Do you sit out here a lot?" Andrews asked then, not bothering to look at him.

He nodded to Dana, not at all fazed by the sudden change of subject. "Guess I do, come to think of it. I like to watch the world drive by, see who's going where. People around here, those that work on post or at McGuire, they have their military doctors, and the others…" He shrugged. "Not a lot left, but I guess you already noticed that."

Scully also noticed that he didn't seem to mind. Although he was too young to step down yet, he appeared to be resigned that this practice wasn't going to get him a retirement home in a better location, and that, for whatever reason, was all right with him. "Oh, we have our moments," he said, startling her. "And it beats all to hell working an ER."

She wasn't inclined to disagree, thanked him for his time, and told him where she was staying in case he thought of something else.

"I already know that," he said. And grinned.

Back in the car, Andrews shook her head in disbelief. "You know, you can't breathe around here without somebody knowing it. Hardly any privacy at all." She forced herself to shudder. "That's too weird for me."

Dana grunted, but she wasn't really listening. There was something not quite right here, something she and the others had missed. She didn't think it was tied directly to the killings, but it was, somehow, important. Small, but important. She knew Mulder felt it as well. In spite of the afternoon's attack, she knew it bothered him, and maybe by the time they returned to the hotel and he had rested, he would know what it was.

As long, she added glumly, as he doesn't call it a damn goblin.

\\\\\\\\\\\\\\\\\'

The motel lights were all on when they returned, highlighting the crown façade, flooding the parking lot with dull silver, making the clouds seem even lower and thicker than they were. After sending Andrews to fetch her interview notes, she pushed through Mulder's door just in time to hear him say, "... a multitude of sins."

"What sins?" she demanded. "And why aren't you in bed?"

He sat in shirtsleeves at the room's tiny table, his back to the wall, papers spread in front of him. Webber was on the bed, propped up by pillows, knees drawn up to serve as a rest for a legal pad.

"Hi, Scully," Mulder said. "I'm cured."

Webber refused to meet the rebuke in her eyes as she dropped into the chair across the table. "You're not cured, and you've been working." But the scolding was, as always, a waste of time; he would only give her one of two looks—the hurt little boy, or the sly-fox, lopsided grin—and do what he wanted anyway.

He settled for the grin. "We've been checking up on Major Tonero."

"It's weird," Webber commented from the bed. "His office confirms he's head of Air Force Special Projects, like he told us, but they wouldn't explain what that means."

"Which," Mulder continued, "covers a multitude of sins." He shook his head slowly. "Curiouser and curiouser. Why would an Air Force major, who isn't even medical personnel, be assigned to an Air Force hospital on an Army post? Which, for the most part, is used as training for reservists, and a jumping-off point when troops have to get overseas in a hurry." Then he pointed at her before she could answer. "And don't tell me there's a perfectly rational explanation."

Oh, Lord, she thought; he's in one of his moods.

"And," Webber added eagerly, "why would he be so interested in the ambush? And why were his people there, too? Those two doctors, scientists, whatever."

Scully stared at him for so long, he began to look embarrassed. "Well... it's a good question, isn't it?" He scratched the back of his head. "I mean, isn't it?"

"Yes, Hank, it is," Mulder said when Scully didn't answer. "And I'll bet I have a possible answer."

"Mulder," Scully said, her voice low and warning. "Do not read into this more than there is."

"Oh, I'm not," he protested lightly. "I'm not even going to begin to suggest that maybe these goblins have something to do with the major." He leaned back in his chair. "I wouldn't think of it."

"Of course you wouldn't," she said. "Because you already have. Now look, we've got a—"

Andrews walked in then, smiled a not very sincere apology for being late, took a reluctant seat on the bed, and said, "So now what?"

Dana checked her watch; it was after five. "So now I think we'd better break for a while and have something to eat." A look shut Mulder up. "There's been too damn much excitement around here, and I want us to cool down for a while before we end up on horses."

"What?" Hank said.

"A definition of confusion," Mulder explained, hands clasped behind his head. "He jumped up on his horse and rode off in all directions." He winked. "Scully likes wise sayings like that. She hoards fortune cookies, you know."

Hank laughed; Andrews only snorted and shook her head.

Dana, for her part, did her best not to react, because she recognized the signs—he was high on an idea, the bits and pieces of the puzzle beginning to give him some kind of picture. The problem with him was, that picture was often one no one else saw but him.

It was what made working with him at once so fascinating and so damn exasperating.

Rather than try to derail him, however, it was better to give him his head and go along for the ride. For a while.

So she suggested they clean up and meet in the restaurant in half an hour or so for coffee. Her tone brooked no argument. When Andrews left without a word, Scully's expression sent Hank along as well, deciding it would be a good thing to take a walk around the building.

When they were alone, Mulder's expression sobered. "I saw it, Scully. I'm not kidding, I really saw it."

"Mulder, don't start."

He spread his hands on the table. "It's not like I'm the only one, you know. Even Chief Hawks admitted there were others." He held up a palm to keep her quiet. "I saw it—okay, just a glimpse—but I also touched it. It wasn't my imagination, it wasn't wishful thinking. I touched it, Scully. It was real."

She leaned away from him, thinking. Then: "I'll grant you it was real. He was real. But it wasn't any goblin, no supernatural creature."

"The skin—"

"Camouflage. Come on, Mulder, Fort Dix is a training base. That means there are personnel who are experts in all sorts of weaponry... and camouflage. God knows how elaborate they can be, but it's probably a lot more now than just smearing greasepaint on your face."

He tried to stand, grimaced, and sagged back. "My jacket." It had been tossed on the dresser. She fetched it and looked it over.

"I hit it twice, once pretty hard." He leaned forward under the light. "There's nothing there, Scully. No paint, no oil, no nothing."

She dropped the jacket onto the bed. "A suit, that's all. Skin-tight, latex, who knows? No goblins, Mulder. Just people in disguise." She pointed at the bed. "Lie down."

She knew he still wasn't feeling well when he made no cracks, just nodded wearily and shifted stiffly to the mattress. As he settled down, she brought him a glass of water and aspirin and watched him drink.

"What about the major and his people?" he asked. His eyelids fluttered. "Hank's right, that's kind of fishy."

"Later," she ordered. "You're not doing anybody any good, least of all yourself, when you can't think straight." Her frown deepened. "Get some rest. I'm not kidding. I'll drop by later to see how you're doing."

"What about the others?"

She smiled prettily and headed for the door. "Oh, I think we'll manage. We'll muddle through somehow."

She opened the door and looked over her shoulder. He hadn't closed his eyes; he was staring at the ceiling.

Then his gaze shifted. "Scully, what if I'm right?"

"Rest."

"What if I'm right? What if they're out there?"

She stepped out, the door closing behind her. "They're not, Mulder. For God's sake, rest, before I—"

"How do you know they're not? You can't see them, Scully. They're out there, somewhere, and you can't see them."

FOURTEEN

The room was empty.

Rosemary didn't really expect to find anyone there; it was too soon after the woodland incident, and it also wasn't easy for it to get away without being noticed.

What she hadn't expected, however, and what frightened her, was the destruction.

She stood on the threshold, one hand absently rubbing her arm, a faint chill slipping across the back of her back. Although she couldn't hear it, she swore she could feel the wind pummeling the hospital, could feel the building's weight settling on her shoulders.

The notion made her angry, but she couldn't shake it off.

Damn, she thought, and passed a weary hand over her eyes.

The mattress had been sliced open in a score of places, the stuffing strewn across the floor; the desk was overturned, one leg snapped off; the chair was little more than splinters.

The Blue Boy had been yanked off the wall and shredded. In its place, scrawled in black letters:

I'm looking for you.

\\\\\\\\\\\\\\\\\\\

Major Tonero sat at his desk, hands folded on the blotter, staring at the telephone.

He was neither panicked nor overconfident, but since leaving the site of the shooting, he had begun to review his options. By the time he had stopped pacing the office, he knew what had to be done. And it galled him. Not that he considered the Project a failure; too much had been learned from it, too much progress gained. No, what galled him was—

The telephone rang.

He listened to it without moving.

At the seventh ring he cleared his throat and picked up the receiver.

"Good afternoon, sir," was followed without prompting by a detailed summary of what had happened that afternoon, and what connection he suspected it had with the two incidents he had previously reported to those in charge. He spoke crisply and flatly, no emotion at all. When he finished, he listened.

He did not interrupt, speaking only when asked a question, his spine rigid, his free hand still flat on the blotter.

The voice at the other end was calm, a good sign, but he did not, could not, put himself at ease.

When the conversation arrived at the crux, thirty minutes had passed.

The last question was asked.

Tonero nodded. "Yes, sir, I do, with your permission." He inhaled slowly. "I believe it's time to explore other venues; there are several mentioned in my December report. This one, through no fault of ours, has been contaminated. I also believe the additional personnel now on site will not be put off, most especially after this afternoon's incident. That they are from the Bureau means we can neither control nor contain them with any true degree of effectiveness or guarantee of success. However, I have no doubt we can make the transfer without discovery, and then the Bureau people can investigate all they want. They won't find a thing."

He listened again, and for the first time, he smiled.

"Yes, sir, I do believe you're right—sometimes you win, sometimes you lose. But we are still light years ahead of where we were the last time. This, I think, argues well for our eventual success."

His smile broadened.

"Thank you, sir, I appreciate that."

The smile vanished.

"Indispensable? No, sir, to be honest, he is not. His objectivity and full commitment have been lost, I believe, and, frankly, his nerves are shot. I do not believe another relocation would be in the Project's best interest. Dr. Elkhart, however, has been most helpful. It would be a severe loss if she were not to remain."

He waited.

He listened.

"Forty-eight hours, sir."

He nodded.

He replaced the receiver and for several long seconds sat without moving.

Then, as if he'd been struck across the shoulders, he sagged, and whispered, "Jesus!" His hands began to tremble, and there was sweat on his brow.

\\\\\\\\\\\\\\\\\\\\

Barelli sat at a window table in the diner, beginning to wonder if he had, in fact, wasted his time. Not that he didn't doubt his reporter's skills; that he was good was a given. But after nearly an hour with that police sergeant, with some comments from the others as they drifted in and out of the station, he had learned practically nothing he hadn't known before—Frankie was dead, the killer was still out there, and nobody had a clue what the hell was going on.

And that goblin shit—Jesus Christ, what the hell did they think he was?

A round-faced wall clock over the register ticked closer to six as he sipped at cold coffee and stared at the traffic. The weather hadn't discouraged anyone, it seemed. Men in uniform, soldiers in civilian clothes trying not to look like soldiers, strolled or drove past, filling the diner, moving into the bars that served food, lingering in front of the movie theater a block west of the police station.

Friday night in the middle of nowhere.

His stomach complained of all the caffeine he had drunk, and he popped an antacid tablet into his mouth, chewed it absently, and wondered what the hell he was going to do now. Of course, there was still that "date" with Babs Radnor to keep. If he wanted to. And right about now, it looked as if it was the only game in town.

Another antacid, another scan of the street, and he dropped a few bills onto the table and went outside.

He scowled at the overcast. He hated this kind of day. If it was going to rain, he wished it would do it and be done with it; otherwise, why the hell didn't those clouds just blow away?

He headed for the corner; his car was still parked in front of the police station.

Along the way he passed an old woman dressed in black from a heavy topcoat to a long scarf wrapped around her head. She held a large purse close to her chest, and an idle glance there made him stop and turn slowly.

What he had seen was the orange top of a spray paint can, and it didn't take a genius to figure out who she was. He hurried after her, came abreast and said, "Miss Lang?"

She stopped and glared up at him. "Ms. Lang, if you don't mind. Who are you?"

"I'm a reporter," he explained, best smile, best voice. "I'm looking into the..." He lowered his voice, slipping her into his confidence. "Into the goblin affair."

He waited patiently, watching her debate both the truth and the sincerity of what he had said.

A bus coughed past them.

Three young airmen on the corner broke into song. Elly Lang eyed him suspiciously. "You think I'm a nut?"

"He killed a friend of mine. That's not crazy at all." When she didn't walk away, he touched her arm lightly. "I'd be pleased if you'd join me for dinner."

"And pump me, right?" she snapped.

The smile turned up a notch. "That, and for the company."

She shook her head. "You're full of it, mister, but I'm not going to pass up a free meal." She took his arm and led him up the street. "You going to be cheap, or are we going someplace good?"

He didn't laugh, but he wanted to; instead, he promised her the best meal this town could provide, which seemed, for the moment, to satisfy her. And as long as he didn't run into Mulder or Scully, he had a feeling this was going to be a most informative, and lucrative, night.

\\\\\\\\\\\\\\\\\\\

Tonero wasn't in his office, wasn't anywhere on post that she could tell, but Rosemary ordered herself not to panic. There was still time to make corrections. There was still time to salvage something of the years she had put in.

She returned to the hospital, nodding silently to the receptionist and making her way down a corridor to an elevator stenciled AUTHORIZED PERSONNEL ONLY. From her pocket she took a small key ring and inserted a silver key into a vertical slot where, ordinarily, a summons button would be. When the door slid aside, she checked the hall and stepped in.

The key took her down.

She didn't bother to watch the floor indicator; the elevator only stopped at three levels—the second floor, where the major's office was, the main floor, and a subbasement.

The car stuttered to a halt and the door opened; she stared uneasily down the length of the dimly lighted corridor.

It seemed a lot longer tonight, and her heels a lot louder on the concrete floor.

The faint thrum of distant machinery was the only other sound.

As if performing for an invisible audience, she made a show of smoothing her smock over her chest, of caressing a palm over her hair as she walked. Confidence, outside and in, was the key. As long as she kept to her plan, as long as she didn't lose her head, everything would be fine.

She tested Tymons's office door; it was locked.

She opened the Project Center door and nearly screamed when she saw him bending over one of the computers.

"Jesus, Leonard," she said, stepping in. "I didn't know you'd be here. What are you—"

He turned to face her, and in his right hand was a rectangular block of black metal about six inches long. In his left hand was a gun. "Just stay where you are, Rosemary, all right? Just… stay where you are."

"Leonard, what the hell are you doing?"

He smiled wanly. "Correcting a few things, that's all."

She looked around the room, not seeing anything out of place until her gaze reached the first computer screen. Though the machine was on, the screen was blank. So was the second one.

He waved his right hand. "It was so easy, I don't know why I didn't think of it before." He held up the block. "Why go through the whole mess when all you need is a magnet."

"My God, Leonard!"

"One pass, and poof!" He dropped the magnet on the shelf. "Poof. All gone."

Outrage prevented her from speaking, and fear of what Joseph would do when he found out. "The thing is," Tymons said calmly, and put a bullet through the nearest computer.

She jumped, but the gun kept her from fleeing.

"The thing is, you see, nobody's ever really going to know, are they? I mean, there's no sense going to the papers or the TV stations, because no one would ever believe it."

He shot another one, showering the floor with splintered plastic and shards of glass.

She took a step back.

He glanced at her sideways, his expression rueful. "I'm still going to try, though. Despite the odds, I'm really going to try."

"You can't," she said hoarsely, her throat lined with sand. She cleared it and tried again. "You can't." Her left hand fluttered helplessly from her chest to her throat and back again. "All those years, Leonard, all the work we've done. All the time. For God's sake, think of all the time!"

"All the failures," he said flatly. "All that time, and all those failures." He spat dryly. "Buried, Rosemary. We had to bury our failures."

He's insane, she thought; my God, he's insane.

"Listen, Leonard, if that's what... if you don't care about the work... think about—" She jerked a thumb at the ceiling. "You can't."

"Why? You mean those stupid oaths we signed?" He fired at the third and last monitor and hunched a shoulder to protect himself against flying shards. "Meaningless, Rosemary. By the time I'm through, they won't mean a thing."

"I'll deny it," she threatened. "I'll tell anyone you tell that I don't know a thing."

He straightened. "My dear doctor, I'm sorry, but you won't live long enough to have the chance."

She backed up hastily until the wall stopped her, the open door to her right. She couldn't think, could barely breathe, and a small fire in the workings of one of the destroyed computers had begun to lift feathers of smoke into the room.

"They'll come after you, Leonard," she warned, swallowing hard, fighting the nausea that roiled in her stomach. "Even if you can get off post, you won't be able to hide for long. A week, maybe a month." Sweat stung her eyes, but she didn't dare move her hands to wipe it away. "You've just signed your own death warrant."

He shrugged. "Like I care, Rosemary? Like I really give a damn?"

Without warning he emptied his clip into the shelves, the explosions deafening, damage almost total. She couldn't help but scream then, more in rage than fear, hands up to protect her face from the spinning, flaming debris. Before she could move, he had replaced the clip with a fresh one from his pocket.

And pointed the gun at her head.

Her eyes fluttered closed.

All she could think was *This is crazy, this is wrong.*

"Go away."

She didn't move, didn't understand.

"Rosemary, go away."

When she looked, the gun was at his side, but the defeat in his voice wasn't reflected in his face.

"Maybe," he said, "you'll last longer than I."

Disgust twisted her features, but she refused to say a word for fear he would change his mind. Although she wanted desperately to rail against the destruction of all their work, she wanted more desperately to get out of this alive.

"Go away," he whispered, and shook the gun at her.

Without further urging, she bolted clumsily into the corridor, and hadn't taken two steps toward the elevator when she kicked herself in the ankle and fell hard into the wall. She cried out, more in surprise than pain, and cried out again when she heard a gunshot.

Another.

At that she ran, keeping her stinging arm braced against her side, fumbling with her free hand for the keys.

At the elevator door the key slid off the control plate twice before she was able to insert it properly. "Come on, damnit," she whispered urgently, willing her nerves to settle down. "Come on, come on!"

The door opened and she virtually threw herself into the car, spun around and inserted the key a second time.

It wasn't until the door had hissed closed that she realized she wasn't alone.

No, she thought; not after all this, no.

"You know," said a rasping voice behind her, "I'm getting pretty good at this, don't you think?"

FIFTEEN

Andrews wasn't in the room when Dana returned, and she decided to take some of her own advice and scrub some of the afternoon away. Maybe some time alone would help her figure out the purpose of today's attack. So little of it made any real sense. If it had been meant as intimidation, as a warning to stay away and drop the investigation—for whatever reason—it certainly wouldn't work, and surely whoever was behind it knew that as well; if it had been meant to stop them permanently, that had failed, too, and she couldn't convince herself that the shooter hadn't been aiming to kill.

"Unless," she thought aloud, "he wasn't an expert."

She pushed a hand back through her hair, and rubbed the back of her neck. There had been a lot of wind, lots of leaves and things blowing around. Branches moving, targets moving. Plus, they had been shooting back.

So maybe, she thought, just maybe, they had gotten a little lucky.

That particular idea unnerved her more than anything. Especially when she realized that the shooter really could have killed her and Webber at practically any time before they had ducked into the trees.

They had been in the open far longer than Mulder.

But he hadn't.

The more she thought about it, the more she believed he had only been trying, and succeeding, to pin them down. To take them out of the game as much as he could.

What he had actually been trying to do was put a bullet in Mulder. The man at the Jefferson Memorial:

you have no protection, Mr. Mulder, you still have no protection.

"Oh, brother," she whispered. "Oh, brother."

Think. She needed a clear head to think this through, or she'd end up just as paranoid as her partner.

Once stripped and in the shower, however, it wasn't the shooter she concentrated on—for some reason, she couldn't stop thinking about Mulder's other assailant. The explanations she had given him were more than likely correct, or at the very least, parameters. Which did not, under any circumstances, include anything like a goblin.

And yet...

She made a noise much like a growl.

And yet there had been times past when she had been forced to the unwelcome conclusion that explanations could very well be only rationalizations in disguise.

She growled again and turned away from the shower head, letting the hot water slam against her back and splash over her shoulders. Her eyes half-closed. Her breathing steadied as she willed the memory of gunfire to a safer distance.

Steam rose gently around her, condensing on the narrow pebble-glass window in the white-tiled wall, running down the translucent sliding door.

She felt nothing but the water.

She heard nothing but the water.

The perfect time, she thought suddenly, for good old Norman Bates to slip into the bathroom, knife held high and at the ready. Effectively deaf and vision blurred, lulled by the comfort of steam and heat, she wouldn't know it was over until the end had begun; she wouldn't know, because all she could see was a smeared shadow on the door.

Standing there.

Watching.

Biding its time.

The shadow, of course, was the drape of bath towels over their rack by the door.

She knew that.

No; she assumed that.

Her eyes closed briefly as she damned Mulder for sparking her imagination; nevertheless, she couldn't stop herself from holding her breath to brace herself, and opening the shower door, just a little.

Just to be sure.

"Mulder, I swear I'm going to strangle you," she whispered in relief and mild anger when she saw the towels, and the rack, and not a single place in the tiny room for anyone to hide.

The steam flowed over and around her, twisting in slow spectral ribbons, creating the momentary illusion she had stepped into a light fog.

She shivered.

The room was chilly.

And the steam that should have filled it flowed and twisted, because the bathroom door was open.

\\\\\\\\\\\\\\\\

He didn't want to sleep.

There was too much to do.

But the pain had finally ebbed, weariness taking its place, and he couldn't keep his thoughts in an orderly line. They drifted, fading and dancing.

mulder, watch your back.

Patches of skin like snapshots, flashing too rapidly for him to focus on, barklike skin without the roughness of bark, without the texture, although he couldn't really be sure because contact had been so brief.

mulder

The voice was muffled by sleep and time, yet it sounded maddeningly familiar despite the fact that it belonged to no one he knew; a roughness here, too, and forced, as if the speaker, the goblin, was either suffering low-level pain or hadn't yet gotten used to the voice that it had.

watch your back.

And if it was true, that he had to watch his back, why hadn't he been killed, like the others?

I don't know, he answered, but the voice and the nightmare wouldn't stop.

\\\\\\\\\\\\\\\\

Rosemary couldn't take it anymore. Her knees buckled, and she sagged weakly to the floor, her back against the elevator wall.

"Are you all right?"

Hoarse, painful to listen to.

She nodded.

"What happened?"

Gone, all gone, she thought; everything's gone and Joseph will kill me and it's gone, damnit, all gone.

"Dr. Elkhart, what's wrong?"

She raised her head and gestured defeat.

"Dr. Elkhart, say something. You're scaring me."

"My dear," she said with a brittle bitter laugh, "you have no idea what scared is."

A shuffling, a shifting, a soft hand brushing across her ankle.

"Can I help?"

She made to shake her head, and stopped. She stared at the elevator door, seeing the two of them, reflections twisted out of recognition in the polished steel, and before long she felt her lips pull back into what might have been a smile.

"Yes," she said at last. "Yes, dear, I think you can."

\\\\\\\\\\\\\\\\\\\

Scully's purse was on the floor between the toilet and the tub. She reached through the gap and fumbled it open, pulled out her gun, and straightened, staring intently at the bathroom door, still open about an inch. Her left hand shut the water off; her right wrist slid the shower door away.

Once on the bath mat, she grabbed a towel and wrapped it hastily around her; it was no protection at all, but it made her feel less vulnerable. Her teeth chattered and her lower lip quivered as the room's chill raised a pattern of gooseflesh on her skin.

She switched off the light.

Water dripped too loudly from the shower head.

The only illumination in the outer room came from the brass lamp on the nightstand between the two beds, just as she had left it.

There was no sound or movement.

Using her left hand, she opened the door as slowly as she could, crouching low until she could slip over the threshold and duck behind the nearest bed. The gun barrel swept the room just ahead of her, but no one else was there.

Don't assume, she told herself; never assume.

Feeling like a jerk now—*never assume, Scully, never assume*—she half-crawled around the footboard to be sure her visitor wasn't hiding between the beds. Once satisfied she was indeed alone, she sat on the mattress and tried to remember if, maybe, she hadn't left the bathroom door open by mistake; or maybe she had closed it, but the latch didn't catch; or maybe Andrews had returned, heard the shower, and decided Scully didn't need to be disturbed.

But if that were true, if she had heard the shower, why had she opened the door?

A trickle of water slipped out of her hair and down her spine.

"All right," she said aloud, as much for the sound as the comfort. "All right. It's all right, you're alone."

That didn't stop her from turning on the hanging lamp over the table to help banish the room's shadows, or from drying off as fast as she could, with the bathroom door wide open. Once that was accomplished, dressing was quick and easy—blouse, skirt, matching wine jacket. By then she was almost calm, and she looked in the dresser mirror as she smoothed the blouse over her chest, deciding that one of these days, Bureau or not, she would get herself a fashion life.

Back into the bathroom, then, to wield a brush through her hair, using her reflection as a sounding board as she practiced telling Mulder what his stupid notions were doing to her. It didn't help. Her reflection just gave her the same sardonic look he would when he heard. If he heard. By the time she was finished, she had decided this was something her partner did not need to know.

A lopsided smile sent her into the front room, where she started and gasped when she spotted someone pacing her at the corner of her vision.

\\\\\\\\\\\\\\\\\\\

"Listen carefully," Rosemary said urgently. She stabbed a thumb at the door. "He's trying to destroy us. Tymons. He's afraid, and he's a coward. He doesn't care about you, me, or the Project. He wants... he wants us all dead."

A silence then, and she held her breath, praying.

"He didn't approve of me from the beginning, you know." Still hoarse, now with sullen rage. "He thought I was too... emotional."

Rosemary agreed silently.

A giggle: "He's really scared of me, you know."

"Yes. I know."

The giggling stopped. "What can I do? I'm not stupid, Dr. Elkhart. I know what'll happen if you stop helping me. What can I do?"

Rosemary tried to think, tried to set the priorities that would keep her intact.

"Do you need him? Dr. Tymons?"

There wasn't a second's hesitation: "No. No, we don't."

"Others?"

"Three," she said without having to think.

Then concern made her stand when a wrenching cough made her wonder if they could pull it off. "Can you do it, dear? Are you well enough?"

"I can do it. Really. But it'll take time. A couple of days, maybe. I can't—"

The coughing increased, grinding into spasms that made Rosemary reach out a hand, grip a shoulder, and squeeze until it was over.

"It's okay," she whispered, rubbing now, soothing. "It's going to be okay." And she believed it. It would be all right. Everything would be all right. Then she spoke the names.

\\\\\\\\\\\\\\\\\\\'

Scully's right hand was already reaching for the gun on the bed when she realized the movement was only her reflection in the dresser mirror.

Too damn many mirrors around here, she thought sourly, and pointed at it as if to order it to find someone else to scare.

She froze.

Something moved on the wall behind her. A slight movement she would have missed had she simply glanced in that direction.

She watched, waiting, thinking maybe it had only been a shadow cast by a passing car.

It moved again, and she turned and made her way between the beds.

A moth fluttered its wings slowly and began to make its way toward the ceiling.

Fascinated, licking her lips, she climbed onto the bed, balanced herself, and looked away.

Looked back, and it took a full second before she could find it again.

"Well," she whispered.

A tentative smile came and went.

Then she bounced on the mattress, just high enough to snatch the moth away in a loose fist. Feeling its wings beat against her palm. Whispering to it as she opened the door and flung it away. Standing back, rubbing her chin thoughtfully.

She needed another test, and footsteps outside made her think fast.

With the hanging lamp on again, the nightstand lamp off, she sat on the far bed and pushed herself back until she rested against the headboard, legs crossed at the ankles. She could barely see herself then, but she could see just the same.

A key turned in the lock.

She heard it but didn't move.

The door opened and Licia stepped in. "Scully?"

Dana opened her mouth, but kept silent.

Andrews headed for the bathroom. "Scully, you in there? Look, are you going to leave me with that boy all night? Damn, you should hear—" She pushed the door open and cut herself off, sighed, turned, and yelped when she noticed Scully sitting on the bed, pointing at her.

"Jesus!" Her hand splayed across her chest. "God Almighty, Scully, I didn't see you there. Why the hell didn't you say something?"

Scully smiled. "You didn't see me."

Andrews scowled. "Of course not. It was dark. You're sitting in the dark."

Scully pushed at the hanging lamp. "Not really. But you see me now, right?"

Andrews didn't know how to answer, her lips working without a sound. Finally she said, "Well… yes. I guess so." She laughed at herself. "Of course I do. The light was—"

Scully pushed off the bed, shoved her gun into her purse, and reached for her coat. "Go get Hank," she said. "Meet me at Mulder's."

"Again?"

"Again." Scully pushed her gently but firmly outside. "God help me, but I have a feeling Mulder is right."

Andrews gaped. "Goblins? About the goblins?"

"Something like that." She couldn't believe she had just said it. "Yes, something like that."

SIXTEEN

Wrapped in nothing but a thin stubby towel, Mulder examined his reflection in the steam-shrouded mirror. He looked drawn, and probably a little too pale. But he certainly didn't look like a man who had almost been killed. Twice in the same afternoon. However a man like that is supposed to look, that is. He rose up on his toes and inhaled sharply when he saw the full extent of the size and shape of the bruise below his ribs. That, he knew, was going to be hell in the morning.

He toweled off slowly so as not to aggravate either the bruise or the hammer and anvil gearing up in his skull. Deliberately slowly, because, as Scully had already sensed, he had begun to feel that electric spark of anticipation, the one that signaled the true beginning of the hunt.

He suspected that right now, Webber was having fits, and Andrews was pacing whether she was standing up or not. It was only natural. A little ordinary poking around had ended up in a deadly firefight, and they probably couldn't stop the adrenaline from flowing. Action, they no doubt thought, was the key now, not methodical investigation. It didn't matter that nothing but casings had been found at the site, and nothing at all at the site of his ambush.

Action. Get moving. Keep moving. Sitting down, having coffee, talking things out, was definitely not the way things were supposed to be.

As he dressed, he glanced around the room, not really seeing the furniture or the dingy walls. Hints and whispers had come to him while he'd let the warm water and steam do their work.

Hints and whispers.

Not all of them clear.

Still, the fever dreams he had had—and there was no other way to describe them—refused to let him go. Every throb in his skull, every touch of fire below his ribs, reminded him of what he had seen.

Not what he thought he had seen.

He slipped stiffly into his jacket, stuffed his tie into one pocket, and grabbed his topcoat. And stopped. What he should do now was head straight for the Queen's Inn to meet the others.

Or he could slip away for a while, away from Scully's watchful doctor's eye, and—

The door opened suddenly.

He stumbled back, tripped over the edge of his bed, and fell on the mattress, his head nearly exploding.

"Jesus," he said angrily.

Scully looked down at him without any sympathy at all. "I have an idea," was all she said.

\\\\\\\\\\\\\\\\

Major Tonero sat on the porch of his modest Cape Cod on the outskirts of Marville, a cigarette in one hand, a tumbler of scotch and soda in the other. Although he had been expecting the FBI to call on him since meeting those agents this afternoon, he wasn't disappointed when they hadn't. Their attention was elsewhere now. Whoever had ambushed them had unwittingly done him a great favor.

Now all he had to do was tell Rosemary about his conversation with their superiors, and they could begin the relocation procedure. By Sunday afternoon they would, with a little luck, be on their way.

He sipped, and blew a smoke ring.

It was chilly tonight, but not enough to keep him inside.

Besides, he preferred it out here. The neighborhood was small, quiet, so perfectly ordinary that there were times, both night and day, when he felt as if his superiors had dropped him into the middle of a television series, circa 1955. But it was definitely better than living with them, shortsighted and single-minded officers who lived and died for the service without once ever understanding what true potential there was.

He toasted that truth with another drink.

There were, now that he thought about it, only two problems remaining: what to do with Leonard Tymons, and what to do with the Project's subject.

He wasn't worried, though. The answer would come. It always did.

A car sped up the block. He frowned, hating the disruption of his quiet evening, the frown deepening when the car squealed to a halt at the curb. He leaned forward—Rosemary?

After several seconds she climbed out and ran-staggered toward the house. He was up and at the steps before she reached them, taking her arms and hushing her until they were inside.

"Leonard," she gasped, and dropped heavily onto the couch.

She looked like hell; in fact, she looked like a corpse, her hair damp with perspiration, her cheeks flushed with an unnatural color that unpleasantly accentuated her already pale face.

Shit, he thought angrily; why the hell can't it be easy, just for once?

"Tell me," he said, keeping his voice low.

He didn't move when she told him what had happened at the Project lab, didn't touch her when she began to tremble so violently she had to hug herself to calm down, didn't offer a word when she finished and looked up at him, beseeching him for comfort.

He turned to the window and looked out at the lawn, hands clasped behind his back. When he turned back, he smiled. "Are you sure he's dead?"

"He… he has to be by now."

"There were backups, correct?"

She passed a hand over her face, forcing herself to think. "Yes." She nodded hesitantly. "Yes, of course. Although I don't know how recent they would be. Leonard was always—"

"No matter." He took a step toward the couch. "In his office?"

"Yes."

He rubbed the side of his nose thoughtfully. "And what about our friend?" His eyes widened in slight alarm and he glanced at the front door.

"No, don't worry." She inhaled deeply, slowly, and leaned her head back wearily, closed her eyes, as her left hand unbuttoned her coat and pulled it away as if she needed room to breathe. "We were in the elevator, and then… I don't know where."

Another step: "I'm correct in assuming that, without the proper medication, our friend will eventually…" His smile flashed and vanished. "Fade away?"

"Damnit, Joseph, what's the matter with you? Haven't you listened to a word I've said?"

He held out his hands, palms up, beckoning until she took them and allowed herself to be pulled to her feet and into his arms. He kissed her ear, her cheek, her lips.

"Joseph?"

She was cold; cold with fear.

And trembling.

He whispered of the telephone call, and of the problems he had had until the problems, it seemed, had decided to take care of themselves. He whispered of the support he had given her to those in charge during that call. He suggested, in a whisper, that they take her car back to the hospital, to Dr. Tymons's office, and retrieve the backup computer disks. Although no one had access to the Project level except themselves, it seemed as if they might be leaving earlier than expected.

"Or," he whispered after she snuggled, wriggled closer, and kissed him back, hard, "we could always wait until morning."

It was her turn to whisper as she began working on his shirt: "Joseph, you can be one arrogant bastard, do you know that?"

"But for good reason, Dr. Elkhart. And don't you ever forget it."

\\\\\\\\\\\\\\\\\\\\\\

Barelli almost felt guilty leaving the old woman alone at the Company G, but since everyone there seemed to know her, and like her, the guilt passed as soon as he was outside.

It had been, from the beginning, an evening of surprises.

The establishment itself, around the corner and halfway down the block from Barney's, was a low clapboard building outlined in soft blue neon. In its large front window a neon trooper marched guard duty around stencil-style letters that spelled out COMPANY G. A shiny black film over the glass prevented anyone from seeing inside, but once through the door he had been pleasantly surprised. The restaurant-lounge was a single large room, softly and indirectly lighted, with black plastic and glass, gleaming chrome and brass. A bar ran along the left-hand wall, and the carpeted floor held a score or more tables, about half of which were taken. A dance floor took up most of the back, with a low stage against the wall.

The food, too, had been more than decent, and the drinks inexpensive. Elly Lang ordered well and ate carefully, as if expecting to make the meal last all night. When he asked her about herself, she smiled and told him little except for the reputation the community had given her.

All because of the goblins.

By the time he had finished he knew he had heard all she had to say. Not ranting, exactly, but it sounded like a story she had told a hundred times, and not much different from what he had learned at the police station.

She had, pleasantly, dismissed him when his mind began to wander, and although he stopped short of kissing her on the cheek, the almost-gesture had made her laugh and shoo him away.

Now, on the street, he considered returning to the station to have a talk with the dispatcher. Because of their job, they usually knew more than anyone, and he remembered Sergeant Nilssen telling him their regular operator was a young woman, Maddy Vincent.

Which was when he remembered his date with Babs Radnor.

"Shit," he muttered. "Damn."

He would have to go back and make some kind of excuse. She had been taken with his reporting reputation, he knew that much, so maybe she wouldn't be all that unhappy when he assured her he wasn't about to head home right away. A rain check until tomorrow seemed the most likely way out.

He hurried up toward Main Street, changing his mind about driving, deciding that a phone call would do. If he played it right, sounded right, she might even be excited for him, now and later.

He shivered then and wished he had brought a topcoat with him.

True night had settled over the town, starless, feeling like rain. Houses and buildings slipped into the protection of the dark, neon and streetlamps giving the street needed color, and a semblance of life it didn't have when the sun shone. There were just enough pedestrians to make the district seem almost lively; a street cop spoke to a disgruntled knot of teens; a cruiser trolled slowly westward, not caring about the traffic it backed up behind it; several shops were open late, ghosts of customers inside.

The wind had died.

Still, he hunched his shoulders as he hurried westward, grumbling when he reached the police station without finding a public phone. He looked over, shrugged a *what the hell*, and took advantage of the first break to sprint to the other side. Once in, he had to wait for several minutes. Unlike his earlier visit, tonight the station was busy—two cops leading two lurching drunks back toward the cells, the radio in constant chatter, a man in plainclothes at a desk arguing with two women, one of whom had a bloody bandage wrapped around her hand. When he finally caught the desk sergeant's attention, he was told brusquely that Officer Vincent wasn't on this shift, he would have to wait until morning.

He couldn't.

The idea had taken hold, and now he couldn't shake it.

A handful of smiling lies inflating Vincent's importance to his story gave him an address and directions; a flourish of notebook and pen proved to the officer that Barelli wasn't about to spell his name incorrectly.

By the time he was back on the sidewalk, he realized he was out of breath.

Easy, boy, he thought; take it easy, don't blow it now.

Two blocks up, one block down, the sergeant had told him. An easy walk, and a chance for him to think of the questions he'd need to ask.

The house was easy to find—it was the only one on the street without any lights.

He knocked, rang the bell, even wandered around to the back door and knocked again, but Officer Vincent wasn't answering.

No matter, he decided, and parked himself on her front steps; she has to come home sometimes, and when she does, I'll be waiting right here to make her famous.

He sat, he smoked, he listened to the neighbors on the left have a beast of a battle. He walked around for a while to keep warm, but always within sight of the house. And when he checked his watch under a streetlamp and realized it was only a few minutes past eight, it occurred to him that Maddy Vincent might not be home for hours. It was Friday night, and she was single, and what the hell had he been thinking?

He was nearly at the corner when he stopped cursing his stupidity and trotted back across the street, pulling his notebook out of his jacket pocket. Just to be sure she'd be around, he would leave a note. Not too obvious, a little mysterious. Pique her policewoman's interest. He would save the sweet talk for when he saw her.

It took him four tries before he was satisfied and tore the page free. The next thing was a place to put it so the wind wouldn't blow it halfway to the next county.

He settled for folding it in half and sticking it between the door and the frame.

Then he turned around, dusting his hands, and saw the shadow standing on the porch.

"Who the hell are you?" he demanded.

"It doesn't make any difference," the shadow said.

Barelli didn't see the blade until it was too late, and there was nothing left to do but open his mouth and try to scream.

SEVENTEEN

A single light over the table, barely reaching the first bed, and the second one not at all.

Scully sat with her back to the window, Mulder by the door, Webber on the edge of the dresser, Andrews on the edge of the near bed.

Mulder didn't like it. He couldn't see expressions; they were too much like spirits at the fringe of a seance, floating in and out of the dark as if they wore veils.

Scully's fingers pushed at nothing on the table's wood-grain surface. "I've been thinking about a moth I found on my wall."

She hadn't seen it right away, not only because it was too small, but also because its coloration almost blended in with the paint. That made her think of camouflage, and the goblin, who was able to hide in an alley without being seen, and hide in the woods without Mulder seeing. Despite what she had said before, she couldn't quite bring herself to believe that tactics like that were supported by an arsenal of camouflage suits and greasepaint, burnt charcoal, twigs and leaves worn as aids to blending in.

Although it was possible, it also required advance knowledge of where the target victim would be.

"And I don't think such a package could be carried on someone's back. It would be inefficient and clumsy."

There was, for example, no way the killer—the goblin, if they had to call it that—could have known that Grady Pierce would pass by that alley that night, at just that time. Webber's interview with the bartender had established that more often than not, Noel brought the ex-sergeant home himself. And they themselves hadn't decided to visit the site of Corporal Ulman's murder until they had finished lunch in the diner.

"Two questions," she said, eyes down, as if speaking to the table.

"How did it know where to be?" Webber said.

She nodded.

"Unless it knows magic," Andrews said, a smile in her voice, "how could it be ready with… whatever it wore to hide itself?"

Scully nodded again.

Mulder watched her fingers move, dusting, tracing circles.

"For now, let's set aside the why of it, the killing. And the who." She looked up, too pale in the light, and Mulder looked away. "The how, on the other hand…"

No one spoke.

A car backfired in the parking lot, and only Webber jumped.

An engine raced on the county road, another followed, and there were horns.

Mulder shifted stiffly as he watched her face. It bothered him sometimes, how smooth it was, without many lines, because it prevented him from really knowing just what she was thinking. Too often a mask. But her eyes, they were different. He could see them now, shadowed by the light over her head, and he could see that she was struggling with a reluctant decision.

He brushed a strand of hair from his brow.

The movement made her look, and when she looked, she inhaled slowly.

"Special Projects," said Webber, startling them all. "That Major Tonero and his Special Projects."

"I think so," she answered. "But exactly what, I'm not sure."

"Yes, you are," Mulder said gently. "It's not a goblin, at least not like Elly Lang says it is."

Andrews made a faint noise of derision. "So what is it? A ghost?"

"Nope. It's a chameleon."

\\\\\\\\\\\\\\\\\

The wind rose.

A draft slipped through the window and fluttered the curtains.

Andrews slapped her thighs. "A what? A chameleon? You mean, a human chameleon?" She waved a hand in disgust. "No offense, Mulder, really, but you're out of your mind. There's no such thing."

He didn't take offense, although he knew she wanted him to. "There are lots of things that are no such thing, Licia. Some of them aren't, some of them are." He scooted his chair closer to the table. "I think Scully's right. This is one of them that is."

Andrews appealed to Scully. "Do you have any idea what he's talking about?"

A corner of Scully's mouth pulled up. "This time, yes."

He made a sour face at her, then swiped at his hair again. "A chameleon—"

"I don't need a biology lesson," Andrews snapped. "Or zoology. Whatever. I know what they can do."

"They change colors," Webber said anyway. "To fit their background, right?" He stepped away from the dresser. "Wow. Do you really think this is what we've got?"

Mulder held up a finger. "First, you're wrong. Sort of. Chameleons can't change color to fit every background. They're limited to only a few, like black, white, cream, sometimes green." He grinned. "Put him on a tartan tablecloth, he'd probably blow his brains out."

Webber laughed, and Scully smiled.

Mulder's fingers began to tap eagerly on the table. "But within certain limits, yes, he can adjust his pigmentation."

"I don't believe this," Andrews muttered. "I swear to God, I don't believe it."

Mulder ignored her; he wanted Scully to follow and watched her as he spoke, in case he made a mistake.

"Now, contrary to popular opinion, chameleons don't change at will, right?" She nodded. "It's things like temperature or emotion that cause the coloration to alter. When they get scared or angry. I don't think they sit down at breakfast and decide to be green for a day." He sat back, then stood.

"Careful, Mulder," Scully cautioned.

"But we can't do that," he said to Webber. "Right?"

"Change color? Hell, no. Except when we get tan or something."

"Right." He moved to the door, snapping his fingers at his side, turned and gripped the back of his chair. "But suppose our Major Tonero and his group— Tymons, right? and Elkhart—suppose they've been able—"

Around the edges of the drapes he spotted flashing lights and yanked open the door. In the parking lot below he saw a police cruiser, warning bar alit and swirling color. A patrolman looked up. "Hey, you the FBI?" he called.

Mulder winced and nodded. The policeman beckoned sharply. "The chief wants you right away. We got another one."

\\\\\\\\\\\\\\\\\\\

Two patrol cars, parked sideways, and a quartet of orange-stained sawhorses bracketed a fifty-yard section of the street. An ambulance was parked nose-in to the curb, and two attendants leaned against it, smoking and waiting. Blue and red lights swarmed across branches and tree trunks, and the faces of two dozen onlookers gathered on the sidewalk opposite the scene. Flashlights danced in back yards, and in the distance a siren screamed.

There was very little talk.

Mulder and Scully followed their driver around the barrier; Webber and Andrews were behind them in the other car.

Hawks met them at the foot of a gravel driveway. "Man walking his dog," he said, pointing to a young man standing in the street, a terrier in his arms. "He found him." He sounded angry.

"Are you sure it's the same?" Scully asked.

Up the drive two men knelt beside a body in high grass between the gravel and the porch; one of them was Dr. Junis.

"See for yourself."

Mulder moved first, but he didn't have to go all the way before he saw the victim's face. "Damn!" He turned to block Scully. "It's Carl."

"You know him?" Hawks demanded.

Scully inhaled sharply and stepped around the two men, nodding as Junis glanced up and recognized her.

"He's a reporter," Mulder explained, disgust and sadness in his voice. "A sports reporter."

"Sports? Sports, for God's sake? So what the hell was he doing here?"

"Corporal Ulman's fiancee was his cousin. He wanted me to come up and look around. I guess... I guess he was doing a little looking on his own."

"Jesus." Hawks clamped his hands on his hips, glowering, breathing heavily. "Son of a bitch, what the hell's going on around here? Mulder—" He stopped and wiped a hand over his face. "Mulder, is there some shit you're not telling me?"

A man on the porch called the chief, who hesitated before telling Mulder to stay where he was. When he left, Mulder scanned the growing crowd, and the shadows the cruiser lights created between the trees, between the houses. It was bad enough when the victim was a stranger, but this... He crammed his hands into his pockets and stared at the ground until footsteps on the gravel made him look up.

"Come on," Scully said gently, her voice trembling slightly.

Hawks called them from the steps, and held out a piece of paper found jammed into the doorframe. It was a note from Barelli, requesting an interview which, he promised, would be paid for by a complete dinner at the best restaurant in town.

"Who lives here?" Mulder asked.

The house was rented by Maddy Vincent. The day-shift dispatcher, Hawks added. A gesture to figures moving around the inside told him the woman wasn't home, and no one knew where she was. "No surprise, it's Friday night," the chief said in disgust. "Shit, she could be in Philadelphia for all I know. Or..."

Mulder checked the porch, the blood on the flooring and on the door. Carl was attacked here, he thought, and the force of the attack, and his probable retreat from it, sent him over the railing. Where he bled to death without ever getting his story.

"Damnit," he said, and stomped down the steps. "Damnit!"

An hour later, Carl's body was gone and those neighbors who'd been home had all been interviewed.

No one had seen anything; no one had heard anything. A call had gone out to Officer Vincent's friends in the vain hope she hadn't left town. A check with the station told them Barelli had stopped in only a short while ago, specifically looking for the dispatcher.

"But why?" Hawks leaned heavily against his patrol car, his face drawn and tired, his voice hoarse. Most of the crowd had retreated to nearby houses; two of the cruisers had left. "What the hell did he think he knew?"

Mulder held up a small notebook. "Nothing that he wrote down." He handed it over. "He had dinner with Miss... Ms. Lang, and wanted to see your dispatcher. All he had were more questions."

"He's not the only one," the chief growled.

Mulder sympathized with the man's frustration, but it didn't extend to telling him about the major. That, he decided grimly, was someone he wanted to talk to himself, without the complications Hawks was bound to create.

The chief finally mumbled something about getting back to his office, and Mulder wandered over toward his car, where the others waited. They said nothing as he turned to stare at the empty house, ribboned now in yellow, a patrolman on the steps to keep the curious away. The dusting had been completed, but he doubted they would find any useful prints besides Barelli's and Vincent's.

Goblins, he thought, don't leave handy clues.

He was angry. At Carl, for playing in a game well out of his league, and at himself, for the helplessness he felt for not knowing enough. It was a waste of energy, he knew that, but there were times, like now, when he simply couldn't help it.

He walked back to the middle of the street and stared at the house, ignoring the damp wind that whipped hair into his eyes.

Carl was a big man, and definitely not soft. He had to have been surprised. A single blow, and it was over. He had to have been surprised.

"Mulder." Scully came up beside him. "We can't do any more here."

"I know." He frowned. "Damn, I know." He rubbed his forehead wearily. "Major Tonero."

Scully looked at him sternly. "In the morning. You're exhausted, you're not thinking straight, and you need rest. He's not going anywhere. We'll talk to him in the morning."

Any inclination to argue vanished when she nudged him into the car; any inclination to do some work on his own vanished as soon as he saw the bed.

But he couldn't sleep.

While Webber snored gently, and murmured once in a while, all he could do was stare at the ceiling, wondering.

Finally he got up, pulled on his trousers and shirt, and went out onto the balcony, leaning on the railing while he watched the trees across the road move slowly in the slow wind.

He thought of Carl and the times they had had; he thought of the man who had tried to kill him that afternoon, an afternoon that seemed years distant, in another lifetime; he shivered a little and rubbed his arms for warmth as he wondered why Carl had wanted to talk to Officer Vincent. Elly Lang was obvious, but what did Hawks's dispatcher have to do with the goblins?

"You're supposed to be sleeping."

He didn't jump, didn't turn his head. "The day you figure out how to turn off my brain, Scully, let me know." He shook his head, but carefully. "Amazing, isn't it."

"Your brain?" She leaned her forearms on the railing. "It's okay, but I wouldn't call it amazing."

"Chameleons," he said. He nodded toward the woods. "Somewhere out there somebody has figured out a way, maybe, to create natural protective coloration in a human being. I don't know what you'd call it. Fluid pigmentation?"

"I don't know. I'm not sure that's—"

"It was your idea."

"Yeah, but I still don't know. Do you have any idea what kind of genetic manipulation that would require? What kind of control on the cellular level that would mean?"

"Nope." He glanced at her sideways. "But if you tell me, maybe I'll be able to get some sleep after all."

She rolled her eyes as she straightened. "Go to bed, Mulder. Just go to bed."

He smiled at her back, suddenly yawned, and did as he was ordered.

Sleep, however, was still hard to come by.

Aside from the aches in his head and side, he couldn't help thinking about the possibility that there could be someone in the room right now, standing against the wall there.

Invisible, and watching him.

Waiting.

And he wouldn't know it until a knife tore out his throat.

EIGHTEEN

There was no dawn. There was only a gradual shift from dark to shades of grey, and a falling mist just heavy enough to keep windshield wipers working, to raise the sharp smell of oil and tar from the blacktop.

Mulder was not in a good mood.

Following Scully's orders, Webber had let him oversleep, and it was close to ten before he finally opened his eyes to a note on the pillow that told him the others would be waiting in the Queen's Inn. He was also not miraculously cured. Although his head seemed fine except for a small lump beneath his hair, his side felt as if it had been set in cement. Every time he moved, he thought his skin would rip open.

He supposed he ought to be grateful for the extra healing time, and for the concern Scully showed him, but knowing that didn't make it happen. He showered and dressed as quickly as he was able, thinking that he would eat quickly, check with Chief Hawks on the slim to none chance there had been any new developments overnight, and then... he smiled mirthlessly as his brush fought with his hair... then he would have a few words with Major Joseph Tonero.

His stomach growled as he knotted his tie, and he snarled at it to hold its horses. Then he grabbed his coat, stepped outside, and was pleased to see that the weather perfectly complemented the way he felt.

I live for days like this, he thought gloomily as he descended the center staircase.

Scully recognized his mood immediately, and after a quick check to be sure he was all right, she hustled them through breakfast and outside, with a reminder that while they were heading for the post, there was also someone else out there, the shooter, they had best not forget.

Andrews still thought the so-called goblins and the shooting were related; when no one rose to the bait, she slumped into her corner and glared at the passing scenery.

There was no sound then but the rhythmic thump of the wipers and the hiss of the tires.

It wasn't until they had passed through town that Mulder remembered wanting to have a word with Hawks. He punched his leg lightly and scowled, and ordered himself to get with it, or he'd blow it all because he wasn't thinking straight.

Once this is done, he promised; I'll talk to him when we're done here.

Fifteen minutes later they passed between two simple brick pillars that marked the post entrance. No guards, no guardhouse; a stretch of woods that quickly fell away to the post's main complex—barracks, administration buildings, and on-post housing. A transport plane from McGuire lumbered and thundered overhead. A squad of troopers double-timed across an intersection, their dark green ponchos slick with water. They passed a construction site for a new federal prison twice before Scully finally gave up and made Hank ask directions. An MP gave them, and within minutes they were on New Jersey Avenue; it didn't take them long to find what they were after.

"Brother," Webber muttered as he pulled up in front of Walson Air Force Hospital. It was a seven-story light tan brick structure, but it somehow seemed a lot smaller.

Because, Mulder realized, it was mostly empty. A lot of empty rooms and offices, a lot of space for things to happen without anyone being any the wiser.

He sat up and watched the entrance, something quickening inside when he noted that hardly anyone went in, and no one came out.

"What makes you think he'll be here?" Andrews asked, rousing herself from her sulking.

"If he's working on a project," Scully answered, "he will. Something like this doesn't often hold over weekends."

Something like this, Mulder thought.

"But do we have any authority?"

Mulder opened the door, slid out, and poked his head back in. "We've been asked in by a U.S. senator, Licia. The senator the major himself called. So if he wants to argue, he can write his congressman."

A civilian receptionist sat just inside the entrance, a multiline telephone and a logbook the only items on her small desk. Mulder wished her a good morning, showed her his ID and asked directions to Major Tonero's office. She wasn't sure the major was in, and because of her standing orders was reluctant to give him the instructions until he insisted; then she pointed to a bank of elevators to their left.

As they moved away, he heard a noise and looked back.

Webber had his finger on the telephone's cut-off button. "I don't think so," he said politely, with a wink. "Government business, okay?"

Mulder couldn't believe it when the woman suddenly grinned. "Sure. Why not?"

Pancakes and women, he thought; the guy's got it made.

`````````````````

The major was in.

But it didn't look to Mulder as if he'd be there very long.

The office was a two-room suite on the second floor. When Mulder ushered the others in ahead of him, he saw a handful of packed cartons against one wall and an empty bookcase behind what he assumed was Tonero's secretary's desk. The door to the inner office was open, and he gestured the others silent as he approached it. He could see the major standing in the middle of the room, back to the door, speaking quietly but angrily to someone seated at his desk.

"Damnit, Rosie, I don't give a damn who—"

He turned and saw Mulder, and forced a smile. "My goodness, Agent Mulder, what is this, a raid?" He laughed as he shook Mulder's hand and nodded to the others.

The person behind the desk was Dr. Elkhart.

Mindful of protocol and egos, Mulder allowed Tonero to direct the conversation, politely answering questions about his health while he noticed that Dr. Elkhart, in a lab coat, was not as composed as she wanted him to
`````````````````

think. Although she sat back in the major's chair, her legs crossed, her hands on the armrests, her cheeks were lightly flushed, and her attempt at a bland expression was nearly a total failure.

She was, he thought, royally pissed off. What, he wondered next, is wrong with this picture?

"It's a real tragedy about Carl," Tonero said, stepping back to perch on the edge of his desk, ignoring Elkhart completely. "I want you to know that I am not going to rest until this matter is solved."

"I appreciate that, Major," Mulder said, sensing rather than seeing Scully take a chair just behind and to his left, while Webber and Andrews flanked the door. It was a large room, but their positions and attitude now made it seem much smaller. "I can assure you that we're not going to let it rest either."

He smiled quickly.

Dr. Elkhart uncrossed her legs.

"Well, good!" Tonero smiled purposefully at each of them in turn before rubbing his hands briskly together. "And what can I do to help?"

Mulder raised his eyebrows—*Gee, sir, I'm not really sure*—and glanced at Scully as if looking for guidance before facing the major again. "Well, I guess you could tell me what your project has to do with goblins."

Tonero sputtered into a laugh that proved he could appreciate a good joke when he heard one; but the laugh faded into a scowl when neither Mulder nor the others joined him. His back straightened; his expression became somber.

"I'm sorry, Agent Mulder, but what we do here is classified. I'm sure you understand."

"I do, believe me," he answered agreeably "The DoD can be pretty tough sometimes."

"Absolutely. Now—" He waved one hand to indicate the closing and packing he had to do. "As you can see, we're being transferred—the orders came just this morning—and we're in a hell of a mess." A look over his shoulder that Dr. Elkhart ignored. "Dr. Tymons—you may recall meeting him yesterday—seems to have gone ahead without telling us, so it's kind of hectic around here at the moment."

He stepped forward, with the intention of easing the agents back into the outer room.

Mulder sidestepped around him, his right hand brushing across the edge of the desk before he leaned on it and turned his head. "Dr. Elkhart, where were you last night? I don't know, about nine?"

Elkhart started, and blinked. "What?"

"Last night," he repeated.

"Now look here, Agent Mulder," Tonero snapped. "Dr. Elkhart is one of our most—"

"Home," the woman answered, crossing her legs again. "I was home. Watching TV." Her smile was crooked. "Why, Agent Mulder? Am I a suspect?"

Mulder matched the smile, didn't answer the question as he turned his back to her. "And you, Major?"

"How—" Tonero's face darkened. "What do you think you're doing? Do you know who—"

"Chameleons," said Scully mildly from her chair.

"Lizards," Elkhart responded immediately, not quite as mildly. "Not, I'm afraid, from the goblin family."

"Goblins?" The major's voice rose. "Goblins? What are you talking about? What does some old woman's rantings have to do with my cousin's murder?"

Mulder shrugged. "I don't know, Major. But just as you have to explore all possibilities within the scope of your projects, so do we, in murder investigations." He turned to Scully. "Do you think we should come back later? I think they're in a hurry."

Scully agreed and headed for the door with the others.

Mulder, however, didn't move. "Major, can I assume you'll be around later this afternoon? Just in case?" He scanned the room. "Looks like you have a lot of work left here. And in your project office, too, I would guess."

"Absolutely, absolutely." Tonero moved again, and this time Mulder gave way. "Just call ahead, if you don't mind. I have—" He gave Mulder a brief martyred look. "Superiors, if you know what I mean. This relocation makes them nervous."

"I'll bet," Mulder said. "Nice to talk to you again, Dr. Elkhart," and was gone before the woman could reply.

Once in the silent corridor, the door closed firmly behind them, he held up a palm to keep the others from talking, then checked left, toward the elevator bank, before looking in the opposite direction, where he saw another, single elevator. A snap of his fingers sent Webber there on the silent run, and a sign that told him there was no button to push.

"Well?" Andrews demanded when they reached the lobby.

"Well," Mulder said, "they sure don't make majors like they used to." He took his left hand out of his pocket and held out his palm, showing them the key ring he'd lifted from the major's desk.

"Not a word, Scully," he said lightly when she began to object. He told Webber and Andrews to get back to town and track down Aaron Noel, Barney's bartender, to see if the man knew how close Pierce and Ulman had been, and if Barelli had been in asking questions.

"And find out where that dispatcher—"

"Vincent," Webber said.

"Right. Find out where she was last night, what time she came home. You know the drill."

"What about you?"

Mulder shrugged. "If we leave now, whatever this key takes us to will be gone before we get back. We're going to snoop around a little."

"But isn't that against—"

Mulder hushed him with a look and hurried outside with them.

The post looked deserted.

Nothing moved but a light rain that shifted now and then as a light wind passed through it.

He opened the door for Andrews, then stood back and wondered what the mighty Douglas would say when he found out that the other car was Swiss cheese and useless. He could see Webber and Licia arguing heatedly inside, but with the windows up, he couldn't hear a word.

He almost intervened, rolled his eyes and changed his mind. That woman will be the death of me yet, he thought, and wished they'd be gone. Now. He wanted to be sure; he didn't want them suddenly turning up again.

The car jerked forward a few feet and stalled.

He smiled gamely and decided to get inside before he added pneumonia to his ills. He mimed giving the car a push with one foot, waved when Webber saw him in the rearview mirror, and trotted back to the lobby when the engine fired and held. The receptionist was clearly puzzled, but he assured her they had only forgotten something in Major Tonero's office and would be gone before she knew it.

The woman seemed to doubt it.

"Mulder," Scully said as they walked purposefully toward the elevator bank, "if we get caught…"

He didn't answer.

After a check over his shoulder, he took her elbow and ducked around the corner.

The corridor was empty, and only half the lights embedded in the ceiling's acoustic tiles were lit.

Whispers from the front, echoing softly.

He found the right key on the second try, and held his breath until the door opened onto an empty car. Once in, he inserted the key again and sent them down.

Scully said nothing; she had been on this road with him too many times before. The obligatory warning had been given—if we're caught; now she would be focused.

He wouldn't disturb that; it was too valuable.

He only hoped the major was still too angry to think straight, and realize what was going on.

NINETEEN

The corridor was short, and the air not quite stale. No ceiling lights here— just a hooded bulb at the far end, and one at the entrance. The floor, like the walls, was unpainted concrete.

"Like a bunker," Scully whispered.

In and out was the order of the day. They hurried to the first door, and Mulder turned the knob. It was unlocked and, when he looked in, empty. A desk, metal shelves on the wall, a small, open safe on the floor beside the desk, and a blackboard.

Nevertheless, they searched, checking drawers and corners. Tonero had said that Tymons was already gone, but Mulder doubted it was to the relocation point. By the looks of it—the papers and pads left behind in the desk, the handful of books on the shelves—this room had been emptied in a hurry.

"I smell gunpowder," Scully said, returning to the corridor. "And smoke." She wrinkled her nose. "Something else. I'm not sure."

The middle door was unlocked as well, and open a few inches. Mulder pushed it with his foot and stood back, shaking his head.

"Jesus."

What was once on the single shelf was now on the floor, smashed and scattered, some of it scorched or charred. He counted the hulks of at least three monitors and a pair of keyboards; he counted at least a half-dozen bullet holes in the wall beneath what looked to be a one-way window.

Without speaking, they sifted through the wreckage, not knowing exactly what they were looking for, knowing only that they'd know when they saw it. Then Scully rocked back on her heels.

"Mulder."

He joined her, dusting his hands on his coat, and saw the blood. Lots of it, dry, and buried beneath plastic and blank sheets of paper.

"Not a gunshot wound, I think," she said.

"Goblin."

"I don't know. It's been here a while, though." She poked at a large stain with a forefinger. "But not that long. We're not talking about days." He guessed that the room on the right had been Tymons's office, and Tymons's alone. It didn't have the feel of being shared with someone, like Rosemary Elkhart. This one had been the Project's heart and control center. From here... he stood at the shelf and looked into the next room.

"Oh, boy," he said. "Scully."

She looked, and her eyes widened.

Mulder checked his watch. "Time, Scully. Not much left."

The last room was a shambles as well, but it was the walls that fascinated him—one cream, one sand, one green, one black.

His fingers began to snap unconsciously.

This was it.

This was where the goblin was tested. One wall, one color.

Scully wasn't sure. "So what did they do, Mulder? Line him up against the wall and wait? They could have done that with a sheet on a bed."

Mulder looked at her sharply, and looked around the room again. His lips moved as if he were talking to himself before they parted in a satisfied grin.

"Training," he decided, and stood against the cream wall, unable to disguise the excitement in his voice. "Scully, it's a training room." He pointed. "Bed, desk, CD case there in the corner. Somebody lived here—no, somebody stayed here temporarily, maybe overnight, maybe for several days at a time." He spread his arms along the wall. "Somebody who—"

Scully whirled on him. "Don't say it, Mulder! I'm having a hard enough time as it is. Do not make it more complicated than it has to be."

"But it's not, Scully," he insisted, pacing now, rubbing at his chin, his cheeks, pushing a hand back through his hair. "This is where the goblin learned how to change." He turned in a slow circle. "Learned how to will the change, Scully, not wait for the change to happen." He took a step toward her, and was stopped by her frown. "You said it yourself, right? He can't carry every contingency around on his back. It's impossible. Even for the most basic circumstances, it would be, for him, a dangerous hindrance."

He looked to the door.

"A trained killer needs as few obstacles as possible. He needs a smooth way in, a smooth way out. No stops along the way for adjustments to a costume. No ripples. The quicker, the better."

He looked around again, closer now, searching for something, anything personal, that would give him a hint to the room's sometime occupant. But there was nothing left, and there was nothing left of the time he had hoped they would have.

On the way back to the elevator, Scully ducked into the control room and came out folding several pieces of paper she tucked into her shoulder bag. Blood samples. Not, Mulder thought, that they really needed them.

He knew who the blood belonged to.

\\\\\\\\\\\\\\\\\

On the way through the lobby, Mulder dropped the keys onto the absent receptionist's desk, then followed Scully outside, anxious to get back to town.

The light rain had grown heavier, the air darker for it.

Another squad of soldiers marched by, absolutely silent.

"Mulder," Scully said, "in case you haven't noticed, we don't have a ride."

It hadn't occurred to him, and he didn't think it mattered.

"And we don't have an umbrella, either."

She slapped him lightly on the arm and returned inside to use the phone. He didn't follow.

He watched the rain.

A human chameleon, he thought, slipping his hands into his pockets. An effective assassin, who could theoretically slip through the tightest of cordons.

In, and out.

No ripples.

Or, more frighteningly, a small army of them, living shadows slipping through the night.

No ripples.

Only death left behind.

It wasn't a perfect disguise. It probably wasn't effective in broad daylight, and the goblin—he couldn't stop thinking of it that way—wouldn't be able to stay in the same room for very long. Even Scully had eventually spotted the moth.

Nevertheless… living shadows.

He shifted from foot to foot impatiently.

No question about it, Major Tonero was the project's shepherd. He knew all of it, which meant he probably knew that Tymons was dead. Killed by the goblin? If so, was the goblin under the man's direction?

But why kill the head of such a project?

Too easy—Rosemary Elkhart was second-in-command. There was no reason to believe she couldn't, or wouldn't, take over if she had to. And the best way to ensure that would be to make herself indispensable to those who were in charge. He pictured her in the major's chair, and suddenly realized that was what had bothered him earlier. *She* was in *his* chair. She was comfortable using it. She had used it before.

"Well," he whispered. "Well, well."

"Stop thinking, Mulder, and move it," Scully told him. She snapped open a large black umbrella, took his arm, and hustled down to the sidewalk.

They hadn't gone a dozen paces before he took it from her before she poked his eye out. "Where did you get this?"

"You'd be surprised what you'll find in the ladies' room on a rainy day." She hugged his arm tightly, quickly. "I called Chief Hawks, he's on his way to pick us up."

"So why—"

"The major isn't going to stay in that office, Mulder, not when he finds out his keys are gone. He'll check that setup first, using Dr. Elkhart's keys, then probably come after us. I would like to be long gone before that, if you don't mind."

"He'll follow us."

"No, I don't think so. We can't disappear, Mulder. The senator, remember?"

He almost stopped then, but her momentum pulled him along.

"Carl."

"What about him?"

Mulder stared into the rain, willing Hawks to come in at speed. "According to his notes, he was asking around about the goblin." His chest tightened, his stride quickened. "Cleaning up, Scully. I think someone's scared, and the goblin's cleaning up."

\\\\\\\\\\\\\\\\\\\\

The telephone rang only once before Rosemary snatched up the receiver. She listened and said, "What are you doing, calling here? Suppose he had answered?" Without thinking, she began to weave the cord between her fingers. "Well, you're lucky he's not. He's downstairs now. Those FBI agents were here, and he thinks they lifted his damn keys." She watched the door without seeing it. "I think, if they didn't know before, they know now."

Her gaze shifted to the window, to the trails of water almost invisible against the grey air, the grey sky.

She stiffened.

"You can't do that. No. It's bad enough, but you can't touch them."

The goblin cleared its throat painfully. "Yes, I can."

Rosemary almost rose out of the chair. "Damnit, will you listen to me? Just… just what we agreed, all right? Don't make it worse than it already is."

"Doctor, I can do whatever I want."

She couldn't believe it. First Tymons, now this.

"In fact, I think all that stuff you've been telling me is plain bullshit."

"Look—"

"You know, I don't think I'm affected much at all." It laughed softly, and wheezed. "And if I am, Doctor… whose fault is that?"

She did stand then, angrily shaking her hand until the cord fell off. "Goddamnit, listen to me, you idiot! If I have to—"

"Doctor." The voice was calm. Very calm.

Rosemary closed her eyes and took a deep breath. "What?"

"We have an agreement. I'll do what you want."

She leaned forward, bracing herself on the desk with one hand. "Thank you. It'll be fine, just fine, as long as we don't panic."

"I'll do what you want."

She nodded. "Yes."

"Are you listening?"

"Yes, of course."

"Then don't, Doctor. Don't *ever* talk to me like that again."

"Oh, really? And what if… hello? Damnit, hello?"

The line was dead.

She gaped at the receiver, then slammed it back onto its cradle. Calm again; she had to regain calm again, be the eye in the storm. It was not, yet, a disaster that those damn agents probably knew something. They could snoop around all they wanted, but they didn't know it all. As long as she made sure she, and Joseph, didn't panic, they never would.

At least not until it was too late.

But she was afraid for the goblin. Despite her assurances, she knew what little control she had was practically gone. Like all the others, those too deep in the woods to be found—here, and elsewhere—the strain and the treatment had proved too much.

This one had lasted the longest, however.

This one was the proof of her triumph.

She grabbed her purse and coat and hurried from the office. Joseph would have to come to her for a change, once he stopped blowing off pompous steam. She still had some last-minute packing to do.

Just a few more weeks, she prayed as she made for the elevators; just get me out of here in one piece, give me a couple more weeks, and it'll be over.

Really over.

The door slid open as the overhead bell chimed softly

She took a step, and froze.

The car was empty. She could see that, but she still couldn't bring herself to go in.

With a low groan of frustration she used the fire stairs instead, yanking on her coat, cursing her own weakness, but oddly grateful for the harsh sound of her heels on the steps.

TWENTY

Scully decided her vacation hadn't been nearly long enough, not by half.

A Marville patrol car had picked them up minutes after they left the hospital, just about the time the rain had stopped. The driver, though polite, refused to answer any of Mulder's questions.

"Talk to the chief," was all he would say. It sounded to her as if Hawks's equanimity at having the FBI in town was being sorely tested.

Now they sped toward town, and she couldn't help feeling that everything was moving too fast. She needed time to think, and she wasn't getting it. She was reacting, rather than acting; otherwise, she never would have taken Mulder's leap from experimental camouflage to full-blown, controlled human chameleon, with no stops along the way.

It wasn't like her; not at all.

She braced herself when the car momentarily lost traction on its way around a bend, and wished she had tried to get a hold of Webber instead. And when the driver said, "Sorry, ma'am" once he regained control, she almost snapped his head off.

Not like her at all.

Then Mulder folded his arms on the back of the seat and rested his chin on them. He said nothing, but she could feel him at her shoulder. Her eyes closed briefly at a flurry of leaves across the windshield.

"Mulder, I'm sorry about Carl."

He grunted.

She realized then that that was part of her problem. She hadn't liked Barelli; he was crude, too slick, and too full of himself. But for reasons she would never understand, he had also been Mulder's friend, and she hadn't said a single word of sympathy, of commiseration. The moment she had seen the reporter's body, she had clicked into professional mode.

She hadn't let the murder touch her.

It had obviously touched her friend.

"We have to get to Elly," he said at last.

She agreed, and asked the driver to take them there instead of the station.

"I don't know," he said doubtfully. "I was told—"

"Don't worry about it," Mulder said. "We'll take the heat. You can tell him we pulled rank. FBI, pushy feds, stuff like that."

For a second, Scully thought the man would flat out refuse. Then he grinned, shrugged, and: "Whatever you say, sir."

"So punch it."

"You got it."

And it took all of Scully's self-control not to grab the dashboard.

\\\\\\\\\\\\\\\\\\\

Traffic increased as Marville began, Saturday shoppers and wanderers taking their time to make the business district last as long as they could make it. The driver took a back-road, corner-cutting shortcut to avoid the main street, and pulled up smoothly in front of the apartment building.

"You want me to wait?" He sounded hopeful.

"Yes," she told him as she opened the door.

He took the radio mike and called in: "Maddy, this is Spike. We're at the Goblin Lady's place. Maybe the chief should meet us here, huh?"

The radio hissed. "I'll tell him. Watch your back."

"You got it," he said, and hooked the mike back on its cradle.

"That's it?" Mulder asked, sounding disappointed.

"You mean, ten-four, that kind of stuff?" The driver shook his head. "The chief hates radio talk. He says it makes us sound too much like cop shows." He laughed. "Besides, half the guys keep getting the numbers wrong anyway. Maddy knows what we're saying, so…" He shrugged.

Scully was already outside, looking up at the bay window. The curtains were closed. She turned slowly as Mulder left the car, and clamped a hand hard against her chest.

"Mulder!"

Immediately she ran across the street without checking for traffic, heading straight for the small park and Elly Lang, sitting motionless on her bench. The old woman faced the empty ball field, bundled in a black coat, a black umbrella canted over her head.

She didn't turn when Scully called her name.

No, she thought, leaping the curb and racing across the wet grass; damnit, no.

"Elly!"

She heard Mulder behind her, drifting to her right to come up on her flank.

"Elly!"

She grabbed the bench back and propelled herself around, damning herself for not thinking of this sooner.

If they were too late, she would personally rip Tonero's medals off, one by one, and pin them back on his bare chest. One by one.

Suddenly a hand snapped out from beneath the umbrella, and she yelped as she jumped to one side when a stream of bright orange nearly caught her on the chest.

The old woman stared at her without blinking. "Oh. It's you." And she tucked the spray can back into her purse. "I must be getting slow."

Scully didn't know what to say, could only nod while she tried to catch her breath. "I thought—"

"Yes," Elly said. "I can see that." Her gaze shifted when Mulder came up beside her. "They won't hurt me, you know. Never have. I figure they figure an old lady can't do them much harm."

"Ms. Lang," Mulder said, "this one is different."

Scully dropped onto the bench and gently pushed the umbrella to one side. "It's killed at least three people that we know of, Ms. Lang. We think you could be in danger."

Elly humphed. "You don't know much about goblins, young lady." She shook a bony finger in Scully's face. "You should study more. You're a smart girl. You should learn more. Goblins," she said, "don't kill anyone. Never have."

Dana looked to Mulder for support, and he hunkered down in front of the old woman, one hand gently on her knee so he wouldn't topple. "Ms. Lang, this one is sick."

"They don't get sick."

He shook his head. "Not that kind of sick."

He tapped his temple. "This kind. It isn't like the others. It's…" He swallowed, and let his hand slide away. "It's evil, Ms. Lang. I don't know any other way to put it."

Scully saw it then, the doubt and the birth of fear in the woman's face. Suddenly she seemed two decades older. "You shouldn't be sitting out here," she said quietly. "You should be someplace warm. It'll rain again soon."

"The children," Elly whispered.

"I don't think they'll be playing much today."

She stood, sliding her hand along the woman's coat until she grasped her hand. The fingers twitched, then curled around hers, and she pulled Elly slowly to her feet, the umbrella dropping forgotten to the ground.

Mulder retrieved it as Scully pointed to the cruiser. "See that man there? His name, if you can believe it, is Spike. I think I can talk him into staying with you for a while."

Arm in arm they walked across the grass.

"Is he married?" Elly asked.

"I don't think so."

Mulder went ahead, keeping himself between the women and the driver as he spoke. Scully blessed him for that. "He's a nice boy," Elly said, using her chin to point at Mulder.

"Yes. I know."

In the middle of the street, Elly stopped, her lower lip trembling. "Is he right about this goblin?"

She nodded.

"I'm not ready to die yet, you know."

Dana squeezed the woman's arm. "I know. And you won't."

"Too mean, too cranky." Dana smiled, although the woman didn't see her. "Well… I don't think so." She urged them forward again. "You're just tough, that's all. A good thing to be."

"Are you?"

Scully didn't know how to answer that one, and was saved from stumbling by Todd Hawks's arrival. It didn't take long to get Elly camped in her apartment, and not much longer than that, once they were outside again, to tell the chief they suspected that someone attached to, or working for, the

Special Projects Office at Fort Dix was responsible for the murders. Someone, she added, who was extremely skilled at blending in.

"Disguises, you mean?" Hawks asked.

"You could say that."

"A real expert, one of the best," Mulder said, following her lead. Then he smiled so quickly she almost missed it. "You could say it gives a whole new meaning to the word wallflower."

"Son of a bitch." Hawks checked the sky as if daring the rain to add to his misery. "Damn, I don't need this. I really don't." He shook his head and looked up at Elly's apartment. The curtains were open; a lamp burned in the window. "If you don't mind telling me, you got anyone in mind?"

He sounded neither bitter nor imposed upon; he only sounded as if he wanted this to be over, so his town could get back to what passed for normal.

"Because," he added flatly, "what I've got is three goddamn corpses, and three families and some local politicians on my ass demanding explanations." He looked at Mulder then, eyes narrowed. "And would you happen to know why, while I was poking around Vincent's house this morning, a United States senator called my office?"

Oh, great, she thought; just great.

Though she could hear traffic in the distance, the neighborhood was quiet. A few lights on porches, in front windows; an old black dog trotting along the gutter; a large crow strutting across the ball field.

Like her, it seemed in a state of anticipation.

"Chief, can you patch Mulder through on your radio, to try to locate the rest of our team?"

"No problem," he said with a wry smile. "They were on their way to the station when I left, trying to find you."

When Mulder questioned her with a look, she shook her head slightly, waiting until Hawks was on the radio. "We've been sloppy," she said, matter of fact, not a scolding. "The major's ready to bolt, and all we've been able to do is run from one killing to another."

"The restaurant," he suggested.

She frowned. "Why?"

"Hank does his best thinking in front of a plate of pancakes."

"Mulder," she started, then waved herself silent. "Okay."

Then she hurried inside to be sure Elly was all right, a concern quickly allayed when she saw Spike on the stool, cap in his lap, avidly listening to the old woman describing her lifelong hunt for goblins.

Neither noticed her in the doorway; neither noticed when she left.

Hank was at the curb when she reached the sidewalk, Mulder already in the car, waving her around the back to the other door. The chief stopped her at the rear bumper.

"You'll let me know what I need to know?"

She promised, then swore when her shoulder bag slipped off and hit the ground. I have got to get control, she snapped at herself, and was grateful when Hawks crouched down to help her fetch her things. She had to kneel to grab a pen that had rolled beneath the car, only half-listening as Hawks made some lame jokes about a woman's purse.

She leaned over, saw the pen, and reached for it.

And froze.

"You need help?"

She shook her head and backed out, the pen retrieved and in her pocket. Then, as he helped her to her feet, something about the license plate puzzled her, froze her again until she saw it.

"Listen, Agent Scully, if there's something the matter—"

"No." She waved off his offered hand. "No, thank you, I'm fine. I just thought of something, that's all." She knew he didn't really believe her, but didn't know the right question to ask. "Thanks," she said, and slipped into the car.

As soon as she was settled, Andrews turned around to ask what next. As far as she was concerned, all they were doing was chasing their own tails, and widened her eyes when Scully said, "Exactly. That's why we're going to the restaurant, order a long lunch, and get things straight before we start tripping over ourselves."

"And what about our goblin?" Mulder asked quietly.

"Our goblin," she said, "won't be out again until tonight."

TWENTY-ONE

Despite the day's gloom, the Queen's Inn's lights were kept low, giving the room an evening feel. Two diners sat at the counter, each reading a newspaper; a family of six sat in the last booth, one of the children describing the movie he had seen on TV that morning, complete with explosive sound effects and dialogue quotations. A busboy swept the already gleaming floor. In the parking lot, a trailer truck took its time making a wide U-turn, causing a minor backup and a brief flurry of angry horns.

"Another peaceful day in the country," Mulder said glumly. He sat by the window, pushed into the corner, his topcoat draped over the seatback. Although his head no longer throbbed to distraction, his side refused to give him respite. He squirmed, thought he was settled, and then a quick stitch made him shift again.

The others didn't seem to notice his discomfort.

Hank sat across from him, gleefully, for Scully's benefit, attacking a steak with all the trimmings he'd been able to think of, while Andrews and Scully settled on salads. All he could think of was pancakes and bacon, so forced himself to order just a sandwich. Two seconds later, he had forgotten what kind it was.

The truck finished its turn.

The kid finished the movie to the laughing applause of his family.

Mulder shifted again. "Do you know what W. C. Fields said about children?"

Licia asked him who W. C. Fields was.

"I'm not old, you know," he said to Scully's infuriatingly blank expression. "Really. I am not old."

"Eat, Mulder," she ordered. "We have work to do."

There was, then, mostly silence as they finished their meal. And once the table had been cleared, Scully flipped over her paper place mat and pulled out her pen, and looked to Mulder, who nodded it was her show, be my guest.

The family left.

The men at the counter paid and left as well.

"Pierce," Scully said, lightly jabbing the placemat with her pen, "was killed on a Saturday night. So was Corporal Ulman. Almost a pattern until last night." She paused, and Mulder was grateful she didn't mention Carl's name. "It's my guess Dr. Tymons is dead, too. Probably sometime yesterday." She filled them in quickly on what they had seen at Walson after the others had left, but gave neither of them a chance to comment. "The Project, whatever it is, is over."

"For now," Mulder added.

"All right. For now. And we don't have much time." She tapped the place mat again. "All the deaths are the same—throat slashed, deeply. This isn't a professional's attack. The violence… and the fact that each one came from the front, not behind…" She took a breath and shook her head. "It's almost psychotic. And the strength to do this indicates it's probably a man. Or," she added, when Mulder opened his mouth to comment, "a woman, okay. These days, there are a lot of women who go for weight training, defense training, things like that. We can't rule that out."

"Which means," Andrews said sourly, "we've narrowed it down to about eight or nine thousand people, right?"

"Wrong."

Mulder sat up, staring at the doodles Scully had drawn on the paper.

"While Pierce may have died just because he was in the wrong place at the wrong time, it's pretty obvious the others are connected. The corporal worked for Major Tonero—although we can't guarantee he knew everything that was going on, Carl Barelli was asking questions about goblins, and Dr. Tymons was the Project head."

She scribbled Tonero's name and circled it.

"I also think Mulder's right—the Project's in danger, and the goblin is cleaning house. Which is why we have someone staying with Ms. Lang." She circled Rosemary Elkhart's name. "That gives us motive. Hide the mistakes, bury the evidence. Literally."

"But if Tymons really is dead," Webber said, "won't that kill the project for good?"

"Oh, no. Not by a long shot. Dr. Elkhart, no matter what the major thinks, is in charge now. Nothing we said in that office fazed her, while the major was only partly acting. So I'm assuming she's gotten hold of the records, and I don't doubt she'd be able to have another center up and running before very long."

Andrews leaned forward eagerly. "She could have been planning it, you know. For weeks. Months, even. Something about the project, maybe it's almost ready, you know? I mean, done. Maybe she wants all the glory."

Scully tapped the name again. "I don't think there's any maybe about it, Licia."

"Then she did it!" Webber exclaimed.

Mulder blinked. "What? You think she's the goblin?"

Webber nodded, then shook his head, then threw up his hands. "Seemed like a good idea at the time." He brightened. "But she could be directing it. I mean, wouldn't she know who was a threat and who wasn't?"

Scully smiled. "Weekend nights," she reminded them. "Only weekend nights."

"So what are you saying?" Andrews asked with a frown. "We narrow it down to only those people who are free on weekends?" She shook her head. "Give me a break, okay?" She reached out to push at the place mat. "Do you know how many troops there are at Dix, for one thing? And every one of them—"

"Damn!" Mulder said.

Scully jumped, and he apologized with a quick gesture, but he had followed her road, marked the signposts, and the more he thought about it, the more he realized he already had the answer.

"What?" Webber said anxiously.

"Louisiana," he answered, speaking to Scully.

All she could do was look.

"That guy in Louisiana, he was supposed to have disappeared in the middle of a circus ring. Walked through a crowd of people and didn't come out the other side. But he was still there, Scully. He just didn't look the same way."

"And how do you know that?"

His left arm rested along the back of the seat, forcing him to turn toward her. "You'll be happy to know that I don't think he just disappeared in a puff of sawdust. He had to be there; he was just different, that's all. The police were looking for one thing, so they didn't see anything else."

"Okay, so things weren't what they seemed. What does that have to do with this?"

"Ghosts and goblins, Scully. Ghosts and goblins."

"Meaning?" Andrews said testily.

"Meaning our field of suspects has just been made considerably smaller."

\\\\\\\\\\\\\\\\\'

Rosemary stood his pacing, his ranting, for as long as she could. Then she came around the desk and said, "Joseph."

He ignored her. "God damn them, anyway. Did you see the way they spoke to me? Who the hell do they think they are?"

"Joseph."

He shook his head in exasperation. "This is too much. It's just too much." His face reddened, and he aimed a kick at one of the cartons. "And I even packed my damn keys away! Jesus H. Rosie, the whole world's gone nuts!"

She leaned back against the desk.

"Son of a bitch bastards are not—I repeat, are not—going to get away with it. I'll call that goddamn senator myself and—"

"Joseph!"

He whirled on her, one fist up, but she didn't flinch. She only softened her expression, and beckoned with a crooked finger. "Joseph." Her voice deep in her throat. "Joseph."

His chest rose and fell, the fist trembled and fell away.

"Joseph, there's nothing to worry about."

"What? How the hell—"

"Nothing to worry about," she repeated calmly, and beckoned him again.

This time he moved, close enough for her to place a hand on his shoulder.

"Everything we need from downstairs we already have. Everything we need from here is ready to ship."

"Yes, but—"

She hushed him with a finger on his lips. "And everything you need is right here, too."

She kissed him softly, quickly, and used all her remaining control to stop herself from slapping him.

"You have the orders?"

He leaned around her and yanked open the center drawer, pulled out a folder and handed it to her. "Signed and sealed, Rosie."

"Good." She pressed the folder against her chest. "Now we can either forget about downstairs altogether, because no one will see it for weeks, maybe even months. Or we can get Captain Whatshisname from Battalion to clean it up." She smiled. "After all, what are soldiers for?"

"I say we just leave it." The flush had receded from his cheeks and brow. He puffed a little, slipping back into his role. "And I say we don't wait for tomorrow morning."

"I don't mind."

"I can get us a flight tonight."

She considered it, and nodded. "Not too late, though. I want to get there in time to get a decent night's sleep."

His expression made her shudder. "Who says we'll get any sleep?"

"I do, you dope." She slapped his shoulder playfully and slipped around him, heading for the door. "We sleep, we see the right people, you take that leave, and then… who knows?"

Tonero laughed. "Okay, Rosie, okay." Then he frowned. "But what about—"

"All taken care of, darling." She picked up her coat from the chair. "All it takes is one phone call."

She waved, showed him a little chest movement, and left before he could think of anything else. There was no doubt he would make all the proper arrangements; she trusted him that much. As for the actual flight itself… she never had minded traveling alone.

\\\\\\\\\\\\\\\\\

In Elly Lang's apartment, the telephone rang.

\\\\\\\\\\\\\\\\\

Mulder knew that Scully was about to tug on the reins, haul him in before his excitement got the best of him. Nevertheless, he couldn't help the way his hands moved, darting from the notes on the place mat to his uneaten sandwich to tracing diagrams in the air only he could see.

"Civilian, first." He made sure they were listening with a look and a gesture. "Dr. Elkhart has no influence over military personnel without Major Tonero. And Tonero isn't about to use the military for project experiments. If it blew up, he'd lose his ticket to whatever election he's hoping to win when he retires."

Hank gaped, astonished. "How—"

"Us, second." He touched Scully's shoulder to keep her attention, and looked at Andrews. "It wasn't magic that told the goblin where we were yesterday. It wasn't magic that told the goblin where Carl would be last night." He scratched through his hair, then slapped it impatiently back into place. "Somebody knows us. Somebody who knows where we are most, if not all, of the time."

"Damn," Hank said. "Somebody who even knows what the hell we had for breakfast!"

It was all Mulder could do to keep the young man from jumping out of his seat.

"Right," Scully said, her eyes slowly widening. "And she was supposed to have a date with him last night. It was in his notes." She slipped out of the booth and grabbed her shoulder bag. "We talk to her now. Before—"

"Absolutely," Mulder agreed. "But not for the reason you think."

"But it has to be," Andrews protested. "God, it all fits. She's alone, so she comes and goes whenever she wants and nobody to question her, she has that equipment to keep in shape—" She grabbed Webber's arm, to pull him from the booth. Her voice began to rise. "She—"

Scully silenced her with a harsh wave and stared at Mulder. "Well?"

He moved more slowly, wincing when his side stabbed him again, dragging his coat along behind him. "She's not going anywhere, Scully." He tilted his head toward the window. "It's still too light."

He urged the others ahead with a nod, then tugged on Scully's coat to keep her back.

"It's not her," he said, keeping his voice low.

"How can you know that?"

He shook his head—tell you later—and gestured to Webber to cover the back, Andrews to stay outside.

"I don't know," Scully said, following him into the office.

"Three against one?" He banged the counter bell. "Come on, that's a bit much, don't you think?"

"She's psychotic," she reminded him when he hit the bell again. "And she's strong, Mulder." Her hand slipped into her purse, and didn't come out.

Mulder struck the bell once more, then rounded the counter and pushed through the beaded curtain. "Mrs. Radnor?" A staircase immediately to his left was dark. From the room at the back he heard muffled music, and hurried down the short hall.

"Mrs. Radnor!"

He stepped into the room, where the motel owner pumped furiously on a stationary bike, headphones on, listening to music from a cassette player lashed to the handlebars. She started when she saw him, her eyes wide and mouth open when she saw Scully, and the drawn gun.

"What the hell?" She held up one hand while the other very slowly pulled the headphones off and switched off the player. "Mr. Mulder, what's going on?"

"You don't seem terribly broken up about Carl Barelli," Scully said, keeping the gun at her side.

Mrs. Radnor tried to speak and couldn't; she could only look at Mulder for help, and an explanation.

He grabbed the handlebars and leaned toward her. "Mrs. Radnor, I haven't got time to explain, but I need to know something."

"Hey, I run a clean place here," she said. "You can't—"

"Frankie Ulman."

"I—what about him?"

"You told Agent Andrews you saw the corporal bring a date here every so often." The woman nodded, her hands shifting to grip the towel draped around her neck. "You told her you didn't know who the woman was."

"Well... yes."

"Why?"

"I didn't have time, for one thing." She forced a laugh. "She was in such a hurry, I don't think we talked more than five or ten minutes."

Mulder frowned, but shook it off. "You lied, Mrs. Radnor," he said carefully, and shook the bike slightly when she started to protest. "You knew who it was. You know just about everyone around here, and you knew who it was."

She mopped her face, a stalling tactic, until Scully cleared her throat and made sure she remembered the gun. "I don't want to get people in trouble, you know? It's bad for business. Word gets around and—"

"Mrs. Radnor," he snapped, "we don't have time for this, okay? I'm only going to ask you once: Who was that woman?"

When she told him, he whirled. "Scully, get the car and Webber." He turned back as Scully charged from the room. "Mrs. Radnor, I have a favor to ask."

"What?" She couldn't believe it.

He smiled, and she softened almost immediately. "I need to borrow your car."

"What?" This time she almost yelled.

Jesus, woman, he thought, would you please stop—

"Commandeer," he said quickly. "I must commandeer your car."

Her face brightened. "Wow. You mean, like in the movies."

"Exactly." He took her arm and pulled her gently from the bike. "Just like the movies."

"But you had two—"

"The other one was shot up. But you know that already, right?"

Excited, flustered, she fumbled in her purse, held out the keys, and snapped them back. "Is this one going to get shot up?"

"I sincerely hope not," he said truthfully, took the keys from her hand before she could change her mind, and ran.

"But what if it is?" she yelled after him.

"The President will buy you a new one!" he yelled back, slammed through the front door, and grabbed the edge to swing him back inside.

"Pink," Mrs. Radnor called. "It's the pink Caddy in back."

Pink, he thought as he ran out again; terrific.

And thought *terrific* again when the storm finally broke, and broke hard.

TWENTY-TWO

"Vincent?" Scully gripped the dashboard as Mulder squealed out of the parking lot. The Caddy took a second to grip the slick tarmac and soon lost the Royal Baron in a swirling, twisting mist. "Officer Maddy Vincent?"

Webber and Andrews followed behind, their car nothing more than a smear of headlights.

Despite the storm, Mulder didn't bother to check his speed. Either what traffic there was got out of his way, or it didn't, it was their choice. He had a difficult enough time seeing through the rain.

"It's why Carl wanted to talk to her," he explained. "He wanted what he thought she knew about who was what, where, at the time of the killings." He grunted as the car threatened to fishtail. "Who else knows where all the cops will be, Scully? Who else knew where we would be yesterday?"

"Mulder, that's not enough."

He knew that. "Watch your back."

"Huh?"

"The goblin said 'Watch your back' to me, out there in the woods. Just before I was clobbered. This morning, on the way back from Tonero's, Vincent told Spike to watch his back." He glanced at her. "The same voice, Scully. It was the same voice."

He plowed through a lane-wide puddle, sending a wave soaring over the shoulder onto someone's front lawn.

Ahead, a pickup doused the windshield with backspray, and he cursed as he set the wipers to their highest speed.

It was almost enough.

At the corner of his vision he saw her shift so she could watch him and the road at the same time. "The makeup," she said, recognition hitting home. "The calamine lotion. It's—"

He listened to her mumble to herself, then catch her breath as he pressed on the horn and rocketed past the truck.

She had caught it now; she had caught the scent.

"It's breaking down." She was thinking aloud. "Whatever treatment they were giving her is breaking down. If… if it works correctly, she ought to be able to revert to normal color with no residual effects. It isn't happening. Mulder, it isn't happening, and she has to hide it somehow."

He had no argument.

The Project had failed; he guessed it wasn't the first time. He also suspected that Elkhart and Tymons had come closer than they ever had before, which was why the doctor and the major were packing to leave.

They were going to try again.

And he still couldn't shake the image of shadow armies, sliding through the night.

Another car ahead, its taillights flaring red as the driver pumped his brakes. Mulder grunted and swerved quickly into the other lane without reducing speed, and frantically spun the wheel right when the blinding bright headlights of an oncoming van blurred across the windshield.

It was too late to slow down.

He swung around the leading car on its right, fighting the wheels' stubborn inclination to take them straight into the woods, ignoring the frightened, angry blare of the other car's horn. His side began to burn. The Caddy jounced through a pothole, and he was on the road again.

"Mulder," Scully said calmly, "we can't help anyone if we're dead."

He stared at her in near panic. "Jesus!" He slapped the wheel with a palm. "Elly! If she's cleaning up… Elly!"

"But how?"

"Vincent's the dispatcher. All she has to do is call—who cares with what excuse?—and Spike is gone on some fool's errand. And Elly is alone."

He swung to the shoulder and braked, was out with the engine still running, instantly drenched and waving his arms. The car he had just passed swept by and honked loud and long as it emptied a puddle onto his legs. But Webber saw him and pulled up, Andrews rolling down her window before the car had fully stopped.

Mulder grabbed the door and leaned in. "Get to the station Hank. Find out where Vincent is, go there, and wait."

"Vincent?" Webber said incredulously. "You're kidding. Vincent?"

"Just do it, Hank," he ordered. He turned, and turned back. "And be careful. If Scully's right and she's gone off because something's gone wrong, she definitely won't hesitate to cut a couple of FBI throats."

There was no time for details. He jumped back into the Caddy and pushed the accelerator all the way down. The rear wheels spun, kicking pebbles and mud before they found traction and leap onto the blacktop again.

Webber's car had already vanished into the rain.

\\\\\\\\\\\\\\\\\\\\

Elly Lang jumped when a gust of wind rattled the bay window. But she wouldn't panic. She had her spray can, she had the cane with the large ivory knob Officer Silber had found in her bedroom closet, and she had his promise he would be back in less than ten minutes.

Still, she was frightened.

The storm had come so suddenly, after so long a wait, and the light had dimmed so fast, that it was hard to believe it was only a few minutes past noon.

It wasn't, she told herself; not really.

It was midnight.

Time for the goblins to make their rounds.

Shadows snaked down the wall behind her, over her, while the rush of water in the eaves sounded too much like thunder.

She had been told to leave the lamp on, but soon after Silber left, she had turned it off. It was better this way. She could see outside better, and she hoped it would be harder for someone to see in.

The window rattled again.

The rain fell harder, and pellets of hail shotgunned against the panes.

I'm ready, she thought; I'm ready.

And then she wondered if she had locked the back door.

\\\\\\\\\\\\\\\\\\

Rosemary Elkhart stood in the middle of her living room and decided it was hopeless. She hadn't been here five minutes, had barely taken off her coat, when Joseph had called, demanding reassurance that he wouldn't be burned, that his reputation would be intact, that no one would find Tymons's body in the woods. She had done her best, but second thoughts changed her mind after his third call.

He was hopeless.

After all this time, after all the bases and posts and installations they had been on, working through the kinks and dead ends of Leonard's discovery, Major Tonero had become, virtually on the night of their success, hopeless.

And a hell of a pain in the ass.

Worse; she had been around him long enough to know what that meant—cut your losses, cover your ass, offer the sacrifice, and start again somewhere else.

With someone else.

She looked with regret at the suitcases waiting near the door. To give him his due, he had bought her a lot of nice things, jewelry and clothes, some of which she had begun to convert to cash as soon as it became apparent that this phase of the project, while not perfect, was nearing its end.

A girl, she thought, can't be too careful.

Cover your ass.

Cut your losses.

And something else:

Travel light.

She picked up the bag at her feet, made sure Leonard's disks were inside, then zipped it closed and reached for her coat. A cab to Philly would be expensive, but she considered it an investment. God knows there were plenty of private businesses out there, not necessarily in this country, who would be more than willing to learn what she knew.

She checked the bag again, recognizing her nervousness, and reminded herself that somehow, between here and the airport, she'd have to lose the gun.

"Okay," she said, and smiled at the room. "Okay."

At the moment she didn't give a damn for Madeline Vincent. The woman would have to learn to fend for herself. For what little time she had left.

She hadn't taken two steps when someone knocked on the door.

\\\\\\\\\\\\\\\\\\

Mulder swore and slapped the steering wheel angrily when storm-slowed traffic finally forced his speed down.

Dana didn't scold. She had been infected by his urgency as well, to the extent that she lowered her window and tried to see if there was a way he could pass again on the right. Parked cars lined the curbs, however; for as far as she could see, and she didn't see suggesting he use the sidewalk as a lane.

If she did, he'd do it.

"Two blocks," she told him. "Just two blocks."

Equally frustrating was the lack of communication between here and the others. If she had a radio, she could have called ahead to Hawks and double-checked on Webber, and on Silber's being at the apartment.

She sighed and opened her bag, to be sure her weapon was loaded and ready.

Her hand touched something else.

Oh God, she thought, and debated for nearly a full minute before making up her mind.

The drum of rain on the roof forced her to raise her voice: "Mulder—"

"I wish I could fly," he said, glaring at the windshield as if that would give his vision a better chance. As it was, the rain was so hard, with the wind blowing now, that it seemed as if the street had been invaded by drifting fog.

"Mulder, listen."

He nodded. "Okay. Sorry."

"The shooter."

"What? Now?" He shook his head, and raised his hand to use the horn, changed his mind and throttled the steering wheel instead.

"Yes. Now." She tossed a sprig of pine onto the dashboard, and waited for him to see it. When he looked, she said, "It was caught under the car. Hank's car. I found it when we were at Elly's."

He was bewildered and lifted a shoulder. "So?"

"So Mrs. Radnor only spoke with Licia for five or ten minutes. So Licia has been fighting you every inch of this investigation. So Hank and I are the only ones who have used that car, and I know damn well I didn't hit or run over any tree." She stopped. Looked outside. "Hawks said they found the spot where the shooter had backed off the road into the woods. It wasn't a clear area." Her hands danced an apology over her lap. "I didn't read her notes, Mulder. She said she had them, I even watched her put them in her briefcase... but I didn't read them. And she didn't bring them to your room."

"Scully—"

"I screwed up." Her hands again. "Damnit, I screwed up."

"Nope," he said, rocking back and forth, body English for the car. "If I was dead, then you would have screwed up." She saw the grin. "Then I'd have to haunt you."

"Mulder, that's not funny."

"But you don't believe in ghosts and goblins."

Hail bounced off the hood.

She jumped when a car honked behind them.

"So," he said, "what do we do?"

"We take care of business," she said without hesitation. "And when that's done, we take care of more business."

He nodded, groaned when traffic came to a complete halt, and finally unsnapped his seat belt. "Take the car."

She reached out to grab his arm, but she was too late. "Mulder!"

He stood in the middle of the street, rain dripping into his eyes. He pointed. "I can't wait, Scully. I can't. Just ..." He flapped the hand helplessly. "Just come after me as fast as you can."

He was gone, the cars behind discovered their horns, and she slid awkwardly into the driver's seat, all the while watching him race to the sidewalk and around the next corner.

If there were any rules left in the book that he hadn't broken, she couldn't think of them. All she could think of was, watch your back, Mulder. For God's sake, watch your back.

TWENTY-THREE

He knew he must have looked like a fool, racing headlong through the rain, one hand held loosely over his head in feeble protection against the hail that, so far, was no larger than a pea. That didn't stop it from stinging, however, and stinging badly.

He bolted across the street, veering sharply when a minivan nearly clipped him on his blind side. He skidded, fell into a parked car, and used it to propel him onto the sidewalk again.

The hail stopped.

The rain didn't.

He didn't want to, but he had to slow up—his side had begun to pull, and he couldn't help thinking that something had torn in there.

Hang on, Elly, he thought; hang on.

At the next intersection, he paused under a tree, half bent over, hands hard on his hips, and took precious seconds to get his bearings, and his breath back. Another block west, he thought, swallowed hard, and tried to run, snarling when he couldn't do much better than a fast trot.

A winter-raised section of concrete made him swerve onto a lawn, where he slid on the wet grass and went down on his hands and knees. It felt good, not moving, and it took him a moment to get back on his feet.

He had no choice but to run now, forcing the pain in his side to another place, one that didn't bother him, one he knew would exact a great price when he couldn't concentrate any longer.

The wind pushed a curtain of water into his eyes. He slapped it away angrily without missing a step as he charged off the curb and across the tarmac to the other side. He figured Scully, with her luck, would beat him there anyway, but at least now he was moving, doing something instead of cursing traffic and feeling helpless.

Reaching the next corner seemed to take hours, and when he stopped, he almost panicked.

This wasn't right; he was on the wrong street.

Strings of mist like ghosts moved slowly through the rain; a storm drain overflowed, creating a shallow pond across the intersection. This wasn't right, and he didn't know which way to go.

Then he saw the park across the way and up the block, the benches and ball field obscured by the rain. His lips parted—it wasn't quite a grin—and he moved on, his face turned toward the houses he passed to keep his vision clear.

The police car was gone.

The lamp was out in Elly's window.

He slowed as he approached the front walk, slipping his left hand into his pocket to wrap around his gun. Front or back? Wait for Scully, or do the stupid thing and go in on his own?

He had no realistic alternative.

He reached the front walk just as a horn honked several times in quick succession. Turning as he ran, he saw Scully bump the pink Cadillac up over the curb and practically throw herself into the street.

Sometimes you just live right, he thought, and waved her around to the back, ran up the steps and stopped with his hand on the knob.

The wind shrieked overhead.

Something rattled down a drainpipe.

He fought his lungs into calming, then stepped into the foyer. Slowly now, knowing he wouldn't be able to give Scully enough time, he sidled to the door and put an ear to the damp wood.

Nothing; the storm made it impossible to hear a thing.

He tried the knob, and closed his eyes briefly when it turned, mouthed a *damn*, and turned it, using his shoulder to push the door inward.

The living room was dark, and empty, grey light from the bay window the only illumination. Rain shadows rippled across the furniture and carpet. An ivory-topped cane lay on the floor in front of the couch.

He could see no light in the kitchen, or in the bedroom at the front room's far side.

He chose the kitchen first.

Keeping as close to the wall as he could, he moved down the short hall. As far as he could see, no one sat at the little table, and he could see no welcome, telltale shadow in the back door window.

Water slipped from his hair and down his spine.

A shudder briefly hunched his shoulders.

Closer, gun aimed toward the ceiling, and he braced himself, counted to three, and stepped quickly into the kitchen, sweeping the barrel ahead of him.

No one was there.

He eased back toward the living room, heard a scraping, and spun around as Scully came through the back door, a sharp shake of her head letting him know there was no one outside, and no sign of Elly.

Or the goblin.

No words, then. Hand signals told her they must be in the bedroom. She nodded, once, and he took the hall again, shoulders brushing along the wall-paper.

Listening, and hearing only the wind, only the rain.

When he sensed Scully directly behind him, he stepped in and crossed the floor in four long strides. The bedroom door was open, but it was too dark for him to see much more than the shadowed outline of a brass headboard.

Time, he thought; *no time*.

Scully positioned herself opposite him at the door, and at her nod, they went in, he high, she low.

"Damn." He kicked at the bed.

The room was empty.

They were too late; Elly Lang was gone.

\\\\\\\\\\\\\\\\

Rosemary adjusted the bag's strap over her shoulder, smoothed the lapels of her coat, and shook her head.

"You're an idiot, Joseph," she said, opened the door, and left.

\\\\\\\\\\\\\\\\

"Maybe she's hiding," Scully said.

Mulder doubted it, but together they took less than five minutes looking into every place large enough to hold a woman Elly's size, not at all surprised when all they found was dust and cans of orange spray paint.

He stood in the middle of the living room, absently tapping the gun against his leg.

"Think," he told himself. "Think!" When Scully rejoined him, he shook his head. "She either left on her own, or she's been taken. And I don't think she—"

The front door slammed open, and they instantly dropped into defensive crouches, their guns aimed and ready to fire.

"Hey, no!" Webber cried, throwing up his hands. "Jeez, guys, it's me!"

"Hank," Mulder said, ready to strangle him. He straightened stiffly and lowered his weapon. "You are an idiot. Don't you know better than that?"

Webber tried to point in several directions at once. "I'm sorry. I saw the car, and the outside door was open, and I thought…" He paled. "Jesus. Oh, Jesus." Without looking at either of them, he dropped into the chair and leaned over, hands dangling between his legs. "I could have been killed, you know that? I'm so stupid, I could have been killed."

Scully offered him no sympathy. She stood in front of him, and poked his foot with her shoe. "Where's Andrews?"

"What?" He looked up, confused. "What are you talking about? She was right—"

"Here," Andrews said, standing in the doorway. Her gun was out, and it was aimed at Mulder's head. "Right here."

\\\\\\\\\\\\\\\\\\

"How much do you charge to go to the airport?" Rosemary asked the cabbie.

"Which one?"

"Philadelphia."

"Lady, are you kidding? In this weather?"

"Whatever it is," she said, holding up her purse, "I'll double it. For the trip over. And for your trip back."

He shook his head doubtfully. "Lady, I don't know. They're saying there's flash floods—"

She took out her gun. "You either make money, or you die." She smiled. "Your choice."

\\\\\\\\\\\\\\\\\\

Andrews shifted to her right so she could still keep Mulder in her sights while keeping the wall at her right shoulder.

He held his empty hands wide at his sides. "You're not doing an awful lot of thinking."

She shrugged. She didn't much care. "Do I have to?" She shrugged again. "You're going to die, what's there to think about?"

"One against three is pretty awful odds," Scully said.

"Oh, God," Webber moaned. "I'm gonna be sick."

"Oh, shut up," Andrews snapped. "Christ, how the hell did you ever get in the Bureau?"

Mulder's gun was on the coffee table with Scully's, and all a leap for it would get him would be a bullet in the side, or in the head. Scully, who had been ordered to sit on the couch, was in no better position.

"Look," he said, "Elly is out there somewhere, with the goblin."

Webber sagged forward, one arm across his stomach. He sounded terrified. "Oh Christ." He retched dryly.

"What do I care about an old lady?" Andrews said. "And if you think you're going to stall me long enough for the cavalry to come, forget it. I watch movies, too, Mulder. I'm not as stupid as you think."

He denied any such idea with a shake of his head, and wished Webber would stop that infernal groaning. He couldn't hear himself think, and it was only making Andrews angrier than she already was. Then he snapped his fingers, making Scully jump and Andrews steady her gun hand. "Douglas." He frowned. "You work for Douglas?" His expression hardened. "Of course you do. Because you're not Bureau at all. Which makes me wonder who the mighty Douglas really works for?"

"Time's up," she said blandly.

"Oh, God," Webber gasped and slipped off the chair and onto one knee. "Oh, God, I'm gonna die."

With a look, Andrews dared Scully to make a move, then swung the gun back to Mulder, and smiled him a farewell.

He threw himself backward just before he heard the shot, bracing himself for the impact, landing on his back and rolling to his left when he didn't feel a thing.

He heard Andrews cry out, though, and heard her fall, her gun clattering across the hall floor.

"Nice dive," Scully told him. She was on the floor by the table, her hand around her gun.

Webber pushed himself back into the chair and closed his eyes, his gun hand dangling over the armrest. "I almost missed her," he said to the ceiling. "Christ, can you believe it? I almost missed her."

Mulder jumped to his feet, angry and relieved at the same time. But he said nothing. He picked up his weapon, tucked it into his pocket, and stood over the fallen Andrews. Webber hadn't missed; the entry wound was through her right eye.

He pointed. "You will answer questions later, Hank. Right now, you stay with her. And I mean stay with her."

He didn't argue. His face was pale, his lips trembling; the only sign that he heard was a weak flutter of his hand.

Then Scully looked out the window and said, "Mulder, the park," and he was out the door at a run, taking the three steps at a leap.

She was there, on her bench, huddled beneath her umbrella, and probably had been there the whole time. He had been so intent on getting into the apartment, he hadn't bothered with a single glance across the street once he reached the building.

"Elly, are you all right?"

He slowed when he reached the sidewalk, walked when he started across the grass.

The woman nodded, but the umbrella was loose in her grip, and it nearly fell.

"It's okay, Elly," he said when he reached the bench. He leaned down and brushed a hand over her knee, then held up a hand to shade his eyes from the rain while he looked over the muddy field to the trees on the other side.

She could be there, he thought; damn, she could be anywhere. "Mulder," the goblin said. "I thought I told you to watch your back."

TWENTY-FOUR

With a silent sigh he stared at the ground, at raindrops splashing out of the grass. Then he looked over his shoulder as he turned without haste, blinking the rain out of his eyes.

The umbrella had been discarded.

She sat on the bench back, wearing a long black coat that reached halfway down her shins, her bare feet on the seat, braced to spring. Her short dark hair was matted into a skullcap, her large dark eyes slightly crinkled, as if she were smiling.

Her left hand lay on her thigh, fingers drumming out of rhythm; her right hand held a bayonet, and he could see the gleam of the sharpened edge as she tapped it against her knee.

It was odd, this meeting. Like two friends coming across each other on a rainy day in the park. Only, one of them, before it ended, was going to die.

She raised an eyebrow. "I don't think so, Mulder. Not me, anyway."

"You can read minds, too?"

"No. But you have that gun in your coat, and I have—" She held up the bayonet. "It's not hard to figure out."

The water had taken most of her makeup off, and had washed the white lotion from the backs of her hands. The skin was mottled as if it were dying and ready to slough away in the rain, but it wasn't just gray and black. He could see blotches of pale green, dark green, and near her toes a smear of something almost red.

It could have been blood.

∿∿∿∿∿∿∿∿∿∿∿∿

"Where's Elly?"

Maddy shrugged. "I don't know. I tried to get in the back door, and the next thing I knew I heard the front door slam." She laughed so hoarsely it made his throat ache. "I didn't know an old lady could run so damn fast. I would have gone after her, but as luck would have it, you showed up."

Her eyes shifted away, shifted back.

"Tell her to be careful, Mulder," Maddy suggested. "You may be fast, and a bullet is real fast, but it won't stop me from doing what I have to, understand?"

"I heard," Scully said from somewhere behind him.

He spread his arms. "It's silly, you know. I die, you die, it isn't going to do you any good."

Her voice deepened. "I'm already dying." She held out her hand. "It doesn't work anymore."

He couldn't believe it when her fingers shifted, flesh to splotchy green to smooth cream, and back. Except two of her knuckles stayed dark far longer.

She giggled. "What a bitch, huh? Instead of getting famous, I'm getting dead."

He didn't know what to say. Somehow, "You're under arrest for murder" sounded awfully stupid.

She giggled again, and that was when he saw the madness—in the tilt of her head, the movement of her eyes.

"Why?" he asked, gesturing at her skin. "Didn't you know how dangerous it was?"

"Sure." She waved the bayonet idly. "But do you know how much a cop in a burg like this makes? A dispatcher? Do you know how much that bitch gave me every month?" She laughed and rocked back, rocked forward quickly, bracing herself again. "She had pictures, I saw them, I can read, I knew the risk. Besides…" Her voice faded.

He waited, not moving when she began to toy with the coat's buttons, opening them, closing them, opening some and leaving them.

She wore no clothes beneath the coat, and that didn't surprise him. For what she could do, and had to do, clothes would have been a problem.

What he needed now was for Scully to get into position to cover him when he made his move. He had to. He couldn't stand here, waiting for her to decide it was time, and he wasn't about to let her go. No matter how sorry for her he felt. Which he did as she began to ramble about the tests in the room below the hospital, about the solution baths and the injections, about spying on her friends and on strangers and—

"—feeling such a sense of goddamn power, Mulder. Power." She grinned; her teeth were brown and black. She whispered, "Power."

"Maddy," he said, "don't do this."

"Oh, knock it off," she snapped, straightening, the bayonet catching silver light from the rain. "You can't appeal to my better nature. I don't have one anymore. You can't offer me a cure. You, and you," she shouted to Scully, "can't offer me a damn thing."

"How about living a while longer?"

She laughed, and brushed a strand of hair from her eyes. "Who's going to stop me, you? Her?"

"I can bet Elly's called the police by now. They take one look at you, they won't stop to talk."

"Big deal. I'll be gone." She bounced a little on her rump. "Don't you know I'm the Invisible Woman?"

Her eyes again, shifting, frowning. Scully had moved to his left and was moving to get behind her. One step at a time.

"She's not fast enough, you know."

He lifted his right hand. "Fast enough, if she has to be."

Maddy tensed. He knew it was coming, and as soon as he recognized it, the calm finally returned. The wind nudged her, and she hugged herself, then slipped off the coat.

He only just managed to keep his expression from reacting to the sight of her, skin rough in one place, seemingly raw in another, dark clouds of color rippling across the ridged plane of her stomach.

"You know something?" she said, licking her lips, gauging distance.

"What?" He kept his voice quiet and steady.

"I learned a lot from that bitch. I'm going to tell her that before she dies."

"Like what? What can you learn from killing people?"

She grinned. "That I like it."

He saw her toes flex.

"Please," he said, just before she giggled.

Just before she jumped.

\\\\\\\\\\\\\\\\

There was no time to pull his gun from his pocket. He twisted away from the blade and, at the same time, fired through the coat, lost his footing in the slippery grass and fell on his back.

Maddy screamed when she landed on her hands and knees, spun around, and tried to stand.

"Stop!" Scully ordered, rushing up, aiming low.

Mulder couldn't stand, couldn't move; he could only watch as Maddy Vincent feinted with the blade, then tried to run-crawl at him.

"Stop!" Scully yelled.

Maddy toppled onto one shoulder as if someone had put a boot in her back, and screamed again, stabbed the ground, and slumped whimpering into the mud.

As Mulder pushed himself to his feet, as Scully braced herself behind the woman, he saw the blood seep out from under her arm.

It didn't look black at all.

It looked red, and it didn't stop.

He leaned over and took the bayonet from her hand, held it close to his eyes for a moment and placed it on the bench. Scully pressed three fingers to the side of the woman's neck, then checked her wrist. She rose awkwardly, a hand pushing through her hair, and Mulder took off his coat and spread it over the goblin's body.

He stared at it for a long while, until he laughed once, sharply, realizing he had been waiting for her, like the Invisible Man, to return to normal, now that the adventure was finally done.

But she didn't.

She just lay there.

\\\\\\\\\\\\\\\\\

Mulder didn't know how long it took to answer the questions, for Scully to make sure the body would be placed in the right hands for the proper examinations, for the cold to finally leave him, for him to finally feel dry.

But it was after eleven that night before he was able to sit in the Queen's Inn and stare at the plate of pancakes in front of Hank Webber.

"Please," Hank said. "Don't say it's amazing."

"It is, but I won't."

Scully was at the counter, ordering coffee and tea, and finding out just what the cook would make this late on Saturday night. Mulder waited until her back was turned, then lifted a finger to get Hank's attention.

"Protest not," he said. "Don't insult me with denials. But how many times have you called Douglas since we've arrived, to tell him how many times I didn't follow the book."

Webber almost choked, but he managed to hold up his fork and say, "Just once."

"What?"

He looked embarrassed. "I couldn't. I mean… I like you. And I didn't see that you were doing anything really wrong."

Mulder grinned as he stretched his arm across the back of the seat. "Webber, I don't care—that's damn amazing." He looked out the window, but all he saw was the night and the rain. "You know that Douglas is probably a plant, don't ask me by whom, and he probably won't be there when we get back. You know you'll probably be transferred somewhere else once we get back and the paperwork is done."

"Sure. I figured. But hell, it was fun while it lasted."

Mulder laughed, a little sadly, because he knew poor old Hank probably wouldn't be with the Bureau for very long. "Fun" wasn't exactly the way to describe the way it worked.

"And by the way," he said, "in all the excitement… thanks."

Webber waved it away. "Not needed, Mulder. I was just doing what I had to, you know?"

And he blushed.

Scully slid in then, clucked at Webber's choice of a meal, and fussed with her napkin while she waited for her order. "You do realize, Mulder, don't you, that that was an incredibly lucky shot. By all rights, you should be dead."

He knew that. He had especially known that when he had seen the rent across the front of his coat.

The blade had come a lot closer than he'd thought; it had sliced clear through the cloth.

"Don't ever try that again."

"Believe me," he said. "I won't."

They ate, then, in companionable, weary silence, interrupted only by a phone call he took at the register. When he returned to the booth, he only said, "They found Tonero's body. Shot once. He was in Dr. Elkhart's apartment."

"And her?" Scully asked.

"Gone. Not a trace."

"They'll find her," Webber said confidently. "After this weekend, half the country'll be hunting for her. Don't sweat it, Mulder, the case is closed."

"I suppose," Mulder said. He looked out the window, through the rivulets of rain. "I suppose."

Scully touched his shoulder, light and quick. "Mulder, don't."

He didn't look. "Sure."

They both knew he was lying.

Because, he thought, looking through his dim reflection to the woodland just beyond, what if they don't find her.

What if, next year, or the year after, you're walking down the street or climbing your steps or standing on your porch or you're waiting for a bus, and an arm comes out of a wall or a tree or...

He stretched a finger toward the glass, watching its reflection stretch toward him.

... a simple pane of glass.

The lights flickered for a moment, and for a moment the reflection vanished.

He rubbed his arm absently, watching the headlights of a car he couldn't see float past and disappear.

We'll never know they're out there—

Armies of living shadows.

Slipping through the night.

END

GROUND ZERO

By Kevin J. Anderson

ONE

Teller Nuclear Research Facility
Pleasanton, California
Monday, 4:03 p.m.

Even through the thick windows of his laboratory building, the old man could hear the antinuke protesters outside. Chanting, singing, shouting—always fighting against the future, trying to stall progress. It baffled him more than it angered him. The slogans hadn't changed from decade to decade. He didn't think the radicals would ever learn.

He fingered the laminated badge dangling from his lab coat. The five-year-old picture, showing him with an awkward expression, was worse than a driver's license photo. The Badge Office didn't like to retake snapshots—but then, ID photos never really looked like the subject in question, anyway. At least not in the past five decades. Not since his days as a minor technician for the Manhattan Project. In half a century his face had grown more gaunt, more seamed, especially over the past few years. His steel-gray hair had turned an unhealthy yellowish-white, where it hadn't fallen out in patches. But his eyes remained bright and inquisitive, fascinated by the mysteries hidden in dim corners of the universe.

The badge identified him as Emil Gregory. He wasn't like many of his younger colleagues who insisted on proper titles: Dr. Emil Gregory, or Emil Gregory, Ph.D., or even Emil Gregory, Project Director. He had spent too much time in laid-back New Mexico and California to worry about such formalities. Only scientists whose jobs were in question concerned themselves with trivialities like that. Dr. Gregory was at the end of a long and highly successful career. His colleagues knew his name.

Since much of his work had been classified, he was not assured of a place in the history books. But he had certainly made his place in history, whether or not anybody had heard about it.

His former assistant and prize student, Miriel Bremen, knew about his research—but she had turned her back on him. In fact, she was probably standing outside right now, waving her signs and chanting slogans with the other protesters. She had organized them all. Miriel had always been good at organizing unruly groups of people.

Outside, three more Protective Services cars drove up for an uneasy showdown with the protesters who paced back and forth in front of the gate, blocking traffic. Uniformed security guards emerged from the squad cars, slamming doors. They stood with shoulders squared and tried to look intimidating. But they couldn't really take action, since the protesters had carefully remained within the law. In the back of one of the white official cars, a trained German shepherd barked through the screen mesh of the window; it was a drug-and-explosive-sniffing dog, not an attack animal, but its loud growls no doubt made the protesters nervous.

Dr. Gregory finally decided to ignore the distractions outside the lab building. Moving slowly and painfully in his seventy-two-year-old body whose warranty had recently run out, he liked to say—he went back to his computer simulations. The protesters and guards could keep up their antics for the rest of the afternoon and into the night, for all he cared. He turned up his radio to cover the noise from outside so he could concentrate, though he didn't have to worry about his calculations. The supercomputers actually did most of the work.

The portable boom box tucked among books and technical papers on his shelf had never succeeded in picking up more than one station through the thick concrete walls, despite the jury-rigged antenna of chained paper clips he had hooked to the metal window frame. The lone AM station, thank goodness, played primarily Oldies, songs he associated with happier days. Right now, Simon and Garfunkel were singing about Mrs. Robinson, and Dr. Gregory sang along with them.

The color monitors on his four supercomputer work-stations displayed the progress of his simultaneous hydro-code simulations. The computers chugged through numerous virtual experiments in their integrated-circuit imaginations, sorting through billions of iterations without requiring him to throw a single switch or hook up a single generator.

But Dr. Gregory still insisted on wearing his lab coat; he didn't feel like a real scientist without it. If he wore comfortable street clothes and simply pounded on computer keyboards all day long, he might as well be an accountant instead of a well-respected weapons researcher at one of the largest nuclear-design laboratories in the country.

Off in a separate building on the fenced-in lab site, powerful Cray-III supercomputers crunched data for complex simulations of a major upcoming nuclear test. They were studying intricate nuclear hydrodynamic models—imaginary atomic explosions—of the radical new warhead concept to which he had devoted the last four years of his career.

Bright Anvil.

Because of cost limitations and the on-again/off again political treaties regarding nuclear testing, these hydrodynamic simulations were now the only way to study certain secondary effects, to analyze shock-front formations and fallout patterns. Above-ground atomic detonations had been banned by international treaty since 1963... but Dr. Gregory and his superiors believed they could succeed with the Bright Anvil Project—if all conditions turned out right.

The Department of Energy was eager to see that all conditions turned out right.

He moved to the next simulation screen, watching the dance of contours, pressure waves, temperature graphs on a nanosecond-by-nanosecond scale. Already he could see that it would be a lovely explosion.

Classified reports and memos littered his desk, buried under sheafs of printouts spewed from the laser printer he shared with the rest of his Bright Anvil team members down the hall. His deputy project head, "Bear" Dooley, posted regular weather reports and satellite photos, circling the interesting areas with a red felt-tip marker. The most recent picture showed a large circular depression gathered over the central Pacific, like spoiled milk swirling down a drain—eliciting a great deal of excitement from Dooley.

"Storm brewing!" the deputy had scrawled on a Post-it note stuck to the satellite photo. "Our best candidate so far!"

Dr. Gregory had to agree with the assessment. But they couldn't proceed to the next step until he finished the final round of simulations. Though the Bright Anvil device had already been assembled except for its fissile core, Gregory eschewed lazy shortcuts. With such incredible power at one's fingertips, caution was the watchword.

He whistled along to "Georgie Girl" as his computers simulated waves of mass destruction.

Somebody honked a car horn outside, either in support of the protesters, or just annoyed and trying to get past them. Since he planned to stay late, those demonstrators—weary and self-satisfied—would be long gone by the time Gregory headed for his own car.

It didn't matter to him how many extra hours he remained in the lab, since research was the only thing left of his real life. Even if he went home, he would probably work anyway, in his too-quiet and too-empty house, surrounded by photos of the old 1950s hydrogen bomb shots out in the islands or atomic blasts at the Nevada Test Site. He had access to better computers in his lab, though, so he might as well work through dinner. He had a sandwich in the refrigerator down the hall, but his appetite had been unpredictable for the past few months.

At one time, Miriel Bremen would have stayed working with him. She was a sharp and imaginative young physicist who looked up to the older scientist with something like awe. Miriel had a great deal of talent, a genuine feel for the calculations and secondary effects. Her dedication and ambition made her the perfect research partner. Unfortunately, she also had too much conscience, and doubts had festered inside her.

Miriel Bremen herself was the spearhead behind the formation of the vehement new activist group, Stop Nuclear Madness!, headquartered in Berkeley. She had abandoned her work at the research facility, spooked by certain incomprehensible aspects of the Bright Anvil warhead. Miriel had become a turncoat with a zeal that reminded him of the way some former cigarette smokers turned into the most outspoken antitobacco lobbyists.

He thought of Miriel out there on the other side of the fence. She would be waving a sign, taunting the security guards to arrest her, making her point loud and clear, regardless of whether anyone wanted to hear it.

Dr. Gregory forced himself to remain seated behind the computer workstation. He refused to go back to the window to look for her. He didn't feel spite toward Miriel, just… disappointment. He wondered how he had failed her, how he could have misjudged his deputy so thoroughly.

At least he didn't have to worry about her replacement, Bear Dooley. Dooley was a bulldozer of a man, with a dearth of tact and patience, but a singular dedication to purpose. He, at least, had his head on straight.

A knock came at the half-closed door to his lab office. Patty, his secretary—he still hadn't gotten used to thinking of her as an "administrative assistant," the current politically correct term—poked her head in.

"Afternoon mail, Dr. Gregory. There's a package I thought you might like to see. Special delivery." She waggled a small padded envelope. He started to push his aching body up from his computer chair, but she waved him back down. "Here. Don't get up."

"Thanks, Patty." He took the envelope, pulling his reading glasses from. his pocket and settling them on his nose so he could see the postmark. *Honolulu, Hawaii.* No return address.

Patty remained in the doorway, shuffling her feet. She cleared her throat. "It's after four o'clock, Dr. Gregory. Would you mind if I left a little early today?" Her voice picked up speed, as if she were making excuses. "I know I've got those memos to type up tomorrow morning, but I'll keep one step ahead of you."

"You always do, Patty. Doctor's appointment?" he said, still looking down at the mysterious envelope and turning it over in his hands.

"No, but I don't really want to hassle with the protesters. They'll probably try to block the gate at quitting time just to cause trouble. I'd rather be long gone." She looked down at her pink-polished fingernails. Her face had a fallen-in, anxious expression.

Dr. Gregory laughed at her nervousness. "Go ahead. I'll be staying late for the same reason." She thanked him and popped back out the door, pulling it shut behind her so he could work in peace.

The computer calculations continued. The core of the simulated explosion had expanded, sending shockwaves all the way to the edge of the monitor screen, with secondary and tertiary effects propagating in less-defined directions through the plasma left behind from the initial detonation.

Dr. Gregory peeled open the padded envelope, working one finger under the heavily glued flap. He dumped the contents onto his desk and blinked, perplexed. He blew out a curious breath.

The single scrap of paper wasn't exactly a letter—no stationery, no signature—just carefully inked words in fine black lettering.

"FOR YOUR PART IN THE PAST—AND THE FUTURE."

A small glassine packet fell out beside the note. It was a translucent envelope only a few inches long, filled with some sort of black powder. He shook the padded envelope, but it contained nothing else.

He picked up the glassine packet, squinting as he squeezed the contents with his fingers. The substance was lightweight, faintly greasy, like ash. He sniffed it, caught a faint, sour charcoal smell mostly faded by time.

For your part in the past—and the future.

Dr. Gregory frowned. He scornfully wondered if this could be some stunt by the protesters outside. In earlier actions, protesters had poured jars of animal blood on the ground in front of the facility's security gates and planted flowers alongside the entry roads.

Black ash must be somebody's newest idea—maybe even Miriel's. He rolled his eyes and let out an "Oh brother!" sigh.

"You can't change the world by poking your heads in the sand," Dr. Gregory muttered, turning his gaze toward the window.

On the workstations, the redundant simulations neared completion after eating up hours of super-computer time, projecting a step-by-step analysis of one second in time, the transient moment where a man-made device unleashed energies equivalent to the core of a sun.

So far, the computers agreed with his wildest expectations.

Though he himself was the project head, Dr. Gregory found parts of Bright Anvil inexplicable, based on baffling theoretical assumptions and producing aftereffects that went against all his training and experience in physics. But the simulations *worked*, and he knew enough not to ask questions of the sponsors who had presented him with the foundations of this new concept to implement.

After a fifty-one-year-long career, Dr. Gregory found it refreshing to find an entire portion of his chosen discipline that he could not explain. It opened up the wonder of science for him all over again.

He tossed the black ash aside and went back to work.

Suddenly the overhead fluorescent lights flickered. There was an intense humming sound, as if a swarm of bees were trapped in the thin glass tubes.

He heard the snapping shriek of an electrical discharge, and the lights popped and died.

The radio on his desk gave out a brief squelch of static, right in the middle of "Hang on, Sloopy." Then it fell silent.

Dr. Gregory's failing muscles sent stabs of pain through his body as he whirled in despair to see his computer workstations also winking out. The computers were crashing.

"Awww, no!" he groaned. The systems should have had infallible backup power supplies to protect them during normal electrical outages. He had just lost literally billions of supercomputer iterations.

He pounded his gnarled fist on the desk, then levered himself to his feet and staggered over to the window, moving more quickly than his unsteady balance and common sense allowed.

Reaching the glass, he glanced outside at the other buildings in the complex. All the interior lights were still shining in the adjacent wing of the research building. Very odd.

It looked as if his office had been specifically targeted for a power disruption.

With a sinking feeling, Dr. Gregory began to wonder about sabotage from the protesters. Could Miriel have gone so far overboard? She would know how to cause such damage. Though her security clearance had been taken away after she quit her job and formed Stop Nuclear Madness!, perhaps she had managed to bluff her way inside, to interfere with the simulations only she could have known her old mentor would be running.

He didn't want to think her capable of such action… but he knew she would consider it, without qualms.

Dr. Gregory swatted at the insistent hissing, buzzing noise that hovered about his ears, finally noticing it for the first time. With all the power suddenly smothered and machine sounds damped to nothingness, silence should have descended upon his office.

But the whispers came instead.

With a growing sense of uneasiness that he forced himself to ignore, Dr. Gregory went to the door, intending to shout down the hall for Bear Dooley or any of the other physicists. For some reason, the company of others seemed highly desirable right now.

But he found the doorknob unbearably hot. *Unnaturally* hot.

With a hiss, he yanked his hand away. He backed off, staring down in shock more than pain at the bright blisters forming in the center of his palm.

Smoke began to curl around the solid security-locked doorknob, oozing out of the keyslot.

"Hey, what is this? Hello!" He flapped his burned hand to cool it. "Patty? Are you still out there?"

Contained within the concrete walls of his office, the wind picked up, crackling with electrical static. Papers blew, curled up by a foul breath of heat. The glassine envelope of black powder spilled open, spraying dark ash into the air.

Untucking his shirt and using the tail to protect his hand against the heat, he hurried back to the door again and reached for the knob. By now, though, it glowed red-hot, a throbbing scarlet that hurt his eyes.

"Patty, I need your help. Bear! Somebody!" His voice cracked, growing high-pitched with fear.

Like an elapsed-time simulation of sunrise, the light in the room grew brighter and *brighter*, seeming to emanate from the walls, a searing harsh glare.

Dr. Gregory backed toward the concrete blocks, holding up his hands to shield his face from yet another aspect of physics he did not understand. The whispering voices increased in volume, rising to a crescendo of screams and accusations climbing through the air itself.

Reaching a critical point.

An avalanche of heat and fire struck him, so intense that it knocked him into the wall. A billion, billion X rays brought every cell in his body to a boil. Then came a *burst* of absolute light, like the core of an atomic explosion.

And Dr. Gregory found himself standing alone at Ground Zero.

TWO

Teller Nuclear Research Facility
Tuesday, 10:13 a.m.

The security guard stepped out of a small prefab shack just outside the chain-link perimeter of the large research facility. He glanced at Fox Mulder's papers and FBI identification, then motioned for him to drive his rental car over to the Badge Office just outside the gate.

In the passenger seat Dana Scully sat up straighter. She willed the cells of her body to supply more energy and bring her to full alertness. She hated catching red-eye flights, especially from the East Coast. Already today she had spent hours on the plane and now another hour in the car with her partner driving from the San Francisco Airport. She had rested fitfully on the large plane, managing only a brief nap instead of genuine sleep.

"Sometimes I wish that more of our cases would happen closer to home," she said, not really meaning it.

Mulder looked over at her, flashed a brief commiserating smile. "Look on the bright side, Scully—I know plenty of deskbound agents who envy us our exciting jet-setting lifestyle. We get to see the world. They get to see their offices."

"I suppose the grass is always greener…" Scully said. "Still, if I ever do take a vacation, I think I'll just stay home on the sofa and read a book."

Scully had grown up as a Navy brat. She and her two brothers and her sister had been forced to pull up their roots every few years while they were young, whenever the Navy assigned her father to a different base or a different ship. She'd never complained, always respecting her father's duty enough to do her part. But she had never dreamed that when it came to her own career, she would end up choosing something that required her to travel around so often.

Mulder guided the car to the front of a small white office isolated from the large cluster of buildings inside the fence. The Badge Office appeared relatively new, with the type of clean yet flimsy architecture that reminded Scully of a child's step-by-step model kit.

Mulder parked the car and reached behind him to pull out his lightweight briefcase. Scully flicked down the mirror on the passenger side sun visor. She gave a quick glance at the lipstick on her full lips, checked the makeup on her large blue eyes, smoothed her light auburn hair. Despite her tiredness, everything seemed in place, professional.

Mulder stepped out of the car and straightened his suit jacket, adjusted his maroon tie.

FBI agents, after all, had to appear suitable for the part.

"I need another cup of coffee," Scully said, following him out of the car. "I want to be absolutely certain I can devote my full attention to the details of any case unusual enough to drag us three thousand miles across the country."

Mulder held open the glass door for her to enter the Badge Office. "You mean that 'gourmet' brew on the airplane wasn't up to your exacting standards?"

She favored him with raised eyebrows. "Let's put it this way, Mulder—I haven't heard of many flight attendants retiring to start their own espresso franchises."

Mulder ran a hand quickly through his fluffy dark hair, ensuring that at least most of the strands fell into place. Then he trailed after her into the heavily air-conditioned building. The interior consisted primarily of a large, open area, a long counter that served as a barricade to a few back offices, and some small carrels that held televisions and videotape players.

A row of blue padded chairs sat in front of a wall of windows that had been tinted to filter out the bright California sun, though patches of the modern brown-and-rust tweed carpet already looked faded. Several construction workers clad in overalls stood in line at the counter with hardhats tucked under their arms and folded pink forms in their hands. One at a time the workers handed their papers to the counter personnel, who checked IDs and exchanged the pink forms for temporary work permits.

A sign on the wall clearly listed all of the items that were not permitted inside the Teller Nuclear Research Facility: cameras, firearms, drugs, alcohol, personal recording devices, telescopes. Scully scanned the list. The items were familiar from her own experience at FBI Headquarters.

"I'll check us in," she said and flipped open a small notebook from the pocket of her forest-green suit. She took a place in line behind several large men in paint-spattered overalls. She felt extremely overdressed. Another clerk opened a station at the end of the speckled counter and gestured Scully over.

"I suppose I must look out of place here," Scully said and displayed her badge. "I'm Special Agent Dana Scully. My partner is Fox Mulder. We're here to meet with—" she glanced down at her notebook, "a Department of Energy representative, a Ms. Rosabeth Carrera. She's expecting us."

The clerk straightened her gold-rimmed glasses and shuffled through some papers. She punched in Scully's name on her computer terminal. "Yes, here you are, 'Special Clearance Expedited.' You'll still need to be escorted everywhere until official approval comes through, but we can issue you badges to allow you access to certain areas in the meantime."

Scully raised her eyebrows, keeping her best professional Meet-the-Public composure. "Is that really necessary? Agent Mulder and I already have full clearances with the FBI. You can—"

"Your FBI clearances don't mean anything here, Ms. Scully," the woman said. "This is a Department of Energy facility. We don't even recognize Department of Defense clearances. Everybody's got their own investigative procedures, and none of us talks to the other."

"Government efficiency?" Scully said.

"Your tax dollars at work. Just be glad you don't work for the Postal Service," the woman said. "Who knows what sort of background check they'd do."

Mulder came up beside Scully. He handed her a Styrofoam cup full of oily, bitter-smelling coffee he had taken from a pot on an end table piled high with flashy Teller Nuclear Research Facility technical reports and brochures about all the wonderful work the R&D lab was doing for humanity.

"I paid ten cents for this," he said, indicating the contributions cup, "and I'll bet it's worth every penny. Creamer, no sugar."

Scully took a sip. "Tastes like it's been on that warmer since the Manhattan Project," she said, but grudgingly took another sip to show Mulder that she appreciated his gesture.

"Think of it as fine wine, Scully: perfectly aged."

The clerk returned to the counter and handed Mulder and Scully each a laminated visitor's badge. "Wear these at all times. Make sure they're visible and above the waist," she said. "And these." She passed them each a blue plastic rectangle containing what looked like a strip of film and a computer chip. "Your radiation dosimeters. Clip them to your badges. Always keep them on your person."

"Radiation dosimeters?" Scully asked, maintaining a calm tone, devoid of any obvious worry. "Is there some cause for concern here?"

"Just a precaution, Agent Scully. We are a *nuclear* research facility, you understand. Our orientation videotape should answer all your questions. Follow me, please."

She set Scully and Mulder at one of the small carrels in front of a miniature television. She inserted the videotape and pushed PLAY, then went back to the counter to call Rosabeth Carrera. Mulder leaned over, watching the static on the leader before the tape began. "What do you think they'll have, a cartoon or previews?" he said.

"Do you believe a cartoon designed by the government would be funny?" she asked.

Mulder shrugged. "Some people think Jerry Lewis is funny."

The videotape ran for only four minutes. It was a sanitized description of the Teller Nuclear Research Facility, with a perky narrator explaining briefly what radiation is and what it can do *for* you, as well as *to* you. The program emphasized the medical uses and research applications of exotic isotopes, gave constant reassurances about the safeguards used by the facility, and made comparisons to background levels of radiation that one might receive taking a single cross-country flight or living a year in a high-altitude city such as Denver. After a final, brightly colored graph, the cheery voice told them both to have a nice, safe visit at the Teller Nuclear Research Facility.

Mulder rewound the tape. "My heart's just going all pitter-pat," he said.

Together they made their way back to the badge counter. Most of the construction workers had already gone inside the chain-link fence to their work site.

Mulder and Scully didn't have long to wait before a petite Hispanic woman bustled in through the glass doors. She spotted the two FBI agents half a second later and came over, looking full of energy, eager to meet them. Scully immediately sized her up as she had been trained to do at Quantico, visually gathering facts to form an estimation of a person upon first glance. The woman held out her hand and quickly shook with the two FBI agents.

"I'm Rosabeth Carrera," she said, "one of the DOE representatives here. I'm very pleased you could come out on such short notice. It is something of an emergency."

Carrera wore a knee-length skirt and scarlet silk blouse that set off her dusky skin. Her lips were generous, embellished with a conservative lipstick. Her full head of rich brown hair, the color of dark chocolate, was pulled back on her head, held by several gold barrettes, and cascaded down her back in a glorious tumble of locks. She was built like a gymnast, filled with enthusiasm, not at all the type of dry bureaucrat Scully had expected.

Scully caught the look on Mulder's face as he stared into the woman's very dark eyes. Carrera laughed. "I could spot you two right away. This is California, you know. East Coasters and a few high management types are the only ones around here who wear monkey suits."

Scully blinked. "Monkey suits?"

"Formal dress. The Teller Facility is pretty casual. Most of our researchers are Californians or transplants from Los Alamos, New Mexico. A suit and tie is a rarity here."

"I always knew I was somebody special," Mulder said. "I should have thought to wear my surfing tie."

"If you'll follow me," Carrera said, "I'll take you into the site and the scene of the… accident. We've left everything the way it was for the past eighteen hours. It's so unusual, we wanted to give you a chance to look at it fresh. We'll take my car."

Scully and Mulder followed her out to a pale blue Ford Fairmont with government plates. Mulder caught his partner's eye and scratched the side of his head in a chimpanzee imitation. Monkey suits.

"We keep the doors unlocked around here," Carrera said, indicating the car doors as she slipped inside. "We figure nobody'd want to steal a government car." Mulder climbed in back, while Scully took the seat next to the DOE representative.

"Can you give us any more details about this case, Ms. Carrera?" Scully asked. "We were pulled out of bed early and sent here with virtually no background. The only information we've been given is that an important nuclear researcher here died in some sort of freak accident in his lab."

Carrera drove toward the guard gate. She flashed her badge and handed over the paperwork that would allow Scully and Mulder to enter the facility beyond the fence. Receiving the counter-signed papers, she drove on, biting her lip as if mulling over the details. "That's the story we've released to the press, though it won't hold up long. There are too many questions yet—but I didn't want to prejudice you before you saw the scene yourself."

"You certainly know how to build suspense," Mulder said from the back seat.

Rosabeth Carrera kept her eyes on the road while they drove past office trailers, temporary buildings, a cluster of old dilapidated buildings with wooden siding that looked like something from an old military installation, and finally to the newer buildings that had been constructed during the large defense budgets of the Reagan administration.

"We called the FBI as a matter of course," Carrera continued. "This is possibly a crime—a death, maybe murder—on federal property, so the FBI has automatic jurisdiction."

"You could have worked through your local field office," Scully pointed out.

"We called them," Carrera said. "One of the local agents, a Craig Kreident, came out for a first glance last night. Do you know him?"

Mulder touched his lips, as he searched his excellent memory. "Agent Kreident," he said. "I believe he specializes in high-tech crimes out here."

"That's him," Carrera said. "But Kreident took one look and said this one was out of his league. He said it looked more like an 'X-File'... those were his words... and that it was probably a job for you, Agent Mulder. I don't understand what an X-File is."

"Amazing what a reputation can do for you," Mulder murmured.

Scully answered the question. "'X-Files' is a catchall term for investigations involving strange and unexplained phenomena. The Bureau has numerous records of unsolved cases dating as far back as the early days of J. Edgar Hoover. The two of us have had numerous... experiences looking into those unusual cases."

Carrera parked in front of the large laboratory buildings and got out of the car. "Then I think you'll find this one to be right up your alley."

Carrera led them at a brisk pace through the building, up to the second floor. The dim echoing halls, lit by banks of fluorescent lights, reminded Scully of a high school. One of the tubes overhead was gray and flickering. Scully wondered how long it had needed to be replaced.

Cork bulletin boards lined the open spaces of cement-block walls, posted with colorful safety notices and signs for regular technical meetings. Handwritten index cards announced rental properties and time-share condos in Hawaii, cars for sale; one card offered "slightly used rock-climbing equipment." The ubiquitous security awareness posters seemed to be left over from World War II, though Scully found none that said "Loose Lips Sink Ships."

Up ahead an entire corridor had been blocked off with yellow barrier tape. Since the Teller Nuclear Research Facility couldn't be expected to have CRIME SCENE barricades, they had settled for CONSTRUCTION AREA tape. Two lab security guards stood posted on either side of the corridor, looking uncomfortable with their assignment.

Carrera didn't need to say a word to them. One guard stepped aside to let her pass. "Don't worry," she said to the man, "you're on a short shift. Replacements are coming in a few minutes." Then she gestured for Mulder and Scully to follow her as she ducked under the flimsy yellow tape.

Scully wondered why the guards should be so concerned. Was it the simple superstition of being too close to a possible murder scene? These guards probably had very little outright crime to investigate, especially not violent crime like murder. She supposed the body hadn't been removed yet, which would be very unusual.

Down the hall beyond the yellow tape, all other offices stood empty, though their still-running computers and full bookshelves showed that the room had been occupied until recently. Coworkers of Dr. Emil Gregory's? If so, they would have to be interviewed. No doubt all of the workers had been relocated, pending investigation of the accident.

One office door, though, was tightly shut and sealed with more of the barrier tape. Rosabeth Carrera stood beside it and pulled off her laminated picture badge from which dangled a dosimeter and several keys. She searched for the key with the appropriate ID number and slipped it into the intimidating-looking lock in the doorknob.

"Take a quick look," she said, pushing the door open and simultaneously turning her face away. "This is just first glance. You've got two minutes."

Scully and Mulder stood beside each other at the threshold and peered inside.

It looked as if an incendiary bomb had gone off in Dr. Gregory's lab office.

Every surface had been singed with a burst of heat so intense, yet so brief, it had curled and crisped the papers attached to Gregory's bulletin board—*but had not ignited them.* His four computer terminals had melted at the edges and slumped in on themselves, the heavy glass cathode-ray tubes of the screens tilting cockeyed like the gaze of a dead man. Even the metal desks bowed and sagged from the brief molten weakness.

An erasable white board had turned black, its enamel finish dark and blistered, though the colored trails of scrawled equations and notes left identifiable paths in the soot.

Scully spotted Gregory's body against the far wall. All that remained of the old weapons researcher was a horribly crisped scarecrow of a man. His arms and legs were drawn up from the contraction of muscles in intense heat, like some sort of insect sprayed with poison and curled up to die. His skin and the twisted rictus on his face made him look as if he had been doused with napalm.

Mulder stared at the destruction in the room, while Scully focused on the corpse, her mouth partially open, her mind already set in that curious mixture of human horror and detached analysis she slipped into when inspecting a crime scene. The only way she could stave off her revulsion was to look for answers. She stepped forward.

Before she could enter the room, though, Carrera placed a firm hand on her shoulder. "No, not yet," she said. "You can't go in there."

Mulder gave Carrera a sharp look, as if she had just pulled on his leash. "How are we supposed to investigate a crime scene if we can't go inside?"

Scully could tell that her partner's interest had already been piqued. From what she could see at first glance she was going to have a hard time coming up with a simple, rational explanation for what had happened here in the sealed lab.

"Too much residual radiation," Carrera said. "You'll need full contamination gear before you go inside."

Scully reflexively touched her dosimeter as she and Mulder both backed away from the door. "But according to your video briefing none of the labs supposed to contain dangerously high levels of radiation. Was that just government propaganda?"

Carrera pulled the door shut again and favored Scully with a tolerant smile. "No, it's true—under normal circumstances. But as you can see, things aren't normal in Dr. Gregory's lab. Nothing any of us can understand… not yet, anyway. There should not have been any radioactive material here; yet we found high levels of residual radiation in the walls, in the equipment.

"But don't worry, those thick concrete blocks shield us out here in the hall. Nothing to worry about—if you stay away from it. But you'll need a much closer look. We'll let you continue your investigation. Come on."

She turned, and they followed her down the corridor. "Let's get you both suited up."

THREE

Teller Nuclear Research Facility
Tuesday, 11:21 a.m.

The thick outfit made Mulder look like an astronaut. He found it difficult to move, but his eagerness to investigate the mysterious death of Dr. Emil Gregory convinced him to put up with the difficulties.

Health-and-safety technicians adjusted the seams of his anticontamination suit, pulling the hood down over his head, fastening the zipper in back, then sealing it with another flap Velcroed over the top to keep chemical or radioactive residue from seeping through the seams.

A transparent plastic faceplate allowed him to see, but condensation formed on the inside, and he tried to control his breathing. Canisters of compressed air on his back connected to a hood respirator that echoed in his ears and made it difficult to exhale. The joints in his knees and elbows ballooned as he tried to walk.

Mulder felt detached from his surroundings, armored against the invisible threat of radiation. "I thought lead underwear went out of style with bell bottoms."

Standing next to him, still clad in her stunning blouse and skirt, the dark beauty Rosabeth Carrera stood with her hands at her sides, looking uncertain as to what she should do. She had declined to suit up in anticontamination gear and accompany them onto the scene.

"You're free to go in and look around as much as you'd like," Carrera said. "Meanwhile, I've arranged for the paperwork to allow you free access to the site—you'll have a 'need-to-know' clearance for this case only. The Department of Energy and Teller Labs are eager to find out what caused Dr. Gregory's death."

"What if they don't like the answer?" Mulder said.

Swathed in her own billowing hood in the anti-contamination suit, Scully flashed him a warning look, one of the usual glances she gave him when he followed his penchant for blundering down a dangerous road.

"Any answer's better than nothing," Carrera said. "Right now all we have are a bunch of disturbing questions." She gestured up and down the hall where the offices of Gregory's co-researchers had been sealed off. "The background radiation in the rest of this building is perfectly normal, except in Gregory's office. We need you to find out what happened."

Scully asked, "I know this is a weapons research laboratory. Was Dr. Gregory working on anything dangerous? Anything that could have backfired on him? A prototype for a new weapons system perhaps?"

Carrera crossed her arms over her small breasts and stood confident. "Dr. Gregory was working on computer simulations. He had no fissile material whatsoever in his lab, nothing that even remotely approached the destructive potential that we see here. Nothing at all deadly. The equipment was no more dangerous than a videogame."

"Ah, videogames," Mulder said. "Could be the heart of our conspiracy."

Rosabeth Carrera gave them each a handheld radiation detector. The gadgets looked just like the kind Mulder had seen in dozens of 1950s B-movies of uncontrolled nuclear tests that accidently created mutations whose bizarreness was limited only by Hollywood's meager special effects budgets of the era.

One of the health-and-safety technicians gave them a quick briefing on how to use the radiation detector. The tech swept the sensor end up and down the hall, taking a sample of normal background readings. "Seems to be functioning properly," he said. "I checked the calibration just a few hours ago."

"Let's go inside, Mulder," Scully said, standing at the door, obviously impatient to get to work.

Carrera used the key on her badge again, pushing the lab door open. Mulder and Scully entered Dr. Gregory's laboratory—and the radiation detectors went wild.

Mulder watched the needle dance high up on the gauge, though he didn't hear the frying-bacon crackle of Geiger counters used so often in films. The silent needle's signal was ominous enough.

Within its concrete-block walls, this office had somehow been the site of an intense burst of radiation that had blistered the paint, seared the concrete, and melted the furniture. The flash had left residual and secondary radioactivity that still simmered, only fading gradually.

Behind them Rosabeth Carrera closed the door.

Mulder's breathing resonated in his ears in the self-contained suit. It sounded as if someone were breathing down his neck, a long-fanged monster riding on his shoulder… but it was only echoes inside his hood. Claustrophobia hammered around him as he stepped deeper into the burned laboratory. Looking at the melted and flash-burned artifacts sent a shudder down his spine, tapping into his long-standing revulsion of fire.

Scully went straight to the body, while Mulder stopped to inspect the heat-slumped computer terminals, the melted desks, the flash-burned papers on the bulletin board and on the work tables. "No indication of where the burst might have originated," he said, poking around the debris.

The walls were adorned with images of Pacific islands, aerial photos as well as computer printouts of weather maps of the ocean wind patterns, storm projections, and blistered black-and-white prints of weather satellite images—everything centered on the Western Pacific, just past the International Date Line.

"Not the sort of stuff I'd expect a nuclear weapons researcher to collect on his office walls," Mulder said.

Scully bent over the scarecrowish burned body of Dr. Gregory. "If we can determine what he was working on, get some details of the weapons systems and any tests he was planning to run, we might come up with a more clear-cut explanation."

"Clear-cut, Scully?" Mulder said. "You surprise me."

"Think about it, Mulder. Despite what Ms. Carrera said, Dr. Gregory was a weapons researcher—what if he was working on some new high-energy burst weapon? It's possible he had a prototype in here and he accidentally set it off. It could have flash-fried everything you see here, killed him… if it was just a small test model, its effect would be limited. It might not destroy the entire building."

"Good for us," he said. "But look around—I don't see the remains of any weapon, do you? Even if it exploded, there should be some evidence."

"We should still look into it," Scully answered. "I need to take this body in for an autopsy. I'll request that Ms. Carrera find us a local medical facility where I can work."

Mulder, preoccupied by Gregory's bulletin board, reached out with a gloved hand to touch one of the curled papers still fastened by a slagged push pin to the crisped cork board. When he brushed the paper with his fingertips, it crumbled into ash, rippling away into the air. Nothing remained but a powdery residue.

Mulder looked around for thick stacks of paper, hoping that something might have been left intact, like the photos on the walls. He searched Dr. Gregory's desk for piles of technical reports or journal articles, but found nothing. Then he noticed the unburned rectangular marks on the charred desktop.

"Hey, Scully, look at this," he said. When she came over, he pointed to the pale rectangular patches. "I think there must have been documents here, reports left on top of his desk—but somebody's removed the evidence."

"Why would anyone do that?" Scully said. "The reports themselves probably still have significant residual radioactivity—"

Mulder met her gaze through the thin faceplates on their hoods. "I think somebody's trying to do us a favor. They've 'sanitized' the murder scene to protect us from classified information that maybe we shouldn't be seeing. For our own good, of course."

"Mulder, how can we possibly expect to solve this if the crime scene has been tampered with? We don't have the complete picture here."

"My feeling exactly," he said.

He knelt to look at Dr. Gregory's two-shelved metal credenza. It was filled with physics textbooks, computer-code user's manuals, a copy of *Lagrangian-Eulerian Hydrocode Dynamics*, and straightforward geography and physics texts. The bindings were burned and blackened, but the rest of the books remained intact.

He looked at the burn marks on the shelves themselves. As he had expected, several books had been removed as well. "Somebody wants a quick answer to this, Scully," he said. "A simple answer. One that doesn't require us to have all the information."

He looked toward the closed lab door. "I think we should inspect each of these other offices down the corridor, too. If they're the offices of Dr. Gregory's project team, somebody might have forgotten to yank out the information that was carefully deleted from this scene."

He went back to the bulletin board and touched another piece of the crumbling paper. The ash flaked off, but he was able to distinguish two words before it disintegrated.

Bright Anvil.

FOUR

Veteran's Memorial Hospital
Oakland, California
Tuesday, 3:27 p.m.

The safety technicians and radiation specialists at the Teller Nuclear Research Facility had assured Scully that any residual radiation in Dr. Emil Gregory's corpse remained low enough to pose no significant safety hazards. Scully found it faintly amusing that none of the other doctors in the hospital wanted to be with her in the special autopsy room they had prepared.

She was a medical doctor and had performed many autopsies, but she preferred working alone—especially in a case as disturbing as this one.

She had dissected corpses in front of her students at the Quantico FBI Training Facility many times, but the condition of Dr. Gregory's body, the specter of a radioactive disaster, bothered her enough on a gut level that she was glad she could think her own thoughts and not be distracted by questions or perhaps even rude jokes from the new students.

Rather than providing general autopsy facilities, the Veterans Memorial Hospital had placed her in a little-used room especially reserved for severely virulent diseases, such as strange tropical plagues or unexpected mutations of the flu. But the room had what she needed. Scully stood in front of Gregory's body. She tried to swallow, but her throat was dry. She should get to work.

She had performed more autopsies than she could remember, on bodies in far worse condition than this burned husk of an old man. But the thought of how Dr. Gregory had died brought back the nightmares she had suffered while in her first year of college at Berkeley: grim and depressing imaginings of the world's dark nuclear future. She had awakened to thoughts of these horrors in the middle of the night in her dorm room. By day she had read the propaganda slogans, the overblown antinuclear brochures designed to foster fear of the atom.

Before this autopsy, she had reviewed medical texts, concise and analytical treatments that avoided the inflammatory descriptions of radiation burns. She was ready.

Scully drew a long, deep breath through the respirator mask. The dual air-filtering cartridges hung heavily from her face, like insectoid mandibles. She wore goggles as well, to keep any of the cadaver's fluids from spraying into her eyes. She had been assured that this simple protective clothing would be sufficient against the low radiation levels in Dr. Gregory's body, but she thought she could feel invisible contamination like gnats on her skin. She wanted to hurry and get this over with, but she was having a hard time getting started.

Scully inspected the surgical implements on the tray next to her autopsy table, but it was merely a stalling tactic. She chided herself for avoiding the corpse. After all, she thought, the sooner she got to it, the sooner she could be finished and out of there.

At the moment, though, she would much rather have been with Mulder interviewing some of Dr. Gregory's fellow scientists—but this was her job, her specialty.

She switched on the tape recorder, wondering if the radiation seeping out of the body might affect the magnetic tape. She hoped not.

"Subject: Emil Gregory. Male Caucasian, seventy-two years of age," she dictated. Curved mirrors reflected the harsh white fluorescents overhead down onto the table. These, along with the surgical lamps, washed away all shadows, allowing no secrets to be hidden.

Gregory's skin was blackened and peeling, his face shriveled to a burned mask over his skull. White teeth poked through the split and charred lips. His arms and legs had been drawn up, folded together as his muscles contracted with the heat. She touched him with one heavily gloved finger. Flakes of burnt flesh fell off. She swallowed.

"Apparent cause of death is sudden exposure to extreme heat. However, other than the several external layers of complete charring…" she nudged the burnt layers that peeled away, revealing red, wet tissues underneath "…the musculature and internal organs appear relatively intact.

"There are some indications of the damage normally seen when a victim dies in a fire, but other indicators are missing. In a normal fire, body temperature rises throughout, causing extreme damage to internal organs, massive trauma to the entire bodily structure, rupture of soft tissues. However, in this case it appears that the heat was so intense and so brief that it incinerated the subject's exterior, but dissipated before it had time to penetrate more deeply into his body structure."

After finishing with her preliminary summary, Scully inspected the tray and took a large scalpel, holding it clumsily in her gloved hands. When she cut into Dr. Gregory's body cavity, the sensation was like sawing through a well-done steak.

In the background the Geiger counters clicked with stray bursts of background radiation, sounding like sharp fingernails tapping on a window pane. Scully froze, waiting until the counts died down.

She adjusted the lamp overhead and went back to work, probing in detail for any clues the old man's body had left for her to find. She dictated copious notes, removing the intact organs, weighing each one, giving her impression of their condition—but as she proceeded, it became clear to her that something was terribly wrong.

Finally, still wearing her gloves, she went over to the intercom mounted on the wall, glancing back over her shoulder at the remains of Gregory's body. She punched in the extension for the Oncology Department.

"This is Special Agent Dana Scully," she said, "in Autopsy Room..." she glanced up at the door, "2112. I need an oncology expert to suit up and come down here briefly for a second opinion. I've found something I'd like to have verified." Though Scully had requested consultation with a specialist, she was already virtually certain as to what they would find.

The voice on the other end of the line reluctantly acknowledged. Scully wondered how many of the specialists would suddenly disappear for lunch breaks or rush off to long-forgotten games of golf, leaving the remaining few to draw straws to see who would have to come in to the room with her and study the burned corpse.

She went back to the body on the polished metal table and looked down, still keeping her distance. Her inhalations through the respirator packs at her mouth hissed like the steaming breath of a dragon.

Long before Dr. Emil Gregory had died from his fatal flash burn, his entire bodily system had been ravaged from within. Tumors upon tumors permeated his system, disrupting his functions.

Even without this bizarre and extreme death, Dr. Emil Gregory would have succumbed to terminal cancer within a month.

FIVE

Vandenberg Air Force Base, California
Underground Minuteman Missile Control Bunker
Tuesday, 3:45 p.m.

A boring routine in a buried trash can that somebody considered an office. Some assignment.

Captain Franklin Mesta had once thought being a missileer would be exciting, protected in an underground fortress with the controls of nuclear Armageddon at his fingertips. Dial in the coordinates, turn the keys—and the fate of the world rested in your hands, just waiting for a launch order.

In reality, it was more like solitary confinement... only without the privacy of solitude.

Mesta was stuck down here in a little cell, his only company a randomly assigned partner with whom he had little in common. Forty-eight straight hours without seeing the light of day, without hearing the wind or the ocean, without stretching his muscles, or getting a good workout.

What was the point of being stationed on the spectacular central coast of California if he had to pull duty down here under a rock? He might as well have been in Minot, North Dakota. One underground control bunker looked like any other underground control bunker. They all had the same interior decorator—no doubt a low-bid government contract.

Maybe he should have asked for EOD duty instead. At least Explosives Ordnance Disposal offered the *chance* that something unexpected and exciting would happen.

From his chair he turned to look at his partner, Captain Greg Louis, who sat out of arm's reach in an identical scuffed red Naugahyde chair. The chairs were mounted to steel rails on the floor that kept the two missileers permanently at right angles to each other. Regulations required that each man remain buckled in his seat at all times.

A circular mirror mounted in the corner between them let the two men look into each other's eyes, but prevented them from being able to touch physically. Captain Mesta supposed there had been instances at the end of a long shift where stir-crazy missileers had tried to strangle each other.

"What do you suppose the weather's like top-side?" Mesta asked.

Captain Louis worked intently on a pad of paper, scribbling calculations. Distracted, he looked up, blinking at Mesta in the round observation mirror. Though Louis's flat face, wide set eyes, and full lips gave him a perpetually stupid expression, Mesta knew his partner was a whiz at math.

"Do you want me to call up?" Louis asked. "They can fax us a full report."

Mesta shook his head and looked aimlessly around the old metal control banks. Everything was painted battleship gray or, even worse, sea-foam green, with clunky black plastic dials and analog numerical readouts—technology straight from early Cold War days.

"No, just wondering," he said with a sigh. Louis could be so literal. "What are you figuring out now?"

Louis set down his pencil. "Taking the projected area of our chamber here, and our depth beneath the surface, I can estimate the volume of material in a cylinder above us. Then I'm going to use the average density of rock to calculate the mass. When I'm done, we'll know exactly how much stone is hanging over our heads."

Mesta groaned. "You've got to be kidding, man! You're psycho."

"Just occupying my mind. Aren't you curious?"

"Not about that."

Mesta slid his chair along the rail bolted to the floor, allowing him to check another station, one he had inspected only five minutes earlier. All conditions remained the same.

He looked at the heavy black phone at his station. "I think I'm going to call up and get permission to use the head," he said. He didn't really have to go, but it was something to do. Besides, by the time the decision came down from the watchdogs, his bladder might well be full.

"Go ahead," Louis answered, intent on his calculations again.

A single cot sat behind a heavy red curtain that provided minimal privacy— and minimal stretching space—but each man was allowed to use it only once during a shift, and Mesta figured he could stay awake a while longer.

Then the red phone rang.

Both men instantly transformed into crack professionals, alert and aware, snapping into the programming that had been hammered into them. They knew the drill, and they took each alarm seriously.

Mesta picked up the phone. "Captain Franklin Mesta here. Prepare for code verification." Grabbing the black three-ring binder, he flipped through the laminated pages, searching for the proper date and authorization phrase.

The voice on the phone—flat, high-pitched, and oddly genderless—rattled off numbers in a crisp, precise drone. "Tango Zulu Ten Thirteen Alpha X-ray."

Mesta followed the digits with his finger, repeating them into the phone. "Tango Zulu One Zero One Three Alpha X-ray. Verified. Second, do you concur?"

At an identical phone, Captain Louis studied his own three-ring binder. "Concur," he said. "Ready to receive targeting information."

Mesta spoke into the handset. "We are prepared to input coordinates."

Mesta felt his heart pounding, the adrenaline running through his veins, though he knew this had to be just an exercise. It was the military's strategy to keep the men from going insane with boredom—putting the teams regularly through routine drills, constant practice in aiming their missile, their personal Big Stick, housed in a silo elsewhere at Vandenberg.

In addition to providing simple practice and relief from the tedium, Mesta knew, the constant and unforgiving drills were designed to program the missileers into following instructions without thinking. Buried under however many tons of rock Louis had calculated, the two partners were so isolated they could never know whether they were preparing for a real launch, or just going through the paces. That was exactly the way their superiors wanted it.

But as soon as the coordinates came in, and both captains dialed them in using analog numerical wheels, Mesta knew the launch could never be real. "That's out in the Western Pacific... somewhere in the Marshall chain," he said. He glanced at the world map taped up on the metal wall, its edges curling from age. "Are we nuking Gilligan's Island, or what?"

Captain Louis answered in a terse, no-nonsense tone. "Probably in keeping with the government's new nonthreatening posture. The Russians don't like us even pretending to aim the birds at them."

Mesta punched in the TARGET LOCK VERIFIED sequence, shaking his head. "Sounds like somebody just wants a few radioactive coconuts."

Still, he thought, the very possibility of an actual launch, a no-turning-back instigation of nuclear war, was enough to bring out a cold sweat—drill or no drill.

"Ready for key insertion," Louis prompted.

Mesta hustled, ripping open his own envelope to pull out the metal key on its dangling plastic chain. "Ready for key insertion," he repeated. "On my mark—three, two, *one*. Keys in."

Both men jammed their metal keys in the slots, then simultaneously let out a relieved sigh. "Exciting, isn't it?" Mesta said, breaking through his professional demeanor. Louis blinked and looked strangely at him.

Now it would all depend on the command station, where someone else in some other uniform would arm the missile, de-safe the warheads, the small conical cluster of atomic bombs. Each component of the MIRV, the multiple independently targeted reentry vehicles, packed hundreds of times the wallop of the Hiroshima or Nagasaki bombs.

The voice on the telephone spoke. "Proceed with key rotation."

Mesta gripped the round end of his key in the slot, feeling perspiration slick his fingertips. He glanced up at the round observation mirror to see that Captain Louis had done the same, waiting for him to give the order. Mesta began his short, careful countdown.

At "one" they turned their keys.

The lights went out.

Sparks flew from the old control panels, transistors and capacitors—possibly even obsolete vacuum tubes—overloading.

"Hey!" Mesta shouted. "Is this some kind of joke?"

Despite his bluster, he suddenly felt a primal fear of being trapped in absolute darkness, buried deep underground in a metal cave swarming with tar-like blackness. He thought he could sense every single ounce of the overlying rock Captain Louis had calculated. Mesta was glad his partner could not see the expression on his face.

"Searching for emergency controls," Louis's voice called, eerily disembodied in the blackness. His voice remained pretend-calm, professional, but with a ragged edge that belied his cool demeanor.

"Well where are they?" Mesta said. "Get the power back on."

Images of suffocation and doom swirled in Mesta's mind. Without power, they wouldn't have air, they couldn't call up topside and request an emergency evacuation.

What if the launch had been real? Had the United States just been obliterated in a nuclear fire? Impossible!

"Switch on the damn lights!" Mesta shouted.

"Here they are. No time for a self-diagnostic." Instead, Louis's voice howled in pain. "Aaaah! The controls are hot! I just fried the palm of my hand."

Mesta could make out the silhouettes of the control banks as the metal racks began to glow a deep brownish red, like a stove burner. A renewed shower of sparks skittered across the electronics. Then another, brighter glow seeped through the wall plates themselves.

"What is going on here?" Mesta said.

"Phone's dead," Louis answered, maddeningly calm again.

Mesta swiveled back and forth in his chair, sweating, hyperventilating. "It's like we're in a giant microwave oven! So hot in here."

The seams in the steel-plate walls split. Rivets shot like bullets from one side of the enclosed chamber to the other, ricocheting and shattering glass instrument panels. Both men screamed. Blazing light poured in.

"But we're underground," Louis gasped. "There should be only rock out there."

Mesta tried to leap to his feet, to run to the emergency ladder, or at least to the secure elevator—but the straps and seatbelts trapped him in the uncomfortable chair. Smoke began to rise from the upholstery.

"What's that noise?" Louis asked. "Do you hear voices out there?"

Light and heat rushed in through the cracks in the walls, like a blinding storm from the core of the sun. The last thing Captain Mesta heard was a raging roar like a whirlwind of vengeful whispers.

Then all the seams split in the walls as the last barrier evaporated. A tidal wave of blazing, radioactive fire flooded over them, engulfing the chamber.

SIX

Teller Nuclear Research Facility
Tuesday, 3:50 p.m.

With his visitor's badge firmly clipped to his collar, Mulder felt like a door-to-door salesman. He followed his map of the Teller Facility on which Rosabeth Carrera had circled the building number where Dr. Gregory's project team was temporarily stationed.

He found the building, a dilapidated, ancient barracks, two stories tall, with windowpanes so old that the glass had begun to ripple with age. The doors and window frames were painted a putrid, yellowish tan that reminded him of the Number 2 pencils given out for standardized tests in public schools. The exterior walls were sided with composite shingles, flexible asphalt sheets slapped on in a repetitive overlapping pattern. They looked like the wings of a freakish mutant moth grown to gargantuan size.

"Nice digs," Mulder said to himself.

From a brochure he had picked up in the Badge Office, Mulder knew that the Teller Nuclear Research Facility occupied the site of an old U.S. Navy weapons station. Looking at the barracks, he decided that these must be a few of the original structures that had just barely held on while others were demolished and replaced with prefabricated modular office buildings.

He tried to guess what groups would be relegated to these forlorn places: projects winding down after losing budget battles, new employees awaiting their security clearances, or administrative staff who didn't need the high-tech laboratories of the bread-winning nuclear researchers.

It looked as if Dr. Gregory's project had lost a bit of prestige.

Mulder trudged up the old wooden stairs and yanked at the door, which stuck briefly in its frame before opening. He entered, ready to flash his visitor's badge and his FBI ID card, even though Rosabeth Carrera had assured him this section of the research facility was open to approved visitors. The building was inside the perimeter fence and therefore remained inaccessible to the general public, but no classified work could be performed in any of these offices.

The hall was empty. Mulder saw only a kitchenette with a coffeemaker and a big plastic jug of spring water perched on a cooler. A laser-printed sign on salmon-colored paper was tacked to the wall, and Mulder saw several other copies posted up and down the hall on doors and bulletin boards.

WARNING, ASBESTOS AREA.
THE HAZARD REMOVAL TEAM WILL BE WORKING
THE FOLLOWING DATES: _____

Naturally, the dates handwritten on the blank line were precisely the days he and Scully planned to be in the area.

Beneath, in a brush-stroke script, as if someone had gotten cute changing fonts on their word-processing program:

"Please pardon the inconvenience."

Mulder followed the short kitchenette-hall to where it intersected with the main corridor of offices. The ceiling creaked, and he looked up to see water-stained acoustic tiles barely hanging on to a suspended structure around fluorescent lights. Footsteps on the second floor continued; the old support beams groaned with weariness.

He stopped at the end of the hall. The entire area to his left was swathed in plastic wrap, as if some mysterious preservation activity was underway. Workers wearing overalls and heavy, full-facepiece respirators wielded crowbars behind a translucent plastic curtain, tearing the sheetrock off the walls. Others used high-powered shop vacuums to suck away the dust that came out. They made a tremendous racket. Yellow tape blocked the corridor farther on, with another handmade sign dangling from the flimsy X barricade.

ASBESTOS REMOVAL OPERATIONS IN PROGRESS.
DANGER!
DO NOT CROSS.

Mulder glanced at the little yellow note of paper on which he had written Bear Dooley's temporary office number. "I hope it's not down there," he said, looking at the asbestos work site. He turned right instead and began checking doorways, most of which were closed—not necessarily because the rooms were empty, but because the people couldn't work with so much noise in the halls.

He followed the room numbers down the hall, listening to the construction workers batter away, excavating the old asbestos-contaminated insulation, which would be replaced with new approved materials. Asbestos insulation had been considered perfectly safe decades earlier. But now, because of new safety regulations, the workers seemed to be creating an even larger hazard. To fix the problem, they gutted the old building, spending huge amounts of the taxpayer's money, and quite probably releasing far more broken asbestos fibers into the air than would ever have been released in the natural lifetime of the building during normal use.

He wondered if, a decade or two down the road, someone would decide that the new material was also hazardous, and the entire process would repeat itself.

Mulder remembered a joke from an old *Saturday Night Live* that he had considered enormously funny while sprawled out on his sofa late one Saturday evening. The Weekend Update commentator proudly announced that scientists had at last discovered that cancer was actually caused by... (drum roll) *white lab rats!*

Now, though, the joke didn't seem quite as humorous.

He wondered how Scully was doing with her autopsy on Dr. Gregory's body.

He finally reached Bear Dooley's half-closed office door, which was burdened with numerous layers of thick brown paint. Inside the dim room, a burly man wearing a denim jacket and flannel shirt and jeans stacked boxes onto tall black file cabinets, arranging items hastily retrieved from his old office.

Mulder rapped on the door with his knuckles and pushed it farther open. "Excuse me. Dr. Dooley?"

The broad-shouldered man turned to look at him. He had long, reddish brown hair and a shaggy beard that looked like it was made of copper wire, except for a striking shot of white down the left side of his chin, as if he had spilled a dribble of milk there. His mouth and nose were covered with a white filter mask.

"Get a mask on—are you crazy?" he said. Dooley moved like a quarterback to the battered temporary desk, where he popped open the top right-hand drawer and snatched out a filter packet. With his meaty hands he tore off the plastic and tossed the mask to Mulder. "You FBI guys are supposed to be so smart—I'd think you could manage a few simple safety precautions."

Mulder sheepishly fastened the mask around his face with a long elastic band and breathed through the paper-smelling covering. He held his badge in his hand, flipping open his ID to display the photo and badge. "Bear Dooley, I presume? How did you know I was from the FBI?"

The big man let out a loud laugh. "Are you kidding? A suit and a tie means you're either with the DOE or the FBI—and with Dr. Gregory's weird death I assumed you were FBI. We were told to expect you and to cooperate."

"Thanks," Mulder said, coming in and sitting in a chair next to the man's cluttered desk without being invited. "I've got only a few questions for you at the moment. I'll try not to take too long. We're still at the beginning of our investigation."

Dooley continued to unload his possessions from cardboard boxes, shoving folders into file-cabinet drawers and dumping pens and notepads into the long center drawer on his desk.

"First off," Mulder said, "can you tell me about the project you and Dr. Gregory were working on?"

"Nope," Bear Dooley said, turning back to pull out framed photos and some sheaves of what appeared to be weather satellite printouts, technical reports, water temperature maps of the oceans. "Can't tell you about that. It's a classified project."

"I see," Mulder said. "Well, can you think of any *unclassified* way that any part of this project might have backfired and killed Dr. Gregory?"

"Nope again," Dooley said.

Mulder got the impression that Bear Dooley was usually this gruff with newcomers—that he did not suffer fools gladly—but that right now the man was particularly distracted. Perhaps he was more than a little overwhelmed to have the entire project thrust upon him so suddenly. Mulder watched the engineer's movements, listened to his abrupt answers. He tried to piece together a scenario where Dooley, wanting to become the new big shot, would arrange for the death of the real project head, thereby setting himself up to become the obvious successor....

But it didn't ring true. Dooley didn't seem to be enjoying himself.

"Maybe we'd better try a safer area. How long have you worked for Dr. Gregory?" Mulder asked.

Dooley stopped and scratched his head. "Four or five years, I guess. Most of the time as a technician. Thought I was working hard *then*, but now he's left me with a set of big shoes to fill."

"How long have you been his deputy project director?"

Dooley answered that one more quickly. "Eleven months, ever since Miriel flaked out on us."

Outside in the hall a circular saw made a loud racket, followed by a sharp yelp. The clanging sound of metal and dropped pipes, crashed sheetrock and wood prompted a brief outburst of cursing and a scurry of frantic efforts to get the hazardous asbestos under control. It made Mulder think of a dentist drilling deep into a patient's molar, and suddenly whispering "Oops!" under his breath. His stomach knotted.

"What is all this stuff about the South Sea Islands?" he said, gesturing to the photos. "Aerial images and weather patterns."

Dooley shrugged and hesitated a moment as he concocted an explanation. "Maybe I'm planning a vacation—get away from it all, you know. Besides, that's the Western Pacific, not the South Seas."

"Funny. Dr. Gregory had similar photos in his office."

"Could be we had the same travel agent," Dooley answered.

Mulder leaned forward. He found it difficult to conduct a serious interrogation while both of them were wearing these absurd filter masks. His breathing made his cheeks and lips hot. His voice was muffled and subdued. "Tell me about Bright Anvil."

"Never heard of it," Dooley answered crisply.

"Yes you have."

"You don't have a need-to-know," Dooley countered.

"I have a security clearance," Mulder said.

"Your FBI clearances don't mean a damn thing to me, Agent Mulder," Dooley said. "I've signed papers. I've gone to my security briefing. I know the level of classification my work falls under. Unlike certain other assistants of Dr. Gregory, I take my oaths seriously."

Dooley pointed a blunt finger at Mulder. "You might not realize this, Mr. FBI—but you and I are on the same side. I'm fighting for this country, doing what our government deems necessary. If you want a blabbermouth, why don't you go see Miriel Bremen at her Stop Nuclear Madness! headquarters? You can find the address in any one of the thousand or so leaflets they left scattered in the ditches and along the fence yesterday. Go ask her your questions. Then arrest her for divulging national security information.

"In fact, why don't you ask her a lot of questions. She was around when Emil Gregory died, and she had plenty of motive to mess up our project."

Mulder looked sharply at him. "Tell me more."

Bear Dooley's color deepened as his long-standing resentment boiled to the surface. "She and her protesters were here the whole time. They threatened to stop at nothing—nothing, if you take the clear implications of that word—to sabotage our work. Miriel would know how to do it, since she worked here long enough. Maybe she's the one who planted something in Gregory's office. Maybe she's behind it all."

"We'll check it out," Mulder said.

Dooley set a box full of office supplies down heavily on the desk. Pens and pencils and scissors clattered next to his stapler and tape dispenser.

"Now I've got a lot of work to do, Agent Mulder. I was already up to my nose in responsibilities, and now it's gotten even worse. Add to that the fact that I've been pulled out of my comfortable offices and stuck in this godawful hole trying to make do, working on a project in a barracks building where I can't even pull out any of my classified papers."

Mulder thought of something else as he stepped to the door. "I noticed in Dr. Gregory's office that some of his reports and papers had been taken away from the death scene. Disturbing the evidence at a crime scene is a serious offense. You didn't have anything to do with that, did you?"

Bear Dooley emptied the last items out of a cardboard box, then upended it on the floor and took great pleasure in stomping the cardboard flat. "All of our project reports are controlled documents, Agent Mulder—numbered and assigned to a specific user. Some of Dr. Gregory's reports were one-of-a-kind. Maybe it was something we needed for our work. Our project takes precedence."

"Over a murder investigation? Who told you that?"

"Ask the Department of Energy. They might not tell you much about the project, but they will tell you that much."

"You sound pretty confident," Mulder said.

"As my old girlfriend used to say, self-confidence isn't one of my weak points," Dooley said.

Mulder pressed the issue. "Could I get a list of the documents that you took from Dr. Gregory's office?"

"No," Dooley answered. "The titles are classified."

Mulder kept his cool. He reached into his pocket and removed one of his cards. "This is the main office of the Bureau. You can reach me through the federal telephone system here on your lab phone, or call me on my cellular if you think of anything else you can tell me."

"Sure." Dooley took the card and offhandedly opened up the center desk drawer already cluttered with pens and rulers, push pins, paper clips, and other debris. He tossed the card inside, where he would probably never be able to find it again, even if he wanted to.

Mulder didn't get the impression Bear Dooley would want to.

"Thank you for your time, Dr. Dooley," he said.

"That's *Mister* Dooley," the engineer said, then lowered his voice. "Never finished my Ph.D. Been too busy working to worry about things like that."

"I'll let you get back to your project then," Mulder said, and slipped out into the hall, where the construction workers continued to rip out sheets of asbestos-containing material behind thin curtains of plastic.

SEVEN

Gregory Residence, Pleasanton, California
Wednesday, 10:28 a.m.

The key fit the lock, but Mulder knocked loudly anyway, pushing the door open a crack before poking his head inside. "Ding, dong—Avon calling," he said.

Emil Gregory's home greeted him with only a shadowy silence.

Beside him, Scully pursed her lips. "There shouldn't be anyone here, Mulder. Dr. Gregory lived alone." She opened the folder that she had been holding against her dark blue jacket. "It says in this report that his wife died six years ago. Leukemia."

Mulder shook his head, frowning. He thought of the terminal cancer Scully had found while doing the autopsy on Gregory's body the previous afternoon. "Doesn't anyone die peacefully in their sleep of old age anymore?"

The two of them hesitated outside the cool, dusty house that sat alone at the end of a cul-de-sac. The architecture of Gregory's home seemed out of place compared to the neighboring houses, its rounded corners and curving arches reminiscent of a Southwestern adobe mansion. Colorful enameled tiles lined the front doorway, and grapevines coiled around an arbor that shaded the porch area.

After waiting a few extra seconds, Mulder pushed the door all the way open. In the foyer, they walked across large, cool terra-cotta tiles and took two steps down to the main living level.

Though Gregory had died only a day and a half before, the place already had an abandoned feel to it, like a haunted house. "Amazing how fast that oppressive atmosphere can settle in," Mulder commented.

"It's obvious he was a bachelor," Scully said.

Mulder looked around and saw no particular untidiness to the house. In fact, it reminded him of the condition of his own apartment much of the time. He wondered if she was somehow ribbing him.

The main room had all the usual furniture—sofa, love seat, a television, a stereo set—but it didn't look as if it had been used terribly often. On the coffee table in front of the sofa a pile of old magazines lay partially buried under a dozen technical reports bearing the logo of the Teller Nuclear Research Facility and several more from the Los Alamos and Lawrence Livermore National Laboratories.

The pale tan walls had a smooth and buttery appearance, like soft clay. Alcoves molded around a fireplace displayed an assortment of small knick-knacks. Painted Anasazi pots sat on small shelves; bright spirit-catchers decorated the walls. A wreath of dried red chili peppers hung centered over the mantel.

The entire house had the authentic Santa Fe flavor, but Mulder got the impression these decorations must have been artfully arranged by Dr. Gregory's long-dead wife, and the old scientist had not had the stamina or the incentive to redecorate the main part of the house in his own style.

"After he lost his wife, Dr. Gregory didn't seem to have any interests aside from his work," Scully said, flipping through the dossier again. "According to this record, he took a two-month leave of absence to arrange for the funeral and to get his mind back on things—but apparently he didn't know what to do with himself. Since his return to work at the Teller Nuclear Research Facility, his employee file is stuffed with commendations. It seems he threw himself into his research with complete abandon. It was his entire life."

"Any record there of what he was really working on?" Mulder asked.

"Because his project was highly classified, it doesn't specify."

"Same old story," Mulder said.

In the kitchen Scully found several bottles of prescription pain killers on the countertop. She shook them and studied the labels. Some of the bottles were half empty.

"He was taking some pretty heavy medication… analgesics and narcotics," she said. "The pain from his cancer must have been incredible. I haven't gotten his personal medical record unsealed yet, but Dr. Gregory undoubtedly knew he only had a few months to live."

"Yet he still went to work every day," Mulder said. "Now that's dedication."

He wandered around in the empty house, not sure what he was looking for. He crossed the living room and stepped down a side hallway that led to the back bedrooms and study. Along these walls, in the private part of Gregory's home, was a completely different style of decoration.

Framed photos adorned the wall in a haphazard arrangement that implied a man with a hammer and a nail, but without the patience or desire to use a yard-stick and level. It looked as if the photos had been mounted as Dr. Gregory collected them over the years, one at a time, and placed wherever he found room.

Each image was different, yet with one striking similarity: the repetitive fury of huge atomic mushroom clouds, nuclear blasts, one after another—some more powerful than others. Mulder spotted a desert backdrop behind some of the blasts, while many others showed the ocean and Navy destroyers. Teams of scientists, identifiable in their cotton shirts and black-rimmed glasses, smiled for the camera beside military officers and other men in uniforms.

"And to think some people collect paintings of Elvis on black velvet," Mulder said, studying the mushroom clouds.

Scully came up beside him. "I recognize some of those pictures," she said. "Classic photos. Those were the Marshall Islands hydrogen bomb detonations of the mid-fifties. These others… I think they were aboveground blasts at the Nevada Test Site, a few shots from Project Plowshare." She stared at the photos. Mulder looked at her, surprised by the disturbed expression on her face.

"Something wrong?"

She shook her head, then tucked a strand of light auburn hair behind her ear. "No… no, it's not that. I was just remembering that, according to his file, Dr. Gregory had worked on nuclear weapons since the days of the Manhattan Project. He was present at the Trinity Test, then worked at Los Alamos. He took part in many of the H-bomb detonations in the fifties."

Mulder stared at what appeared to be the largest mushroom cloud, an enormous eruption of water and fire and smoke out in the ocean. It looked as if an entire small island had been vaporized. Handwritten on the bottom border of the glossy were the words "Castle Bravo."

"Must have been quite something to see," he said.

Scully gave him a quick surprised look. "Not something I'd ever want to see," she said.

He quickly ran a hand through his mussed hair. "Rhetorically speaking, I meant." He read the strange names scrawled on each of the photos. They had been written with different pens but obviously by the same hand. Some of them had faded over the years; others had retained their color and darkness better.

"Sawtooth"

"Mike"

"Bikini Baker"

"Greenhouse"

"Ivy"

"Sandstone X-ray"

"What's this, some kind of code?" Mulder said.

Scully shook her head. "No. Those were the names of the test shots, different bomb designs. Each one was given a kind of nonsense name. The tests themselves weren't a particular secret, just the details of the device, time, anticipated yield, and core assembly. One whole series of underground blasts out at Nevada was named after California ghost towns. Another series used the names of various cheeses."

"What a bunch of funny guys."

Mulder left the photo gallery behind and stepped into the large, disorganized office where Gregory had done his work at home. Despite the clutter of papers, notes, and books scattered in various piles around the room, he suspected that Dr. Gregory could have found any item at a moment's notice. A den or an office in the home was a man's private sanctum, and, despite the random appearance of all the paraphernalia, over the years the old scientist must have gradually arranged it exactly the way he wanted.

Now, seeing unfinished ideas jotted down on yellow legal pads and in bound lab notebooks, Mulder experienced the poignant sense of a life suddenly stopped. It was as if an amateur filmmaker had placed his videocamera on

PAUSE while Dr. Emil Gregory did an EXIT STAGE LEFT, leaving all the props in place and untouched.

Mulder carefully looked at the notes, papers, technical reports. He found a stack of colorful travel brochures for various small Pacific islands. Some were flashy and produced professionally while others appeared to be crudely made by people who didn't exactly know what they were doing.

"You don't expect to find anything here, do you?" said Scully. "It's unlikely that Dr. Gregory ever took any classified work home."

"Probably not," Mulder said. "But he was brought up during the Manhattan Project days. Security was a little more lax than it is now, since everyone was working on the same team against the same bad guys."

"And here we are still building bombs to fight against the bad guys—yet we're not at all certain who the bad guys are anymore," Scully said quickly, almost as if by reflex.

Mulder looked sidelong at her, raising his eyebrows. "Was that an editorial comment, Agent Scully?"

She didn't answer. Instead she picked up a framed certificate that had been taken off the wall and set atop one of the low bookshelves. Mulder could still see the naked nail on the wall where it had hung.

"I wonder why he took this one down," she said, tilting it so he could see.

The certificate was a competently made printout from a laser printer with a logo designed with a low-end computer art program—just a joke, but someone had obviously spent a lot of time on it. The symbol in the center of the parchment was a stylized bell with a clapper dangling beneath its shell. Superimposed on top was the slashed circle of the universal "No" symbol. The words underneath read, "This prestigious NO-BELL prize awarded to Dr. Emil Gregory by the Bright Anvil Project staff."

"No-Bell prize," Mulder said with a groan. "The strangest part, though, is that Bear Dooley—Dr. Gregory's number one man—insisted to me vehemently just yesterday that the Bright Anvil Project doesn't exist. Who signed that certificate?"

Scully glanced down. "Miriel Bremen—the woman who used to work for Gregory but then quit to become a protester."

"Ah," Mulder said. "Based on this, and what Bear Dooley told me yesterday, I think it's time we spoke with Miriel Bremen. The offices of the protest group are in Berkeley, aren't they? Not far from here."

Scully nodded, preoccupied. Her answer surprised him. "I'd like to go see her by myself, Mulder."

"Any particular reason why you're giving me the afternoon off?"

She shook her head. "Old stuff, Mulder. Nothing to do with this case."

Mulder nodded slowly. He knew enough not to push her when she didn't want to come out with what was bothering her. He trusted his partner to tell him in her own time.

EIGHT

Teller Nuclear Research Facility
Wednesday, 12:08 p.m.

Two days of maniacal asbestos-removal construction—*destruction*, actually—had left a disconcerting whitish film all over Bear Dooley's desk, his notebooks, his computer terminal, and his telephone.

Using an industrial-strength paper tissue, he wiped down the exposed surfaces, telling himself that it was probably just flakes of drywall, gypsum from the plasterboard, nothing hazardous. All of the stray asbestos fibers would certainly have been removed with meticulous care. The contractors were, after all, government employees.

That thought sparked uneasiness in him all over again.

Dooley wanted his old office back. He passionately disliked these temporary quarters. He felt as if he were camping in his own workplace. "Roughing it," Mark Twain would have called it.

Such distractions annoyed him. The Bright Anvil project was too important for him and his coworkers to "make do" while the investigation into Dr. Gregory's death continued. What did that have to do with the progress of the test? Who set the priorities around here, anyway? The project had a very narrow window of time, and conditions had to be exactly right. A murder investigation could continue indefinitely, regardless of the time of year or weather conditions.

Just let Bright Anvil go off without a hitch, he thought, and the FBI agents could have all the time they wanted.

He glanced at his watch. The new satellite images were ten minutes overdue. Dooley reached for the phone, then heaved a sigh of disgust. It wasn't his own phone in his own office with numbers preprogrammed on the dialing pad. Instead he had to ransack the desk drawers for a facility phone book and flip through the pages until he found Victor Ogilvy's extension. He punched it in, rubbing his fingers together and looking at the fine white dust he had picked up. Scowling in disgust, Dooley wiped his hand on his jeans.

The phone rang twice before a thin voice answered.

"Victor, where's that weather report?" he said without wasting time on greetings or cordialities. His young assistant could certainly recognize his booming voice by now.

"We've got it, Bear," came the researcher's nasal reply. "I was just double-checking and triple-checking the meteorological projections. Uh, I think you'll like them this time around."

"Well, get 'em over here," Dooley said, "so I can check them a fourth time. Things have to be exactly right."

"On my way!" Victor hung up the phone.

Dooley sat back in the creaking old chair, trying to get comfortable. The air-conditioning was turned up too high in the old barracks building, so he had not taken off the denim jacket that covered his red flannel shirt. With his long hair and bushy beard he looked like a mountain man.

His demeanor intimidated many of the people around him, particularly those who didn't work for him. Bear Dooley didn't think he was all that difficult a taskmaster, so long as everyone did what they were expected to do. If they weren't willing to do their jobs, then they shouldn't have bothered to apply in the first place. Victor and the other engineers who had been on Dooley's team for several years understood that he was perfectly easy to get along with, that he trusted them and their abilities—but his team members also knew they'd better run for cover if they ever let him down.

Out in the halls, the construction workers continued their hammering and pounding, tearing down the walls. Plastic sheeting lay draped over everything as the laborers ransacked another wing of the building.

The barracks' outside door opened, and redheaded Victor Ogilvy bounded up the wooden stairs, then down the linoleum hallway to Dooley's temporary office. He burst in, his face florid, grinning with the eagerness of

Jimmy Olsen hot on a news story. His wire-rimmed glasses slipped down his nose.

"Here's the satellite printouts," he said. "And here's the overlays." He spread the projections on Dooley's cleared desk, weighting the curling edges with a stapler and a pair of scissors.

"See the storm clouds here, Bear? Ninety-five percent probability that this depression will follow the path I've marked with red dashes." He traced a big-knuckled finger along a contour in the Western Pacific, just past the International Date Line in the Marshall Islands. "I've looked for projected landfalls, and there seems to be an absolutely perfect target—right here." Victor's finger completely obscured a minuscule dot that looked like a printer's error in the middle of the ocean. "Bingo!"

Dooley looked down. "Enika Atoll."

"It's in the ephemeris," Victor said, then jerked his head over to Dooley's bookshelf.

Dooley leaned back in his chair to grab the thick book, blowing the white gypsum dust from its spine. He riffled the pages, studying the nautical coordinates and finding the brie listing for Enika.

"Oooh, exciting," he said, reading the brief description. "A big flat rock out in the middle of nowhere. No recent photos, but it sounds tailor-made for our purposes. No existing settlements, not even any history."

"Nobody will ever notice anything there," Victor agreed.

"Let me see those weather charts again." Dooley reached forward, snapping his fingers to make Victor hurry. The younger man spread out the charts again, showing the angry-looking knot of cloud swirling across the ocean like a clenched fist.

"Hurricane warnings have gone out to all the adjacent islands. There's not much in the vicinity, only a few sparsely populated islands such as Kwajalein and Truk. It's even in U.S. protectorate waters."

"And you're sure the storm is going to hit land there?" Dooley asked. He was already convinced, but he wanted someone else to say it.

Victor gave an exasperated sigh. "Look at the size of that storm system, Bear! How could it miss? We've got a week until projected landfall—that's an eternity as far as weather projections go, but not much time to set up our preparations... if we decide to go, that is." The whip-thin redhead stepped back, shuffling his feet as if he had to go to the bathroom badly.

Dooley fixed Victor with his best don't-give-me-any-bullshit glare. "What do you mean, if we decide to go? Is there anything to recommend against it? Be straight."

Victor shrugged. "Nothing that I can see—but it's still your call, Bear. Without Dr. Gregory, you're the one pulling all the strings."

Dooley nodded, knowing full well when he could trust his people—and this was one such time. "All right, let's start making phone calls. As of right now I am activating Bright Anvil. We're on our way. Let's get the Corps of Engineers flown out to Enika, get our destroyer on standby down at Coronado Naval Base ready to move out as soon as we arrive."

Victor nodded quickly. "We've already done the paperwork with the Department of Transportation for the SST. The Bright Anvil equipment, diagnostics, and the device itself will be shipped down to San Diego posthaste. The Coronado Base is waiting to receive it."

Dooley nodded. Sending the SST, or Safe Secure Transport, was no minor task, requiring clearances from numerous counties, the federal highway system, as well as city commissions.

"Pull everybody's travel papers. We need to get a move on," he said. "I'll be with the first crew going out to Enika. Support Team B—that's you, Victor—will be ready to take a transport plane out to the islands once everything's set up."

Victor scrawled copious notes in handwriting that Bear Dooley had once foolishly tried to decipher, but never again. Breathless, Victor looked as if he might suffer from a stroke in his excitement.

"Let's go. No time to waste," Dooley said.

The young assistant scuttled toward the door, but Dooley called after him. "Oh, and Victor?" The other man turned, blinking owlishly behind his glasses, his mouth partly open. "Don't forget to pack your swim trunks."

Victor laughed and disappeared down the hall.

Dooley stared down at the maps and weather charts again, letting a smile creep across his face. Finally, after all this time, they were moving on to the next step. There could be no turning back once the wheels started moving.

Besides, he had to admit he wasn't terribly sorry to get away from those nosy FBI investigators. He had work to do.

NINE

Stop Nuclear Madness! Headquarters
Berkeley, California
Wednesday, 12:36 p.m.

Scully took the rental car and drove alone into Berkeley, following once-familiar highways. Now, though, she sensed she had become an intruder in a place where she had previously felt at home.

Heading down Telegraph Avenue toward the campus, Scully saw that the university remained basically unchanged. It stood like an island of ferociously independent culture—the People's Republic of Berkeley—while the rest of the world went on its way. The unbroken string of pizza joints, student art galleries, falafel stands, and recycled clothing shops made her feel warm with nostalgia. She had spent her first year of college here, getting her first taste of independence, making her own choices on a day-to-day basis.

Scully watched the usual smattering of students, some on old bicycles wearing white helmets, some jogging, some even Rollerblading. Young men and women wore clothes that were somehow one step sideways from fashion; they moved as if their every action was a Statement. Behind the steering wheel of the new car—itself out of place—Scully surprised herself by looking down at her conservative business jacket and slacks, her professional briefcase, with some measure of embarrassment.

As an undergrad at Berkeley, Dana Scully and her friends had laughed at people very much like what she herself had become.

Scully parked in a public ramp and walked out into the sunshine, pushing sunglasses up on her nose and scanning the streets to get her bearings. She walked along, glancing at kiosks that announced student film festivals, rallies, and fund-raising events.

A black dog lay panting beside a tree to which it had been leashed. A long-haired woman sat on a blanket in front of a strewn display of handmade jewelry for sale, though she seemed more interested in strumming her guitar than in pressuring potential buyers. Outside the door to an old apartment complex, a cardboard box stuffed with ragged paperbacks begged for customers; a sign taped to the box announced that the books were "50 cents each!" A coffee can sat next to the box, awaiting contributions.

Tracking addresses by the numbers on the sidewalk, Scully finally found the Stop Nuclear Madness! Headquarters in a tall old building that looked as if it could have been the set for a courthouse in an old black-and-white movie. A diner and coffee shop shared the street level of the building with a large new-and-used bookstore that catered to students buying and selling their used textbooks as well as grabbing a quick read between exams.

A short flight of concrete steps led down from the sidewalk to below street level. An easel propped beside the stairs held a posterboard with stenciled letters announcing the protest group and something called the "Museum of Nuclear Horrors."

Scully went down the stairs, her heels clicking on the cement. The place was typical of temporary headquarters on any university campus, she thought. The owners of these old buildings specialized in low-rent, short-term-lease offices, utilizing their extra space as quick-setup bases for political campaigns, activist groups, and even tax-preparation businesses around April.

On the building's outside wall she noticed a faded Civil Defense symbol, the three-bladed radiation sign surrounded by deep yellow, identifying the lower levels of the building as a bomb shelter in the event of a nuclear emergency. Scully stared at the symbol for a minute, thinking of the irony… and experiencing a sense of familiarity as well. She had been in places like this many times during her own student days.

She pushed open the basement door and entered the Stop Nuclear Madness! Headquarters. She felt transported back in time. She remembered when she had been younger, filled with enthusiasm to change the world.

Even in her first year she had been a good student, dedicated to her physics classes and to learning. She knew how much money her parents were spending on tuition, a good portion of her father's Navy salary, just to give her the chance to go to a big university.

But swept up in the alienness, the excitement of a culture so different from her military upbringing, Scully had flirted with activism. She read the pamphlets, listened to her fellow students talk far into the night, and grew more and more upset at what she heard. Believing everything she read and discussed, she had spent long sleepless nights in her dorm room, imagining what she could do to Make a Difference. She had even contemplated joining one of the protests scheduled out at the Teller Nuclear Research Facility—but ultimately she had been too practical to follow through on the idea.

Still, her involvement had been enough to let her engage in spirited discussions—no, she decided to be truthful with herself: they had been outright arguments—with her father, a conservative and dignified Navy captain stationed at the nearby Alameda Naval Air Station. It had been one of the first subjects on which she and her father had truly disagreed. That was before she had decided to join the FBI, which had also brought her parents' disapproval.

Scully loved her father greatly. She had been profoundly affected by his recent death just after the Christmas holidays. He used to call her Starbuck, she called him Ahab… but that was all in the past. She would never see him again.

Scully had spent only a year at Berkeley before the Navy had transferred her father, and she herself had gone to the University of Maryland to study. Most of their wounds had been bandaged a long time before, and no doubt her father had simply considered her brush with the protesters to be an example of the brashness of youth.

Now that she stood on the threshold of the Stop Nuclear Madness! Headquarters, those sore spots grew tender again. But Scully had not come here to join in the protest movement this time. She had a death to investigate. And some of the clues had led her here.

As she entered the small offices, the woman behind the desk turned to give her an automatic smile—but froze with instant suspicion upon seeing her professional garb. Scully felt a sinking in her stomach.

The young receptionist was in her early twenties, with skin the color of light milk chocolate and bushy hair knotted into a medusa swirl of dangling dreadlocks. Her necklace consisted of enormous rectangles of enameled metal; the voluminous wrap covering her body was a dizzying geometric pattern—some sort of Swahili tribal dress, Scully decided.

She glanced down at the fancy engraved nameplate—probably a minor concession of importance for the volunteer workers—on the table that served as a makeshift front desk. "Becka Thorne." Beside the nameplate, the table held a telephone book, telephone, an old typewriter, and some preprinted leaflets.

Scully pulled out her ID. "I'm Special Agent Dana Scully from the FBI. I'm here to speak with a Ms. Miriel Bremen."

Becka Thorne's eyebrows went up. "I... I'll see if she's here," she said. Her voice was cold and uninviting, her guard up. Again Scully felt a pang of disappointment.

Becka Thorne seemed to be pondering whether or not to lie. Finally she got up and glided to the back of the offices, her colorful wrap swishing as she moved. Somewhere out of sight behind movable fabric partitions Scully could hear an overworked photocopy machine churning out leaflets.

While she waited, Scully studied the posters and photo enlargements mounted on the wall, presumably the Museum of Nuclear Horrors promised on the sign outside.

A computer-printed banner had been tacked up at ceiling level, proclaiming in large dot-matrix letters: "WE'VE ALREADY HAD ONE NUCLEAR WAR—WE MUST PREVENT THE NEXT ONE!" Grainy black-and-white enlargements of awesome mushroom clouds adorned the painted cinderblock walls. They reminded her of the hallway in Dr. Gregory's home. There, though, the photographs had been trophies occupying honored positions. Here they were accusations.

One poster listed known international atomic bomb tests and the amount of radiation each above-ground blast had showered into the air. She saw a chart with rising bars that showed the increase of cancer in the United States attributed to such residual radiation, particularly strontium 90 contamination in grass consumed by dairy cows, which was then carried into their milk and ingested by children who poured it over their artificially sweetened breakfast cereals. As the bars rose from year to year, the numbers appeared staggering.

Another display listed the islands that had been destroyed in the Pacific Ocean, with pathos-filled photographs of natives from Bikini Island and Eniwetok Atoll as the U.S. military evacuated them from their island paradises to make way for atomic bomb tests.

At the time, the evacuation efforts had been undertaken at enormous cost. For years the Bikini Islanders had petitioned the United States and the United Nations to be allowed to return to their homeland, but only after the United States footed the atrocious bill to remove the residual radioactivity from their coral reefs, their beaches, their jungles.

Thinking of the island photographs on Dr. Gregory's walls, as well as the satellite images and weather projections in his lab office, Scully inspected the exhibit with greater interest.

In 1971 the Bikini Atoll had been declared safe, and the islanders were allowed to return. But tests in 1977 showed that the atoll still seethed with dangerous levels of radiation, and the inhabitants were forced to evacuate again. Residents of Eniwetok Atoll, which also was used for a prolonged series of hydrogen bomb tests, returned to their homes in 1976, only to learn that a nuclear waste dump on the islands would remain contaminated for thousands of years. In the early 1980s it was found that residents of islands even one hundred and twenty kilometers away from the original tests had developed an unusually high incidence of thyroid tumors.

Shaking her head, Scully moved on to the worst part of all, the centerpiece of the museum—a gallery of gut-wrenching photos showing the blasted remains of Hiroshima and Nagasaki, burned corpses left in the wake of the fireball that had blazed across Japanese skies a half-century before. Some of the bodies had been incinerated so completely that nothing remained but greasy shadows of black ash splashed against the walls of surviving buildings. Worse even than the corpses were the blistered and suppurating survivors.

As Scully looked at the photos she noticed an unsettling familiarity between those bodies and the corpse of Dr. Emil Gregory in his own radiation-washed laboratory.

"Yes, Agent Scully?" a woman's terse voice said.

Scully turned to see Miriel Bremen, a tall woman with short, wavy mouse-brown hair cut in an unflattering squarish style. Her chin was long, her nose pointed, and her gray eyes seemed weary. She was not an attractive woman, but her bearing and her voice bespoke a no-nonsense quality of intelligence.

"So now what did we do?" Miriel said impatiently, not allowing Scully to speak. "I'm getting tired of all this harassment. We've filed the appropriate papers, given the required notices, obtained the correct permits. What on earth has my group done to attract the attention of the FBI?"

"I'm not investigating your group, Ms. Bremen," Scully said. "I'm looking into the death of Dr. Emil Gregory two days ago at the Teller Nuclear Research Facility."

Miriel Bremen's cool mask cracked, and her whole body sagged. "Oh," she said. "Emil... that's different."

She paused, gripping the receptionist's table with one hand and took a deep breath. Becka Thorne watched to see if she could help, then surreptitiously disappeared to attend to the photocopy machine. Miriel glanced around as if for reassurance at the posters of Nagasaki victims, at the forlorn Bikini Islanders.

"Sure, let's talk, Agent Scully—but not here."

TEN

Triple Rock Brewery and Cafe
Berkeley, California
Wednesday, 1:06 p.m.

Miriel Bremen led the way to a small microbrewery and restaurant only a few blocks' walk from the heart of the university. Scully followed Miriel through the wood-framed glass doors into a room full of booth tables layered with a thick armor of glossy varnish, and a bar lined with empty stools. The droning background noise of pedestrians on the sidewalk and constant traffic on the main streets faded as they stepped inside.

Metal signs advertising long-out-of-business beer manufacturers from the 1940s and 1950s covered the walls. Above the brass-railed bar, a chalkboard listed the four handmade brews on tap. On the back wall, next to a dartboard and pool table, a large green slateboard suggested deli sandwiches, hot dogs, nachos, or salads from the food-prep window.

"You order food over there," Miriel indicated a smaller counter. "Vegetarian chili is their specialty, but the soup's pretty good, too… and of course a sandwich is a sandwich is a sandwich. People come here for the beer. Best you'll find anywhere."

She left Scully to prop her briefcase in one of the booths far from the door and gestured with her shoulder at the list of house beers on tap. "What are you having?" Miriel said. "The stout is to die for."

"I'll just have an iced tea," Scully said. "I'm on duty."

Miriel frowned at her. "Listen, Agent Scully—the whole point of going to a microbrewery is to taste some decent beer. This isn't Budweiser Lite, you know. They'd probably throw us out on our ears if we ordered iced tea in here."

Scully didn't think the manager would do any such thing, but the place did remind her of her student days enough that she felt a pang inside. She wasn't much of a beer drinker, but Scully couldn't afford to scorn an overture of friendship, if she wanted Miriel to open up and answer probing questions.

"All right, let me try one of the stouts, then. But just a small one—and only one."

Miriel forced a faint smile onto her hard face. "That'll be up to you to decide." She went to the bar while Scully perused the list of sandwiches. "Get me a hot dog and a cup of chili," Miriel called back. "I take it Uncle Sam is paying?"

"I am," Scully said, noting the prices and realizing that they both could get by on less than ten dollars for lunch.

When they returned to their table, Scully sat down, reaching across the table to pick up her pint of dark malty stout. "Looks thick enough to hold up a spoon," she said.

She took a sip and swallowed, surprised at the density of the drink. The taste was overpowering, almost chocolaty. A true liqueur of a beer, not the light, sour-tasting stuff she occasionally drank very cold out of a can at picnics or birthday parties. Scully raised her eyebrows and nodded in approval at the woman in the seat across from her.

She tried to think of where to begin, but Miriel pre-empted her. The protester seemed to have no problems with self-expression, bypassing time-consuming pleasantries and the dance of conversational give-and-take before Scully could get around to the real questions.

"So, let me tell you why I think you're here," Miriel Bremen said. "It's one of two possibilities. Either you think I, or someone from my protest group, has in some way caused the death of Emil Gregory—or you've been stymied by your escorts at the Teller Facility, your lack of appropriate security clearances, and your inability to access classified documents. Nobody'll tell you anything, and you've come to me thinking I have some answers."

Scully spoke slowly. "A little of both, Ms. Bremen. I've completed the autopsy on Dr. Gregory. There's little doubt as to the primary injuries that resulted in his death, but I haven't yet been able to determine how they came about. What could Dr. Gregory have stumbled into that caused his death?

"I'll have to admit that your protest group does have a credible motive for wanting Dr. Gregory out of the picture, so I have to look into it. I also know that Dr. Gregory—a man you worked with—was involved in some sort of classified weapons project, something called Bright Anvil. But nobody will tell us what that is. And here you are, Ms. Bremen, at the intersection of both of my lines of investigation."

"Well then, let me tell you something," Miriel Bremen said, folding her hands around her pint of dark beer and taking a long swallow. "It sounds clichéd to say that I have nothing to hide—but in this instance I truly don't. It works to my benefit to tell more and more people about what's really going on at the Teller Nuclear Research Facility. I've been trying to blow the whistle on them for the past year. Here, I brought along some of our group's brochures." She reached into her pocket and handed over two of the hand-folded, photocopied pamphlets that some volunteer had no doubt designed on a personal computer.

"Back when I worked at the Teller Facility, I was quite a devoted assistant to Emil Gregory," she said, settling her long chin into her hand. "For many years he was my mentor. He helped me through the politics and the paperwork and the progress reports so I could do some real work.

"Your imagination is probably going to blow this out of proportion, thinking we were lovers or something—but that's just plain wrong. Emil was old enough to be my grandfather, and he took an interest in me because he saw that I had the talent and the enthusiasm to make a good partner. He coached me, and we worked well together."

"But you had some sort of falling out?" Scully said.

"In a sense… but not exactly the way you might be thinking," Miriel said, then sidestepped the question. "You want to know what Bright Anvil is? It's an unorthodox type of nuclear explosive. These days, despite the end of the Cold War and the supposed downscaling of nuclear weapons development, we're still designing new ones. Bright Anvil is a very special type of warhead using a technology that…" She paused, then stared at the walls, her eyes unfocused, as if she was thinking of anything but the decorative metal signs.

"A technology that…?" Scully encouraged.

Miriel sighed and met Scully's gaze. "It's a technology that seems to operate beyond the laws of physics, as I know them—and I do know physics, Agent Scully. I'm not aware of how much physics they taught you in your training as an FBI agent, but—"

Scully interrupted her. "My undergraduate degree was in physics. I spent one year here at Berkeley before I transferred to the University of Maryland. I wrote my thesis on Einstein's Twin Paradox."

Miriel's eyes widened. "I think I might have read that." She contemplated. "*Dana* Scully, right?"

Scully nodded, surprised. Miriel sat up and looked at her with greater respect. "That was interesting stuff. Okay, now I know I don't have to put it in kindergarten terms—but I wish I could, because I don't understand it myself.

"The whole Bright Anvil Project was funded by non-traditional means, invisible on the ledger sheets, money skimmed from other projects, to pay for new tests, cutting-edge research, unorthodox concepts. Bright Anvil was never listed on any budget submitted to Congress, and you won't be able to track it down.

"Emil had worked in the nuclear weapons industry for decades. He was even at the Trinity Test, back in 1945." She smiled wanly. "He used to tell us stories...." Her lips trembled for just a moment, but she covered it by eating some of her vegetarian chili. "But by now he was at the end of his career. He thought he was hiding it from all of us, but I don't think he was in very good health."

"No, he wasn't," Scully said.

Miriel nodded, but asked no further questions. "Emil wanted to do something important to end his career on a high note. He wanted to leave a legacy behind. But all the work he'd been doing in the past decade or so was just 'fine tuning a paper bag,' as we physicists call it.

"Then Bright Anvil fell in his lap. Someone else had done the preliminary physics. We got designs for exotic, high-energy, pulsed-power sources. It was a done deal. The components worked. I couldn't figure out *how* or *why*—but Emil didn't worry about that. He got all excited. He saw how such technology could be used to create a fundamentally new kind of warhead. Emil took it and ran with it.

"Even from the start, I had my doubts—but I kidded myself. I followed along because Emil had done so much for me. This was our new project. I helped him run simulations, scenarios that had little likelihood of ever coming about for real. But the more I worked with it, the creepier it became. Bright Anvil was just too weird. It didn't seem to come from any physics I was ever taught in school. No technology I know can do what it does. Some of the components of the device were fabricated elsewhere. We never knew where or how—we just *received* them from the program offices in Washington."

Miriel finished off her beer. She glanced over at the bar as if she wanted to order another one, but instead settled back to look across the table where

Scully sat in rapt attention. Miriel leaned over, placing her elbows on the polished tabletop.

"I'm a scientist by training. But for me to understand, my science has to have some foundation. And Bright Anvil has no scientific basis that I can grasp. It's something so exotic I couldn't conceive of it with my wildest imagination. So I backed off, I raised too many objections, and in the process made a lot of enemies.

"Then, in one of those serendipitous occurrences, I went to a conference in Japan. Just out of curiosity I took a side trip to Hiroshima and Nagasaki—you know, a weapons researcher's pilgrimage. Both cities have been rebuilt, but it's like putting makeup over a scar. I began to check into things. I read the literature that I'd studiously avoided before, not wanting to look too closely at my own conscience.

"Do you know what they did to the Marshall Islands with the nuclear tests in the fifties? Do you know the horrible aboveground tests they did out in Nevada, staking out livestock at various distances from Ground Zero just so they could analyze the destructive effects of the blast and flash on living tissue? Do you know how many Pacific Islanders were booted off their homes, their peaceful idyllic island existence destroyed, just so somebody could blow up a big bomb?"

"Yes," Scully said. "I know."

Miriel Bremen shoved her plate away, having finished most of her lunch. She brushed off the front of her shirt. "I apologize. I was giving you a sermon." She nudged the Stop Nuclear Madness! brochures across the booth closer to Scully. "Read these if you want more information about it, and about us. I won't take up any more of your time." She slipped out of the seat.

Scully glanced down and saw that she had eaten only half of her own meal. Miriel Bremen had already ducked out the door, leaving Scully alone in the restaurant before she could think of an intelligent follow-up question.

Considering what she had just learned, Scully picked up her sandwich and chewed slowly. Someone dropped a quarter in the jukebox, which began blasting a classic Bob Seger single that seemed too rowdy for the lunch hour.

Scully quickly finished her meal and picked up the protest brochures before stepping outside to head back to the parking ramp. Mulder would be interested in the details, the new developments. She stopped on the sidewalk at a wire trash can as a big city bus heaved by, belching oily blue-gray exhaust. A skate-boarder rattled past, dodging pedestrians with reckless ease.

Scully stood tapping the homegrown pamphlets against her palm, on the verge of tossing them into the wastebasket. Then she reconsidered. "STOP NU-CLEAR MADNESS" the title proclaimed.

Giving herself the excuse that she could consider them evidence, Scully pocketed them instead.

ELEVEN

Coronado Naval Base
San Diego, California
Thursday, 10:15 a.m.

From the Coronado shipyards the ocean sprawled westward, stretching toward the curve of the earth, deep blue and dazzling with reflected morning sunlight. The downtown skyscrapers rose high and white across the narrow San Diego Bay. Cruise ships waited like colorful behemoths at the public docks; a maze of piers bristled with the masts of sailboats.

The weather struck Bear Dooley as incredibly mild, sunny but cooled by fresh breezes, so that even his flannel shirt and denim jacket were tolerable. While riding in the taxi from the airport, he drank in the colorful and clean city, surprisingly pleasant for such a large urban area. But here, on the thin peninsula, the naval base looked like a naval base, and the ships at the restricted docks demonstrated quite clearly why the color had been named battleship gray.

A young officer in white dress uniform met Bear Dooley at the docks. Dooley didn't know the regulations of when sailors were supposed to wear certain uniforms, but he got the impression that this blond-haired, clean-cut Navy man might be someone of more-than-average importance.

The sailor—Dooley corrected himself: they probably wanted to be called "seaman"—gave him a smart salute, though Dooley didn't believe he warranted one, according to military protocol. He clumsily returned the salute without knowing whether that was correct either.

"Mr. Dooley, sir," the man said, "I'm Commander Lee Klantze, executive officer of the USS *Dallas*, here to escort you on board our ship. If you'll follow me, sir, Captain Ives is ready to see you. We've recalled the entire crew and kept them busy provisioning the ship and preparing to shove off. We'll be ready to get under way as soon as you're situated."

Dooley's jeans and flannel shirt were a marked contrast to the razor-folded and bleached-white uniform of the Navy destroyer's exec officer. But Dooley wore his own personality like a shield. He never let his attire bother him. He had been hired for his abilities, not for his appearance.

Dooley had trimmed his beard and shaved his cheeks and neck that morning before rushing off to the San Francisco Airport for a quick shuttle flight down the coast. He had spent the last two hours in the air and then being taxied through the sparkling city of San Diego over to the spit of land that held the Coronado Naval Base.

He had then wasted another half hour bulldozing his way through paperwork and clearances and approvals, even though everything had already supposedly been taken care of. Dooley hated to think of what hassles he would have encountered if everything hadn't been in order. The military did have its way of doing things, and little short of an all-out war could get them to streamline their operations.

"How was your trip?" Klantze asked. "No complications other than the military inefficiency getting on the base?"

"Yeah, the flight was fine, but nobody will give me a straight answer," Dooley said. "Did the SST arrive okay, all equipment safe and on board?"

"I believe so, sir," Klantze answered. "Sometime late last night. Sorry for all the added security." He pushed his wire-rimmed glasses up on his nose. Their Photogray lenses had turned dark, so Dooley could not see the man's eyes directly.

The disguised and armored semi truck, the Safe Secure Transport, had left at sunset the previous day and driven south through the night on the California freeways to reach San Diego. The drivers were escorted front and back by armed, nondescript vans, whose drivers and passengers had orders to shoot to kill, no questions asked, should anything threaten the nuclear device. No part of the caravan was allowed to stop for so much as a bathroom break.

Dooley was glad he didn't have to bother with those difficulties. He would have preferred to have the entire expedition depart from the Alameda Naval Air Station, a short hop away from the Teller Nuclear Research Facility. But the

Navy destroyer assigned to take them out to the Marshall Islands was docked in San Diego. It was easier—and less conspicuous—to move the Bright Anvil device and all its equipment than it was to move an entire destroyer.

Klantze turned about, ready to march off, then glanced over his shoulder in sudden embarrassment. "Oh, excuse me, sir—may I take your duffel, or your case?"

"Sure." Dooley handed over the soft-sided satchel that contained a week's worth of clothes crammed into its various pockets. "I'll carry the briefcase though," he said—not that it was handcuffed to his wrist as in a spy thriller, but it contained classified documents crucial to the Bright Anvil Project. It was securely locked, and Dooley planned to hold on to it.

"As you wish, sir."

The two of them strode along the dock, past several other chain-link fences and gates guarded by armed military police. Dark, creosote-covered planks formed the edge of the dock, while a narrow paved road ran along the center. Klantze walked down the middle of the road, keeping an eye out for government vehicles and puttering Cushman carts that traveled up and down the dock on military business.

Finally, Dooley saw the large Navy destroyer that had been assigned to his project. The enormous, sleek ship looked like a skyscraper in the water, with weapons mounts and control towers, radar antennas, satellite uplink dishes, meteorologic instruments, and various superstructures Dooley could not identify. Navy stuff, he figured.

Along the deck ran barricades of rope mesh, painted to look remarkably like a chain-link fence. Everything was the same shade of gray—the rails and pipes and rigging and steps and ladders. Even the long cannons. Only the bright orange life preservers mounted every fifty feet along the hull provided a few spots of color. The U.S. flag and Navy flags flew from all four corners of the ship.

Dooley stopped and looked along the length of the gigantic cruiser. Despite his usual gruff demeanor, he was impressed with the vessel.

"There she is, Mr. Dooley," Klantze said. He snapped to attention and began to rattle off the ship's statistics. They seemed to be a matter of pride with him, rather than a memorized speech.

"The *Dallas*, Spruance Class, built in 1971—Five hundred sixty-three feet overall length, powered by four sets of GE gas turbines. She's got a small captain's gig for quick trips ashore, plus an entire surface-to-air missile battery, antisubmarine weapons, and torpedo tubes. This class of destroyer was designed primarily for antisubmarine warfare, but she's lightly armed and carries a minimal crew. The *Dallas* is the finest vessel in her class, if you ask me, sir. She'll get us out to the islands, no matter what the weather."

Dooley looked sharply at the exec. "You already know the details of our mission, then?" He had thought that very few of the crewmembers would have been briefed on the assignment out to Enika Atoll.

"Captain Ives has explained it to me, sir," Klantze said, then smiled faintly. "I am the executive officer, if you'll recall. If my information is correct, and if your device is successful, nobody on board is going to be unaware of the test."

Dooley agreed. "I suppose it's tough to keep a secret on board a ship."

"It's also difficult not to notice a giant mushroom cloud, Mr. Dooley."

The exec led him up a wide gangplank the size of a freeway entrance ramp and marched him across the deck and up several flights of hard metal steps to the bridge tower, where he introduced Dooley to the captain of the *Dallas*.

"Captain Ives, sir, this is Mr. Dooley," Klantze said after he had exchanged salutes with the captain. The executive officer nodded to Dooley. "I'll take your duffel to your stateroom, sir. I'm sure Captain Ives wishes to speak with you privately in greater detail."

"Yes I do," the captain answered. Klantze spun about sharply, like a mechanical marionette on a glockenspiel, and marched off.

"Pleased to meet you, Captain Ives. Thanks for your help." Dooley extended his hand, and the captain took it with a firm shake. The captain's arms, contained within his captain's uniform, had muscles like steel wires. Dooley got the impression that he could crack walnuts in his fist.

Ives was a lean man in his late fifties, as tall as Dooley but less burly. His stomach remained washboard flat. He moved with a spare grace, as if every exertion counted for something important. His chin was narrow, his eyes slate gray under heavy salt-and-pepper eyebrows. A bristling mustache rode his upper lip, and steel-gray hair lay neatly beneath his white captain's cap. He showed no sign of sweating in the heat. Perhaps he didn't allow it.

"Mr. Dooley, I'm sure your first concern is for your delicate equipment. Let me reassure you that everything arrived safely and intact, as far as we can tell."

"Good," Dooley said, his voice curt. He wanted to make certain at the outset that the captain understood that *Dooley* was in charge and that his instructions were not to be questioned. "If that equipment is damaged, we might as well not even bother to go. When do we set sail?"

"The *Dallas* can leave port at about four o'clock this afternoon." Captain Ives said. "But you may have noticed that this vessel has no sails."

Dooley blinked at him, then understood. "Oh, just a turn of phrase," he said, annoyed. "Do you have any weather charts or updates for me?"

"We received an encrypted signal," the captain said, "a report from a fast flyby of an aircraft out of our Kwajalein tracking station. Enika Atoll checks out. We'll be heading out for the Marshall Islands at full throttle, but it'll still take us five days."

"Five days?" Dooley said. "I was afraid of that."

Ives met his look with a steely gaze. "This isn't an aircraft, Mr. Dooley. It takes a long time to get a ship this size across that much water."

"All right, all right," Dooley said. "I suppose I knew that. Do we have weather satellites? Is the storm system still doing what we expected?"

Ives led him over to a chart table where weather maps and satellite photos lay spread out. With one long finger the captain indicated the swirl of clouds out over the deep, featureless water. "The tropical depression is worsening, as expected. Within a few days it should be at full hurricane strength. According to our projections it is heading straight toward the atoll."

"Good, good." Dooley leaned over, rubbing his hands together. Though he was a physicist and an engineer, he had learned a great deal about meteorology during the preparations for this test.

Captain Ives leaned closer and lowered his voice so that the other crewmen would not hear him from their communications or navigation stations. "Let me be blunt, Mr. Dooley. I have already notified my superiors of my extreme objections to the entire purpose of this mission. I have grave doubts about the wisdom of resuming aboveground nuclear tests, no matter where they occur."

Dooley stiffened, pausing just a moment to scratch his beard and allow his blood pressure to drop slightly. "Then maybe you just don't understand the necessity, Captain."

"I understand all right—more than you know," Ives replied. "I've been present at several hydrogen bomb tests already, one of which I doubt even you know about, since all results were highly classified."

Dooley raised his eyebrows. "When?"

"Back in the fifties," Ives said. "I was just a seaman recruit then, but I was there, out in the islands, Eniwetok, Bikini, even Johnston Atoll near Hawaii. I worked with plenty of eggheads who were completely amazed by their own calculations, absolutely confident in what they had invented. But I can tell you this, Mr. Dooley: every single time, those weapons developers, like yourself—people who were so smug about their own abilities—were literally turned to jelly with awe when they watched their devices go off."

"I look forward to it then," Dooley said crisply. "You have your orders. Let me take care of the test details."

Captain Ives stood straight, backing away from the chart table. He adjusted his white cap. "Yes, I have my orders," he said, "and I will follow them, despite my objections—not the least of which is that it goes against all of my years of seamanship to head deliberately into a brewing hurricane."

Dooley walked around the bridge, puffed up with his own importance, glancing offhandedly at the outdated computer monitors, the various tactical stations. He turned to look back at the reluctant captain.

"The hurricane is the only way we can pull this test off. Let me do my work, Captain Ives. You just keep the ship from sinking."

TWELVE

Jornada del Muerto Desert
Southern New Mexico
Thursday, 3:13 p.m.

As if playing a scene from an old John Wayne movie, Oscar McCarron slid out of the saddle and tied his horse, a spry two-year-old palomino mare, to the fence post outside the General Store. He made sure to stomp his worn, pointy-toed cowboy boots on the boardwalk porch. The spurs gave a satisfying jingle as he ambled—the English language had no other word for it—to the store entrance.

McCarron's face was as seamed and leathery as his old boots, and his pale blue eyes wore a perpetual squint from a lifetime spent in the pounding desert sun. He eschewed sunglasses—they were only for sissies.

He had shaved this morning for his weekly trip into town, though the grizzled old whiskers could barely punch their way through his tough cheeks anymore. He didn't bother wearing gloves; with the several layers of calluses on his hands (calluses that penetrated to the bones themselves) gloves would have been redundant. His squash-blossom silver-and-turquoise belt buckle was so large it could have been used as a coaster for cold drinks; it was one of his most prized possessions.

McCarron rode into the don't-blink-or-it's-gone town from his outlying ranch no more often than once every seven days to pick up his mail. There were limits to the amount of human companionship one man could stomach.

The door creaked as it always did when he stepped inside the General Store. He moved his left boot over by one floorboard so he wouldn't step on the loose plank.

"Afternoon, Oscar," said Fred, the store owner. His elbows rested on the countertop, but other than shifting his gaze, Fred didn't move a muscle.

"Fred," he replied. It was all the greeting he could manage. A man who was eighty years old couldn't afford to change his public personality this late in life. "Get any mail this week?"

He had no idea what Fred's last name was. He still considered the shopkeeper a newcomer to the area, though Fred had bought the General Store from an old Navajo couple a full fifteen years earlier. The Navajos had run the store for thirty-five years or so, and McCarron had considered them part of the landscape. Fred, on the other hand… well, Fred he still wasn't too sure about.

"We've been waiting for you to come in, Oscar. You've got the usual junk mail, but there's a letter here from Hawaii. Postmark says Pearl Harbor. Imagine that! It's a package. Any idea what it is?"

"What it is, is none of your damn business," McCarron said. "Just get me my mail."

Fred levered himself off of his elbows and disappeared behind the counter to the small post office and storeroom in the back. McCarron brushed his hands down the snaps of his denim shirt and pants, knocking the whitish desert dust away. He knew everyone else called them "blue jeans" these days, but he hadn't gotten used to thinking of them as anything other than dungarees.

Fred returned with a handful of mail, junk newspapers, solicitations, advertising circulars, a few bills, and no letters. Nothing interesting—except for a medium-sized padded manila envelope.

McCarron took the stack and deliberately flipped through the junk mail first, driving back his own curiosity, knowing it would fluster Fred to no end. The junk mail always did a good job of starting his campfire when he slept out under the stars every Thursday night after coming into town. Finally, he held up the padded envelope; squinted at the postmark: *Honolulu, Hawaii.* The package bore no return address.

Fred leaned over the counter, cracking his big knuckles and blinking his brown eyes eagerly. His cheeks sagged on his lantern-jawed face. When he got a little older the shopkeeper would have jowls like a bulldog's. "Well, aren't you going to open it?" Fred asked.

McCarron glared at him. "Not in front of you, I ain't."

He had never forgiven Fred for his blatant indiscretion two years back of opening one of McCarron's packages when he was a day late coming into town. It had happened to be a boxed set of videotapes, the old *Victory at Sea* series, one of McCarron's favorites. He had always been fascinated by World War II.

Fred had been scandalized, not because of the subject matter of the tapes— McCarron suspected the old store owner had a few girlie films hidden back in his own house behind the store—but because Oscar McCarron had ordered the tapes at all, thereby exposing the secret that the old man actually had a television set and a videotape player. That went completely against the rancher's carefully cultivated image of living off the land and scorning all modern conveniences.

Back at his own ranch, McCarron kept an outhouse in plain sight of the main building and had a pump out front for water that came up pure and sweet from the White Sands aquifer. But in truth, he had modern bathroom facilities inside the house, electricity, and not only a TV and VCR but also a large satellite dish hidden back behind the adobe main house. He had purchased all the equipment up in Albuquerque, had it brought down and installed without telling anyone in the small town. McCarron enjoyed keeping up his "old codger" image, but not at the expense of his own comfort.

Fred had indeed kept his mouth shut over the past two years, at least as far as McCarron could tell, but he would never forget the offense.

"Awww, come on Oscar," Fred said. "I've been waitin' all day for you to come in just so's I could see your smiling face."

"Ain't that sweet," McCarron said. "Next thing, you're gonna be asking me to marry you, like one of them California faggots." He slapped the padded envelope unopened on the top of his junk mail and tucked the pile under his armpit. "If the package contains anything that concerns you, I'll be sure to tell you next time I come in." He turned and ambled back toward the door, intentionally stepping on the creaking board this time.

Outside, the still-hot afternoon sun had turned a buttery yellow as the light slanted toward the black lava teeth of the San Andres Mountains.

The palomino whickered when she saw him and stamped her foreleg, impatient to be off and trotting again. Seeing no one else out on the sleepy street, McCarron allowed himself to break into a smile of delight. The young mare was so eager. She seemed to love these pack trips even more than McCarron did.

His curiosity burned within him to see the contents of the mysterious envelope. But his pride wouldn't allow him to show any outward interest, not within sight of the General Store, where Fred was probably even now peering at him through the fly-specked windows.

He untied the horse and mounted up, stuffing the mail into one of the saddlebags before he rode off down the street, and then headed east overland into the sprawling open desert of the White Sands Missile Range.

Through long habit, McCarron found the loose gate in the barbed-wire fence that ran for hundreds of miles along the government-owned wasteland. He slipped the wire loose and led the palomino through the fence, fastening the gate behind him.

He fingered the bent but laminated old pass card that had been issued to him so long ago that every one of the original signers had died years ago. Oscar McCarron's right to go onto the missile site hadn't been questioned for several years now, not even by the hot-rodding young MPs who loved to roll over the dazzling gypsum sands in their all-terrain vehicles, as if they were surfers in dune buggies going to a beach party. But McCarron had a deep respect for authority and for the government itself, after all Uncle Sam had done for him.

Besides, he didn't want to mess with patriotic young enthusiasts who were willing to defend even such a desolate wasteland against foreign invaders. That kind of mindset was something you didn't play around with.

McCarron rode toward the low craggy foothills. The desert was stark and flat, like a huge stretch of Nebraska sprayed with weed killer, then plopped down inside a ring of volcanic mountains. The bleakness somehow had made it an appropriate place to have hosted the world's first atomic explosion.

Oscar McCarron's family once had owned all of this land, a worthless swath of New Mexico, not good for ranching or even mining, since it was devoid of desirable minerals and ore. But back in 1944 the Manhattan Engineering District had expressed a passionate interest in the land—and McCarron's father had been only too happy to strike a deal. He had sold the spread for a small price, but still far more than it was worth.

The government paid extra when McCarron's father agreed to allow them to doctor the Land Bureau documents, removing his name from original ownership, keeping the land transfer secret so that it would show on archival documents that the government had leased it from a fictitious ranch family, the McDonalds.

The government and its Manhattan Project engineers had erected farm buildings and a windmill, concocting a story of the McDonalds who had lived at the Trinity Site. Only later, after the Trinity atomic bomb test in July 1945, had McCarron understood the reason for such secrecy. The nuclear detonation had taken place in what would have been the landowners' backyard. But reporters and, much later, protesters never located the mythical McDonalds.

McCarron's father had driven another hard bargain as part of the deal. It was during the bleakest part of World War II, when the Germans seemed to be making great strides toward global conquest and the Japanese Empire was sweeping the Pacific Rim. American soldiers were dying in record numbers. McCarron's father had not wanted to count his young, strong son as one of the casualties. He had exchanged the land in a secret transfer in order to make his son forever exempt from military service.

Also, because he loved the land despite its seared countenance, he and his family were guaranteed permanent access, if they chose to visit. Because that had meant so much to his father, dead these thirty-four years now, Oscar McCarron had made it a tradition to spend at least one night a week out in the open, reveling in the solitude under the vast desert skies on the land they had once owned.

The palomino enjoyed the desolate landscape, and without encouragement from McCarron, broke into a trot that gradually gave way to an all-out gallop as the energetic horse stretched her muscles, leaping over low basalt outcroppings and pounding across the baked hardpan. McCarron had his favorite camping spot, and the palomino knew full well how to get there.

They reached the bowl-shaped depression with daylight to spare. Hardy lichens spattered the black rocks, showing off their vitality with a display of bright colors. Gypsum sand filled the depression, as if a hot blizzard had cascaded across the desert. A sinkhole between the rocks cradled a small, pure pool from a spring that bubbled up, filtered clean through yards of fine sand.

McCarron went first to the spring and took deep gulps of water, which was cool from being in shade all day long. He swallowed the sweet wetness, not wanting to waste the water in his canteens. The palomino nudged his shoulder, urging him to hurry. But McCarron took his time, enjoying the water before the palomino could slobber all over inside the spring. Then he let her drink her fill.

He unsaddled the horse and tied her to a gnarled stump. He went out with his hatchet to chop up some of the dead mesquite brush and haul it back to his makeshift firepit. The fire would burn hot, crackling and popping into the night, filling the still air with a rich aromatic smoke.

Taking his mail out of the saddlebag, he held the mysterious padded envelope for an extra second, then decided to let the curiosity tickle his belly a little more. Oscar McCarron got few surprises in his life these days.

He rolled up the advertising flyers and junk mail and placed them under the chopped mesquite wood, then lit the fire with a single match, as he usually did. The twigs were so dry they practically ignited themselves.

McCarron unrolled his blanket and thin sleeping bag, then got out the cooking utensils. Looking up into the sky, he watched a shower of stars spray across the deepening darkness, the swarms of bright lights twinkling with a diamond richness that city dwellers never saw in their light-polluted skies.

As the resinous flames blazed bright and hot, McCarron finally sat back on his favorite rock, took the padded envelope, and tore it open. He dumped the contents into his callused palm.

"What the hell?" he said, disappointed after his hours of anticipation.

He found only a scrap of paper and a small glassine envelope filled with a powdery residue, some sort of greasy black ash that squished in his fingers as he pressed the envelope. A scrap of paper also fell out, displaying a message inked in precise razor-edged letters.

"FOR YOUR PART IN THE PAST."

No signature, no date, no address.

"What the hell?" he said again. "For my part in the past of what?"

He cussed at the horse, as if the palomino might somehow be able to give him an answer. The only thing of significance Oscar McCarron could think of having done in his entire lifetime had been an accident, a coincidence of fate—having owned the land on which the Trinity Test had taken place.

He did feel deeply proud of that part in his country's history, helping to spark the beginning of a nuclear age that had ended World War II and prevented those bloodthirsty Japanese from conquering half the world. That single successful atomic test had, in effect, begun the Cold War, leading to the development of more powerful superweapons that had kept the Commies in check. Sure, Oscar McCarron had been proud of his part in all that... but it wasn't as if he had actually *done* anything.

What else could the mysterious message mean?

"Some crazy nutcase," he muttered. With a rude noise, he tossed the note and the package of ash into the crackling mesquite fire.

He unbuckled his food pack and pulled out a can of chili, which he opened with a handheld can opener. He dumped it into a pot, which he hung from a tripod above the flames. He took out his special treasure, plastic zipper-lock bags of jalapenos and fresh-roasted Hatch green chilis, which he added to the mix to give the bland, commercialized recipe a little more bite.

As the food simmered, he listened to the utter quiet, the absence of birds or bats or insects. Just the desert silence, an opaque stillness that allowed him to hear himself breathe, hear the pulse in his ears, hear his own thoughts without being disturbed by a chatter of background noises. He let his eyes fall closed as he inhaled deeply of the stinging spices in the sizzling chili.

The palomino snorted and whinnied, breaking the silence.

"Awww, shut up," McCarron said, but the mare blew loudly through her nostrils again, stomping from side to side as if afraid of something. She tossed her head, sniffing and snorting.

"What is it?" he asked, slowly rising to his feet on creaking old knees. The horse acted as if she had scented a cougar or a bear, but McCarron knew that was ridiculous. Nothing larger than a few lizards, rattlesnakes, and kangaroo rats could survive out here in the Jornada del Muerto Desert.

Then he heard the voices, whispering, like a wind of words in a foreign language, a chant, drumbeats, building to a scream. The hissing white background noise reminded him of the harsh static he heard when his TV was turned up too loud and the videotape ran out.

"What the hell is it?" he said. "What's out there?"

McCarron stood and went to his saddle to pull out his rifle. The wind picked up, and he felt a hot breeze against his leathery cheeks—much hotter than the desert night. A dust storm? Brush fire?

The palomino thrashed back and forth, straining against the rope. Her eyes rolled, wild and white. The mare reared and then leaped sideways, crashing into the rough lava as if pinned to the walls of the shallow depression.

"Easy, girl! Easy!" McCarron turned to see a smear of blood on the rock from where the horse had scraped her flanks raw. But he didn't take the time to soothe his horse.

He waved the rifle's barrel back and forth into the buzzing, roaring night air. Somebody, or something, had to be out there.

"If you think you're gonna mess with me, you got another thing coming!" he shouted. His eyes watered, stinging. He fired a shot into the air, a warning, but the crack of the rifle vanished in the rising, howling noise.

The desert air seared his mouth like a blast from the hottest oven, parching his throat, burning his teeth. He backed away. The horse squealed in terror, a bizarre animal insanity that frightened the old man more than his own confused senses possibly could.

Suddenly the night around McCarron exploded as the angry presence behind those voices, behind the whispers and screams and the sudden heat, surged into the depression, as if someone had dropped a miniature sun right into his lap.

Oscar McCarron's world filled with an intolerable burst of atomic fire.

THIRTEEN

Trinity Site, near Alamogordo New Mexico
Friday, 11:18 a.m.

Scully took her shift driving south from Albuquerque across the flat, dry southern half of New Mexico. The air-conditioning in the rental Ford Taurus began to complain as she drove up a steep grade and then began the long descent into the deeper desert.

Beside her in the passenger seat Mulder folded and unfolded his copy of the faxed Unusual Occurrence Report that DOE representative Rosabeth Carrera had given him early that morning.

"Thought you might find this of interest, Agent Mulder," the dark-haired woman had said, pointing to the brief description that had come to her office on a standard distribution list from the Department of Energy headquarters. "The DOE requires that certain people be notified of unusual accidents relating to radiation. I'm one of those people—and this incident certainly qualifies."

Scully had taken the sheet from her partner, scanning the description of yet another mysteriously burned body, presumably washed by a flood of radioactive fire. This one had occurred far from the Teller Nuclear Research Facility, out in the White Sands Missile Range, near a barren memorial that Scully knew of all too well—the Trinity Site, the location of the first test of an atomic explosion back in July 1945.

"But how can this incident be relevant to Dr. Gregory's death?" Scully had asked. "The victim was an old rancher, with no connection to current nuclear weapons research."

Rosabeth Carrera simply shrugged. "Look at the details. How could it *not* be related? These sorts of deaths don't occur every day."

Mulder had eagerly taken back the Unusual Occurrence Report, rereading the summary. "I want to check it out, Scully. This could be the lead we've been lookng for. Two clues instead of one."

Scully sighed and agreed. "The very fact that they seem so unrelated could be the break we need… once we figure it out."

And so they had raced to the Oakland airport, hopped a Delta flight to Salt Lake City, and then down to Albuquerque, where they had rented a car for the long drive south.

Scully kept the car at ten miles over the speed limit, but the traffic still roared by in the fast lane. She gripped the steering wheel more tightly as a large three-trailered semi truck exploded past.

Scully ran ideas by her partner as she drove. "Mulder, so far our working theory is that a weapons test went wrong in Dr. Gregory's lab, or possibly that a protester engaged in some sabotage that led to his death. I don't see how any of that fits with a dead rancher out on a deserted missile range."

Mulder folded the Unusual Occurrence Report and stuck it in the pocket of his jacket. "Maybe we're not thinking big enough, Scully. Maybe there's a broader connection, an overall relationship to nuclear weapons. Missile range... nuclear research lab...."

"You may as well include the whole government, Mulder," she said.

"At least it gives us plenty of room to maneuver," he said.

After a brief moment of silence, Mulder narrowed his eyes and looked at Scully. "We'll know more when we get there, I hope. I made a call back to Headquarters while we were at the airport. I'm expecting the people at White Sands to have some information faxed to them, a broader ID check on Oscar McCarron. We'll see just how disconnected he is from Dr. Gregory. It might be something really obvious."

Scully returned her attention to the road unreeling ahead of her. "All right, we'll see."

They decided to table further discussion until they actually arrived at the site where the old rancher's burned body had been found.

Mulder fidgeted, trying to avoid the heat that baked through the windows. "Next time let's find out if the car has black seats before we sign the rental papers," he suggested.

"I agree." As Scully drove, letting the speedometer top seventy-five, then eighty, she recalled that New Mexico with its desert highways had traditionally been the first state in the country to raise its speed limits, to the cheering of the state's residents.

They passed signs on the highway that read, "NOTICE! DO NOT PICK UP HITCHHIKERS. PRISON FACILITIES NEARBY."

"Charming place," said Mulder.

The Ford Taurus reached a small town past Socorro, called San Antonio, where they turned east, heading deeper into the Jornada del Muerto—the aptly named "Journey of Death" desert. At Stallion Gate, the northern entrance to the White Sands Missile Range, they stopped at a guard checkpoint and flashed their papers. A military escort came out to meet them, and then waved them through onto the bleak missile test site.

Scully shaded her eyes and looked at the uninviting landscape—like the corpse of a once fertile land. She had seen the place in photos, but had never made it down to visit.

"These gates are opened once a year," she said, "so that tourists and pilgrims can go out to the actual Trinity Site and see what's left of the McDonald Ranch. That's ten miles deeper into the missile range, if I remember correctly. Not much to see, just a cairn of stones and a commemorative plaque."

"Just what I want to do on my summer vacation," Mulder said. "Go out and stand right on Ground Zero."

Scully kept her silence. She didn't think her partner knew about her peripheral involvement in protest activities in the past, and she preferred to keep that bit of her life private. It made her uncomfortable, though. She had always shared so much with Mulder. This uneasiness felt foreign to her, and she tried to identify her feelings. Embarrassment? she wondered. Or guilt? She drew a deep breath. They had a job to do here.

Two military policemen pulled up in a Jeep. Scully and Mulder reluctantly left the air-conditioning of their Taurus and climbed down to meet the MPs. Neither of them was dressed properly for driving across the dusty gypsum sands, but the MPs didn't seem to notice. They motioned for the two FBI agents to join them. Mulder secured their briefcases under the seat, then helped Scully climb into the back of the vehicle.

The two of them sat on hot seats in the jouncing vehicle, holding on for dear life as the Jeep roared across the rutted flatlands, oblivious to the lack of any road. The MPs tightened their helmets and gritted their teeth against the flying dust.

They arrived at a bowl-shaped depression where a dozen other MPs and Air Force officers stood at a cordoned-off site. Someone wearing anti-contamination clothes and carrying a handheld Geiger counter had stepped deeper into the blockaded area, inspecting the site.

Scully got out, ignoring the pain in her stiff legs. She felt dread build within her. Mulder walked silently beside her as they came to the edge of a depression bordered by dark volcanic rock.

It looked as if the entire hollow had been melted.

She and Mulder introduced themselves. A colonel waiting there had expected them. He handed Mulder a drooping sheet of thermal fax paper. "This came from your Bureau Headquarters, Agent Mulder," he said, "but I could have told you that information. We know all about old Oscar. That's how we found him there."

"So tell me," Mulder said, raising his eyebrows hopefully. "We need every detail you can give us."

"That rancher is an old fart who's come out here practically every week since before the Red Sea parted. He and his father originally owned the ranch land around here that was deeded to the Trinity Site—for the test, you know—but because of some wartime secrecy act, the names were changed on the paperwork so it couldn't be discovered who had originally owned the land. I guess they were afraid of crazy protesters even back then, or maybe Nazi spies." The colonel nodded down toward the blasted bowl. "And maybe they had good cause, considering what's happened."

Scully couldn't tear her eyes from the scene. The gypsum sand had been roasted by such extreme heat that it had become like a pottery glaze, turning into hardened glass with a greenish, jadelike consistency.

"Trinitite," she said.

"What's that?" Mulder asked.

She nodded toward the glassy fusion that lined the sands. "I'll bet we'll find out that glassy sand and rock is Trinitite. Around Ground Zero during the Trinity Test the heat was intense enough to fuse the surrounding sand into a glasslike solid. Very unusual. People even collected the stuff."

"Come on, we can go closer," the colonel said. "You'll want to take a look if you're to get any information from this."

"Thank you for your cooperation, Colonel," Scully said.

The gaunt, sunburned man turned to her. "We sure don't want to have to solve this one, Agent Scully. You're welcome to it."

She followed the colonel past the cordon, and down toward the flash-burned sands. Against one rock wall they could see the sprawling bowl glittering in the sunlight where the gypsum had turned molten.

Fused into the ground by the intense heat were the blackened remains of two burned figures, a nearly disintegrated man, and a horse, flattened and incinerated, pushed into the melted sands. The hardened glass had frozen the corpses into an eerie tableau, like tortured insects in amber.

Mulder shuddered and turned away from the crisped horror of the victim's face. He grasped Scully's arm briefly for support. "I really hate fire," he muttered.

"I know, Mulder," she said. She didn't tell him how much she herself hated the threat of radiation and fallout. "I don't think we should stay here any longer than we have to."

As she turned away, all she could think of were the hideously burned corpses, the photographs of Nagasaki victims at the Stop Nuclear Madness! museum in Berkeley.

How could it be happening again, here?

FOURTEEN

Historic Owl Cafe
San Antonio, New Mexico
Friday, 1:28 p.m.

Before reaching the interstate on their trip back to Albuquerque, Scully and Mulder decided to stop at the "Historic" Owl Cafe, a rusty-tan adobe building that looked like an abandoned movie set. The large building seemed the only thing of note in the entire city of San Antonio, New Mexico. The gravel parking lot hosted four battered and dirty pickup trucks, two Harley-Davidsons parked side by side, and an old-model Ford station wagon.

"Let's risk it, Scully," Mulder said. "We've got to grab lunch anyway. It's a long drive north."

Scully folded the highway map and climbed out of the car into the sweltering heat. She shaded her eyes. "I wish at least one other city in this state had a major airport," she said. She followed Mulder to a big glass door encrusted with road dust. He held it open for her, and she noted from the sticker on the glass that the restaurant was AAA approved.

Inside, the place was a dim and noisy dive, just the type of place she generally avoided. Mulder adored it. "Come on, Scully," he said. "It's *historic*. Read the sign."

"Wait," she said. "I think I've even heard of this place before. Something to do with the Manhattan Project or the Trinity Test."

"Then we've stopped at the right place," Mulder said. "Our hamburgers will be work-related."

Shadowy figures hunched over the counter: ranchers who had not deigned to take off their wide cowboy hats, a few truckers wearing old baseball caps, and a tourist or two. Someone played pinball in the far corner. Neon signs for various brands of low-end beer flickered over the bar and in the dining area.

"Looks like genuine Naugahyde seats," Mulder said. "This place is great."

"You *would* think so, Mulder."

A big Navajo man with long gray-black hair tied in a ponytail came around the corner to the cash register. He wore jeans, a checked cotton shirt with mother-of-pearl snaps, and a turquoise bolo tie. "Take any seat," he said, gesturing to the array of empty booths like an ambassador welcoming them into his kingdom. He went back to wiping down the Formica counter where others were eating and swapping loud unbelievable stories.

The walls of the Owl Cafe were dotted with posters, framed photographs of White Sands experimental missile launches, along with official-looking certificates of participation in Nuclear Emergency Search Team exercises. Photographic prints of mushroom clouds from desert detonations hung framed on the paneled walls, while smaller reprints were available for sale in the small glass display case near the old cash register... as were glassy jade-green rocks—Trinitite.

"I'd like to look around, Mulder," Scully said. "Might be some interesting stuff here."

"Let me just grab us a seat," he said, "and I'll order for us."

"I don't know if I should trust you to do that," she said.

He waved good-naturedly at her. "Have I ever been wrong?" He disappeared deeper into the dim labyrinth of Naugahyde booths before she could give him an honest answer.

She waited by the display case beneath the cash register and picked up a small mimeographed brochure showing a grainy photo of the Owl Cafe. The poorly written text described the restaurant's claims to fame. She scanned the words, refreshing her memory—and it all carried back to her from when she had obsessively studied the Cold War and the arms race and the beginnings of the U.S. nuclear program.

In the days before air-conditioned cars, the Owl Cafe had been an unofficial stopping place for Manhattan Project scientists and engineers during their frequent long drives from the northern mountains at Los Alamos down to the Trinity Test Site. They had no interstate highways, only state roads, and the trip must have been gruesome in the heat of summer in 1945.

Technically, the crews were not allowed to stop along the way. They were ordered by the military to drive straight through. But the Owl Cafe, isolated at a desert crossroads out in the middle of nowhere, was ideal for the small automobile convoys to stop at before heading east into even more murderous terrain. The crew couldn't help but want lunch or a cold drink before heading out to the restricted land area the government had set aside for the first atomic bomb blast.

The big Navajo saw Scully standing by the display case and came over, speaking in a rich deep voice. "What can I get for you?"

Startled, Scully looked down and pointed to the selection of small rocks. "I'd like one of those pieces of Trinitite, please."

"That five-dollar one?" Without another word the broad-shouldered man pulled out a little key and opened the rear of the display case, removing one of the smallish rocks. After a pause, he set it back down on the shelf, selecting a larger sample instead. "Here, take this one," he said. "They're all overpriced anyway."

Scully took the glassy lump and squeezed it in the palm of her hand, trying to imagine the hellish fury that had created it—not any geologic process deep in the core of the earth, but a man-made inferno that had lasted only a few seconds. The stone was cool and slick on her palm; any tingle she felt came strictly from her imagination.

Scully paid for the rock and wandered over to the other exhibits.

An old bottle collection covered half of one wall. Brown glass, green glass, clear glass, even a few bright blue bottles, were all on display without identifying tags—except for a single typewritten sheet of paper, yellowed with age, tacked to the wall.

The bottle collection had been there since before World War II, the prized possession of another old Navajo who had originally owned the Owl Cafe. The former owner knew nothing of the secret nuclear project or the impending test, although he couldn't help but notice the official government vehicles, military brass, and the suit-and-tie engineers who could never disguise themselves as local ranchers or reservation Navajos.

In fact, Scully thought, the Manhattan Project engineers must have looked as out of place as she and Mulder did this afternoon. She continued reading.

Several days before the actual test explosion in July 1945, one of the engineers, a regular—if unofficial—customer at the Owl Cafe, had tipped off the old owner. He gave no classified details, said only that it might be wise to take down the fragile bottles for a few days. The skeptical Navajo owner had complied... and thus the bottle collection had been saved when the Trinity blast had rattled walls as far away as Silver City and Gallup, nearly two hundred miles distant. The name of the considerate Manhattan Project engineer was not mentioned, no doubt to keep the man from getting into trouble.

Taking her Trinitite souvenir, Scully wandered back into the dining room in search of Mulder. He was slumped back comfortably on the Naugahyde seat as he reread the fax he had received out at the White Sands testing range. He sipped iced tea from a red plastic cup.

Scully slid into the padded seat across from him and saw that he had ordered her an ice tea as well. She set the lump of glassy rock on the Formica table in front of him. He picked it up, turning it over in his hand with curiosity.

"You once called me a sucker for buying souvenirs at a tourist-trap cafe like this one."

"This is different," she said.

"Of course." He gave her a wry smile.

"It *is*. That's Trinitite," she said, "the stuff I was telling you about."

He studied it under the dim light cast by a flickering Coors sign. "Looks just like the stuff out at the death site."

She nodded.

The waitress interrupted by bringing their meals. She gave each of them a basket of sizzling french fries and an enormous burger so juicy it had to be wrapped in paper to catch the grease.

"You're gonna love this, Scully," he said. "The house specialty, a green chili cheeseburger." Mulder held his up, took a big bite, and spoke around a dripping mouthful. "Delicious! They grind their own meat here, and the green chilis really enhance the flavor. You can't get this stuff in Washington, D.C."

"I'm not sure I'd want to," Scully said, picking up her own huge burger. She inspected it to determine the best method of attack, making sure she had plenty of napkins within easy reach. Despite her skepticism, though, she found the meal absolutely delicious, the bite of green chilis unlike anything she had ever expected.

"So, Scully," he said, finally getting down to business, "let's see what we can come up with. We now have two bodies—three, if you count the horse—killed by a sudden flash of heat like a miniature atomic explosion. One in an isolated weapons lab office, and another out here in the middle of the desert."

Scully held up one finger, saw that some ketchup had run down to her knuckle, and plucked up a napkin to wipe it clean. "The laboratory death site was being used by a nuclear weapons researcher developing a secret and intense new atomic device, and the second death occurred out in the White Sands Missile Range, where the military might be expected to test such a device. Could be a connection."

"Ah," Mulder pointed out, "but Dr. Gregory's office was not an engineering and experimental lab. In fact, it wasn't much more than a room full of computers. You wouldn't find a nuclear warhead stashed in his file cabinet drawer. And, if the military intended to test this Bright Anvil device, why do it out at White Sands? The government already has a perfect nuclear testing site in Nevada. It's official and everything, with all the security they could ask for. Besides, did you get the impression that the colonel at White Sands *expected* this?"

Scully had to admit he was right. "No, he didn't seem at all prepared to deal with the situation."

Mulder wiped his mouth with a napkin. "I think we should look for a broader connection—and it might not have anything at all to do with Bright Anvil."

"If not Bright Anvil, then what do you have in mind?"

Mulder finished the last bite of his cheeseburger, then set to work on his remaining fries. "Emil Gregory and Oscar McCarron had a few obscure connections dating all the way back to World War II. Oscar McCarron was an old rancher who had probably never set foot out of New Mexico in his entire life. Dr. Gregory was also from New Mexico. He worked on the Manhattan Project more than fifty years ago, then spent time at Los Alamos before coming to the San Francisco area to work for the Teller Nuclear Research Facility."

"So what are you suggesting, Mulder?"

He shrugged. "It's only a shot in the dark, and I'm not sure I've come up with anything yet. Just thinking that maybe we should use our imaginations a little, consider alternative possibilities. What else could those two men have in common? We know Gregory worked on the Trinity Test, and McCarron's family owned the land where the test took place."

Scully picked up a french fry and ate it quickly. "Mulder, sometimes your imagination is far too active."

He pointed to himself, miming *Moi?* "And how often are my alternative solutions proven to be correct, Scully?"

Scully ate another fry. "That all depends on who you ask."

Mulder sighed. "Scully, you're an impossible skeptic sometimes—but I like you anyway."

She rewarded him with a smile. "Somebody's got to keep you in line."

Wiping his hands on another napkin, Mulder pulled out their map of New Mexico. "I wonder how far Roswell is from here?" he said. "It might be worth a side trip."

"Absolutely not," Scully said. "We've got a plane to catch."

He looked at her with a *Gotcha!* expression to show that he hadn't been serious. "Just thought I'd ask."

FIFTEEN

Kamida Imports
Honolulu, Hawaii
Friday, 2:04 p.m.

Sitting at his impeccably neat and carefully arranged desk in the high-rise office building, four floors of which were devoted to his own imports company, Ryan Kamida carefully addressed a padded envelope.

His calligraphic pen moved in precise strokes, and the letters came out perfectly, the wet black ink like scorched blood.

Expansive windows covered two walls of his corner office, offering a panoramic view of Oahu. But Kamida kept the mini-blinds half-closed most of the time. He dearly loved feeling the gentle warmth of the sun, letting its heat bathe his scarred skin, soothing, caressing his body, as it had in the barely remembered idyllic days on an isolated Pacific island.

But too much bright sunshine felt like fire to him. It reminded him of that other blaze from the sky, the searing flash so intense that it had set the air molecules themselves on fire.

Kamida's snow-white hair lay neatly on his head, thick and perfectly maintained. Because of the almost supernatural good fortune he had experienced during his adult life, Kamida had plenty of money for things like that: clothes, grooming, possessions.

But his money couldn't buy everything. He didn't *want* everything.

His lumpy, wax-textured hands gripped the polished pen as if it were a weapon—and in a sense, it was. The words resounded in his head. He filled out the address in a careful, perfect script, feeling for the right spot on the padded envelope. He could sense the accuracy of his letters.

Satisfied, Kamida rested the pen in the familiar groove on his desk next to the ink reservoir. Then he reached out to hold the special envelope, feeling its edges, the sharp corners. He took it on faith that he had filled out the address correctly. He would never ask anyone else to double-check it, though he could not see it himself.

Ryan Kamida was completely blind.

The list in his mind grew shorter and shorter with each package sent, each target identified. Kamida had the names of those responsible etched clearly in his well-honed memory.

As he sat at his desk with the warm Hawaiian sun suffusing around him through the mini-blinds, letting him feel its kind touch, he felt very alone— though he knew he had asked for this. He had sent all the workers on this floor home for the afternoon. They had objected, pointing out the work they had to do, shipping records, finders' fees, sales commissions. Kamida simply offered them time-and-a-half pay, and they went home satisfied. They were well accustomed to his eccentricities.

He now had the offices to himself to do his important work.

No doubt to assuage its unacknowledged pangs of guilt, the government had assisted Ryan Kamida through the years, sometimes offering veiled handouts, at other times blatantly approving his bids and choosing him over his competitors. He was a handicapped businessman, an ethnic minority—though here in Hawaii being a Pacific Islander was hardly remarkable. Between the Japanese tourists and the Pacific Islanders who made their homes here, middle-class Caucasian families were the true minorities.

Kamida had used every resource at his disposal to help his company succeed. His business specialized in exotic imports from little-known Pacific islands—Elugelab, Truk, Johnston Atoll, the entire Marshall chain—impressing tourists with trinkets that came from faraway places with interesting names.

He needed the money to accomplish his true mission.

Kamida fingered the envelope, stuffed the hand-written note and a small glass vial inside, then sealed it. That simple act of closure brought a shudder of relief to him, but it lasted only a moment.

No matter how many such packages he sent, no matter how many of the guilty he identified, he could never make up for the loss of his people. It had been a completely successful genocide, more thorough than anything Adolf Hitler had accomplished. In a single stroke Ryan Kamida's family, his relatives, his tribe… his island had vanished in a surge of light and flames. A small boy was the sole survivor.

But Kamida did not consider his survival to be either a miracle or a blessing. He had been given an entire lifetime to endure the memory of those few seconds, while for all the others it had been over in an instant.

Or so he had thought.

The voices in his head had not stopped screaming since that day when he was ten years old.

Setting the envelope aside, Kamida sniffed the stuffy air in his office. He tilted his burned face and blank white eyes toward the ceiling. He couldn't see, but he could feel, could sense the gathering storm.

A seething sea of white-hot luminescence boiled in a suspended pool against the acoustic tiles, like froth in a pot, swirling with spectral screaming faces. Though blind, he *knew* they were there. They wouldn't leave him alone.

The ghosts of his incinerated people grew more and more restless. They would strike out at their own targets if he refused to offer them a victim of his own choosing. The ghosts had waited so long, and Ryan Kamida could no longer keep them under control.

Walking with the grace and confidence of a sighted man through the familiar offices, he picked up the hand-addressed envelope and left his room, taking it to the mail drop, from which the package would be rushed to an airplane and shipped to the United States. He deemed the expense of overnight mail delivery across the Pacific insignificant. The envelope would be delivered to a particular low-profile but very important official at the Department of Energy headquarters near Washington, D.C.

It was probably already too late to stop Bright Anvil, Kamida supposed, but perhaps this would be enough to prevent the nightmare from occurring again.

SIXTEEN

Teller Nuclear Research Facility
Monday, 10:16 a.m.

After an uneventful weekend—for once—Mulder drove back to the Teller Nuclear Research Facility, whistling "California Dreaming." Scully pretended to heave a long-suffering sigh, as if to say that since he was her partner, she would put up with his odd sense of humor. Mulder smiled at her in appreciation of her tolerance.

The condition of the old rancher's body at the Trinity Site had been so unmistakably similar to that of Dr. Emil Gregory that Scully couldn't discount some sort of connection. But they had come back to the San Francisco-area nuclear weapons laboratory with more questions than before.

They stopped at the guard gate, flashing visitor's badges and FBI credentials. They needed to talk to the rest of Dr. Gregory's Bright Anvil team—deputy project head Bear Dooley and the other researchers and engineers. Scully still insisted there must be some technical explanation for the deaths, a test of a small yet powerful nuclear device, something that had backfired on Dr. Gregory, something that had been tested out in New Mexico.

That didn't ring true, though, to Mulder. He thought there must be some reason they hadn't considered yet, though Scully would hold onto her explanations until she found a better, more logical one.

After they passed through the guard gate, Mulder reached over to unfold the map of the Teller Facility. He traced the access roads with his finger to find the main lab building where Dr. Gregory had died and the temporary barracks offices to which Bear Dooley and the other team members had been relocated.

"Now that you've found out some details about Bright Anvil through, uh…" Mulder raised his eyebrows, "shall we say, 'unofficial means,' let's see what Mr. Dooley has to say for himself. Solid information is our best weapon."

"I just wish we had the information to solve this case," Scully said.

"If wishes were horses . .. " Mulder began.

Scully shuddered, thinking of the equine corpse at the White Sands Missile Range. "I withdraw the comment."

They arrived at the converted barracks building and left their car in a Government Vehicle Only parking space. This time, Mulder knew to take a paper respirator mask to protect himself from wild asbestos fibers floating in the air. Handing another mask to Scully, he helped her fasten it over her hair. He carefully scrutinized his partner's new appearance.

"It's a fashion statement," he said. "I like it."

"First dosimeters and now breathing masks," Scully said. "This place is a health nut's paradise."

Down the corridor the construction workers had moved the translucent plastic barrier curtains after demolishing another entire section of the wall. A loud generator roared, maintaining negative air pressure in the enclosed work area, supposedly to prevent the lightweight asbestos fibers from drifting past the barricade.

"Down here," Mulder said, turning right and motioning for Scully to follow. "Bear Dooley's new office makes my basement at Bureau Headquarters look like Club Med."

When they reached Dooley's temporary office, the door stood wide open, despite the racket of crowbars and the generator and shouts from the workmen.

"Excuse me—Mr. Dooley?" Mulder called. "I don't know how you can work in this environment."

But when Mulder popped his head inside, the office appeared abandoned. The desk had been cleared, the file drawers taped shut. Framed photos were still stacked in cardboard boxes and various office paraphernalia lay scattered in disarray, as if someone had packed up frantically, leaving unnecessary items behind. Mulder pursed his lips and glanced around.

"Looks like nobody's home," Scully said.

Suddenly a young redheaded man entered the office. With his glasses, plaid shirt, and pocket stuffed full of pens, he looked like a poster boy for the "nerd's dress code." His badge identified him as Victor Ogilvy. Mulder couldn't tell if the young man was smiling or frowning behind his white breathing mask.

"Are you the Department of Defense people?" Ogilvy asked quickly. "We've got the preliminary reports ready, but nothing else I can deliver to you just yet."

"We're looking for Mr. Bear Dooley," Mulder said. "Can you tell us where he is?"

Behind his round eyeglasses, Victor Ogilvy blinked rapidly. "Well, that was in the initial briefing. I'm sure of it. He left for San Diego last Thursday morning. The *Dallas* should arrive at the atoll in another day or two. The rest of us are getting all packed up to be flown out."

"Flown out to where?" Mulder asked.

The question took Ogilvy entirely by surprise. "What do you mean? Are you sure you're from the Department of Defense?"

Scully stepped forward. "We never said we were, Mister Ogilvy." She flipped out her badge and ID. "Federal agents. I'm Special Agent Dana Scully, and this is my partner Agent Mulder. We need to ask you a few questions about Bright Anvil and the death of Dr. Gregory... and this test that's taking place out on an atoll in the Pacific," she said.

Mulder was amazed at how quickly and easily she had put together the details into a rapid, professional-sounding string of inquiries.

Ogilvy's eyes bulged out so far that they practically bumped the lenses of his glasses. He stumbled over his words. "I... I don't think I should say any more," he said. "It's classified."

Mulder noted how intimidated the young man was and decided to press his advantage. "Didn't you hear what Agent Scully said? We're with the *FBI*." He said the words with dire import. "You have to answer our questions."

"But I could lose my clearance," Ogilvy said.

Mulder shrugged. "One way or the other. Would you like me to start quoting you FBI statutes? How about this one: if you refuse to cooperate with our ongoing investigation, I just might cite you under Statute 43H of the FBI Code."

Scully quickly squeezed his arm. "Mulder!"

He shook his head. "Let me handle this, Scully. Victor here doesn't know what kind of trouble he could get himself into."

"I..." Victor Ogilvy said, "I think you should talk to our Department of Energy representative. She's authorized to answer those types of questions. If she gives me the go-ahead, then I can respond. You'll have no cause to cite me. Honest!"

Mulder sighed. He had just lost this round. "Well, get her on the phone so we can talk to her."

Ogilvy rummaged around Bear Dooley's abandoned desk until he found a Teller Nuclear Research Facility phone listing. He nervously paged through it, then punched in the number for Rosabeth Carrera.

Scully leaned over and whispered in his ear. "Statute 43H?"

"Unauthorized Use of the Smoky the Bear Symbol," Mulder mumbled, smiling sheepishly. "But he doesn't know that."

Within moments Rosabeth Carrera was on the phone. Her voice started out rich and sweet, its Hispanic undertones mostly hidden. She sounded polite, helpful. "Good morning, Agent Mulder. I didn't know you had returned from New Mexico."

"Seems like a lot has happened over the weekend," he said. "Most of Dr. Gregory's team has disappeared, and we can't get any answers on what's happened to them. Since they are quite clearly involved in this case, we'll need to interview them further—especially now that we've uncovered a clear connection between Dr. Emil Gregory and the other victim at White Sands."

Scully's eyebrows shot up. Mulder was overstating his case, but Carrera had no way of knowing it.

"Agent Mulder," Carrera said, her voice a bit crisper now, "Dr. Gregory was working on a very important project for this laboratory and for the United States government. Such projects have milestones and schedules and a great deal of momentum behind them. People in very high political circles have a lot at stake in seeing that the research continues as planned. I'm afraid we can't call our scientists back on a whim."

"This is no whim, Ms. Carrera," Mulder said, growing more formal. "Your main researcher is dead under highly suspicious circumstances, and now another victim has turned up at the White Sands Missile Range, killed by the same means. I think that's ample reason for proceeding with caution and asking a few more questions before moving on to the next stage. I'd like you to postpone this Bright Anvil test."

"Bright Anvil? No such test has been announced," Carrera answered.

"Let's not play games," he said. "It wastes valuable telephone time."

"I'm afraid that's impossible," Carrera said dismissively. "Dr. Gregory's work will go on, as planned."

Mulder took the challenge. "I can make some calls to Bureau Headquarters, and I've got a few connections in the Department of Defense."

Carrera's tone was brisk, almost abrupt. "Make whatever phone calls you feel you have to, Agent Mulder. But Dr. Gregory's test will take place as scheduled. No question about it. The government has many priorities, and I have no doubt that you will find that your murder investigation is rather far down the list compared to the national interests that are at stake."

After he hung up, Scully said, "From the look on your face, I take it Rosabeth Carrera didn't bend over backward to offer you her assistance."

Mulder sighed. "I've had more helpful conversations."

Victor Ogilvy hovered nervously by the door. "Does that mean I don't have to answer your questions?"

Mulder shot him a quick glare. "Depends on how badly you want to be on my Christmas card list."

The young redhead quickly ducked out of sight.

Scully put her hands on her hips and turned to face Mulder. "Well then, I guess it's my turn to ferret out some details," she said. "Time to check my other source of information."

SEVENTEEN

Stop Nuclear Madness! Headquarters
Monday, 3:31 p.m.

Scully returned to the headquarters of the Berkeley antinuclear protest group, but when she trudged down the half-flight of stairs to the bomb-shelter basement, she found the temporary offices in the sort of chaos that might be expected at a fly-by-night business suddenly afraid of a bust.

A group of student volunteers busied themselves removing the posters of Nagasaki victims from the walls, the poignant photographs of homeless Bikini Islanders, the long listing of aboveground atomic bomb tests, and the colorful graphs showing cancer statistics.

Scully stepped through the door and stared at all the movement, the confusion, the shouting. Behind the fabric room dividers, the exhausted photocopier still whirred, working overtime.

Standing on a stepstool, the receptionist, Becka Thorne, yanked push pins from the wall to release the draped, dot-matrix banner that warned against a second nuclear war. The black woman turned, her dress an even more dizzying riot of colors than her previous voluminous wrap had been, her hair still clumped together in its lumpy, tentacular dreadlocks.

"I'm looking for Miriel Bremen again," Scully shouted into the chaos. "Is she here?"

Becka undid a last push pin, and half of the paper banner drooped to the floor like a falling streamer of fireworks. She climbed down off the stepstool and wiped her hands on her colorful dress. "You're that FBI lady, right? Well, Miriel's not here. As you can see we're shutting down the office. No more Stop Nuclear Madness!"

"You're shutting down the office?" Scully asked. "Are you moving to a new location?"

"No. Miriel just up and pulled our lease. We only had a month left in it anyway, but she handed it over to the next group coming in. These office spaces on campus are in great demand, you know."

Scully tried to understand. "Did your organization lose its funding unexpectedly?"

Becka laughed. "Not in the least. We were probably the healthiest group Berkeley has seen in five years, lots of money dumped in from some corporation in Hawaii. But Miriel just pulled the plug and told us to call the next group on the waiting list. Said she had a change of heart, or something. Guess she became 'born again' again, but in another direction this time."

"What's moving in here now?" Scully asked, still taken aback by the protester's sudden disappearance. What could have driven Miriel Bremen to give up the work that had so ignited her passions that she would jettison her career and her security clearance, leaving a blot on her employment record that would haunt her for the rest of her working days.

Becka Thorne gestured to the other volunteer workers. "It's an environmental activist group," she said. "I can show you some of their posters—very disturbing. They're calling attention to increasing levels of environmental pollutants in our groundwater, how toxic chemicals are seeping into every part of our daily lives and causing an avalanche of health problems."

The receptionist flipped through several large foam-core posters, some with tables that listed organic and toxic chemicals discovered in a sample of everyday tap water. Scully recognized many of the organic substances, but others seemed like the ingredients from a chemistry set. Some of the listed concentrations gave Scully cause for concern, and she wondered if their "random" analysis was reproducible.

She flipped to another chart that showed cancer statistics rising year after year—only this time they were blamed on toxic pollutants in the groundwater. The graph looked identical to the one used by Stop Nuclear Madness! that had connected the same increase in cancer to background radiation from nuclear tests in the 1950s.

One of the student workers slid the stepstool to the other side of the wall with a loud rattling sound, then climbed up to pluck the remaining push pins. The entire paper banner fell rustling to the floor.

"So what will you do with yourself now, Ms. Thorne?" Scully asked. "Does your group give you a reference to find a job someplace else?"

Becka Thorne blinked at Scully with her huge brown eyes. "No, I'll just work for the new group. I follow the protesters. Whatever cause they've got is fine with me. They're all interesting. And everybody's got a point, as far as I can see. Can't trust anybody these days, you know—especially not the government. Uh, no offense to you."

Scully smiled. "I think my partner might agree with you."

Becka Thorne gave a quick smile, then wiped the perspiration off her forehead. "Well, send your partner down here then. We always need new recruits for our work."

Scully had to keep herself from laughing. "I think he's too preoccupied for that—on this case, for instance." She finally succeeded in getting back to the point. "We really need to talk to Miriel Bremen. Do you know how we can get in touch with her?"

The receptionist looked at Scully carefully. "She didn't leave a phone number, if that's what you're after—but mostly likely she's gone to the islands, or something. When her conscience gets too bad, she sometimes goes off on these pilgrimages. She even went to Nagasaki once, another time to Pearl Harbor. Who knows where else? She's a pretty private person, our Miriel."

Scully furrowed her brow. "So she's somewhere in 'the islands,' but you have no idea where she might have gone? Jamaica? Tahiti? New Zealand?"

Becka shrugged. "Look, Miss FBI—Miriel was in one hell of a hurry to get out of here. Came in last Friday afternoon and told us we were done—done. Just like that. She was turning over the lease, and the rest of us were on our own.

"Oh, she thanked us for our efforts and told us to use her as a reference if we ever needed it—as if a big company would pay the slightest bit of attention to a reference from someone like Miriel Bremen! She's just lucky most of us have our own connections with the protest groups around here. We're not going to starve."

Scully handed Becka a business card. "If you learn where she is, Ms. Thorne, or if you get in touch with her, have her call me at this number. I think she'll be willing to talk to me."

"If you say so," the receptionist said. "We need to get back to work now. The environmental group wants to hold a rally this Saturday, and they've got flyers to go up on all the kiosks and light posts. We've got about a thousand phone calls to make. No rest around here. I sure wish I could go to the islands for a vacation."

Scully thanked her again and then left, climbing the concrete stairs to street level. She was deeply troubled. First Dr. Gregory had been killed in his office, and then Bear Dooley and his team had suddenly pulled up stakes and fled to the Pacific to set up their secret test, and now Miriel Bremen, former member of the Bright Anvil Project and outspoken radical protester against the test itself, had also left abruptly, heading out for "the islands."

Could it be a coincidence? Scully didn't like coincidences.

And how did old Oscar McCarron fit in?

The pieces of the puzzle seemed too widely separated, yet connected by invisible threads. Scully just had to feel around until she found the connections that bound the mystery together. She and Mulder would just have to keep looking.

The truth was out there. Somewhere.

EIGHTEEN

Scheck Residence
Gaithersburg, Maryland
Monday, 6:30 p.m.

Late afternoon in the Washington, D.C., area, hot and humid.

The air hung as thick as a damp rag. Brooding thunderheads in the sky promised only an oppressive increase to the mugginess, rather than a refreshing and cooling rain shower.

On days like this, Nancy Scheck felt that the hassle of maintaining an in-ground swimming pool in her fenced backyard paid off.

She let the front screen door close by itself as she entered her brick-front house with the black shutters. Flowering dogwoods and a thick, well-trimmed hedge surrounded its white colonial pillars. It was just the kind of imposing mansion an important Department of Energy executive was supposed to own, and she relished it.

Since she had been divorced for ten years and her three children were all grown and away at college, the place gave her plenty of room to breathe, space to move about. She enjoyed the freedom, the luxury.

Such a mansion was far more than she needed, but Nancy Scheck didn't like the implications of settling for a more modest dwelling, not now. All her career she had been concerned with moving *up* in the world, clawing her way to the top. Exchanging an impressive big house for a smaller one did not fit in with the plan.

She dumped her briefcase on the small Ethan Allen telephone table in the front hall, then shucked out of her stifling business jacket. Her entire career had been inside the Beltway, and she was used to dressing in conservative formal outfits and uncomfortable pantyhose. At her level, such items were just as much of a required uniform as the quaint outfit a teenager wore behind the counter of a fast-food restaurant.

At the moment, though, Nancy couldn't wait to peel off her clothes, get into her sleek black one-piece swimsuit, and take a long, luxurious dip in the pool.

She snagged the usual pile of mail and dropped it unceremoniously on the kitchen counter. She punched the answering machine to listen to the two recorded messages. The first was an offer from a company eager to come and give her a free, no-obligation quote for aluminum siding.

She snorted. "Aluminum siding on my house? I think not."

The second message was in a rich, familiar voice. The words sounded formal and innocuous, but she could detect the hidden passion behind them that went orders of magnitude beyond a mere business relationship... or even good friendship.

In her persona at work and at DOE social functions, she called him "Brigadier General Matthew Bradoukis." During his frequent visits here in her backyard or on the patio, she allowed herself to call him "Matthew"—and while they were in bed, she moaned endearing and never-to-be-repeated names into his ear.

He didn't identify himself on the answering machine, not that he needed to. "It's me. I'm a little late at the office so I won't be over until seven-thirty or so. I'm going to stop by my house and pick up the two Porterhouse steaks I've been marinating in the fridge all day. We'll throw them on the barbecue grill, then we can take a swim and… whatever. With so many parts of the project coming to a *head*, reaching their *climax*—"

Nancy giggled, knowing he had picked the turn of phrase intentionally. She found it very erotic.

"—we both need a little release from our tension." The tone beeped, and the tape rewound.

In her bedroom, she shed her clothes and, smiling to herself, she yanked down the satin sheets on her bed before changing into her bathing suit, black and smooth and slick.

She admired herself in the mirror. At forty-five she knew she wasn't as gorgeous or sexy as she might have been at twenty-five, but she had a body that stood out above most other women her age. She kept in shape. She dressed well. She exercised, and she had retained her appetite in sexual pleasures. Her hair was short and neatly trimmed. Luckily, blondes didn't become gray—instead they turned "ash."

Nancy grabbed one of the plush beach towels from the closet and went through the kitchen, pausing to pour herself a gin and tonic. She swished the alcohol and mixer around with the ice, making it good and cold. No sense not getting the buzz started before Matthew got here. He would fix his own drink when he arrived.

With the towel slung over her shoulder, Nancy took the mail and her drink out the back patio door to sit by the pool. She pulled a chaise lounge up to her small patio table, then went to turn on the bug lights. The mosquitoes and gnats never relented, especially not near sunset. Finally, she picked up the pool skimmer and swept the net around the surface of the water, removing the drowned bugs and the leaves that had fallen from the neighbors' trees. When the blue water sparkled clean and inviting, she returned to her shaded chair.

Nancy settled back to relax, sipping the strong drink, tasting the tonic and the Tanqueray that burned along the back of her throat and into her sinuses. She imagined the taste of the rich steaks Matthew would soon be cooking. She could imagine the salty sweet flavor of his kisses as their breath mingled.

She squirmed in anticipation on the lounge chair, then ran her hands over the swimsuit.

It was so good to have a man whose security clearance was as high as her own, someone who worked on the same classified project, who knew about the money skimmed off the operating budgets of other programs, leaving no paper trail of funding. No accounting could ever be made for highly sensitive projects such as Bright Anvil.

She didn't have to worry about pillow talk when she needed conversation, since Brigadier General Matthew Bradoukis handled the Department of Defense's operations of the new warhead concept, while she took care of the DOE side. No worries there. He was her perfect match... for now.

Nancy slicked baby oil on her bare legs and arms and shoulders, massaging it into her neck... imagining Matthew's strong fingers working it there. She had to stop herself from thinking like that, or she wouldn't be able to stand waiting until he arrived.

She tried to distract herself by opening the mail, sifting through the form letters, advertising circulars, and junk mail without interest—until she came upon an express-delivery package with a postmark from Honolulu but no return address.

"Maybe I won a free trip for two," she said, and tore open the envelope. To her disappointment, she discovered only a small glass vial of fine black ash and a scrap of paper. The message was written in neatly printed, razor-edged letters, carefully formed capitals, in a hand that showed elaborate patience.

"FOR YOUR PART IN THE FUTURE."

She frowned at the note. "What's that supposed to mean?" Out of curiosity, she shook the vial of black ash, holding it up to catch the light. "Am I supposed to convince people to stop smoking cigarettes?"

Nancy stood up, disgusted at somebody's lame idea of a joke. Whoever was trying to threaten her, or pull her leg, couldn't succeed unless she understood what the point was. "Next time try adding a few more details," she said, tossing the note on the patio table.

Nancy decided not to worry about it. The sun was dropping lower, though the humidity would hold the heat in the air for a long time to come. She was wasting good swimming time.

By the edge of the pool, the bug light crackled and snapped. She watched it give off blue sparks as it fed upon whatever gnats or mosquitoes had been lured to their doom in its voltage differential.

"Take that," she said with a grin. "Hah!"

Then the other bug lamps began to spark, frying loudly, buzzing, popping. The lights flickered violently. The sparks returned like miniature lightning storms.

"What is this, a June bug invasion?" Nancy said, looking around. Only the large beetles would cause the lights to sizzle so much. She wished Matthew would hurry up and get here—she wanted him to see this craziness.

Finally, one by one, each bug light erupted like a small bomb, with a geyser of blue electrical sparks like a Roman candle into the air. Nancy groaned in disgust. Now they would have to waste valuable weekend time replacing the fixtures.

"What's going on here, dammit?" Still holding the weird vial, Nancy slammed her drink down, somehow managing not to shatter the glass and dump ice cubes across the concrete patio. She felt unprotected and defenseless out here wearing nothing but her black bathing suit. Maybe if she could get to a phone....

Voices came at her from all sides, speaking in some strange and primal tongue, swirling invisibly around her ears—but she could see nothing.

The air itself sparkled and discharged, as if every object on her patio had become a lightning rod. Blue-white arcs shot from her lounge chair to the patio table. "Help!" she cried.

Nancy turned to run, but slipped and reached out instinctively for support. When she touched the chair, skittering electricity shot up her arms in a burning discharge.

She opened her mouth to scream, and sparks danced from the fillings in her teeth. Her ash-blond hair rose up into the air like serpents, waving from side to side, spreading into a nimbus around her head.

Nancy staggered toward the edge of the pool, desperately seeking sanctuary there. Her skin crawled and burned, alive with static electricity. She dropped the vial of ashes into the water.

A gathering storm of harsh light surrounded her. The screaming voices grew louder.

Critical mass.

A sudden rush of thunder engulfed her.

The intense firestorm crisped her eyes. The force of the blast of heat and radiation slammed her back.ward into the pool with a surge of light. A cloud of vaporized water swept upward like a fog bank into the sky.

The final afterimage on Nancy Scheck's optic nerve was of an impossible, spectral mushroom cloud.

NINETEEN

Scheck Residence
Tuesday, 1:06 p.m.

The body looked the same as the others, Mulder thought—severely charred, crackling with residual radiation, twisted in a flash-burned, insectlike pose that reminded him of that famous lithograph by Edvard Munch, *The Scream.*

Somehow, though, finding a radiation-blasted corpse in the backyard of an expensive suburban home seemed far more eerie. The mundane surroundings—swimming pool, lounge chairs, and patio furniture—gave the death scene a more frightening aspect than even the blasted bowl of glassy sand out in the New Mexico desert.

A local policeman blocked them from entering the pool area, but Mulder flashed his badge and ID. "Federal agents," he said. "I'm Special Agent Mulder, this is Agent Scully. We've been flown in to look at the site and examine the body."

A homicide detective was studying clues and taking notes around the pool and patio. He looked baffled. He overheard Mulder's introduction, and looked up. "FBI? Now that's calling in the big guns. Why were you brought here?"

"We might have a certain background on this case," Scully answered. "This death may be related to another investigation we're working on. There have been two similar deaths in the past week."

The detective raised his eyebrows, then gave a weary shrug. "Anything you guys can do to help. Takes work off my shoulders. This is a weird one, all right. Never seen anything like it."

"No question: this one goes in *your* special file cabinet," Scully said quietly to Mulder.

Scully began a perimeter inspection of the crime scene, working around the bustling evidence technicians and detectives. She took out a small knife to probe a large charred patch on the redwood fence that bounded the Scheck property.

"The burn doesn't go very deep," she said, flaking away an external film of charcoal. "As if the heat was intense, but very brief."

Mulder inspected the mark she had made with her knife. Then he noticed the shattered bug lights around the pool. "Look, they're all destroyed," he said. "Like some sort of power surge blew them up, every one. Doesn't happen every day."

"We can check electrical company records to see if there were local power fluctuations at the estimated time of death," Scully suggested.

Mulder nodded. He placed his hands on his hips and turned slowly around, hoping that an answer would jump out at him. But nothing did. "Okay, Scully," he said. "This time we're not at a nuclear research lab or a missile testing site—just somebody's patio in Maryland. How are you going to explain this one scientifically?"

Scully sighed. "Mulder, right now I'm not even sure how *you're* going to try to explain it."

"Not necessarily by the book," he said. "First off, I'm going to see if there was any connection between Nancy Scheck and Emil Gregory and Oscar McCarron. Or nuclear weapons testing. Or even the Manhattan Project. It could be anything."

"She wasn't old enough to be involved with the Manhattan Project in World War II," Scully pointed out. "But she did work for the Department of Energy, an important person, according to the dossier. But that's a tenuous link at best. Tens of thousands of people work for the DOE."

"We'll see," Mulder said.

The coroner had already wrapped up the charred body in a black plastic bag. Mulder went cautiously over to the coroner and motioned him to unzip the body bag so he could study again what remained of Nancy Scheck.

"Weirdest thing I ever saw," the coroner said. He sneezed, then sniffled loudly, and muttered something about his allergies. "Never seen a death like it. Isn't just a burn victim. Can't imagine offhand what could blaze that hot. I'm going to have to dig in my reference books."

"An atomic bomb could have done it," Mulder said.

The coroner gave a nervous chuckle, then sneezed again. "Yeah, good one. Everybody has an A-bomb go off in their backyard. Must have been some argument with the neighbors! Unfortunately, no witnesses reported seeing any mushroom cloud."

"I'd agree that it sounds preposterous—" Mulder said, "if this weren't the third identical death we've seen in the last week or so. One in California, one in New Mexico, now here."

"You've encountered this before?" the coroner perked up, then rubbed his reddened eyes. "What on earth caused it?"

Mulder shook his head and allowed the stocky man to zip the bag shut again. "Right now, sir, I'm as stumped as you are."

A man in a general's uniform stood just outside the glass patio doors speaking with two policemen, who took copious notes in their small notebooks. The general was short, broad shouldered, with close-cropped black hair and a swarthy complexion. He appeared deeply distraught. The scene instantly captured Mulder's curiosity.

"I wonder who that is," Mulder said.

"I heard one of the policemen talking," Scully said. "I think he's the one who discovered the body last night."

Mulder hurried over, eager to pick up on what the general was saying and ask a few questions of his own.

"The concrete was still hot when I got here," the general said, "so it couldn't have been long. The back fence was smoldering. The paint was bubbling, and *the smell* ..." He shook his head. "The smell!" The general turned to look at Mulder, standing beside them, but didn't seem to register his presence. "Listen to me—I've seen combat before, and I've witnessed some accidents, awful ones... even helped recover the bodies from a plane crash once, so I've gotten a glimpse of death and how hideous it can be. But... in her own backyard...."

Mulder finally managed to read the general's engraved plastic name tag. "Excuse me, General Bradoukis—did you work with Ms. Scheck?"

The general seemed too much in shock to challenge Mulder's right to ask questions here. "Yes... yes, I did."

"And why were you here last night?"

The general stiffened, his eyebrows drawing together. "We were going to have dinner. Steaks on the grill." His wide face flushed somewhat. "Our relationship was not a complete secret, though we were discreet."

Mulder nodded, understanding the general's extra measure of distress. "One thing, General—I understand that Ms. Scheck was a fairly important person in the Department of Energy, but I'm not sure I know which program she ran. Can you tell me?"

Bradoukis averted his black eyes. The two policemen fidgeted, as if uncertain whether they should chase away this new investigator, or let the FBI agent ask their questions for them.

"Our... uh, Nancy's work wasn't much talked about."

Mulder felt a quick thrill of excitement, a new trail to follow. "You mean it was one of those black programs, an unofficially funded project?"

The general cut him off. "The media call them 'black programs.' There's no official designation for them. Sometimes it's necessary to get certain things done by nontraditional means."

Mulder leaned forward like a hawk swooping in for the kill. Everything depended on the next question. "And was Ms. Scheck's work connected with a project called Bright Anvil?"

The general reared back like a startled cobra. "I'm not at liberty to discuss that project, especially not here in an un-secured area."

Mulder gave him an understanding smile. "That won't be necessary, General." Bradoukis's reaction had been answer enough. The sound Mulder heard in his mind was the clicking of puzzle pieces falling together. Things were still not entirely in place, but at least they were arranged into some semblance of order. He decided his best tactic would be to leave the distraught man alone for now.

"That's all for me, General. Sorry to have bothered you during this time of great distress. I take it you have an office in the Pentagon? I may visit you in person if I have further questions."

Bradoukis nodded without enthusiasm, and Mulder stepped over to the pool, looking down at the blistered, blackened paint that had once been sky blue around the concrete rim. Half of the water had boiled away in the flash of intense heat, leaving the pool warm and murky with brownish scum collecting in the corners.

The fireball must have been utterly intense—yet it had not set Nancy Scheck's home on fire, nor had it spread to the neighbors' yards. Almost as if it had been *directed*, intentionally focused in a specific area. Several people on the block claimed to have seen a brief, bright flash, but had not bothered to investigate. Neighbors kept to themselves in these upscale areas.

Mulder's usually sharp eye glimpsed an object floating near the bottom of the pool, a small glass bottle that drifted about as if only partially waterlogged. He searched until he found a skimmer net and yanked it off its hooks near the patio doors. The flash of heat had twisted the handle, but the net remained surprisingly serviceable.

Mulder took it to the edge of the pool and dipped the skimmer deep, swirling it around until he succeeded in netting the dark object and fishing it out. Water trickled off the edges of the skimmer.

"I found something here," he called. He lifted free a small vial that contained a black substance. Some pool water had leaked into the vial, but just a few drops. The detective and Scully came over to look. Mulder held the vial between his thumb and forefinger, tilting it to the light. The object seemed very odd to him, and by its sheer oddness he decided it must be important to this case.

He offered it to Scully, and she took it, shaking it to disturb the contents. "I can't say what it is," she said. "Some sort of black powder or ash, but how did it get to the bottom of the pool? Do you think it has something to do with her death?"

"Only one way to find out, Scully," Mulder said. He turned to the homicide detective in charge. "We have exceptional analytical facilities at the FBI crime lab. I'd like to take this back with us to run a full analysis. We'll copy you on all reports, of course."

"Sure," the detective said. "One less thing for my people to do." He shook his head. "I've never seen anything like this case, and I think it might be beyond me. Do me a favor and figure this one out." With one hand, the detective brushed his hair back. "Sheesh, give me a stabbing or a drive-by shooting any old day."

TWENTY

FBI Headquarters
Washington, D.C.
Tuesday, 3:10 p.m.

After so much time on the road, Scully found it comforting to be working in her own lab for a change, even on as gruesome a subject as this.

She basked in the solitude and familiar surroundings. She knew where all her equipment was located. She knew whom to call for help or a technical consultation. She knew specialists whose skills she respected in case she needed an unbiased person to verify what she found.

The FBI crime lab was the most sophisticated facility of its type in the world. It was filled with an oddball assortment of experts in the forensic sciences whose unusual interests or skills had proven time and again to be the keys to solving bizarre and subtle cases: a woman genetically predisposed to detect the bitter-almond odor of cyanide that many people could not smell, a man whose interest in tropical fish had led him to identify a mysterious poison as a common aquarium algicide after all other methods of analysis had failed, another man who specialized in identifying the type of photocopying machine that had made a particular copy.

In their numerous X-Files cases, Scully and Mulder had stretched the capabilities and imagination of the FBI crime lab more often than most other field agents.

The labyrinth of labs lay on an interconnecting grid supposedly designed to facilitate cooperation between separate units, each with its own jurisdiction and expertise: Chemistry/Toxicology, DNA Analysis, Firearms and Toolmarks, Hairs and Fibers, Explosives, Special Photography, Video Enhancement, Polygraph, Latent Fingerprints, Materials Analysis, and other more esoteric specialties. After her years with the Bureau, Scully still didn't understand the actual organization of the units. But she did know where to find what she needed.

Scully entered the main lab of Berlina Lu Kwok, in the receiving area for the Biological Analysis Unit, where specimens were given their first cursory inspection before being subjected to other, more specific analysis routines. When she stepped through the door, the stench that assailed Scully's nostrils was far worse than usual, and the heavyset Asian lab director was in a foul mood.

"Agent Scully!" Lu Kwok said, her sharp voice slicing through the air, as if Scully were somehow to blame for the smell. "Is it too much to ask? Don't we have clear-cut and regularly posted procedures for submittal of samples? Isn't it as easy to do it the *right* way as to do it the *wrong* way?"

Scully clutched a packaged sample of the black residue Mulder had retrieved from Nancy Scheck's backyard pool; she shifted it to her side in embarrassment. "I thought I'd fill out the forms in person—"

But the lab director was determined to finish her lecture, sniffing the sour air with disgust. "The FBI has every right to expect that local law-enforcement officials will make some sort of *attempt* to follow simple procedures, isn't that correct? It helps us all out, doesn't it?"

She waved an old memo in her hand, squeezing the edge with fingers powerful enough to snap wooden boards. Without pausing for a response, she began to read from it. "'All submissions should be addressed to the FBI's Evidence Control Center. Bullets should be sent by the United Parcel Service, registered mail, or private courier. Human organs should be *packed in dry ice* and sent in plastic or glass containers via UPS, private express mail, or special delivery.'" Berlina fluttered the memo in the air to fan away the stink.

"Now some podunk town in South Dakota has sent me a victim's liver for toxicology analysis. They stuffed it in a zipper-lock plastic bag labeled with handwriting on masking tape—and they didn't even pay for overnight express." She snorted. "Economy two-day!" The memo floated to the floor as Berlina tossed it away. "It'll take us weeks to get rid of the smell around here, and we probably won't be able to find out much from the tissue, either."

Scully swallowed, hoping to deflate the other woman's tirade. "If I submit a sample using proper procedures, may I request a favor?"

Berlina Lu Kwok fixed her with a glare from narrowed almond eyes. Finally she laughed with a sound like a storm breaking. "Sorry, Agent Scully. Of course. Is this for your DOE exec murder? We've been told to give you high priority."

Scully nodded and handed over the sample, along with a note Mulder had written expressing his suspicions as to the identity of the substance. Lu Kwok scanned the words. "Interesting," she said. "We can check out Agent Mulder's speculations fairly quickly—but if it doesn't match, we could be weeks identifying the substance."

"Do what you can," Scully said. "And thanks. Meanwhile, I've got two autopsies to perform."

"Lucky you," the Asian woman said, scrutinizing the powdery sample. Still muttering to herself about the stench in her lab, she turned and walked back toward her equipment.

\\\\\\\\\\\\\\\\\\\

It was a messy and exhausting afternoon.

Scully completed the autopsy on Nancy Scheck, as well as the old rancher, Oscar McCarron, who had been packaged and shipped to her lab—following proper procedures, she hoped—thanks to the helpful people at the White Sands Missile Range. Scully suspected they simply wanted to wash their hands of the matter and let her deal with the questions.

But now that she had studied three victims who had apparently died by the same impossible method, she still had no guess as to what the lethal weapon could have been.

It was easy enough to list the cause of death as "sudden and violent exposure to extreme levels of heat and radiation," but that still didn't explain the source of the exposure. Was it a new kind of death beam, or a pint-sized nuclear warhead?

From her own undergrad classes, Scully knew the physics of nuclear explosions well enough to understand that a warhead could not fit inside, say, a small package bomb or a hand grenade. Critical mass and initiators and shielding required a certain amount of bulk—and such things left debris, none of which had been found at any of the three death scenes. The only piece of trace evidence she had in her possession was the vial of strange black ash Mulder had fished out of Nancy Scheck's swimming pool.

Letting other FBI staffers clean up the autopsy arena and take care of the two burned bodies, Scully moved to her smaller lab, analyzing another portion of the ash. In a sterile metal tray she carefully used a long, narrow-bladed scalpel to spread the greasy, powdery residue flat so she could inspect it. Using a magnifying glass, Scully studied the substance, probing delicately to inspect its material properties.

She took out her tape recorder, inserted a new microcassette, and pushed the RECORD button, letting the voice-activated microphone deal with the long pauses in her narration. She stated the case number, the evidence sample number, and then began her off-the-cuff report.

"The black substance found in the Scheck swimming pool appears to be fine and flaky, partially granular, composed of two distinct components. The bulk of the material is soft, ashen, and appears to be composed of some sort of organic residue. The powder is mostly dry now, although I believe it may have been contaminated by chlorine and other chemicals from the pool. We may have to compensate for those impurities in our final analysis.

"The second component in the mixture is grainy and…" She isolated a couple of the grains with the point of her scalpel and pressed down on one, hearing it pop and skitter to the side of the metal pan. "And it's hard and crystalline, like some sort of rock or… sand. Yes, it reminds me of dark sand."

Scully scooped a small amount of the black substance onto her scalpel blade, spread it on a clean microscope slide, and then slid it under her stereomicroscope. She hunched over the eyepieces and adjusted the focusing knob, studying the substance under low and then higher powers of magnification, using a polarizing filter, prodding with the tip of her scalpel to distribute the tiny pieces more evenly.

"Yes, it does seem to be sand," she said out of the corner of her mouth, hoping the microcassette recorder would pick up her words. She frowned. "One possibility could be that the ash was scraped up from a beach somewhere, and the sand was inadvertently combined with the primary material. This is strictly conjecture, however." She would have to await the results of Berlina Lu Kwok's chemical tests on both components.

On a hunch, but already dreading the answer, Scully went to an equipment cabinet and retrieved a rarely used device she had requested for the autopsies that afternoon—a small alpha counter, a delicate radiation meter that could pick up residual radioactivity beyond the usual background counts.

Scully pointed the sensitive end of the alpha counter, playing the silvery rectangular foil cells over the smear of black ash and sand she had placed in the metal tray. With the detector's output linked to her own computer and running obscure alpha-counting software, she was able to trace a nuclear spectrum. Considering the circumstances of the overall case, she was not surprised to find residual radioactivity in the sample. Fortunately, the specimen was small enough that the dose could not harm her. Its spectrum was slanted to the high end, enough that it was obviously something of unusual origin, something resulting from a high-energy burst.

The software did most of the work for her, comparing the nuclear spectrum with thousands of others it kept in its database, searching for a match it could offset.

Scully heard a knock on the door, and Berlina Lu Kwok came in, holding a folder full of papers. "Here are your results—special delivery for you, Agent Scully."

"Already?" Scully said, surprised.

"What, you wanted me to pack it in dry ice and send it UPS?" Lu Kwok laughed. "I just wanted to get a breath of fresh air from my lab." Scully gratefully took the folder, but before she could say anything else, the Asian woman spun about and marched back down the hall.

Scully looked at the folder, then sat down next to her computer to wait for results from the radiation scan. To her surprise she discovered that during the brief interruption, the computer had already found a match. Before she opened up Berlina Lu Kwok's Biological Analysis report, Scully studied the nuclear spectrum results.

The error bars were large, but due to the unique half-life properties and the unusual nuclear cross section of the sample, its best guess was that this black residue had been exposed to high levels of ionizing radiation between forty and fifty years earlier.

Scully swallowed, deeply troubled. Reluctantly, she flipped open the Biological Analysis folder, already suspecting the answer. The only way Lu Kwok could have identified the substance so quickly was if Mulder's lead had indeed proven accurate.

She scanned through the analysis summary, paging to the end, interested only in the final result for now. Her stomach sank.

The black powdery sample was indeed *human ash*, almost completely incinerated—exposed to high radiation something like forty years ago, mixed with a black grainy sand.

Radioactive human ash four decades old, found at the death site of a victim who had been obliterated by a similar atomic flash.

Sand.

Ash.

Radiation.

Scully sat back in her seat and tapped her fingernails on the folder. Then she picked up the phone. She couldn't put it off any longer. Mulder was going to love this.

TWENTY-ONE

Kamida Imports
Tuesday, 12:03 p.m.

When Miriel Bremen went into the upper floors of the Honolulu high-rise business complex, she felt intimidated. Outside, traffic streamed by in the sunshine, flowing along the seaside, while Diamond Head reared its blocky spire like a sentinel over the waves and the sunbathers. Inside the Kamida Imports office building, Miriel felt as if she had stepped into another world.

She had no interest in the balmy climate, the lovely ocean, the beaches crowded with fishbelly-white American vacationers or swarms of Japanese tourists who stayed up shopping all hours of the night. Her message to Kamida was far too grim to worry about vacation trivialities.

Miriel waited for the receptionist to announce her arrival. She paced in the waiting room, too distracted to read any of the colorful but banal magazines spread out on the low tables.

Miriel had known Ryan Kamida for a year now. She had met him immediately after the personal epiphany that had turned her against nuclear weapons work and transformed her into a vehement protester. The extravagant funding Kamida donated anonymously from the coffers of his successful imports business had kept Stop Nuclear Madness! free of financial worries during its one-year existence.

From their first meeting, Miriel realized that she and the scarred blind man had so many things in common that it was almost eerie. Even so, his very presence sent a thrill of fear through her. She found it hard to understand Kamida's offhanded acceptance of his tragic fate, but he swept such thoughts away with his strange charisma.

As a respected researcher at the Teller Nuclear Research Facility, Miriel Bremen used to feel comfortable meeting many important people, holding her own in any conversation. After she had learned of Ryan Kamida's power and his generosity—and his personal drive—Miriel had promised herself that she would not return to ask more of her benefactor except in the direst emergency.

Circumstances now warranted such a visit.

For months, Kamida claimed to have been making preparations, forming contingency plans, and speaking of desperate measures, as if he could see the future. She did not relish the thought of taking him at his word again. Now she had no choice.

Ryan Kamida emerged from his back offices, led by the receptionist. He maintained only the slightest touch on her shoulder, simply an acknowledgment that he required her to guide him. His eyes were milky, the color of a half-cooked egg; his face was scarred, like the bust of a very proud man done by a poorly trained sculptor.

Kamida cocked his head to one side, as if he could detect Miriel's presence from the faint perfume in the deodorant soap she had used, or perhaps the sound of her breathing. Miriel wondered if he had more abilities than he let on.

"Mr. Kamida," she said, standing up. "Ryan, it's good of you to see me on such short notice."

He came forward, homing in on the sound of her voice and releasing his grip on the receptionist, who took his dismissal as a matter of course. She returned to her station just as the phone began ringing.

"Miriel Bremen, what a pleasant surprise. It's kind of you to come all the way to the Islands just to see me. I was about to go to my greenhouse for lunch. Would you join me?"

"Yes, I would," she said. "We have certain things to discuss."

"I'm sorry to hear that," he said. "Or am I pleased?"

"No, you're sorry," she said. "Definitely sorry."

Kamida turned to the receptionist. "Shiela, please have a nice lunch for two brought into the greenhouse. Ms. Bremen and I would like to relax for some private conversation."

An enormous room on the top floor had been converted into a lush tropical forest. Skylights funneled sunshine through the ceiling, while an entire wall of plate glass allowed daylight to stream in from the side. Mist generators kept the air humid and warm, smelling of damp organic greenery and compost and plant food. Ferns and flowers grew in a wild profusion—not potted or ordered in any way, simply a riot like the dense rainforest one might find on an isolated Pacific island. Several captive birds flitted about in the treetops.

Ryan Kamida walked in without guidance, weaving through plant-bordered aisles. He held both hands out in front of him like a preacher giving a benediction, going out of his way to brush against the vegetation. He bent over to smell flowers in bloom, inhaling deeply, closing his eyes.

A mist generator spat a rain of spray near him, and he adjusted his hand to touch it, letting the cool droplets form in a glittering sheen on his rough, blistered skin.

"This is my place, Miriel," he said, "a special place where I can enjoy the sound of growing leaves and inhale the smell of fresh earth and blooming flowers. The experience is quite remarkable, from my humble point of view. I'm almost saddened to think of the profusion of windows that your other senses open for you, so that this full and focused experience is denied you."

Though blind, Kamida led the way to a small table nestled in the midst of the dense foliage. He pulled out an ornate metal chair and waited for her to sit down, then pushed her closer to the round glass table. Its size was perfect for two people to dine in the seclusion of a jungle paradise.

"I'm afraid the news is bad, Ryan," she blurted, before he even took his seat.

He felt his way to the opposite chair and sat in it, pulling it snugly up to the table. Before she could continue, though, an employee of Kamida Imports hurried in, bearing two large salads and a plate of fresh pineapple, papaya, and mango slices. She fell silent, looking at him while waiting for the employee to leave.

Ryan Kamida had used his handicap to great advantage, Miriel thought, as if he were watched over by angels. Blessed in business, he had developed his exotic imports company into a wealthy corporation.

Though she had met him accidentally that first time in Nagasaki, Miriel held the uncertain suspicion that he had set up the entire encounter himself, and that events were even now playing out exactly the way he wished.

Now she shuddered and hunched her shoulders as she bent over her salad.

When she had turned away from her mentor, Emil Gregory, Miriel had looked to Kamida as a new supporter, someone who shared her vehement beliefs. Ryan Kamida knew an enormous amount about nuclear weapons testing, about the entire military industry. He was someone to whom she could divulge the dire designs concocted by unenlightened weapons scientists, the blueprints passed along to her through a few sympathetic workers who remained at the Teller Nuclear Research Facility.

Miriel had told Kamida everything, without qualms about spilling classified information. She had vowed to devote her life to the cause; she now responded to a higher calling, not one decreed by the military industrial complex (who had, after all, caused so many of the problems in the first place). She knew what she was doing was right.

Now the time had come for their work to reach its climax. If they could not stop Bright Anvil soon, then all their efforts were simply smoke blown in the eyes of people who wanted to believe.

Kamida ate his salad, waiting for her to continue. His stiff, grave demeanor, however, led her to suspect that he had already guessed what she was about to say.

"Everything I've tried has failed," Miriel said, picking at the greens on her plate and then spearing a chunk of pineapple with her fork. "The government has a momentum behind what it decides to do—and no one, not me, not you, can stop it once it's started."

"I take it that means that no one has heard our complaints."

"Oh, they've heard them all right," Miriel said. "They just don't pay attention to them, any more than they would bother with a gnat buzzing in their ears."

The blind man sighed, and his scarred face fell. Miriel continued, speaking louder, leaning across the table toward him—though he could hear her perfectly well. "The Bright Anvil test is going ahead, even without Dr. Gregory. Somewhere out in the Marshall Islands, on an abandoned atoll."

Ryan Kamida sat up sharply. "Of course," he said. "Enika Atoll. That's where it will take place."

"How do you know?" she asked.

"How could it not take place there?" he practically shouted. With a sharp gesture Kamida knocked his salad plate sideways, hurling it off the table. It smashed on the floor of the greenhouse. The noise was thunderous, but he paid no attention to it. He turned and fixed his milky gaze on Miriel Bremen.

"Our greatest nightmares are about to unfold," he said.

TWENTY-TWO

Kamida Residence
Waikiki, Oahu
Tuesday, 11:17 p.m.

A blind man has no need for lights. Alone in his spacious house, Ryan Kamida sat in the darkened living room lit only by outside reflections from the moon shining over the placid ocean and a warm glow from the glassed-in fire-place behind him.

As the evening chill deepened, he had started a fire, carefully stacking small sticks of cedar and pine, aromatic wood that made pleasant-smelling smoke as it burned. Kamida enjoyed the incense of the smoke, the velvet touch of ra-diating heat. He listened to the snapping and popping as the flames gnawed the wood. It sounded like... whispers.

He opened the glass patio door so that the ocean breeze could drift in. In the distance he could hear the gentle pounding of the surf, the steady drone of traffic on the coast highway below. Tourists coming to Oahu from time zones all across the world never slept, but busied themselves constantly, sightseeing, shopping, eating.

Kamida sank back in his chair, scarred hands gripping the rough-textured arms. Waiting. The cushions conformed themselves perfectly to his body. Year after year, the weight of his body had shaped them during this nightly ritual.

The voices would come soon. He both dreaded and anticipated them. This time, though, the dread felt stronger, more ominous. The situation had changed, worsened. He knew it and so did the spirits. A chill swept down his spine, and he turned his head to the left toward the fireplace, feeling the heat spill on his cheek.

Bright Anvil. Enika Atoll.

Kamida was more distressed than Miriel Bremen could ever know. He showed it in a different way. Regardless of the circumstances, though, he could not be with her this evening. He had obligations—to the ghosts.

The spectral voices demanded their share of his time, and he had no choice but to give it. He could not complain. Ryan Kamida was alive, and they were not.

Outside, ocean waves continued to roll in, sounding like pebbles rolling in a steel drum.

On a table next to his chair, close at hand, he kept his collection of tiny soapstone sculptures. He amused himself by picking the small objects up, using the sensitive ends of his fingers to explore the details of their carving. His hands were scarred but his mind was sharp. The intricate yet minuscule figures of dolphins, elephants, dragons, and ancient gods fascinated him.

Heard through the open porch high up on the hillside, the soughing sound of waves became muted. Kamida sensed a static building in the room, a charge in the atmosphere. His hand tightened around the sculpture in his hands, an image of Pele, the female fire god from many Island mythologies.

Then the voices buzzed in his ears, speaking his old, never-forgotten language. The phantoms were clustered all around him.

Kamida had never seen the spectral images directly, though he visualized their distinct shadows in his mind, echoes transmitted by senses other than his fried optic nerves. He knew the spirits bore faces frozen in a shriek at the moment of nuclear conflagration as their every cell became an inferno. He couldn't see the harsh white light that bathed his own face as the spectres swirled in front of him, filling his home with blazing, cold light.

But the apparitions did not harm him. These spirits were not here to destroy. Not tonight. They had another purpose altogether; they had a use for Ryan Kamida, the sole survivor of his people.

The faces separated from the glowing, swirling cloud one by one and floated in front of him, giving him their names, telling of who they had been, describing their lives' triumphs and losses, their stolen dreams.

His people's lives had been cut short, but the phantasms had to relive every moment, force Kamida to witness it all. He *remembered* for them.

Though Enika Atoll had never been heavily populated, the mass of demanding ghosts seemed never-ending as they forced him to think of their lives, their names, one by one… as they had done every night for the past forty years.

Ryan Kamida sat in his chair, helpless, gripping the small figurine of Pele. He had no choice but to listen.

TWENTY-THREE

The Pentagon
Arlington, Virginia
Wednesday, 10:09 a.m.

Following a hunch, Mulder went to see Nancy Scheck's "friend," Brigadier General Matthew Bradoukis, in his Pentagon office.

Mulder thought that he might have to talk fast to bluff his way into a brief meeting with the general, now that the man had had additional time to recover from his shock. Mulder frequently found that people avoided him because of his knack for asking constant, uncomfortable questions. This morning he suspected Bradoukis would be in a convenient meeting or otherwise occupied away from his desk.

Surprisingly, though, the general's administrative assistant spoke quickly into the intercom, then motioned for Mulder to make his way back to the large office Matthew Bradoukis called his own.

The brigadier general stood from behind his desk and extended a beefy hand. His wide, swarthy face looked as if it had been drained of self confidence—a quality few generals lacked. He squeezed his generous lips together as if to squash his nervousness.

"I've been expecting you, Agent Mulder." The general's red-rimmed eyes gave him the appearance of not having slept well in recent nights.

"Frankly, I was afraid you would refuse to see me, General," Mulder said. "Some people don't want me looking into certain aspects of this murder investigation."

"On the contrary." Bradoukis sat back down and folded his hands together, staring at his wooden desktop before raising his eyes to meet Mulder's gaze. "You might not believe this, but I've been looking forward to your arrival— you in particular. I was upset with you yesterday and your embarrassing questions, wondering what the hell an FBI guy was doing at Nancy's house. But then I looked into your background with the Bureau. I've got my sources, and I've learned a bit about your reputation, read summaries of some of the cases you've investigated. I've even met your Assistant Director Skinner. He seems a good enough man. He speaks highly of you, though guardedly."

Mulder was surprised by the information. He and the assistant director had been at odds many times, because of Mulder's insistence on exotic explanations that Skinner didn't want to hear. Mulder couldn't tell which side Skinner was on.

"If you know my reputation, sir, then I'm doubly surprised that you agreed to see me," Mulder said. "I'd have thought my track record would scare you off."

Bradoukis squeezed his hands together as if he wanted to pop all the knuckles simultaneously. His face took on a deeply serious expression. "Agent Mulder, we both know something highly unusual is going on here. I can't say this in any official capacity—but I think your... willingness to accept certain things that others might find laughable could be a great advantage in this investigation."

That got Mulder's attention. "Are you aware that there were two other bodies found, apparently killed by identical means? One was a weapons designer at the Teller Nuclear Research Facility. The other was an old rancher down at the White Sands Missile Range near the Trinity Test Site. The bodies were found in a condition very similar to Nancy Scheck's."

The general pulled open a side drawer and removed a folder. He tossed it across the desk to Mulder. "And two more," Bradoukis said, "two you don't even know about. A pair of missileers at Vandenberg Air Force Base on the central coast of California."

Surprised, Mulder opened the file. Glossy photographs revealed the now-familiar details of the hideously burned corpses. Mulder noted the control racks on the walls, the outdated buttons and oscilloscopes, the plastic knobs blackened and folded in on themselves in what appeared to be a cramped room somewhere, a sealed chamber that had contained the deadly blast.

"Where was this taken?" he asked.

"Deep underground in a buried Minuteman III missile control bunker. Those bunkers are the safest possible construction, which is why we place them so far below the surface where they can survive a nuclear attack. The bunker is hardened against a direct strike. Only those two men were down there. For security reasons no one else is allowed. We have complete records. The elevator was not used."

He tapped the gruesome pictures. "But still… *something came in and obliterated them.*"

Leaving Mulder to stare at the photos, the general leaned back in his chair. "I know one of your operating theories in this investigation is that some new weapon under development at the Teller Nuclear Research Facility was triggered in Dr. Gregory's lab, and that another such device went off at the White Sands Missile Range.

"Such an explanation, however, fails to take into account these two young officers in the missile control bunker, or—" he stopped and swallowed as his voice caught, "or Nancy at her home."

Mulder thought to himself that Scully could probably come up with some far-fetched but scientifically plausible scenario to convince herself that there was still a rational explanation.

General Bradoukis continued. "Believe me when I tell you this, Agent Mulder. I work at the highest levels of the Defense Department. I manage some of those invisible programs you mentioned yesterday. I can tell you with utter certainty that no weapon we are currently considering or have under development can do this."

"So it doesn't have anything to do with Bright Anvil?" Mulder asked, fishing.

"Not in the sense you mean," the general answered, then took a deep breath. "Ah, would you like some coffee, Agent Mulder? I can have some sent right in. Perhaps a pastry?"

But Mulder would not allow himself to be distracted. "What are you saying, 'not in the sense you mean'?" he asked. "How are these events connected with Bright Anvil? Is there a spinoff of the weapons project?"

The general sighed. "Nancy Scheck was in charge of the Department of Energy oversight on the entire Bright Anvil Project, and Dr. Gregory was the lead scientist. The test of the prototype device will be conducted on a small atoll in the Marshall Islands, sometime in the next few days."

Mulder nodded. He had surmised or known all of this information already.

"The Marshall Islands," Bradoukis repeated. "Bear that in mind, because it's important."

"How so?" Mulder asked.

"Immediately before those two missileers were killed," the general said, his voice laden with import, "they had gone through a routine missile-targeting exercise. Since the U.S. and Russia are no longer enemies, we're not allowed to aim our Minutemen toward them, not even for practice." He shrugged. "Diplomatic constraints. For the exercises we choose random coordinates around the world."

"So how does that tie in?" Mulder said.

The general jabbed a finger at him. "For that morning's exercises, their missile was targeted toward a small atoll out in the Marshall Islands—the same atoll where the Bright Anvil test is scheduled."

Mulder stared at the general. "What are you suggesting?"

"I leave that for you, Agent Mulder. You're reputed to have an active imagination. But you may think of some possibilities I couldn't suggest to my superiors because I'd be laughed out of my rank."

Mulder frowned, looking down at the gruesome photos again.

"One other piece of information," Bradoukis said. "The atoll—Enika Atoll—has a bit of history of its own. Another hydrogen bomb test took place there in the fifties—Sawtooth—though you won't find it in any record book. It took place shortly after we went through such enormous efforts to clear those islanders off Bikini Atoll. In this instance, the scientists and the military were in a hurry, and the island wasn't as thoroughly checked as it should have been. There is some evidence that an entire group of indigenous islanders was obliterated."

"My God," Mulder whispered. Sick horror prevented him from saying anything else. The general waited, and finally Mulder said, "And you think this... this tragedy on the atoll forty years ago has something to do with these unexplained deaths today?"

Suddenly he remembered the results of Scully's analysis on the residue in the vial found in Scheck's swimming pool. Human ash, four decades old, and grainy sand. Coral sand.

The general unfolded his hands again and stared at his fingernails. "I suggested no such thing, Agent Mulder. You are, of course, free to think what you choose."

Mulder closed the folder and tucked the photographs into his briefcase before the general could take them back. "Why are you telling me all this?" he asked. "Do you want to make sure someone is caught for Nancy Scheck's death?"

Bradoukis looked deeply saddened. "That is part of it," he said, "but also, I fear for my own safety."

"Your safety? Why?"

"Nancy was the DOE liaison for the Bright Anvil Project. I am the Department of Defense liaison. I'm afraid I might be next on the list. I'm trying to hide—I've been staying in a different hotel every night. I haven't been home in days. Though I doubt such measures will do any good against a force that can swoop down through bedrock and attack two soldiers in an underground missile control bunker."

"I don't suppose you have any suggestions on how we might stop this... thing?" Mulder asked.

The general flushed again. "Bright Anvil itself seems to be the link. Whatever has been awakened, or at least triggered into violent action, came about because of this impending test. There's no telling how long the force has been around, but it became active only recently."

Mulder jumped in. "Then whatever is going to happen, whatever event these killings are building toward, will probably occur out in the Marshall Islands. That's the only place we can be sure of." He plunged ahead without thinking. "General, my partner and I need to be there. I need to be at the site to see what's happening."

"Very well," Bradoukis said, "my feeling is that these attacks could be attempts to prevent the test from occurring, with some of these other murders perhaps being incidental... or it might be the force, whatever it is, lashing out at other targets and then returning its focus toward the main goal. Since the Bright Anvil test is already in place, I believe that is where the next strike will occur. But I'm taking no chances that it won't come after me as a loose end."

"If Bright Anvil is such a highly classified test," Mulder said, "how will my partner and I get out there?"

The general stood up. "I'll make a few phone calls. I'll even call Assistant Director Skinner, if need be. Just be ready to get on a plane. We don't have any time to lose."

TWENTY-FOUR

Mulder's Apartment
Alexandria, Virginia
Wednesday, 6:04 p.m.

With a suitcase lying open on his bed, Mulder dashed back and forth, packing everything he would need for a vacation in the Pacific islands.

Because of the amount of traveling he did for the Bureau, he kept his toiletries already packed in a small dopp bag in the suitcase; all that remained was to throw in sufficient changes of clothes.

Smiling, he carefully removed three garish Hawaiian floral shirts from his bottom drawer and placed them in the suitcase. "Never thought I'd be called on to wear these for business purposes," he said.

Then he packed a pair of swim trunks; he hadn't had a chance for a long, strenuous swim down at the FBI Headquarters pool for more than two weeks, and he looked forward to the opportunity. Unless he exercised regularly, he couldn't keep his body—or his mind—at peak performance.

He stashed a battered paperback of an old Philip K. Dick novel he had been reading and a fresh bag of sunflower seeds in his luggage as well. It would be a long flight across country to the Alameda Naval Air Station, near San Francisco, where their transport plane would depart for Hawaii; then a smaller plane would take them out to Enika Atoll along with the rest of the Bright Anvil team.

In his living room the television blared loud enough for him to hear. He had seen those old movies a dozen times already, but he simply couldn't pass up the "Monster Madness Marathon" of black-and-white films from the fifties, each showing a giant lizard or insect or prehistoric beast that had somehow been awakened or mutated by ill considered atomic tests. The movies were morality plays, chastising the hubris of science while celebrating the genius of the human spirit. Right now, giant ants had infested the cement-lined drainage canals of Los Angeles, much to the consternation of James Whitmore and James Arness.

In his kitchenette several small white cartons of carry-out Chinese food sat on the table, flaps open, next to two paper plates. He'd already heaped one of the plates with steamed rice, kung-pao chicken, and dry-fried string beans with pork. As he packed, he shuttled back and forth between his suitcase, the television, and the kitchenette, grabbing a few bites to eat.

With his mouth full of garlicky string beans, Mulder heard a sharp rap on his apartment door. "Mulder, it's me."

He swallowed quickly before rushing to let his partner in. Dressed in professional, though comfortable, traveling clothes, Scully carried a bulging duffel bag. "I'm all packed. I'm even ten minutes early," she said. "That gives you plenty of time to tell me what's going on."

He gestured her inside. "I've arranged for two tickets to paradise. You and I are going off to the South Seas."

"Your message told me that much," she said. "But what for?"

"We've got a pair of front row seats at the Bright Anvil test. I asked for season tickets to the New York Knicks, but this was the best they could do."

She blinked her blue eyes in astonishment. "The test? How did you manage that? I thought—"

"Connections in certain high places," he said. "One very frightened brigadier general who was willing to go out on a limb for us. I picked up some Chinese carry-out for a quick dinner before we head to the airport." He indicated the extra paper plate. "I got an order of kung-pao chicken—your favorite."

Scully set her duffel bag on an empty chair and looked at him curiously. "Mulder, I don't recall that we've ever gone out for Chinese food together. How would you know what my favorite meal is?"

He favored her with a reproachful look. "Now what kind of FBI agent would I be if I couldn't find out a simple thing like that?"

She pulled up a chair at the small dining room table and scooped out some of the chicken chunks laden with red Szechuan peppers. Taking an appreciative whiff of the aromatic spices, she snagged the extra pair of disposable chopsticks next to the napkins.

Mulder came out of the bedroom, lugging his packed suitcase. He secured the locks, then placed his briefcase on top of it. "I think I told you once, Scully, that if you stuck with me I'd show you exciting lands and exotic places."

Scully shot him a wry look. "You mean like an island about to be flattened by a secret nuclear weapons test?"

Mulder placed his hands in front of him. "I was thinking more of coral reefs, blue lagoons, the warm Pacific sun."

"I thought it was hurricane season out there," she said. "That's what Bear Dooley and the Bright Anvil scientists kept studying on their weather maps."

Mulder sat across from her to eat his food, lukewarm by now. "I'm trying to be optimistic," he said. "Besides General Bradoukis said something about us going on a 'three-hour tour.'"

Scully finished her meal and checked her watch; She reached inside her jacket to pull out the two airplane tickets. "I picked these up from the Bureau travel office on my way over, as you requested," she said. "Our plane leaves Dulles in about ninety minutes."

Mulder tossed their plates in the wastepaper basket, looked at the remains of the Chinese food in the white boxes, and without a thought dumped the remnants of all three dishes together into a single container. Scully watched him in astonishment. "It's good for breakfast that way," he said. "Add a few scrambled eggs—delicious." He placed the container in the refrigerator.

Scully picked up her duffel. "Sometimes you really are spooky, Mulder."

After switching off the television—the giant ants had been superseded by a gargantuan tarantula out in the Mojave Desert—he followed her out.

He noticed that the metal "2" of the "42" on his apartment number had fallen off again onto the floor. "Just a second, Scully," he said, picking up the number.

He ran back in to the junk drawer in his kitchen, where he pulled out a screwdriver. "This number keeps coming off. Very suspicious, don't you think?" He checked it for listening devices on the inside, rubbing his finger along the curve of the thin metal. At one time he'd been certain someone was spying on him, so he had removed every detachable thing in his apartment including the numbers on his door. Now the "2" refused to stay where it belonged.

"Mulder, you're paranoid," Scully said with wry amusement.

"Only because everybody's out to get me," he said.

After reassuring himself that the metal number was clean, he used a spare set of screws to attach it tightly to the door. "Okay. Now we can go. I hope you brought your suntan lotion."

She shouldered her duffel. "Yeah, and my lead umbrella for the radioactive fallout."

TWENTY-FIVE

Enika Atoll
Marshall Islands, Western Pacific
Wednesday (across the International Date Line), 11:01 a.m.

The atoll had recovered remarkably well in forty years. The low, flat island, little more than a massive coral reef with a shallow dusting of topsoil, was once again burgeoning with lush tropical vegetation, breadfruit and coconut palms, vines, ferns, tall grasses, and low taro plants and yams. The reefs and lagoons swarmed with fish; birds and butterflies thronged in the foliage above.

When Captain Robert Ives had left here four decades earlier, he had been a young seaman recruit who had barely learned to shut up and do as he was told. The spectacular Sawtooth nuclear test had been the most awe-inspiring sight his slate-gray eyes had ever witnessed. It had reduced Enika Atoll to a hot, blasted scab, its entire surface sterilized, its coral outcroppings sheared off in the boiling froth of the sea, vegetation crisped, wildlife exterminated.

The intricate network of reefs extended far past the portion of the atoll that actually rose above the surface, in many places lurking only a few feet beneath the water. With amazing recuperative powers, Nature had reclaimed the territory that humans had so swiftly and violently snatched away. Once again, Enika Atoll looked like an isolated island paradise, pristine and uninhabited.

At least Captain Ives hoped it was uninhabited this time.

On the shore of the atoll, sheltered behind the rugged coral rocks that formed the highest point of the island, Bear Dooley and his team of researchers used sailors and Navy engineers to help make preparations for their secret test.

A small landing strip had been cleared along a straight stretch of beach. Bulldozers, off-loaded from the *Dallas*; plowed through the jungle, scratching narrow access roads from the sheltered control bunker to the lagoon on the far side of the atoll, where the Bright Anvil device would be set up and detonated.

Trapped aboard drab gray ships for so much of their tours of duty, the Navy engineers enjoyed the work, riding heavy machinery and knocking down palms and breadfruit trees, leaving naked paths of churned-up coral dirt like raw wounds on the island.

They needed to construct a bunker to house the controls that would run the small warhead detonation. Because the control bunker would be so close to the detonation, it had to be incredibly sturdy. Captain Ives instructed his engineers in an old trick.

After laying down electrical troughs and pathways to a backup generator in a shielded substation next to the blockhouse, the engineers stacked bags of concrete mix and sand around and around a bowed wooden frame in a shrinking circle, creating a structure that looked like an igloo or beehive. Then, with pumps hooked up to clunky ship firehoses thrust into the ocean, the engineers sprayed the outside of the structure, soaking the sand and concrete mixture. After a day or two of hardening in the warm Pacific sunshine, the bunker would be virtually indestructible.

NASA engineers had used the same technique at Cape Canaveral to erect protective bunkers for control systems and observers close to the early rocket launchpads. Such bunkers had withstood the explosive stresses inflicted upon them—and in fact had survived so well that the Corps of Engineers had abandoned the old structures in place out in the Florida swamps because they could think of no way to demolish them!

As the sandbags dried against the reinforced parabolic frames that held them in place, Bear Dooley supervised the installation of his test equipment inside. The broad-shouldered deputy project leader helped install the control racks that had been carefully crated and stored down in the Navy destroyer's hold. He was willing to roll up his sleeves and get his hands dirty to speed up the work.

The bearlike man sweated in the tropical heat, but he refused to wear cooler clothes, treating his flannel shirt and denim pants as required dress. Dooley listened in on the shortwave radio to regular weather updates for the Marshall Islands. Every time the announcement tracked the approaching tropical depression, now nearly a full-fledged hurricane, he grew ecstatic.

"It's coming," Dooley had said to Ives the last time he received such news. "And we've got a lot of work to do. Timing is crucial."

Ives let the man have his way. He had his orders, after all.

He didn't think Bear Dooley was even aware of the previous H-bomb test that had taken place in this same area. Dooley didn't seem the type of man who wasted time studying history or worrying where things came from.

For the rest of his life, though, Robert Ives would be haunted by the knowledge that they had made a horrendous, tragic mistake here at Enika Atoll.

By now Ives had seen the Bikini Islanders repatriated, after the government had stripped the topsoil from their blasted island and replaced it with fresh dirt, replanted the jungles, restocked the lagoons.

The mysterious islanders on Enika, though, had not enjoyed such solicitous treatment.

Sawtooth had been one of the first H-bomb tests, kept quiet at the time, just in case the device failed. During those Cold War years the U.S. couldn't afford to let anyone see that its thermonuclear devices didn't function well enough to keep the Commies awake at night.

But Sawtooth had worked—spectacularly well.

It was in the days before spy satellites, and the perimeter of the atoll had been ringed with gunboats, calmly confident that they wouldn't be seen. These waters were infrequently traveled, and the captains of the cutters had instructions to chase off any fishing boats or sightseers. Even so, the anticipated flash of the Sawtooth device was visible for hundreds of miles across the open water, rising like the brief glow of sunrise in the wrong part of the sky at the wrong time of day.

Everyone had been so naive then. They had assumed that the small, barely charted atoll was uninhabited, and so the scientists and sailors had not looked too hard to find any indigenous islanders.

The Navy expected to find no one on Enika, and so no one had ever really searched.

During preparations for the Sawtooth explosion, the engineers and sailors had not bothered to report signs of encampments, tools, nets found washed up on the rough reefs. They dismissed the junk as old artifacts and looked no farther, because they didn't particularly want to find anything else. Such information might cause problems.

The perimeter boats had all pulled back and the main destroyer, the USS *Yorktown*, had moved out to a safe distance beyond the reef line. Those lucky few observers who had been assigned welding glasses stood on deck to see, while the others promised not to open their eyes at the critical point. Still, when the Sawtooth detonation went off, several dozen crewmen suffered from brief flash blindness.

Ives remembered. Some things were impossible to forget. The roar sounded like the world cracking open, and the mushroom cloud rose like Old Faithful geyser in Yellowstone—only about a million times as big—sucking up vaporized coral and sand along with an immense volume of seawater. The incandescent plume towered like an awesome thunderhead heralding Armageddon. The shockwaves slamming through the water caused the *Yorktown* to rock like a toy boat in a bathtub....

Several hours later, after it was all over and the sea had grown calm again, initial inspection teams from the Yorktown suited up and took their small cutters back to the atoll to plant radiation counters and to map out the effects of the fallout. A seaplane drifted overhead, taking photographs for before-and-after images to determine how the atoll's topography had changed.

Being one of the most junior seamen, Ives had been "volunteered" to be part of a small group on a perimeter cruise around Enika to study any anomalies in the aftermath. What they found proved even more astonishing than the detonation itself.

Standing out in open water more than two miles from shore was a boy about ten years old. All alone. Just waiting.

At first young Robert Ives had quailed in terror, thinking that some vengeful angel had come to punish them for what they had done to the pristine island.

The boy appeared to be standing right on the surface of the water like a marker buoy, aimless and lost. Only later did the rescuers remember that the low reefs stretched in a labyrinth just beneath the surface far from the actual island. The boy had somehow walked on them, following the submerged reefs away from what had once been his island.

They hauled him aboard. He was speechless and shaking, horribly burned, his face puckered, his eyes sunken and sightless from the glare of the blast. Most of his hair had been scalded away, and his skin was an angry red, as if he had been boiled alive. The agony of the boy's burns must have been even greater due to the constant lapping of saltwater that drenched him.

No one expected him to live when they brought him back to the *Yorktown*. In fact, the ship's doctor seemed ambivalent, as if he didn't *want* the boy to survive, because he would be blind and hideously scarred for his entire life… and because the very existence of a survivor was an accusing finger, proof that natives had lived on Enika Atoll. An entire tribe had been wiped out in the Sawtooth blast, save for this sole survivor.

But to everyone's surprise the boy had recovered, despite his festering injuries. He remained utterly silent for days, and then finally croaked out words in a strange language that none of the crew could understand.

The data obtained from the Sawtooth test were filed away with the Defense Department, and the Navy placed the entire event under the strictest order of silence.

When the *Yorktown* finally docked again at Pearl Harbor, the horribly burned boy was taken quietly to an orphanage in Honolulu. Official records showed that he was the only survivor of a terrible house fire that had killed the rest of his family. Having no other living relatives, the boy was raised as a ward of the state, although he received a generous (and mysterious) allowance from the Navy.

Ives had never seen or heard of the boy again, and he wondered how the poor victim had managed to fare in life. He had not thought of the boy in some time, but now all those memories had come flooding back with nightmare intensity—ever since Ives received his orders to take the *Dallas* out to the Marshall Islands.

Captain Robert Ives had hoped never to see Enika Atoll again. But now he had returned… for yet another secret nuclear test.

TWENTY-SIX

Alameda Naval Air Station
Alameda, California
Thursday, 2:22 p.m.

Mulder and Scully arrived in the San Francisco Bay Area, red-eyed and exhausted from the non-stop travel, knowing they had a much longer trip still in front of them.

Mulder rented a car, and they drove toward the Alameda Naval Air Station, then spent the better part of an hour at the gates showing their paperwork, answering questions, and finally arguing with a stoic military policeman who made repeated phone calls to his superiors inside.

"I'm sorry, sir," the MP came back for the third time, "but your story doesn't check out. We have no C-5 transport plane leaving for Hawaii this afternoon. We have no record of you coming, or of your place on board such a plane, if one existed."

Mulder wearily pulled out the paperwork again. "This was signed by Brigadier General Bradoukis, directly from the Pentagon. It's regarding a classified project out in the Marshall Islands. I know you don't have the authorization sitting on the top of your desk, because they wouldn't make it so blatant—but my partner and I are authorized to go on this flight."

"I'm sorry, sir, but there *is* no flight," the MP insisted.

Mulder heaved an angry sigh, and Scully squeezed his arm to calm him. Before he could speak again, Scully broke in, "Why don't you talk to your superior again, Sergeant," she said, "and this time mention two words to him: *Bright Anvil.* We'll wait here until you come back."

The MP retreated to his guard shack wearing a skeptical expression and shaking his head. Mulder turned to Scully in surprise. She smiled at him. "You rarely accomplish anything by getting angry."

Mulder sighed, then forced a chuckle. "Sometimes I wonder if I ever accomplish anything—period."

Within minutes, the MP came back and opened the gate for them. He offered no apologies or any explanations whatsoever. He simply handed them a map of the base and directed them where to go.

"Wasn't your father stationed here at one time?" Mulder asked. He knew how deeply the death of her father had affected her.

"Briefly," Scully said, "around the time I started college at Berkeley." Mulder looked over at her. "I didn't know you went to Berkeley. As an undergrad?"

"Just for my first year."

"Ah," he said and waited for her to continue. But Scully seemed uncomfortable about the subject, so he didn't press her for details.

Exactly where the guard had directed them, they found the whale-sized C-5 transport. Small hydraulic vehicles hauled cargo, stuffing crates into the swollen, olive-colored belly of the plane.

Forklifts raised pallets filled with the final loads of equipment, while civilian passengers and military personnel climbed aboard, using a set of steps that had been hastily rolled up against the plane.

"See, Scully," he said, "they have no C-5 transport plane here on the base, and nothing whatsoever is scheduled to depart." He opened his hands in a helpless gesture. "But then, a tiny aircraft like this must get misplaced all the time."

Scully, who had long ago accepted the secrecy and the denials surrounding classified projects, made no rejoinder. Carrying his suitcase and briefcase, Mulder bounded up the metal steps that led up to the aircraft passenger compartment. "I hope we can get ourselves a window seat," he said. "Nonsmoking."

"I think I'll try to take a nap on the way," Scully answered.

Inside the no-frills transport plane, Mulder looked around the sharply shadowed interior, which was lit from behind and below by the open cargo doors. Other passengers—naval officers and enlisted men, as well as half a dozen nonmilitary types—milled about, finding places to sit.

Mulder saw no baggage compartment, only webbing stretched across the metal wall panels, where others had already secured their personal baggage. He went back to tuck his suitcase into an empty spot, then returned to take Scully's bag, securing it next to his own. He kept his briefcase with him so that the two of them could look over notes and discuss the case during the long flight to Pearl Harbor; after a brief stopover, they would change to a much smaller plane and head out to the Western Pacific.

When he returned to Scully, she reached inside her purse and handed him a few sticks of chewing gum. "What, is my breath bad?" he asked.

"No, but you'll need it for the flight. I've flown on these Navy planes before with my father. They're not pressurized. Chewing the gum helps equalize the pressure in your ears—trust me, it's my professional medical advice."

Mulder took the sticks skeptically and slipped them into his shirt pocket. "I knew we were getting a bargain ticket, but I at least expected some oxygen."

"Blame it on military budget cuts," Scully said.

Mulder and Scully searched for a comfortable seat, but all the chairs were hard and stiff-backed. They both buckled in. Finally, the cargo doors closed, and muffled shouts from inside announced the plane's readiness for departure. One of the sailors pulled the thick passenger compartment doors shut as the engines began to power up with a loud vibrating hum.

"I guess they don't have a first-class section," Mulder said.

He turned around in his seat and recognized some of the civilians already buckled into their seats, scientists and technicians he had seen at the Teller Nuclear Research Facility. Mulder smiled and waved as a bespectacled redhead blushed and tried to look small. "Hello, Victor! Victor Ogilvy—fancy meeting you here."

Victor stammered, "Uh, hello Mr. Agent... I didn't know the FBI was scheduled to watch the test preparations."

"Well, Victor, I told you I was going to make some phone calls," he said feeling like a bully, and somewhat embarrassed at it.

Scully leaned closer to Mulder. "We've got a long flight ahead of us, so let's be friends. We're all here with our country's best interests at heart, right Victor?"

The young redheaded technician nodded vigorously.

"Right, Mulder?" She elbowed him in the ribs.

"Of course, Scully."

The hulking transport plane began to lurch along, lumbering into motion like a behemoth, as aerodynamic as a bumblebee, but orders of magnitude louder. The C-5 accelerated down the runway and gracefully lifted off, hauling its enormous bulk into the air with a roar of jet engines. Before long, the aircraft had gained altitude, circled over the hills east of Oakland, and then headed straight out to sea.

Mulder turned back to look at Victor Ogilvy. "So, Victor, why don't we make this into a regular tropical vacation with sun and surf and sparkling beaches?"

Victor looked surprised. "No such luck, Agent Mulder. Did you both bring along your rain slickers?"

"What for?" Scully asked.

Victor blinked again behind his round eyeglasses. "And I thought you two had done your homework. Maybe you didn't get as many details as you thought.

"The Bright Anvil test—we're heading directly into a hurricane."

TWENTY-SEVEN

Airborne over the Western Pacific
Friday, 8:07 a.m.

Leaving Pearl Harbor behind on a perfect picture-postcard morning, Scully, Mulder, and the entire crew took off in a smaller plane headed out over the monotonously blue, sun-dappled Pacific. While dawn chased them over the horizon, Scully looked out the window, her mind drifting far away.

"So," Mulder said, slouched next to her in a cramped seat, getting comfortable, "did you enjoy our all-expense-paid government trip to Hawaii? A fine day of boredom and waiting, but you can't beat the hospitality."

Scully squirmed in her seat, then pulled down the window shade; she couldn't find a comfortable position as easily as Mulder seemed to. "It was everything I've come to expect from a government-paid vacation."

The plane rattled and hummed as it roared over the ocean. Clouds began to gather in the western skies, and Scully had no doubt that as they proceeded the weather would get worse. Mulder didn't seem the least bit concerned for the safety or integrity of the plane—but then traveling never seemed to bother her partner.

Curious to see how the rest of the passengers were holding up, Scully turned around to look at the small cliques scattered throughout the plane. Victor Ogilvy and some of the other Teller Nuclear Research Facility technicians had gathered in the back and were poring over their notebooks and technical papers.

The Navy troops all sat by themselves, talking loudly, completely relaxed as the plane rattled along. Scully knew from her own background that sailors traveled often on a moment's notice. Thrust together with new groups of seamen, either with plenty in common or few shared interests, they found ways to amuse themselves without difficulty.

Mulder had fixed his attention on two young black men diligently playing a game of Stratego with a travel-sized board that used small magnetic pieces. He watched them for a few moments, then looked away with a troubled expression on his face.

Another group of sailors surrounded a broad-shouldered seaman with close-cropped dark hair and a Hispanic cast to his features; he sat intently reading the latest enormous technothriller by Tom Clancy. The three spectators loudly discussed the merits of Clancy's work and the excitement of being a CIA agent like Jack Ryan. Scully wondered if they had the same view of the exciting life FBI field agents led.

Then the three began discussing the classified information woven through Clancy's work. "Man, if you or I wrote something like that, we'd be thrown in the brig so fast we wouldn't have time to cash our royalty checks!" said one.

"Yeah, but you and I have security clearances—key point. We've signed papers that hold us accountable. Clancy doesn't have any access to that sort of stuff, so who's gonna believe him?"

"Are you telling me he's making it up? He's got a damn fine imagination, if that's the case. Look at all those details."

The critic shrugged. "Doesn't matter. He's just an insurance agent, man. He has no 'implied credibility' like we do, because we work directly with the material."

"I still think somebody should break Clancy's knuckles for letting out classified secrets like that."

"No way," said the third. "He wouldn't be able to write no more books if he had broken knuckles."

"Well, break his kneecaps then."

Paying absolutely no attention to the three spectators hovering over his shoulders and speaking around his ears, the reader casually flipped a page and continued with the chapter.

The aircraft struck heavy turbulence, jouncing the passengers from side to side in their seats. Scully gripped the arms of her chair. Mulder nonchalantly chose that moment to lean forward against the bucking carnival ride and pull out his briefcase. He snapped it open on his lap, ransacking it for papers.

"Let's go over a few things while we have time," he said.

The jostling became so rough that the two sailors playing Stratego finally gave up, brushed their magnetic pieces into the carrying case, and clicked their board shut.

With her teeth rattling together, Scully couldn't imagine how her partner could think clearly—but then she thought Mulder might be doing this to keep her mind off the turbulence. She silently thanked him for it.

"Just what do you expect is going to happen out there on the island, Mulder?" she asked.

"General Bradoukis seems to think that whoever or whatever has been killing people around the country is going to try once more to stop the Bright Anvil test. This is its last chance."

"You keep saying 'it,' Mulder," she pointed out.

He shrugged. "Fill in your own pronoun of choice." He hauled out a map of the Pacific Ocean with the island chains highlighted. He unfolded it on top of the other papers in his briefcase. "If you're still worried about that hurricane, I've got some good news for you."

Scully, still holding tightly to the arms of her seat, looked questioningly at him. The plane continued to rattle. "Right now I'm worried about this plane staying aloft—but if the best you've got is good news about the hurricane, I'd be happy to hear it."

With a mischievous gleam in his eye, Mulder said, "The good part is that we aren't flying into a hurricane after all."

The brief wash of relief surprised Scully, but she knew him better than that. "What do you mean? Have the weather conditions changed? Has it been downgraded to a tropical storm?"

"Not at all," he said, pointing to the map. "Look here, we're heading out to the Western Pacific. Meteorologically speaking, storm systems in this region aren't called hurricanes. They are technically designated *typhoons*. No other real difference, though. Same damage potential."

"What a relief," Scully said. "Aren't semantics wonderful?"

Mulder studied the tiny flyspeck dots out in the vast blue areas of the map. He circled the specks with his finger. "I wonder why they're going way out here. The Marshall Islands are a U.S. protectorate, so I'm sure that has something to do with it. Could it be just to intercept the storm?"

Scully perked up, glad to have a subject on which she could discourse. She forced herself to ignore the rocking turbulence as she added her knowledge to the discussion. "It probably has more to do with the track record of nuclear testing out here. The Marshall Islands chain is where most of the U.S. bomb blasts took place between 1946 and 1963—hydrogen bombs and cobalt bombs, thermonuclear devices, everything too big to be detonated in Nevada. In fact, between 1947 and 1959, forty-two nuclear devices were set off on these islands alone."

Scully was amazed at how these facts came back to her, as if she were reading from a textbook, or a political diatribe, in her mind. "The entire atoll of Eniwetok was like a hopscotch ground. Test detonations stepped from one clump of islets to another, vaporizing one lump of coral, then the next. The inhabitants were evacuated, promised adequate compensation, but Uncle Sam never really came through for them. In all fairness, nobody knew exactly what they were doing at the time, not even the weapons scientists. They made mistakes—some bombs fizzled, others produced a much higher yield than expected. It still amazes me how they just… played with all that destructive potential."

Mulder raised his eyebrows. "You're sounding pretty passionate there. Is this a particular interest of yours?"

She looked at him, feeling her walls go up. "Used to be."

"So what happened?" he asked. "With the testing, I mean."

"All atmospheric testing of atomic explosives ceased in 1963 with the Nuclear Test Ban Treaty. But by that time over five hundred nuclear weapons had already been detonated by the United States and various other countries."

"Five hundred!" Mulder said. "*Above*ground? You're kidding, right?"

"Have you ever known me to exaggerate, Mulder?"

"Not you, Scully," he said. "Not you."

The plane suddenly lost altitude for a terrifying two seconds, then caught itself. The sailors in back whooped and cheered, applauding the pilot. Scully hoped the pilot wasn't about to leave the controls to come back and take a bow.

She sucked in a deep breath. Mulder waited for her to continue. "There's even been an off-and-on moratorium of underground testing," she said. "The French and Chinese and others have continued their work, although they deny it. The French recently resumed testing out on some other islands near Tahiti—and sparked a firestorm of public opinion against them. With seismic surveillance and high-resolution spy satellites, however, it's awfully difficult to mask the signature of a nuclear explosion."

"Ten to one this approaching storm isn't just a coincidence then."

"I think that's a safe bet, Mulder."

TWENTY-EIGHT

Enika Atoll
Marshall Islands
Friday, 2:11 p.m.

The weather grew even rougher, tossing and batting the small plane about as they neared the isolated atoll. Scully found herself wishing for the stability of the immense C-5 transport plane they had flown from Alameda to Pearl Harbor.

The plane circled around to attempt a second approach to the small island's crude landing strip. "They haven't told us to assume crash positions yet. That's a good sign," Mulder said.

Wind shear knocked the aircraft sideways, and even the seasoned sailors embarrassed themselves with nervous gasps.

"Mulder, I didn't realize you were such an optimist," Scully said, but he had distracted her just long enough for the plane to make its final run. Through the rain-splattered window, Scully could make out a distressingly short landing strip that had been bulldozed along a flat stretch of beach.

She squeezed her eyes shut. When the plane finally bounced and rattled to a rough halt, the passengers burst into a round of spontaneous applause.

Sailors already on the island rushed forward, heads bent, to put chock blocks behind the plane's wheels. The side door swung downward on reinforced cables, converting into creaking stairs. The cargo section was pried open from below, and a group of Navy men swarmed out of storm shelters, where they had hidden from the freshening wind and the approaching typhoon. In a well-choreographed routine, they began unloading the remaining crates.

Scully walked on rubbery legs to the airplane stairs, but declined Mulder's help getting down. She stepped onto the hard-packed coral gravel of the "runway," holding the side of the staircase for support, and stared around at the flat, foliage-covered island, the reef outcroppings of coral, and the clean sand.

The bowl of sky surrounding them was a muddy gray-green from the approaching hurricane. The air itself held an ominous crackle of ozone mixed with the salty iodine smell of the sea. The wind gusted in short sharp breezes from random directions.

Scully's light auburn hair blew around her face. Mulder stood beside her, his maroon striped tie flapping up and off to the side of his suit jacket. "See, what did I tell you? Two tickets to paradise."

Scully glanced sidelong at him. "You must have gotten the bargain tickets."

In a sheltered bay farther down the rough shoreline, Scully spotted a small enclosed boat, the captain's gig, used to shuttle crew and materials from the Navy destroyer anchored in view farther out beyond the treacherous reef line. Scully recognized the type of ship, a Spruance-class destroyer, a powerful vessel primarily designed for rapid response and antisubmarine warfare.

"The Navy must be taking this test seriously," she said. "That kind of destroyer isn't something to mess with."

A trim young officer came directly toward them. He had short-cropped sandy hair and eyeglasses with Photogray lenses that had managed to turn dark even in the gloomy light of the rising storm. "You must be the FBI agents," he said and stood rigidly in front of them. "I'm Commander Lee Klantze, the *Dallas's* XO. I'll take you to meet Captain Ives. He's here to supervise the last-minute preparations, though I believe he intends to observe the test from the *Dallas*."

Klantze turned about and then set out along the beach, taking long strides. "We received word from Brigadier General Bradoukis in Washington that you'd be VIP guests, though we're all a bit mystified as to your purpose here. This isn't an FBI matter, as far as I can see."

"It dovetails with a pending investigation," Scully said.

"Oh," Klantze answered.

You could always tell a career military officer, Scully thought with a smile. They *knew* when to stop asking questions.

"We'll take you to the Bright Anvil control blockhouse and let you get on with whatever you need to do. Just try to stay out of the way of the test preparations. Plenty of delicate instruments. Careless hands can cause more damage than the hurricane will… and Mr. Dooley tends to over-react in his protectiveness."

"Thank you," Scully said. She and Mulder followed the executive officer as he struck out toward where coral outcroppings formed the edge of a sheltered lagoon. A high-rising bluff shielded a small cluster of buildings from the opposite side of the island, the direction from which the storm approached.

Mulder turned back and pointed to the cargo being unloaded from the plane. "Our suitcases and bags are over there," he said.

Klantze didn't seem worried. "They'll be taken back to the *Dallas*. We've got staterooms for you to sleep in, although everybody is pretty much going to be working round the clock until the blast goes off. The test is set for oh five-fifteen tomorrow."

"That soon?" Mulder said.

"No choice," Klantze answered as he continued briskly along the beach. Sand whipped around them, stinging their faces. "That's when the storm is due to make landfall."

Scully wanted to ask why they were so concerned about making their test coincide with the hurricane, but she decided to save those questions for Bear Dooley or someone else in charge.

The executive officer led them to an unusual, igloo-shaped control bunker, to which all sorts of generators, air-conditioning units, and satellite dishes had been linked.

"Look, it's the Enika Holiday Inn," Mulder said.

Scully could see many figures moving in and out of the blockhouse, checking generators and electrical connections. A man in a white captain's uniform saw them and waved Klantze over.

Upon approaching the captain, Scully automatically took out her ID, and Mulder did the same. The captain dutifully accepted the FBI badges and studied them, genuinely paying attention before handing them back. "Thank you, Agents Scully and Mulder. I'm Captain Robert Ives," he said, "of the USS *Dallas*."

Scully reached out to shake his hand, surprising herself with a sudden rush of memory. "Yes, Captain. I believe I met you once, when I was much younger, at a Naval reception in Norfolk, Virginia. My father was Captain Bill Scully."

"Bill Scully!" Ives looked astonished. "Why, yes, I knew him. He was a good man. How is he these days?"

Scully swallowed. "He passed away recently," she said.

"I'm sorry." Ives stiffened. "When you're at sea so much of the year, a lot of personal news vanishes before you get a chance to pay attention to it. I'm really sorry."

"Thank you," she said.

Ives cleared his throat as if to banish his discomfort. "Now then, I understand that you're here in regards to something unusual about the Bright Anvil test? General Bradoukis was reluctant to give details. Is there something we should know about?"

Scully looked to Mulder, giving him a chance to recount the odd connections and the strange theory he had proposed. But he just looked back at her, apparently not wanting to bring up the possibilities.

"We're here to observe and gather a few details," she said. "As you may already be aware, there have been several unusual deaths of individuals involved with Bright Anvil."

Just then Bear Dooley came blustering out of the low door in the beehive blockhouse, blinking his eyes into the wind that tossed his long hair and white-shot beard into wild disarray around his face. His eyes fixed on the two FBI agents, and his expression gathered a fury equal to the storm brewing around them. He had obviously been stewing about their arrival for some time.

"I don't know how you two got the authorization to come to this restricted testing site, Agents Mulder and Scully. I can't question it, and I can't send you home right now—unfortunately." He planted his hands on his hips. "But get this straight from the start: stay out of the way. We're busy. We have a test to run and a device to set off early tomorrow morning. I do not have time to babysit a couple of feds in suits."

"I haven't needed a babysitter in at least four years," Mulder said dryly.

"Mr. Dooley," Scully said, "we apologize for coming out here in the middle of your preparations. Trust me, I would've preferred to have all our questions answered back in California. But since you and your entire team disappeared without notifying us, we had no other choice."

Mulder said, "And you didn't exactly overwhelm me with information when I did talk to you."

"Whatever," Dooley said in complete dismissal. He turned away from them and extended a flapping sheaf of papers toward Captain Ives. "New weather projection from overhead satellite feeds," he said. "Exactly as expected. The hurricane center is only two hundred miles out, and it's big enough that there's no chance it'll miss us. No chance at all. We're in luck—Enika is going to be whomped tomorrow morning."

"We're in luck?" Mulder repeated.

Ives scanned the satellite projection and nodded. "I concur."

"Wait a minute," Mulder said. "First things first. Where is this nuclear device? Is it in one of the crates we flew out with, or is it already set up here in the control bunker—what?"

Dooley gave a scornful laugh. "Agent Mulder, you're not impressing me with your expertise. The blockhouse is supposed to be *sheltered* from a nuclear blast. Therefore, the device isn't going to be set up anywhere nearby. Logical?"

The chance to explain things seemed to calm the big engineer. "The Bright Anvil device is on the other side of the island in a lagoon. It came out on the *Dallas* from San Diego. Everything is all set up and ready to go, waiting for the storm."

Scully spoke up. "You've gone to a lot of trouble to make all your preparations in secret—and you've taken great pains to select a deserted island that just happens to be directly in the path of a major storm system. Most people with any sense would head away from a typhoon. Do you have any idea how much damage a storm like that can cause?"

Dooley narrowed his eyes as if about to scold her for her stupidity, then he let out a gruff laugh. "*Of course* I do, Agent Scully. Think about it. With all the damage the hurricane is going to cause when it strikes this island... who's going to notice a little more destruction?"

TWENTY-NINE

Enika Atoll
Friday, 5:18 p.m.

The pressure of the approaching storm felt like a psychological vise tightening down on Scully. Standing on the rough beach, she looked up at the blackening clouds at sunset, the eerie color of the storm-sickened sky.

Outside the control blockhouse, Bear Dooley, Mulder, and Captain Ives stood together in a moment of relative quiet. In the shallow lagoon in front of the blockhouse, the captain's gig bobbed, waiting for passengers. Shielded by the hummock of reefs, the water was glassy smooth in contrast to the roiling choppiness farther out to sea. A line of breakers foamed around coral outcroppings submerged just beneath the angry waters.

One of the Bright Anvil technicians came running out of the blockhouse as Scully walked up to them. The technician looked flustered. "Captain Ives, sir, there's an emergency message for you over the secure telephone line!" Ives looked down at the walkie-talkie on his hip, disconcerted that the message hadn't come to him directly. "It's from the *Dallas*, sir," the technician continued. "The communications officer on the bridge wants to speak with you."

Mulder looked directly at Bear Dooley as he spoke. "Oh boy, maybe they're canceling the test."

"Fat chance," Dooley said.

"I'm sure they'd issue you a raincheck."

Dooley just shook his head, as if wondering where Mulder got his sense of humor.

All five of them ducked inside the claustrophobic blockhouse. Scully was glad to get out of the damp wind that made her skin crawl. Captain Ives went to a phone box that had been bolted to a plywood wall inside the armored bunker.

"Ives here," he said, then listened intently. The expression on his face quickly became grim. "What are they doing out in this weather?" He waited for an answer. "Okay, how far away?" He waited again. "And we're the only ones within range?" He scowled. "Hold on."

He put his hand to the headset and looked at Dooley. "We've just received a distress call—a fishing boat out of Hawaii, Japanese registry. They're in trouble from the typhoon, and the *Dallas* is the only ship in the vicinity. It's a general mayday, but they're requesting an urgent rescue. We can't ignore it."

Dooley turned red with annoyance. "I thought you said this area was cleared. Everything around Enika was supposed to be free of shipping traffic!" He fumed. "And what are those idiots doing out in this weather anyway? It's crazy to go out in a hurricane."

"Sure is," Mulder said, under his breath.

Ives seemed to be fighting to keep his cool in front of Dooley. "Because your people needed to keep this test so *secret*, Mr. Dooley, we weren't allowed to send a fleet of patrol boats out to keep the waters clear. You didn't want anyone to notice the activity. We did our best, but something could easily have slipped through—as this fishing boat apparently has. It's a big ocean, after all."

Dooley heaved a huge sigh and stuffed his big-knuckled hands in his jeans pockets. "I think we should just leave them out there. Those bozos will only get what they deserve for setting out without checking the weather reports."

Ives had had enough of the discussion. "Mr. Dooley, it's the law of the sea to attempt a rescue whenever another vessel signals a distress. It's a law by which I live, and I have spent my entire career on ships. That doesn't change just because of your pet project."

"What are we going to do with the survivors once you take them aboard?" Dooley said. "You can't let them witness the test."

"We'll keep them belowdecks—if we succeed in rescuing anybody."

"But what if it's a spy ship?" Dooley said. "We might not be the only people with an idea like Bright Anvil, you know. Another country could have developed the same concept."

Scully tried not to laugh, but the bearlike physicist seemed completely serious in his suspicion.

"Yeah," Mulder said, "if those Japanese fishermen spies see too much of Bright Anvil, they'll start making inexpensive imitations, and you'll be able to buy your own warhead at the local electronics store."

Dooley glared at him, but didn't seem to know what to do with his own anger. "Well, Captain, at least find out who they are and what the hell they're doing out here. These aren't good fishing waters."

With a sigh, Captain Ives put the telephone to his mouth again. "What's the name of the ship?" he said. "Find out their registry." As he waited for an answer, suddenly Ives's face turned white. "*Fukuryu Maru*," he said. "*The Lucky Dragon?*"

Scully put a finger on her chin, thinking. "*Lucky Dragon*," she said. "That sounds familiar...."

Ives spoke into the phone. "Acknowledge their transmission—tell them we're coming to help. Prepare the *Dallas* for immediate departure." Ives hung up, then he looked at Scully, since she had been the only one to react to the name.

"You're thinking of another Japanese fishing boat with the same identification—the vessel that wandered too close to the Castle Bravo H-bomb detonation on Bikini in 1954. The crew received a huge dose of radiation—the incident caused quite an international scandal."

Mulder perked up. "And now a ship with the same name is straying close to this nuclear test? That can't be a coincidence."

Scully quickly interrupted his train of thought. "Oh no you don't, Mulder. Don't even suggest that this is some… ghost ship of irradiated Japanese fishermen coming back to stop the Bright Anvil test."

Mulder held up his hands helplessly. "I didn't suggest any such thing, Scully. I'd say you've got an overactive imagination." He frowned in feigned contemplation. "Interesting idea, though."

She turned to Ives. "Captain, I'd like to go with you out to that fishing boat." She looked at Mulder, asking with her eyes if he wanted to go along.

"No thanks," he said. "I'll stay on solid ground. I want to keep poking around here." Mulder turned to admonish her as she and Ives headed back out into the freshening wind. "Be sure to wear your life jacket."

Scully tried to stay out of the way on the bridge deck of the Navy destroyer.

Captain Ives directed the helmsman to begin accelerating away from Enika Atoll and into the storm-ragged water. The low coral island dropped away as the battleship left the labyrinth of whitecaps that marked treacherous underwater rocks. The *Dallas* headed out to sea, following their charts to where the hapless fishing boat had gotten itself into trouble.

Scully attempted to start a conversation several times, but couldn't find the words. Ives appeared deeply troubled and preoccupied, his salt-and-pepper eyebrows crinkled together, his lips pursed and pushing up his mustache. Finally, she blurted out, "Captain Ives, you looked shocked when you heard the name of the fishing boat. How much do you know about the *Lucky Dragon*? The original one, I mean."

He glanced over at her, setting his lips in a thin, pale line, then continued staring out the rain-streaked bridge windows of the *Dallas*, watching the rough seas. His Adam's apple bobbed up and down once.

"I was an observer at the Castle Bravo test, Agent Scully. I witnessed a lot of the island detonations during my tour of duty as a young sailor. I was a Navy man through and through, and a lot of us ambitious young recruits sort of 'collected' bomb blasts in those days. We tried to get ourselves assigned to ships that were going out to observe the nukes. We thought it was fun.

"It's an awe-inspiring sight, I can tell you that—but Castle Bravo was something else entirely, a new design, the biggest yield ever measured for a nuclear detonation. The Los Alamos scientists had calculated their cross sections wrong, or so I understand. The yield was supposed to be five megatons… instead, it turned out to be nearly fifteen. An explosion equivalent to fifteen million tons of TNT.

"That number doesn't really mean anything to the human imagination, until you try to compare it. The Little Boy bomb dropped on Hiroshima was about the same as twelve point five kilotons of TNT. That means the blast from Castle Bravo was *twelve hundred times* as powerful as Hiroshima. Twelve hundred Hiroshima bombs all going off at once!" He shook his head. "You should have seen it. The fireball itself was four miles in diameter."

Scully swallowed. "I'm not sure I would have wanted to. Wasn't it dangerous to be so close?"

Ives gave a far-off smile. "A lot of us got a significant dose. This horrendous whitish substance rained down from the sky—we found out later it was calcium precipitated from the vaporized coral thrown up into the air. Obviously, the danger zone from the blast turned out to be much larger than the safe area we had calculated."

Scully continued for him, "And this Japanese fishing boat happened to be in the wrong place at the wrong time."

"The *Lucky Dragon* wasn't so lucky after all," he said. With a crew of twenty-three, they were trolling more than eighty nautical miles east of Bikini—a good distance, but unfortunately it was directly downwind from the fallout.

"Two weeks later the fishing boat came into home port with a sick crew. The U.S. offered radiation specialists to help treat the men, but refused to give any specifics about the content in the fallout. Somebody was afraid the Soviets could derive a bomb recipe from it. One of the fishermen died of a secondary infection.

"Lewis Strauss, the chairman of the Atomic Energy Commission, brushed aside all responsibility and said that those fishermen had been well inside the danger zone—which I doubt very much—and that the *Lucky Dragon* was probably a Red spy ship anyway."

"A Red spy ship?" Scully's throat clenched in a combination of disbelief and anger. She could find nothing else to say.

"His exact words." Captain Ives gave her a hard look with his narrowed eyes. "And so I don't intend to let this other unlucky ship wallow out there at the mercy of deadly fallout, even if they manage to survive the typhoon."

"But as I understand it," Scully said, "there isn't supposed to be any fallout from this weapon. Bright Anvil is only a small-yield device, nothing that should extend far out into the ocean."

Ives looked at her skeptically. "Of course. And Castle Bravo was only supposed to be a third as strong as it turned out to be. I've learned *my* lesson, even if Mr. Dooley hasn't. This Bright Anvil device is brand new technology— and no matter how many computer simulations the scientists run, sometimes they plain forget about secondary effects. I don't want to take any chances."

Scully swallowed and finally asked, "You don't... you don't think there's anything supernatural about the appearance of this other *Lucky Dragon*, do you? At this specific time?"

Ives smiled faintly. "Supernatural? No, it's just a coincidence. For all I know, it could be a common name for Japanese fishing boats. But I'm still not going to let it happen again."

The skies darkened, and the clouds drew in around them like a noose. Before long, the *Dallas's* forward sensors detected the fishing boat and headed directly toward it. Scully could make out the dim shape bobbing on the rough seas. She didn't know what she expected to see. Perhaps something like the *Flying Dutchman*, a battered old hulk barely remaining afloat, a few ragged survivors clinging to the deck rails.

But the *Lucky Dragon* looked perfectly intact, not even struggling much against the waves. Nevertheless Captain Ives hove the Navy destroyer close to the fishing boat. Below, two Asian fishermen stood on deck, drenched with rain and spray, waving their arms for help, while another remained in the control house.

"The boat looks sturdy enough," Ives said. "We should be able to tow the vessel back to the atoll with us."

Scully quickly nodded, not knowing if he was asking her opinion or just stating a fact. Ives tossed her a rain slicker and summoned a team of his crewmen. "Come on, let's get those people on board to safety. Give them warm clothes and some soup."

On the fishing boat two other silhouettes appeared, shadowy figures behind the rain-streaked windows of the bridge deck. As the Navy rescuers crossed over to help the stranded fishermen aboard the *Dallas*, the other figures emerged. The first was a scarred, Hawaiian-looking man who moved carefully. Judging by his milky white eyes, Scully was sure he was blind. When the second shadowy figure reached for the wet ladder that hung down from the destroyer, Scully gasped with instant recognition.

Miriel Bremen climbed up into the rain.

THIRTY

Enika Atoll
Friday, 6:05 p.m.

Mulder looked up at the angry skies. Wistfully, he thought of how beautiful the Pacific sunset should have been. Instead, oily-gray clouds that bore an unnatural yellowish-green tint had spread like gangrene through the atmosphere.

He hummed the first few bars of "Stormy Weather," but didn't try to sing, since he wasn't sure of the words.

"So I'm stuck with you, Agent Mulder," Bear Dooley said, coming to stand next to him. "Did you stay behind because you have a technical interest in Bright Anvil, or because you're afraid of the storm?"

"Yes," Mulder answered cryptically. "That's absolutely right."

Dooley found the answer funny and let out a guffaw that could be heard even through the rising wind. "You're a pain in the butt, and your investigation is getting in the way of this test—but here you are, and I can't keep you from seeing with your own two eyes." He sighed. "And I guess that partial information is more damaging than no information at all. So I may as well fill you in."

Dooley shouted back at the other technicians just inside the bunker. "I'm going to hop on a Jeep and head off to the other side of the island to check on the device one last time." He turned to Mulder. "Come along, and you'll see what this is all about."

Victor Ogilvy came out of the control blockhouse, wiping a few spatters of light rain from his eyeglasses. "According to the reports, they checked it already, Bear," he said. "The team and I went out there first thing after the plane landed. It's all set."

"Fine," Dooley said, his hair and beard whipping around his face. "But I didn't ask if *you* checked it. I said *I* want to see for myself. I'd like a hands-on inspection, all right?"

"We need you here, Bear," Victor said, as if the storm and the impending test had brought him to the verge of panic.

"No you don't, dammit!" Dooley said. "I've got enough trouble babysitting this FBI agent. Can't I trust my own people to do their jobs?"

Victor looked stung, and Bear softened his voice. "Don't worry, Victor. I won't mess with the diagnostics, and you can handle the control blockhouse just fine by yourself. I'll be back in an hour or so. Agent Mulder and I have to get over there and back before full dark—and that'll be any time now, thanks to the typhoon."

Mulder followed Dooley over to a tarp-covered Jeep sitting in the open, but sheltered from the wind by the tan igloo of the blockhouse. Dooley yanked off the thick tarp and tossed it inside a storage shed. He swung into the driver's seat in a manner that reminded Mulder of a burly cowboy climbing onto a faithful horse.

The bearded engineer looked Mulder over as he settled into the passenger seat. Dooley looked warm and comfortable in his denim jacket and flannel shirt. Mulder would have thought the outfit completely inappropriate for a jungle-covered Pacific atoll, but the angry storm had sent a twisted chill through the air. "That fancy suit jacket of yours is going to get wet when the rain starts coming in hard," Dooley said.

Mulder brushed his hands down the fabric of his jacket and loosened his tie. "I've got some nice Hawaiian shirts in my suitcase on the ship, but I never got a chance to change."

Dooley pushed the starter button on the Jeep and roared off. The vehicle jounced along the rough dirt road through the jungle, rocking and twisting like a carnival ride with every rut and root it struck.

Mulder held on, unable to talk because his teeth clicked together every time he opened his mouth. Dooley gripped the steering wheel and kept driving. Watching the road ahead, Mulder finally shouted over the roar of the Jeep and the loud sigh of the wind.

Before long the jungle opened up, and Mulder could see the sprawling ocean again. Large swells rose and fell, creating a dizzying optical illusion, as if the landscape were on some sort of drunken turntable. In a shallow, semicircular lagoon eaten into the storm side of the atoll, rugged reefs sheltered the water from incoming waves. On a raft in the middle of the shallow pool Mulder saw a strange high-tech construction, like a Rube Goldberg machine, or something out of a Dr. Seuss book.

"There's the Bright Anvil device," Bear Dooley said. "Never been anything like it. Isn't it beautiful?"

It looked to Mulder as if an alien ship had crash-landed there. He decided that the most tactful thing would be to grunt noncommittally.

"See those supports, where it's suspended on the raft? We could have done the detonation underwater, but this way it's easier to hook up the diagnostics."

Long metal pipes and tubes stretched out like spiderwebs into the jungle alongside the rutted road. Substations sat at intersections of the conduits. Dooley pointed to them. "Those are light pipes, carrying optical fibers for our diagnostics. They'll be vaporized in the first second of the blast, but the data pulse will be about a millisecond ahead of the shockwave, so our information will manage to outrun the destruction. We'll get some good signals before the whole thing disintegrates, then some sexy analysis codes on the computers back in the blockhouse will crunch the numbers until they're meaningful. We've also got cameras mounted all around the jungle. No telling how many of them will survive both the blast and the typhoon, but the photos should be spectacular."

"A real Kodak moment," Mulder said.

"You bet."

Mulder stared at the contraption. "So you think nobody's going to notice your atomic blast because any destruction will be attributed to the storm? As I understand it, some of the H-bomb explosions literally erased small islands."

Dooley gestured with his hand, as if brushing aside Mulder's comment. "Yeah, but those were big mothers. Bright Anvil isn't nearly so large. In fact, its yield is only about the same as the Nagasaki bomb—really dinky, as far as warheads go."

Mulder thought about the two Japanese cities obliterated by the atomic bombs in World War II and silently questioned Bear Dooley's use of the word "dinky."

"Shoot," Dooley said, "today's ICBMs in their silos contain fifty or a hundred Nagasaki bombs in every single missile—multiple warheads that target independently. Sure, Fat Man and Little Boy were hefty for their time, back in the Jurassic Age, but that's nothing compared to what we can do now."

A splatter of warm rain rushed across the windshield. Mulder shielded his eyes to stare out at the rickety-looking structure on the raft. "Is there really a demand for small-yield nuclear weapons. For shoppers on a tight budget?"

Bear Dooley shook his head. "You're missing the point. Bright Anvil is *fallout free*, man! Some weird technology that Dr. Gregory thought of, burns up all the dangerous daughter products in prompt secondary reactions. I have no idea where he came up with the scheme, but it removes the big political stigma of using a nuclear weapon. Bright Anvil finally makes nuclear weapons *usable*, not just bluff cards."

Mulder looked over at him. "And that's a good thing?"

"Look, you don't want to drop a bomb on a city if it's going to take half a century before the radiation dies away. You'll get cancer deaths for decades and decades after the peace treaty is signed, and then what have you got?" He grinned and held up a finger. "With Bright Anvil, though, you can flatten an enemy city, then move in afterward, set up your headquarters, and reclaim territory. You can begin reparations immediately. It's sort of the opposite of the neutron bomb—remember that one? All lethal radiation and little blast damage."

"I thought the neutron bomb got canceled because of the bad PR, that it was strictly designed to slaughter civilians."

Dooley shrugged. "Hey, I try to stay away from the politics of it all. I just do the physics. That's my part in it."

Mulder pressed him. "So... you created Bright Anvil, a nuclear weapon that our government can use during a conflict, without worrying about the consequences—and you're not concerned with the politics?"

Dooley didn't answer. He got out of the Jeep, leaving the engine running as he checked the connections on the light pipes, pushed testing buttons at the substations to make sure all LEDs on the instrument panels winked green. He was clearly not interested in the moral implications, but he seemed to sense Mulder staring quietly at him. After he had finished tinkering with the diagnostic sensors, he stood up, slowly facing into the wind as he looked back.

"Okay, Agent Mulder, I admit I think about it. I think about it a lot—but the fact is I'm not responsible. Don't go lecturing me."

"A convenient excuse, don't you think?" Mulder said. He was provoking the researcher intentionally, curious to see what Bear Dooley might let slip if he got riled enough.

Dooley seemed oddly calm, intense but not furious. "I read the newspapers. I watch CNN. I'm a reasonably intelligent man—but I don't pretend to know how other governments are going to react, how foreign policy might be made in some other country that's as alien to me as Mars. I'm a physicist and an engineer—and I'm damn good at it. I understand how to make these devices work. That's what I do. If somebody decides that's a good thing, they fund me, and then I do my job. I leave it to foreign policy experts to make the best use of what I make."

"Okay, okay," Mulder said. "So if you've created this new type of warhead, and somebody uses it to, say, wipe out a city in Bosnia, you wouldn't feel the least bit guilty about all those civilian deaths?"

Dooley scratched the white streak in his beard. "Agent Mulder, is Henry Ford responsible for the deaths caused by automobile accidents? Is a gun manufacturer responsible for the people killed in convenience-store robberies? My team has created a tool for our government to use, a *resource* for our foreign policy experts to do their jobs.

"If some nutcase like Saddam Hussein or Moammar Khadaffi wants to lob their own homemade uranium bomb at New Jersey, I want to make sure that our country has the means either to defend itself or to strike back. They are the policymakers. It's their job to see that the tools get used wisely. I have no more business dictating this country's foreign policy than—than a politician has coming into my laboratory and telling me how to run my experiments. That's ridiculous, don't you think?"

"It's one way to look at it," Mulder said.

"The plain fact is none of us researchers knows enough about it," Dooley continued. "If we went messing with things we don't understand, following our consciences based on sketchy information, we could end up like... like Miriel Bremen, a rabid protester who doesn't understand who's pulling the strings and why people make the decisions that they do. And I guarantee you, man, Miriel Bremen isn't any more qualified to run U.S. foreign policy than I am."

Bear Dooley was on a roll, and Mulder listened with fascination, not even needing to prompt him. Dooley looked down at his big hands.

"I used to like her, you know. Miriel's a good researcher. Always came up with innovative solutions when Emil Gregory ran into a problem. But then she thought too much about things that weren't in her job description—and now look at where she is. Bright Anvil has suffered quite a few setbacks, with Miriel leaving the project and Dr. Gregory being killed. I am not about to let Bright Anvil fail now after all this work, all those careers." Dooley pointed a large finger at the device out on its raft. "*That* is my responsibility, out there. I've got to see that it works."

Dooley finished checking the equipment, rubbed his hands hard against his jeans to remove the worst of the dust and grime, and climbed back into the Jeep. "Now, this has been a fine debate, Agent Mulder—but the countdown is ticking even as we speak, and I've got a lot of work to do.

"Bright Anvil is set to go off at 5:15 a.m. tomorrow. Kind of like the Trinity Test, you know? That one was delayed by a storm that whipped up in the middle of the night out in New Mexico. But here we're counting on the storm."

He tromped his booted foot down on the accelerator, and the Jeep sprayed a rooster tail of sand as they spun around and accelerated back toward the control blockhouse.

Mulder glanced at his watch. Only ten hours remained.

THIRTY-ONE

USS Dallas
Friday, 8:09 p.m.

In the full darkness of early night, the roiling ocean had a greasy cast. No moonlight penetrated the barrier of clouds high above. The wind whistled with a cold metallic tang.

Scully shivered as she held the deck rail of the *Dallas*, gray-painted ropes cross-woven to look like a chain-link fence. She watched the recovery operations on the *Lucky Dragon* as seamen swarmed aboard the rescued fishing boat. A team of strong young sailors, wet with spray and perspiration, assisted the three fishermen, the scarred blind man, and Miriel Bremen as they reached the relative safety aboard the destroyer.

Captain Ives stared in stunned amazement at the blind passenger, unable to tear his gaze from the blistered scars on the man's face, the blank look in the refugee's dead eye sockets as he worked his way up the rattling ladder. The blind man reached the deck, seemingly impervious to the gathering hurricane-force winds. He slowly turned and faced Ives, exactly as if he knew the captain was staring at him. A faint smile rippled across his scarred face.

Scully watched the silent encounter curiously, but then turned her attention to Miriel Bremen as the protester came aboard the *Dallas*. For some odd reason Scully felt betrayed, that Miriel had led her along. Scully's stomach tightened with a sinking feeling, and she wondered just what the other woman might have been up to.

Miriel hadn't noticed her yet, and Scully spoke sharply into the sound of the wind and waves, "You don't expect us to believe this is a complete coincidence, do you, Ms. Bremen?"

Surprised, Miriel Bremen turned toward the voice. Then her long-chinned face compressed with sour anger. "So, Agent Scully—it looks like you knew more about Bright Anvil all along. What a sucker I am. You were playing me for a patsy, seeing how much I would tell you."

Scully was taken aback. "That's not true at all. I—"

Miriel just scowled and pushed her glasses more firmly onto her face as the wind whipped her mousy brown hair. "I should have known better than to believe an FBI agent."

Captain Ives stood next to Scully, looking at Miriel's bedraggled form. "You know this person?"

"Yes, Captain. She's a radical antinuclear protester from Berkeley. She was near the scene of the murder of Dr. Emil Gregory, who was originally in charge of the Bright Anvil project."

Captain Ives narrowed his gaze, his eyebrows clenched together as his forehead furrowed. "You chose a convenient place for a pleasure cruise."

Scully frowned again. "And you can bet they selected the name of their vessel quite specifically. *The Lucky Dragon*—that was no accident. Even if they couldn't be sure somebody would recognize it, they must have thought it an amusing joke."

Ives gestured for several of the crewmen to come over. "Take them all below to one of the empty staterooms each. Get their names and make sure they're comfortable, but don't let them cause any trouble. Things might not be exactly what they seem."

He turned sideways to glance at the blind stranger again. The other man stood rigid, with that faint, contented smile on his scarred face. "We'll contact Mr. Dooley and ask his opinion on the subject."

"I think he might be surprised to hear he has more visitors," Scully said. "Especially these."

"Probably," Ives said.

The three fishermen seemed delighted and relieved to be aboard the large and stable Navy destroyer, while Miriel and the blind man seemed to consider themselves prisoners of war. Miriel walked proudly between the sailors as they escorted her to shelter belowdecks.

One of the sailors called up from the deck of the *Lucky Dragon*. "Captain Ives? Sir, I think you should come down here. We found some interesting items on board that you may wish to inspect."

"Very well," Ives answered. "Coming down."

"I'd like to go with you, Captain," Scully said.

"By all means," Ives answered. "You seem to know as many scattered details of these circumstances as I do. It just gets weirder and weirder."

"Unfortunately, none of us has the whole picture," Scully said.

They lowered themselves over the side and climbed down the slick metal ladder to the deck of the fishing boat lashed to the *Dallas*. Scully gripped the rungs against unpredictable gusts of wind from the storm.

Below, the *Lucky Dragon* pitched and rocked, though the large destroyer blocked the worst of the waves. From what Scully could tell, the fishing boat did not appear damaged: its equipment seemed intact, its deck and its hull unscarred—but then she didn't know enough about small marine craft to be a good judge of its seaworthiness.

One crewman came forward to meet Captain Ives and Scully; he rapidly began pointing out some of the anomalies they had found on the *Lucky Dragon*. "All systems appear operational, sir," the young sailor said, raising his voice over the roar of the ocean. "No damage that I can see, nothing that should have caused them to send out such an urgent distress call. This ship wasn't in any trouble."

"Maybe they were just spooked by the storm," Ives said.

Scully shook her head quickly. "I don't believe they were in distress at all," she said. "They wanted us to go out and pick them up. It was the only way they could be certain of getting to the Bright Anvil test site."

Captain Ives worked his jaw and ran his hand over his mustache, but said nothing.

Another sailor popped his head out from belowdecks. "Very unusual hull construction, sir," he said. "I've never seen a small craft designed like this. She's practically armored. I'll bet there's never been a stronger ship this size built."

"Specially constructed," Scully muttered. "I wonder if they were planning to take it into a hurricane?"

"Typhoon," Captain Ives corrected.

"A big storm," Scully said. "You'd need a special design if that was the purpose of your boat."

"But it's a fishing boat," the seaman standing next to them said.

"It's supposed to look like a fishing boat," Scully said.

Ives shook his head. "Look at this equipment, the nets—all brand new. Those nets have never even been dropped into water. They're all props... just for show. I think you're right, Agent Scully—something goes deeper here."

Another sailor emerged from the rear cargo compartment. "No fish down here, sir. No cargo at all, just a few supplies and one storage barrel."

"Storage barrel," Ives said. "What's in it?"

"I thought you might want to take the top off yourself, sir. Just in case it turns out to be something important."

He and Scully descended into the shelter under the deck, to where a single drum had been chained to the hull wall. Seeing it, Scully's mind raced, thinking of Miriel Bremen and her radical protest activities, the suspicion of her involvement in Dr. Gregory's death—and her arrival out here, which was almost certainly to sabotage the Bright Anvil test. Miriel would take whatever measures she deemed necessary....

Ives took a screwdriver from the sailor and began prying up the top of the barrel. Scully looked again at the drum and suddenly cried out. "Wait! It might be a bomb!"

But Ives had already popped the lid off. He froze, as if expecting to be blasted. When nothing happened, he raised the metal lid higher.

"Nothing," he said. "Just powdery dirt. Black ash of some kind."

Scully's heart was pounding as she approached the barrel. One of the crewmen gave her a flashlight, which she shone down into the barrel, illuminating the glittering, powdery black residue. The barrel was nearly two-thirds full of it.

"Why would they bring a drum full of cinders all this way? Is it an incinerator can?" the sailor asked.

Scully carefully reached in and touched the ash, bringing out a pinch between her fingertips. She smeared it around, feeling the greasy and grainy texture. It seemed identical to the residue in the small vial found in Nancy Scheck's pool.

"No, it's not from an incinerator," she said. "But I think this provides direct, clear-cut evidence that Miriel Bremen is involved in the murders of Bright Anvil personnel."

Ives replaced the top on the barrel and turned to the sailors. "Make sure this boat is secure. Agent Scully, let's get back on board the *Dallas*. I need to find out from Mr. Dooley if he knows anything about this."

Scully followed him out, but she knew her first priority would be to speak directly with Miriel Bremen, to try and get some answers.

THIRTY-TWO

USS Dallas
Saturday, 1:02 a.m.

As Scully looked on, the security officer used a jingling ring of keys to unlock the stateroom in which Miriel Bremen had been isolated. He didn't bother to knock; no doubt Miriel had heard them approach. Footsteps rang out on the metal deckplates, even over the muffled echoes of the hurricane.

Scully waited in the corridor, her eyes burning and itchy from too little sleep and too much thinking in the past few hours. The security officer swung the heavy metal door open and gestured for her to enter. Scully swallowed, raised her head, and stepped inside the small room.

Miriel Bremen sat on a narrow bunk, elbows on her knees, long chin in her hands. She glanced up at Scully. Her red-rimmed eyes flashed with recognition, but not hope. "Did you at least bring me some bread and water here in solitary confinement?" she said.

Startled, Scully looked at the security officer, then back at Miriel. "Would you like something to eat? I think we can get a meal fixed for you."

Miriel shook her head with a sigh, running shaky hands through her mousy brown hair. "No, I'm not hungry anyway. It was just a joke."

A thought flashed through Scully's mind, a realization. Miriel Bremen's entire demeanor had changed since their meeting in Berkeley—and now Scully suddenly thought she had pinpointed the subtle difference. The protester remained as determined as before, *but now she appeared frightened.*

Oddly, though, Miriel's fear did not seem to stem from being held prisoner on board a Navy destroyer. After all, she had not done anything illegal, as far as anyone knew, though her intent to impede the Bright Anvil test seemed obvious. No, Miriel Bremen now looked like someone far from home. From the haggard look on her face, Miriel seemed to be in over her head, pushed too far by her own convictions. With the spectre of the upcoming test detonation, her activism had somehow transformed into outright fanaticism, making her willing to abandon all her work in Berkeley and charge headlong into a typhoon in a small fishing boat.

Scully stood just inside the stateroom and tried to cover an uneasiness that ran through her. Ever since meeting Miriel Bremen and setting foot inside the Stop Nuclear Madness! Headquarters, she had been reliving flashbacks from her first undergrad year, during which she had come very close to joining an activist cause herself. Even allowing for the impetuousness of youth, such activities had been very much against her parents' wishes. Then again, joining the FBI a few years later had also been against their wishes. Scully didn't abandon her convictions that easily… but now, looking at what had happened to Miriel Bremen, she saw the fine line that she too could have walked. If things had turned out differently, she might have fallen off a precipice just as sharp.

Scully turned to the guard. "Would you give us a few minutes of privacy, please?"

The security officer seemed uneasy. "Should I wait just outside in the corridor, ma'am?" he asked.

Scully crossed her arms over her chest. "This woman hasn't been charged with any crime," she said. "I don't think she's a threat to my safety." Then Scully glanced back at Miriel. "Besides, I've had combat and self-defense training at the FBI Academy at Quantico. I think I can handle her, if I need to."

The guard looked at Scully with a small measure of dubious respect, then nodded briskly as if barely restraining himself from saluting. He closed the door behind him and marched off down the hall.

"You said it yourself, Agent Scully," Miriel began. "I haven't been charged with any crime. I haven't done anything to you, or to this ship, or to the Bright Anvil test preparations. The only thing I've done is call for assistance out in a storm."

As if hearing her words, the winds outside gusted so loudly that they resonated through the destroyer. Scully could feel the enormous craft rocking in the rough water as they churned back toward Enika Atoll.

"Why am I being held here?" Miriel said, continuing her offensive. "Why was I locked in this stateroom?"

"Because people are nervous," Scully said. "You know about the impending test—don't try to tell me your showing up at this precise location and time was a simple accident. We just haven't figured yet what sort of mischief you might have planned."

"Mischief?" Miriel sat back on her bunk with an astonished expression on her long face. "A fallout-free nuclear weapons test is about to be detonated, in violation of all international laws and treaties—and you're sitting by, a federal representative, condoning it—yet you call whatever I might be up to 'mischief'? What did you think Ryan Kamida and I might do? We have one fishing boat, no weapons on board, no explosives. This isn't a Greenpeace sabotage raid."

Scully said, "You brought a barrel of black ash."

Miriel looked surprised. "So? And what's that supposed to do?"

"Similar black ash was found at the site of Nancy Scheck's murder in Gaithersburg, Maryland."

Miriel stood up from her bunk, brushing down her still-damp blouse. "Commandant Scheck? I didn't even know the witch was dead."

"You expect me to believe that?" Scully said.

"It doesn't really matter to me what you believe," Miriel said, "because you probably *couldn't* believe what's really going to happen, what's really going on around here right under your nose."

"Just prove it to me," Scully said. "Give me some objective evidence, and I'll be happy to believe. But don't expect me to take preposterous explanations at face value. You're a scientist yourself, Miriel. You know what I'm talking about. What do you think is going to happen during the Bright Anvil test? It's less than five hours away."

"I've got a better idea," Miriel said, pulling up a chair from the small half desk, as if she preferred the uncomfortable hard chair to the narrow bunk.

"Let me tell you about something that's already happened, and you can draw your own conclusions. Did you ever hear of the *Indianapolis*, a U.S. destroyer from World War II?"

Scully pursed her lips. "The name sounds familiar." She hedged for a moment. "That was the battleship that delivered one of the first atomic bomb cores out to the island of Tinian, wasn't it? In preparation for the raid on Hiroshima."

Miriel seemed surprised but pleased that Scully knew the answer. "Yes, the *Indianapolis* delivered the uranium core of the Little Boy atomic bomb out to Tinian. The Little Boy bomb was dropped on Hiroshima, the first strike in our world's first nuclear war."

"Spare me the propaganda speeches," Scully said, still annoyed.

A fire grew behind Miriel's eyes as she pulled the chair closer and looked intently at Scully. "Did you know that during the outbound voyage of the *Indianapolis*, the bomb core was actually welded to the floor of the captain's stateroom? No one knew what the thing was, just that it was some ultra-secret, extremely powerful weapon.

"But word got around. Rumors fly on ships, especially during wartime. The whole crew on board the *Indianapolis* believed they were carrying a vital component for victory against Japan. After an uneventful voyage, the *Indianapolis* safely delivered its cargo to Tinian, where it was assembled into the bomb—"

Scully cut her off impatiently. "Yes, and the *Enola Gay* took off and dropped it on Hiroshima, where seventy thousand people were killed. I know all this. Why is it relevant now?"

Miriel held up a long finger. "What's relevant is what happened after the *Indianapolis* completed its mission. Nobody thinks about the aftermath. They just sweep it under the rug. But with such destruction there must be some sort of atonement—don't you understand?"

Scully could only shake her head. Miriel sighed.

"I believe that there is a balance of justice in the world. Such mass murder could not be ignored.

"Three days after the *Indianapolis* unloaded its bomb core, the battleship was torpedoed by a Japanese submarine. A casualty of war, you might call it. But 850 of the 1,196 men aboard survived the sinking of the ship. They got life rafts into the water in time… but they weren't rescued by the Japanese sub. The Japanese did not take prisoners out of the water. The survivors were stranded.

"The men floated in shark-infested waters all alone for five days before a Navy plane spotted the survivors. Five days isolated in the ocean, watching their comrades being eaten alive one by one as the sharks came from all around, smelling the blood in the water, growing hungrier…." Miriel seemed dazed by her own story. "Do you know why it took so long for the search plane?" she asked rhetorically.

Scully didn't even attempt to answer.

"Through a bureaucratic error, the *Indianapolis* had not even been marked as missing. No one had bothered to search for it. They were found by accident! In the end, despite frantic rescue efforts, only three hundred and eighteen people were pulled from the water. Three-quarters of the original crew—two-thirds of those who had survived the actual sinking of the ship— were lost. It was devastating."

"That's horrifying," Scully said, sickened by the thought. "But it still doesn't imply anything unnatural."

"If you think that's horrible," Miriel said evenly, "you should talk to Ryan Kamida and hear *his* story."

"Wait," Scully said, counting the days in her head. "According to what you said, the *Indianapolis* was torpedoed nine days before the Hiroshima bomb was dropped. How could any sort of supernatural revenge be involved for an event that hadn't even taken place yet? Lots of ships were sunk in the Pacific during the war. My father used to tell me the stories. You're picking one that serves to illustrate your own ends—but you're not making your point."

"I'm not sure you're ready to hear my point," Miriel said.

"What?" Scully asked, recalling Mulder's suggestion. "That some sort of atomic bomb ghosts are wreaking havoc among nuclear weapons researchers? That they're using paranormal means to stop this Bright Anvil test? How can you expect me to believe that?"

"I'm not telling you what to believe," Miriel said. She seemed calmer now after having told her story. Her long face wore a hardened, resigned look. "Just go talk to Ryan."

THIRTY-THREE

Enika Atoll
Saturday, 2:19 a.m.

Scully had just returned to her own cabin for a brief rest when Captain Ives appeared at the door.

"Wonders never cease," he said, bracing himself against the doorframe as the ship rocked. "I've finally gotten through to Bear Dooley on the atoll. I couldn't tell whether he was outraged or hopping excited to learn that Miriel Bremen and her friends had come out here."

"So what did he suggest we do?"

Ives shook his head in disbelief. "He wants us to escort the whole group to the blockhouse so they can be present during the test."

"Why would he do that?" Scully asked, then answered her own question. "Ah—I suppose he wants to watch the expression on Miriel's face when the Bright Anvil device goes off."

Captain Ives frowned and gave a slight shrug. "I don't believe it's as simple as that," he said. "I'm sure gloating might be part of it, but I get the impression that Mr. Dooley honestly respects Ms. Bremen and the work she did in the past. Maybe he thinks the excitement of the countdown will bring her around again, show her what she's been missing. He'd love to snatch her back from what he considers to be antinuke brainwashing."

"Okay, I can understand that," Scully said, unzipping her duffel to yank out her extra rain slicker. She had changed into comfortable, dry clothes upon reaching her room on the *Dallas*. "But what about the blind man, Ryan Kamida. Why should Dooley want him there?"

Captain Ives gave a slight smile. "Because that's the only way Ms. Bremen would agree to come along."

Scully shook her head. "They do enjoy playing their games, don't they? All right, how are we going to get over there?"

"I'm staying here on the *Dallas*," the captain answered. "The wind wall of the storm is approaching, and the gale is due to hit maximum force within the next three or four hours. I can't leave my ship. I'm not comfortable having my captain's gig there at the atoll, but my exec, Commander Klantze, is going to ferry it back here."

"So we'll have to wait for the return trip?" Scully asked. By now Mulder would be wondering what had happened to her, probably having uncovered many details on his own that he needed to share… most likely preposterous explanations of supernatural manipulation or alien interference in nuclear weapons development. She could never tell what he might come up with.

"Actually it's more unorthodox than that," Captain Ives said. He stood tall and straight, his feet oddly close together as if he were a statue. "Ms. Bremen suggested we take the *Lucky Dragon*. Two of my seamen will pilot her, although the fishermen want to go along as well. It seems everybody is determined to go joyriding through this typhoon." He shook his head.

"I have to concede that the *Lucky Dragon* is seaworthy, and I'm not entirely comfortable having her lashed up against my ship if we get to rocking and rolling even worse, as I expect we will. Banging hulls together could cause significant damage, either to the fishing boat or to us."

Captain Ives brooded, an uncertain expression on his face. He had been strangely reticent ever since taking the *Lucky Dragon* passengers aboard. Scully finally asked him about it. She slung her duffel over her shoulder and followed him out into the narrow corridor. "Something is really bothering you about this test, isn't it?"

He paused in midstride, but did not turn to look at her. "Just a lot of shadows from my past," he said. "Things I'm being forced to remember that I'd prefer to forget. I had thought them all safely tucked away, but unfortunately such memories have a habit of coming back to haunt you."

"Would you care to elaborate on that?" Scully asked.

Ives finally turned to look at her and shook his head. His slate-gray eyes seemed expressionless, as he brushed his mustache with one finger. "No—no, I don't think I would."

Scully recognized the look, but it seemed quite alien on the face of a hardbitten old captain who had spent many years on the sea.

She saw the fluttering dark wings of genuine fear.

The *Lucky Dragon* easily rode the swells, pulling away from the *Dallas* and heading directly toward Enika Atoll. The boat handled well, according to the seamen Captain Ives had assigned to shuttle it over.

During the brief ride to the island, Miriel Bremen remained with Ryan Kamida, avoiding Scully. The blind man appeared disoriented and agitated, as if afraid of something or overwhelmed by circumstances. Scully wondered what had caused his blindness, the terrible burn scars. She didn't think he could possibly be a Nagasaki survivor. He looked too young, too exotic… too strange.

As the fishing boat rode up to shore and anchored in the sheltered lagoon, Scully spotted Mulder waiting for her under the bright light hung over the door of the control blockhouse. He waved his arms, and his wet suit jacket flapped about in the wild wind. She noticed that he had removed his tie and unfastened the first few buttons of his shirt.

Mulder came to meet her, helping Scully climb off the boat onto the damp sand. She handed him her duffel. "It seems as if I'm spending more time here on the island than aboard the ship, so I thought I might need a few things."

Mulder looked up into the looming storm that looked like a giant fist ready to pound down. "Doesn't appear we'll need the suntan lotion at the moment."

Bear Dooley shuffled out of the blockhouse, haggard and preoccupied with his nonstop preparations. The test was due to go off in less than three hours. He stood with his hands on his waist, staring at Miriel Bremen as she stepped off the boat onto Enika Atoll.

Miriel helped Ryan Kamida step onto the beach—but the scarred man dropped to his hands and knees, not in collapse, but more like an embrace of the crushed coral and sand. He looked up, and Scully saw tears leaking out of his blind eyes.

Miriel stood next to Kamida, a hand supportively squeezing his shoulder. Finally, she directed her gaze toward Bear Dooley.

"Ah Miriel, glad you could join us," Dooley boomed. "You didn't have to go through so much trouble, though. You could have just asked, and we would have included you among the crew."

"I wasn't sure I want to be part of the crew, Bear—not under the circumstances," Miriel said. Her voice remained quiet, but somehow the words cut sharply through the wind. "I trust you didn't have any trouble setting up the test?" Miriel's voice was uninflected, without barbs; Scully thought she sounded defeated, resigned. The Bright Anvil test would indeed go off, despite the protester's efforts to stop it. Scully wondered just how far she had intended to go.

From belowdecks on the *Lucky Dragon*, the three fishermen scrambled up, hauling the half-full barrel of black ash uneasily between them. They nervously carried the sealed drum onto the deck of the boat.

"What are you doing with that?" Dooley shouted. Two seamen prevented the fishermen from taking the barrel over the side of the *Lucky Dragon* and onto the beach.

"We don't want it on our ship," the fishermen said.

"Well, you've had it on your boat all along," one of the Navy men said.

"Now we can take it ashore," the fishermen insisted.

Dooley took two steps closer to Miriel. "What's in that?" he said, "Anything dangerous?"

"It's just some old ash," Miriel said. "Nothing to worry about."

Dooley shook his shaggy head. "Miriel, I used to be able to understand you—but you've been turned into a pod person or something."

The Japanese fishermen managed to bypass the sailors and took the metal barrel ashore. Dooley gestured toward them. "You're not taking that inside my blockhouse," he said.

"But if we leave it here, it'll wash away in the storm," one said.

"Not my problem," Dooley answered.

Ryan Kamida lifted his head and turned a tear-streaked, burned face toward Miriel and then Bear Dooley. "Let them leave it where it is."

Relieved, the fishermen hurried into the shelter of the blockhouse, ducking out of the slicing rain.

"Miriel, why don't you come inside, and I'll show you around our posh quarters," Dooley said. "I'm sure you'll remember some of the equipment."

"Trying to rub my face in it, Bear?" she said.

He blinked his small eyes. "No, I don't think so," he said. "These engineers don't know what I'm talking about half the time, and you at least understand. For old times' sake, for Emil Gregory, come and look at Bright Anvil."

Reluctantly, she tapped Kamida's shoulder, trying to get him to accompany her, but the blind man shook his head. "Let me stay out here for a while longer," Ryan Kamida said. "I will be fine."

Miriel looked uneasy about leaving him there alone, until Scully stepped forward. "We'll stay with him for a few minutes, Miriel. You wanted me to talk to him, remember?" Understanding came to Miriel's eyes, and she nodded before following Bear Dooley and the seamen into the control blockhouse.

On the beach Kamida dug his scarred fingers into the sand, smelling the coral and the water and the spray. He tilted his head up to the greenish-black hurricane clouds. He breathed through his mouth and closed his blind eyes as he sat back, clenching his fists and gritting his teeth.

"Mr. Kamida" Scully said, "Miriel said you might have something to tell us… a terrible story about yourself? She thought we ought to know."

The blind man turned a scarred face toward her, fixing his unseeing gaze to a point directly between Mulder and Scully. "You hope to find answers," he said.

"Do you have any?" Mulder said. "At the moment, we're not even sure which questions we should be asking."

"You shouldn't be asking questions," Kamida said. "You shouldn't be here at all. You are innocent bystanders who could become casualties of war."

Scully said, "Miriel told me that something happened to you, something terrible. Please tell us the story. Is it about how you were blinded and burned?"

His chin twitched downward just a fraction, as if in an unconscious nod. Sitting on the beach with the waves crashing against the reef line out beyond the lagoon, Ryan Kamida spoke with the voice of a ghost in the wind.

"I was born here on Enika—as were all of my people, a small tribe. We lived here… although legends tell us we came from other islands on a long pilgrimage. We found this island and we stayed. It was our place. It was peaceful."

"But Enika Atoll is uninhabited," Scully said.

"Yes," Kamida answered. "Yes, now it is uninhabited—but forty years ago it was our home, when the United States was walking tall, striding across the world, proud in its new status as a superpower. You had atomic weapons in your pocket, and you were still flushed with pride over your victory in World War II.

"But your first atomic bombs weren't big enough, so you had to build fusion bombs, hydrogen bombs, thermonuclear warheads. And in building such bombs you had to test them in places where no one would notice… places such as Enika Atoll, the home of my childhood."

Scully said, "I know the islanders on Bikini and Eniwetok were displaced to other homelands when the atolls were evacuated for nuclear tests. Is that what happened to your people?"

Kamida shook his head. "The government did not bother with that. I was only a young boy, probably about ten. I have since learned that the name of the test was Sawtooth.

"I had grown up here 'primitive and uneducated,' some might say, while others would call it 'idyllic,' an existence in paradise with fine weather and a warm climate, with breadfruit, coconuts, taro, and yams growing in abundance, with all the fish and shellfish we could possibly want given to us by the sea.

"I was young—small and wiry and strong. In the reef rocks around my island there were many caves, small outcroppings and hollows that, had they been underwater, would have been the homes of moray eels and octopuses. But above ground they provided openings for me to worm my body through, to go down into tidepools and mysterious mazes... half-submerged treasure houses where I could find mussels and conch shells and abalone.

"My parents would wait above with my older sisters and my uncles as I wriggled down into the reef caves to search for delicacies." Kamida's rough face wore a half-smile. "I remember it so clearly—memories are all I've been able to see for most of my life."

A blast of wind curled around the coral uplift that sheltered the blockhouse, and slapped down at them. Scully rocked back to keep her balance; Mulder grasped her shoulder. Ryan Kamida didn't seem to notice the gust at all.

"We knew the strange Navy ships had been cruising around our island, long metal monstrosities, bristling with spines. The sailors had landed in their white uniforms, but we hid in the jungles, thinking they were invaders from some other island. If they were trying to locate and evacuate the inhabitants of Enika, they did not search very hard. We were afraid of them, but also curious. We didn't know why they had placed strange machines on our island, unusual structures with amazing blinking substations and other devices. It was magic to us. Evil magic."

He picked up a fistful of the wet sand, letting it trickle through his scarred fingers.

"I remember that day. Many of my cousins had gone to inspect the device the soldiers had left behind ... others watched the destroyers pull away. But I had my day's work to do. My father insisted that the water level was perfect for me to find special treasures in the caves, and so I crawled deep down into the winding passages, carrying only my small knife and a net in which to store the shells that I found.

"I had secured a large abalone, enough for an entire meal, I thought, and a few other shells. When I crawled back out of the cave, my father waited for me, standing out in the sunlight. I could see him towering above the opening of the cave. I held up the net that contained the shells. He bent down to take it from me so that I could climb out of the cave. I looked into his eyes. They were cast into shadow as he leaned toward me...."

Kamida paused. His voice caught.

"And then the sky turned white, a burning white, a blaze of heat, so hot and so fast that it wiped everything clean, blasted every molecule of color from the world. The last thing my eyes ever saw was my father's silhouette, fuzzy around the edges where I could see right through his skin. For the barest fraction of a second, I could clearly make out the skeleton inside his body as the radiation poured through him—until the rest of the shockwave blew him to ashes. And then the light engulfed me as well."

Scully stared at him, wide-eyed, her hand to her mouth.

"Somehow, I survived," Kamida continued. "The shockwave was immense, but I tumbled back down into the caves even as the nuclear detonation flattened my island. The water inside the caves boiled and blasted upward like a geyser. My skin was cooked as if I were a roasting pig.

"A long time later I found myself alive and outside of the caves. Much of the reef overhead had been vaporized. I had been spared, though it was no blessing. No blessing at all.

"I felt my way along the hot steaming rock. I found the lagoon, but it was still boiling hot, scalding my legs... which were already too burned to feel any more pain. I walked and waded out to sea, unable to see anything. Still I continued, sloshing farther and farther from the island....

"They say I made it two miles before I was picked up."

"Picked up?" Mulder asked. "Who picked you up?"

"Navy ship," Kamida said. "Sailors, men assigned to observe the Sawtooth test. They didn't know what to do with me. After their immense technological victory, my survival must have been quite an embarrassment to them."

Kamida stared deeply into his memories for a moment, his eyes too blind to see the present.

"After I recovered, they placed me in the care of an orphanage in Honolulu. They changed all the records, and I survived. Oh yes, I survived—and in later years I made a name for myself. I became lucky. I was talented in business. I have become a wealthy man over the past forty years.

"You'll find no record of the Sawtooth nuclear test, or of my people now annihilated, or even of me, the lone survivor of a test the government would prefer to forget."

"But if there's no record and you were such a young boy," Scully said, "how did you get all this information? How can you remember and be sure of the details?"

Kamida directed his blind gaze at her in a way that so unnerved her, she looked away in embarrassment. His hollow voice sent a shudder down her spine. "Because I have been reminded time and again."

Mulder leaned closer. "How were you reminded?"

"They told me," he said. "The spirits of my people. They come and speak to me. They tell me not to forget them or my own past."

Scully sighed and looked at Mulder, but he ignored her. "In other words, your people were annihilated in this secret atomic bomb test, and because you're the only survivor, you can speak to their spirits?"

Scully stood up, ready to leave the man to his delusions. "Come on. We should get inside the shelter."

"Agent Mulder," Kamida said, though Scully couldn't remember ever having introduced him. "The atomic flash blinded me in an instant, but it also boosted me somehow. My eyes no longer function, but I can see and hear other things. I am linked to the brooding ghosts that remain with me, like afterimages from that blast."

Mulder's eyebrows shot up, and Scully looked at him, amazed to see her partner believing this tale.

"Think of it, my friend," Kamida said to Mulder—the blind man seemed to know intuitively who was most likely to swallow his story. "For four decades, they have been gathering energy. Their screams have finally reached a peak—to deafen those who brought this upon them, and those who would willingly do it again."

"Wait a minute," Mulder said, intrigued, "are you suggesting that the sheer suddenness and high energy of an atomic blast somehow added power to the souls of those people destroyed in it? Made them different from your ordinary, run-of-the-mill ghosts?"

"I am no scientist," Kamida said. "Perhaps the spirits of an entire annihilated people have greater powers than those killed in a more common fashion. Absolute atomic genocide. They do seem to have a greater awareness. They can sense connections, they know who is involved in the development of such weapons—and they also understand that this Bright Anvil test is a very frightening step down a treacherous path for the entire world." He smiled to himself. "Perhaps the spirits of my people are protectors of the human race."

Scully caught the meaning of his words. "Do you mean to say that these ghosts have been killing nuclear weapons researchers and other people who had a connection to the atomic bomb?"

"Agent Scully," Kamida said, "I will confess that I bear some responsibility for the death of Dr. Emil Gregory. I had hoped that removing him would bring this test to a halt. But I was wrong. It was too simplistic. Out of spite I also directed the annihilation of an old man in New Mexico who was in some way linked to the first Trinity Test that unleashed nuclear weapons upon the world. So many of the others are already dead from time and illness. His was the first name I could find.

"I was also responsible for the death of a Department of Energy executive, a woman behind the funding for the Bright Anvil project. Without her support, this test could not have taken place.

"But I waited too long. I have held the ghosts in check for too many months, too many years… and now they're growing restless, striking even at those I have not designated—those they believe are in some way a threat to our island."

Scully thought of the radiation-burned missileers in their underground control bunker, the photos Mulder had showed her.

"Their attention expands. They grow very restless. But in a few hours they will fulfill their destiny and protect this island again."

"Why are you telling us all this?" Mulder asked. "Confessing to murder isn't something people do lightly."

The storm's growl grew to a persistent roar. Scully touched Kamida's elbow, raising him to his feet. "It's not safe to be out here. We need to get inside—all of us."

"Safe!" Kamida laughed. "Safety is a luxury none of us can afford now. I'm telling you this, Agent Mulder, just so you have the answers because you are a curious man—but none of us will get out of this alive." He cocked his head to stare up into the storm, as if calling to something.

He spoke in a mystical whisper. "At last the wave of fire will reach the shore of death."

THIRTY-FOUR

Enika Atoll
Saturday, 4:11 a.m.

As howling darkness engulfed the island, Scully and the others huddled inside the shelter of the supposedly indestructible concrete-sandbag walls of the blockhouse.

Bear Dooley paced the control chamber that smelled of dust, new solder and lubricants, chalky concrete, and fresh-sawed wood. Jury-rigged lightbulbs hung from the support beams overhead, shedding uneven light. Dooley triple-checked every diagnostic system on the equipment racks, then went through the entire routine again.

He flashed repeated suspicious glances at Ryan Kamida and the three Japanese fishermen, who sat at an analysis table that had been cleared of all papers and reports. Dooley pointed his thick finger at the fidgeting fishermen. "Don't touch anything," he said. "Just stay there and keep your hands to yourselves."

He looked sourly at Miriel Bremen, as if accusing her of poor judgment for insisting that a man and three fishermen accompany her to the blockhouse rather than just staying aboard the *Dallas*. Miriel ignored him. She stood rigid, scanning the instrument racks and diagnostic panels, as if reluctant to move forward for a closer inspection.

Dooley studied the big round dial of the watch strapped to his wrist. "It's 4:15," he announced. "Only one hour to go."

Victor Ogilvy nervously hung up the portable phone set at his station. "Hey, Bear—I just got a communication from Captain Ives. He says the storm surges are already at their maximum projected levels. Wind-wall velocity just topped a hundred miles an hour, and the storm isn't due to peak for another fifty minutes."

"Good," Dooley said. Outside, the typhoon boomed like a series of muffled explosions.

"Good?" Miriel said, shaking her head. "Doesn't it bother you, Bear, that regardless of all the moral and ethical considerations you dismiss so easily, this test goes blatantly against international law? Above-ground nuclear explosions have been banned for more than thirty years."

Dooley looked at her, and his broad shoulders sagged. "Miriel, we had a phrase in my high school class. I think it even showed up in the yearbook as our class motto. 'Everything's legal until you get caught.' And we're not going to get caught. This hurricane will mask the test signature. It'll cover all the destruction on the atoll in case anyone's watching with satellites. No problem.

"And because there isn't any fallout from Bright Anvil, weather stations aren't going to report a sudden increase in radioactive daughter products. We've got it all covered." He clasped his big hands in front of him in an unconscious pleading gesture. "Come on, Miriel—you worked on this baby for years. You and Emil solved most of the problems—"

Miriel interrupted him. "I didn't *solve* any of the problems, and neither did Emil. None of us understands the technology behind Bright Anvil, or even where it came from. Doesn't that bother you?"

He shook his head, stonewalling. "I don't understand how my car engine works, either, but I know it starts every time I turn the key... well, usually. I don't know how my microwave oven works, but it reheats my coffee just fine." His wide, bearded face held a boyish sense of wonder, a hope behind it.

"Miriel, I'd really like you to be a part of the team again," he said. "Without Emil, this whole project nearly fizzled. When we lost you, we lost our greatest contender. I've been doing my damndest to keep everything working and running on schedule—but that's not what I'm good at. I'm no match for you, but I'm not going to walk away from my responsibilities. I'm going to see that Bright Anvil goes off as planned, because that's my job."

Scully stood next to Mulder, watching the debate between the two scientists. Mulder seemed intrigued, but Scully felt her abdomen tightening in knots to hear Bear Dooley's unbridled enthusiasm.

"I'm disappointed in you, Bear," Miriel said. His face fell, as if that were the worst thing she could have told him. She remained standing, formal and rigid, one step away from the instrument racks.

"I know you want to test this new weapons system in a 'real use' situation, but I wish you'd let it *bother you* a bit to think of just what that 'real use' may be once Bright Anvil is weaponized. The only advantage to the hydrogen bombs and the enormous thermonuclear warheads we've been stockpiling is that they're too destructive for any sane government to consider using."

Miriel became more animated, waving her hands in front of her like captive birds. "But Bright Anvil gives us precise annihilation, *clean* destruction. It terrifies me to think that the United States may have a brand new warhead it won't be afraid to use."

"Miriel," Dooley said sharply, cutting off her lecture, "I wouldn't want anyone but a professional mechanic to try to fix my car. I wouldn't want anyone but a surgeon to do brain surgery on me—and I wouldn't want anyone but a well-versed diplomat to make decisions on nuclear policy. I know *I'm* not a professional diplomat... *but neither are you.*"

She frowned at his outburst, but Dooley continued. "It's the government's job to use these weapons responsibly," he said, blinking his eyes rapidly as if grains of sand had gotten in them. "You have to trust the government," he repeated. "They know what's best for us."

Mulder looked at Scully with his eyebrows raised, an expression of amazement on his face.

THIRTY-FIVE

Enika Atoll
Saturday, 4:25 a.m.

Mulder watched Bear Dooley stride over to the countdown clock bolted to the uneven wall. The bearded engineer squinted, peering at it as if he could barely make out the regularly descending numbers.

"Fifty minutes," he said. "Everything still check out? I want a verification on each subsystem." He looked around, scanning the faces of his team. The technicians all agreed, studying their own stations, checking instrument racks.

"Good. Countdown's proceeding without a hitch," Dooley said to no one in particular, rubbing his hands together as he stated the obvious.

Just then the heavy door to the blockhouse ripped open with a siren blast of wind. Howling rain pelted in at a nearly horizontal angle, like bullets of water in a shotgun spray. Two bedraggled and shellshocked sailors staggered in, gasping; they worked together to swing the door shut, bolting it into its jamb. They were sopping wet, their uniforms yanked and disarrayed by the violence of the typhoon. In the incandescent light inside the sheltered bunker, their skin had a pasty, grayish appearance, reflecting their deep fear. Even seasoned seamen rarely saw a storm of such incredible magnitude.

"Okay, everybody's inside," one of them shouted, as if he thought the storm would still drown out his words... or perhaps the throbbing gale had partially deafened him.

"Generator's functioning properly," said the other sailor. "It's sheltered from the rain and wind, and it should hold up even if the typhoon gets worse. The center of the wind wall will be here soon."

Dooley nodded, speaking gruffly. "Generator damn well better keep functioning—that power source is running all our diagnostics. If that fails, this whole test will be a bust even if Bright Anvil does go off as planned."

"Don't forget, we've got the secondary generator, Bear," Victor Ogilvy pointed out.

"I'm sure you'll get your data," Miriel Bremen said sourly. "What could possibly go wrong?"

As if to taunt them, the lightbulbs overhead flickered briefly, then came back on with full strength.

"What was that?" Dooley said, looking up at the ceiling. "Check it!"

"Power fluctuation," Victor answered. "The backup UPS modulated it, though. We're fine."

Dooley strutted around like a tiger in a cage. He glanced at the wall clock. "Forty-three more minutes," he said.

While the technicians focused intently on their stations, Mulder watched the scarred blind man who had told them such an unbelievable story only hours earlier.

After adding Ryan Kamida's tale to the details of the mystery as he saw it, Mulder began formulating a hypothesis that fit all the information. It began to make complete, if fantastic, sense to him. He pondered how best to broach the subject with Scully. She would no doubt find the explanation preposterous... but then she often did.

Scully considered it her purpose in life to be Mulder's devil's advocate, to convince him of the logical explanations behind the incredible events they had witnessed in their many cases together... just as Mulder himself accepted it as his goal to make Scully *believe*.

He leaned closer to his partner, speaking in a low voice near her ear, though the roar of the typhoon whipping around the concrete beehive was enough to drown out the words for any eavesdropper.

"I've been thinking, Scully—and I've got an idea. If what Mr. Kamida says is true, then we could be dealing with some sort of... psychic shockwave, a burst of energy that was transformed into something half-sentient during the original H-bomb blast that took place on this island."

Scully looked at him, blinking her blue eyes. "What are you talking about, Mulder?"

"Let's take a look at this, Scully. Imagine the entire population of islanders here, all together, unsuspecting, living out their normal lives—and then suddenly and unexpectedly catapulted across the brink of death by one of the most powerful instantaneous blasts ever recorded on this planet. Isn't it possible that such a blast could have acted as some sort of boost to a... a higher level of existence, crossing some sort of energetic barrier."

"That's not how I see it, Mulder," Scully said.

"Just think about it," he insisted. "Every single one of Kamida's people, all screaming at once, all of them not just killed, but utterly annihilated, practically disintegrated down to their last cells."

"Mulder, if the energy of an atomic blast can somehow turn its victims into—" she searched for words, then shrugged— "into a vengeful collection of radioactive ghosts with superpowers, then how come there aren't a hundred thousand phantom juggernauts running around after the Hiroshima and Nagasaki blasts?"

"I thought of that," Mulder said, "but those were the first atomic weapons. Even though those bombs were powerful, the Fat Man and Little Boy warheads produced just a fraction of the power that was unleashed in the hydrogen bombs that were detonated out here on the Pacific Islands. The test assemblies in the fifties reached ten or fifteen *megatons*, whereas the Hiroshima blast was only twelve point five *kilotons*. That's a big difference—a factor of a thousand.

"Maybe the Hiroshima and Nagasaki blasts weren't quite enough to cross that threshold. And, as far as I know, nobody else was killed directly in any of the other H-bomb blasts."

Scully looked at him seriously. "And you think that this collection of ghosts is hunting down people originally involved in the development of nuclear weapons, as well as individuals in charge of the Bright Anvil test, and… assassinating them out of revenge?"

"Maybe revenge," Mulder said, "or maybe they're just trying to prevent the tests from continuing. Everything points toward stopping the Bright Anvil test, which could well be the start of a whole new series of aboveground blasts, not to mention fallout-free warheads that might be readily used in combat. What if these ghosts are trying to prevent what happened to them from ever happening again?"

Scully shuddered. Mulder supposed that if he had made the same proposal in the light of day in the cool shelter of their offices at FBI Headquarters—or anyplace else that seemed safe—she might have scoffed at his reasoning. But here, in the darkest hour before dawn, surrounded by brooding hurricane-force winds out on a deserted Pacific island, any sort of creepy story had a greater ring of truth.

Mulder suddenly had another thought. "The ashes!" He spun around to see that Ryan Kamida sat placidly at the analysis table, his scarred hands folded atop the smooth Formica surface. His ravaged face was directed toward them. His lips were quirked in a mysterious smile, as if amused at Mulder's explanation; he looked as if he had heard every word.

Mulder hurried over to him. "The ashes—what were the ashes all about, Mr. Kamida?"

The blind man nodded in deference. "I think you know the answer, Agent Mulder."

"Those were the ashes of the victims from your island, weren't they? You're using them as… as signal flags, or magnets to draw the attention of the ghosts."

Kamida turned his face down toward his folded hands. "When I grew older and accustomed to my blindness, after I had developed connections and earned plenty of money, I came back here to Enika Atoll. The spirits of my people had told me their story, told me my life, told me over and over again what had happened here until I was mad with the repetition. I had to come home, for my own sanity."

He quieted and raised his blind gaze to both Mulder and Scully. "Some entrepreneurs will do strange things for eccentric people without asking questions, so long as the money is sufficient.

"I spent many days here on the reefs, crawling over this abandoned atoll that had grown its jungle back again. I was blind, but I knew where to go, I knew where to look, because the voices guided me. With a knife and a trowel and a barrel, I spent days in the hot Pacific sun, working, scraping a few bits at a time. I found the scant ashes of my people who had been incinerated in a flash and burned into mere shadows on the rock.

"Much time had passed, and one might have expected the stains to have been weathered away, returned to the coral and the sand, to be eaten away by rainstorms and the surf. But they were still there waiting for me, like shadows in human form outlined against the sheltered reefs. I collected them one at a time as the spirits guided me.

"I gathered as much of the ash as I could. It seemed a pitifully small amount, all that remained of an entire island population. But it was enough for my purposes... and theirs. When I was ready, I sent samples of the ash, like calling cards, to those people who needed to receive them."

"You sent a vial to Nancy Scheck?" Scully asked.

Ryan Kamida nodded. "And a packet to Emil Gregory. And to Oscar McCarron in New Mexico. The spirits didn't really need the ash. Left to themselves, they could find their own targets. But it helped... and it helped me to direct them."

Mulder felt sick with horror. "Nancy Scheck and the others each received only a tiny sample of that ash—but you brought an *entire barrel* with you here to this island."

He suddenly recalled the three fishermen, terrified, unloading their ominous cargo and setting it on the beach, where it now sat unprotected, because Bear Dooley wouldn't allow it inside the blockhouse.

"It is everything I have left," Kamida said. "It will bring them here. All of them. Finally."

Just then the phone rang. Victor Ogilvy grabbed it. His eyes widened as he pressed the phone headset tight against his head, as if he had difficulty making out distinct words from the transmission.

"Bear!" Victor said, clinging to the telephone, staring at it with his mouth partially open. "Bear, that was a communication from Captain Ives. He said their radar systems aboard the *Dallas* just picked up something big and powerful approaching the atoll. Not a storm. He doesn't know what it is—like nothing he's ever seen before!"

Victor swallowed, waving the phone headset. "And then his transmission cut off entirely. I can't raise him."

"What the hell's going on here?" Dooley bellowed. "We've only got thirty-five minutes until detonation. We can't afford screwups now!"

Then all of the power went out in the blockhouse, plunging them entirely into blackness.

THIRTY-SIX

USS Dallas
Saturday, 4:30 a.m.

Captain Robert Ives didn't know how he could possibly remain standing in the turmoil—but a captain wasn't supposed to fall on his butt on the bridge of his own ship, not even at the height of a typhoon. With his muscular legs planted widely apart and feet braced firmly on the deck, he rode the churning rollercoaster of waves. Loose objects on the bridge deck, from pencils to notepads to crates, slid back and forth.

Fists of rain pummeled the bridge windows, and the sickly sky was filled with an unnatural greenish light. Ives checked his wristwatch, knowing it couldn't possibly be dawn—not yet. The eerie glow made his skin crawl. He had seen hurricanes before, and they always seemed otherworldly, but none more so than this one.

"Wind wall levels reaching one hundred fifteen miles per hour, sir," Lee Klantze shouted from his exec officer station. A three-ring binder that listed international signals and codes popped off its shelf and crashed to the deck, making Klantze jump. "That's well beyond the maximum expected levels for this storm. Something's pumping it."

"How far away is the eye?" Ives asked.

"We don't expect it to come through for another half hour, and then we'll get a little coffee break. For the time being, we just have to hold on."

Ives gripped the rail at the captain's station with white knuckles. The tendons in his neck stood out like steel cords. "Brace yourselves. I expect it'll get much worse."

Klantze looked at him, amazed. "Worse than these levels?" He glanced down at his weather readouts again, then grabbed for balance as the deck lurched. "On what do you base that, sir?"

"On the sense of unrelenting dread building in my gut, Mr. Klantze. Run a check," Ives said crisply. "Make sure every station is secure. Get all nonessential crew belowdecks."

"Already done, sir," Klantze said.

"Do it again!" Ives snapped, and the young executive officer staggered on rubbery legs across the bucking deck to carry out his captain's orders.

"How much longer until Bright Anvil goes off?" Ives said without taking his gaze from the writhing whitecaps in front of the *Dallas*. Though he could look at the chronometer himself, he knew he needed to keep his crew busy doing routine tasks they could understand; otherwise they would spend too much time fearing the damage the typhoon might inflict upon them.

"About half an hour sir," answered one of the tactical crewmen.

"Thirty-eight minutes," said another simultaneously.

"Thank you," he answered. Ives left unspoken his thoughts of how insane these weapons designers must be even to consider conducting a delicate test shot under such circumstances.

A foamy wall of water slammed into the side of the *Dallas*, making the entire hull ring like a struck gong. The destroyer listed to starboard, then slowly righted herself, like a killer whale regaining its balance. Captain Ives held on, riding the motion. He was glad the *Lucky Dragon* was no longer tied to their hull.

Executive Officer Klantze staggered back up to the front of the bridge, leaving behind the intercom station from which he had spoken to various parts of the destroyer. "All stations have checked in secure, Captain," he said. "We're lashed down and ready to withstand anything."

Ives looked at him, forehead furrowed above his salt-and-pepper eyebrows. "Anything, Mr. Klantze? You're an optimist."

"I'm in the Navy, sir." Klantze must have thought his ridiculous answer would impress Ives.

"Captain!" the tactical officer shouted. "I'm picking up something on forward radar. There's—my God, I can't believe it! It's so big."

"What is it?" Ives said swiveling around and nearly losing his balance as another large wave slammed into the side of the destroyer. "Give me details."

The tactical officer remained at his station, peering down at the flickering screen. His eyes were wide and disbelieving. "The thing is huge—and it has extremely high energy. It's heading this way. Other sensors are picking it up as well—even sonar shows a great turmoil in the surface layers of the water, far exceeding the storm disturbance. I don't understand these readings, sir. An electrical storm? A power surge?"

"Contact the Bright Anvil team on shore," Ives said, with a deep foreboding. "Let them know." He lowered his voice so that no one else heard his words. "Maybe it'll give them time to prepare."

"Could it be a glitch in the instruments?" Klantze asked, making his way over to the tactical officer's station.

"Not likely," the officer said. "It's consistent... and the speed—the thing is getting closer and closer, just like we're in a targeting cross."

Ives whirled to look through the rain-splattered bridge windshield. He saw a sickening, washed-out glow across the waves, like a fire far out on the water. It reminded him of a high-intensity miniature sunrise coming out of nowhere.

"There it is," Klantze said, pointing—as if Ives couldn't see it. "What is that thing? It's like an inferno."

As the bridge crew watched, the wall of light grew into an incandescent sphere that rushed toward them, brighter and brighter, even through the murky air of the hurricane.

Ives had seen something very much like this several times at nuclear tests back in the 1950s. The light and the shape of an H-bomb explosion was something he would never forget—and now it came toward him again.

Ives grabbed the ship's intercom at his station and switched it to all decks. "All hands! Brace for impact."

The blaze of radioactive light hurtled toward them, riding the crest of a sharp, boiling wave, a line of angry seawater that churned up and vaporized with the hot blast of a holocaust.

Ives stood at the captain's station staring helplessly out the window. He had no eye protection, but he knew from the depths of his clenched stomach that nothing would make any difference at the moment. So he stared and kept staring as the force slammed into them.

The last thing his eyes registered before his optic nerves surrendered to the onslaught was the sharp bow of his heavily armored Navy destroyer slumping, melting, as the steel plate vaporized.

Then the wall of light and fire swallowed the *Dallas* whole.

THIRTY-SEVEN

Enika Atoll
Saturday, 4:40 a.m.

In the sudden black chaos following the power outage in the blockhouse, Mulder grabbed one of the emergency flashlights mounted on the wall. He switched on the beam, shining it around the control bunker like a bright spear, hoping that its illumination would restore calm and order to the seamen and technicians there.

Instead, he witnessed Bear Dooley and the other Bright Anvil engineers scrambling around, blindly trying to rescue their subsystems.

"Somebody get that generator restarted!" Dooley roared. "We'll lose all our data if it's not up in half an hour."

Mulder shone the flashlight in a slow circle over the rest of the panicked bustle. He saw no apparent damage to the blockhouse itself. Scully stood beside him, holding on to his arm to keep them from being forced apart in the confusion.

"But we just checked the generator," one of the bedraggled sailors said. "It was working fine."

"Well it's not working fine now, and we don't have much time to fix it before Bright Anvil goes off. Get outside and check it out."

"Excuse me, Bear," Victor Ogilvy said, his thin voice quavering with anxiety. "I don't think it's just the generator."

Mulder shone the flashlight over toward him, and the bespectacled engineer held up the phone. "This phone is on the backup source, and it had a full charge—but I can't raise the *Dallas*. I can't even get a whisper of static. It's dead. Everything's dead. All the control panels, all power, even our secondary systems."

Mulder pulled his satellite-uplink cellular phone from his pocket, wondering if he could possibly get anything on that system. But the phone was a silent lump of plastic against his ear; he should have at least heard a hiss or the beep of an improper connection.

Dooley stood with his fists balled at his hips, suddenly overwhelmed. Mulder knew the big man had been just barely holding onto his composure.

"But what could drown everything out like that?" Dooley asked. "What sort of accident did this typhoon cause?"

"No accident," Miriel Bremen said in a calm, strong voice. "Bear, you know what can cause those effects."

"The *Dallas* reported something huge on its radar," Victor said. "With a high-energy signature."

Dooley swung his face toward Miriel, his expression open and lips trembling as uncertainty set in. "I don't know what you're talking about."

She looked squarely at him. The light from Mulder's flashlight reflected in the sheen of perspiration on her face. "Electromagnetic pulse," Miriel said.

"An EMP? But how? That would require a—" He suddenly looked at the protester in horror. "An air burst—a nuclear air burst! What if somebody else is using this hurricane as cover for another test? My God, I can't believe it. Somebody else detonated a device—that's what Captain Ives picked up on his radar. Somebody else is stealing our show!"

He spun around frantically, looking for something to grab, someone to tell. Victor Ogilvy cringed, as if afraid that Dooley would grasp him by the collar. "But who would do such a thing? The Russians? The Japanese? Who would have set off an air burst here? *Here* of all places. I can't believe it!"

"There may not be such a facile explanation," Miriel Bremen said coldly. The heartless conviction in her voice sent a shudder down Mulder's spine. Outside, the wind hissed past the cement-bag walls like water in a boiling cauldron. "It may not be something you can understand at all, Bear," she whispered.

"Don't try to spook me," Dooley shouted back at her. "I don't have time for it right now."

With Scully still grasping his arm, Mulder thought again of the story Ryan Kamida had told. Mulder himself had cobbled together an unlikely explanation from the unfolding tale and the bits of evidence he and Scully had collected.

"Hand me that flashlight, Agent Mulder," Dooley demanded. "I've got work to do. This is no time for a *kaffeeklatsch*," Mulder quickly handed over the light.

Behind him, Mulder heard the clank of a deadbolt being thrown, the click of the latch raising. Then the heavy armored door to the blockhouse blasted inward and the storm exploded into the confined chamber. Papers spiraled into the air on a whirlwind.

In the eerie light of the storm outside, Mulder saw a silhouetted form in the doorway, braced against the gale, pushing himself outside into the jaws of the typhoon.

Ryan Kamida had let himself out.

"It is time," he shouted back at them. "They're coming!" Then, as if drawn by an invisible chain, the blind man plunged away from the blockhouse into the ravening storm.

"Ryan, no!" Miriel Bremen screamed.

Kamida turned back toward her for just a moment before the winds and the darkness swallowed him up.

THIRTY-EIGHT

Enika Atoll
Saturday, 4:55 a.m.

"Don't just stand there," Bear Dooley squawked. "Get that damn door shut."

"Shouldn't we try to get that guy back in here?" one of the sailors yelled.

"You can't just leave Kamida out in the hurricane!" Scully cried, looking helplessly around her. "He'll be killed for certain."

The other team members appeared nervous, but Dooley only scowled. "He shouldn't have run out there in the first place," the big man answered petulantly. "We can't send out search teams now to save an idiot from his own stupidity. Our power is out. The Bright Anvil countdown is still going—and we don't get a second chance! Where are your priorities?"

Mulder watched as two Navy engineers wrestled with the heavy door, pressing their shoulders to it and shoving against the battering ram of wind. Silence fell like a stone in the darkened control blockhouse.

Miriel Bremen stared stricken at the doorway through which Kamida had just vanished. Mulder was surprised to see her standing rigid, holding on to one of the control racks for support. He thought she'd have argued to rescue her friend—but the protester said nothing, apparently resigned to his fate and terrified of her own. "It's what he wanted," she muttered.

The light from a new flashlight made a weird bobbing glow inside the blockhouse. Technicians scrambled to restore their equipment, to get the backup generator jump-started.

"How do we know the equipment out at the device is functioning?" Victor Ogilvy asked, blinking owlishly in the shadows and harsh light. "What if the countdown is frozen because of another dead battery? The EMP could have wiped out everything over there, too."

"We have no proof of any electromagnetic pulse," Scully said.

Dooley tugged at his hair in a comical gesture. "The device itself has a completely different power source, hardened against all accidents, rough weather—and even handling by Navy personnel," he said. "Bright Anvil is one robust sucker." He frowned at Victor. "If you don't believe me, how would you like to take a hike over there and check it out?"

"Uh, no thanks, Bear." The young redhead quickly found something else to do. But from the queasy expression on Dooley's face, Mulder knew that Victor had raised a question the bearded engineer would rather not have considered.

Distraught, Bear Dooley rounded on Miriel, seeking a target for his frustration. He put his face close to hers and yelled so vociferously that in the flickering light from the bobbing flashlight beams Mulder could see spittle flying from his lips. She flinched, but did not back away from him.

"This is your fault, Miriel," he said. "You came to Enika of your own free will, and I welcomed you—but you performed some kind of sabotage, didn't you? What did you do to the generators? How did you shut down all the power? You've been trying to stop this test since the very beginning.

"I thought you were at least honorable enough to be here and witness it with me for old time's sake—but now you've destroyed Bright Anvil, ruined everything. What did you do? Did you do something to Emil Gregory, too?"

"I did nothing," Miriel said. "Or maybe I didn't do enough. But we'll see. The Bright Anvil test will not take place—not this morning, not ever. It's out of my hands."

"See? You admit it," Dooley said, stabbing his finger at her. "What did you do? We have to get these diagnostics switched back on."

"Talk to Agent Mulder," Miriel said, her mouth a grim line above her long chin. "He's figured it out."

Mulder was surprised to hear her—a former weapons physicist—actually agreeing with his bizarre explanation for the events.

"So you're saying *he's* in it, too? He's not smart enough." Dooley's face crumpled into an expression of disgust, and he stormed away from her. "I want nothing more to do with you, Miriel. That's it. Emil would have been ashamed of you."

Miriel looked stung by the last comment, and her posture sagged, but still she held the edge of the control rack. "We're all going to be obliterated," she muttered. "The wave is coming, a flashfire, a wall of cleansing rage from the Enika ghosts. It's already hit the *Dallas*, and it'll be here next."

Mulder went to her side. "You knew about this? You knew it was going to happen?"

She nodded. "Ryan told me it would... but I have to admit—" She gave a short bitter laugh. "A good part of me never actually accepted it. Ryan can be very charismatic, though, and so I went along just to see what I could do to fight with more practical means. But now it's... it's just the way he said it would be."

She drew a heaving breath. "At least Bright Anvil's going to be stopped, one way or another. All the test material will be wiped out here, along with the project people. In the wake of this disaster, I doubt such a weapon will ever be developed again."

Miriel closed her eyes, and a strong tremor ran through her body like a seizure that quickly passed. "I suppose I always knew there would come a time when I'd have to test my convictions," she said. "It's easy to decide to volunteer and hand out leaflets or carry signs. It's harder to say that you're willing to get arrested during a protest: that's a line some people aren't willing to cross." She glanced sharply at Scully, who looked away. "But there are other lines farther down the path, more difficult still—and I think I just crossed another one."

Her eyes wide, Scully looked at Mulder and then at Miriel. "I can't believe what you're saying. You honestly think a cloud of atomic ghosts is going to come and stomp on the Bright Anvil test because they won't condone another nuclear explosion here?"

Miriel just looked at her without answering, and Scully let out a long sigh of disbelief. She turned to Mulder in exasperation.

"I think that's exactly what's going to happen, Scully," he said, surprising her. "I believe it. We're sitting ducks if we don't get away from here."

The three fishermen from the *Lucky Dragon* stood up, looking extremely agitated. "We don't want to stay here any longer," their leader said, waving his hands in front of him as if trying to recapture a spare portion of courage that flitted just out of reach. "This place is a deathtrap. It is a target. We're fools to stay here."

A second fisherman pleaded with Mulder, as if the FBI agent were in charge. "We want to take our chances, get back to our boat."

Scully said, "You can't go out in a boat in the middle of a hurricane. It's safer to stay here."

All three of the fishermen shook their heads vehemently. "No, it is not safer. This place is death."

Mulder said, "You told me yourself, Scully, that their boat's been heavily reinforced, designed to withstand travel through a heavy storm."

Miriel Bremen nodded. "Yes, Ryan wanted to make sure we could make it out here. But I don't know if he had any intention of going back. I don't think he did."

Bear Dooley stormed around, still looking for something to break. "Go on out in the storm—all of you—see if I care. Get away from me. We've got work to do. There's still a chance we can bring this test off. The device is on the other side of the island, and the countdown is going to proceed, whether or not we get these diagnostics up."

Mulder looked at Scully, and in his heart he felt an absolute certainty of what was going to happen—he realized it must be the same confidence that Miriel Bremen and some of the other protesters felt about their personal convictions. The fishermen went to the blockhouse door and worked the bolt to open it.

Dooley stood ranting at them. "You're all insane." Mulder knew that Scully probably agreed with him.

"Come on, Scully," Mulder gestured as he ran to the door. "You've got to go with us."

"Mulder, no!" she shouted, looking torn.

"Then at least help us rescue Mr. Kamida," he said. Her expression changed to one of sudden uncertainty.

The door finally blew open and the storm roared in—though the winds had already blown loose everything that it possibly could. Now, though, the voice of the whirlwind had a different quality, almost like human speech: wailing screams, whispering accusatory voices that lurked behind the gale, growing louder, coming closer.

Mulder's skin began to crawl, and he could see that Scully also felt the violent strangeness, though she probably wouldn't admit it.

With the fishermen beside him, Mulder stood at the threshold, nearly blown back by the storm's force. He looked out at the awesome clouds that hung like sledgehammers ready to pound the island. He could see that, far beyond the brooding presence of the typhoon, something terrible... truly terrible, was coming their way.

"By the pricking of my thumbs..." Mulder murmured.

Scully still resisted, but Mulder finally dragged her close enough to the door so that she could look out. She protested again until she stared into the night and looked up at the sky.

Then all her objections evaporated on her lips.

THIRTY-NINE

Enika Atoll
Saturday, 4:54 a.m.

The storm spoke to him in its power—dreadful voices against those others, welcoming whispers for him. At last.

Ryan Kamida was part of them, a member of their spectral group, yet he was the misfit. Not because he was blind or scarred, but because he was *alive.*

He staggered away from the control bunker, bumping into winds that punched him with the force of a catapult, driving him back—but still he ran. His feet slipped on the rough rock and sand that the gale flung up around him like shrapnel.

Kamida stumbled, fell to his hands and knees, felt his numb fingers digging into the cold, wet beach. He wanted to let it suck him down, to draw him into the sand to become one with the ashes of his people, a part of the scarred atoll.

"I'm here!" he shouted.

The typhoon howled, and the voices of the ghosts grew louder, urging him on. He got up and ran again. A blast of rain-sodden wind with battering-ram strength snatched up his body, yanking his feet off the ground. He flailed his arms and legs in the air, floating like a ghost himself—but it was too soon. It was not completely finished yet.

Kamida fought the chains of the hurricane until his lungs were about to burst. His heart wanted to stop beating from sheer exhaustion, but he plunged ahead, seeking release to join his family, his people—those unseen companions who had appeared to him for decades.

Kamida called out to them wordlessly, trying to make his mouth form words in the tongue he had known as a child but had not spoken aloud in forty years. It didn't matter how well he formed the language, because the spirits would understand him. They knew.

They were coming.

High up on the beach, Kamida tripped over the barrel left there by the fishermen. Instinctively, unerringly, he had found his way to the metal drum filled with the ashes of his tribe, those bits of charred flesh he had painstakingly separated from the coral and the sand of the atoll.

He embraced the barrel, holding it tightly, pressing his cheek against the curved, rain-slick metal that felt cool even against his insensitive scarred skin. He held onto it as if it were an anchor, sobbing, as the hurricane roared around him.

The eerie whispers and screams behind the wind grew louder and louder, drowning out even the storm in the congealing mass of clouds overhead. Ryan Kamida could feel the power growing in the accusing eye of the hurricane—a static electricity, a surge of energy.

Kamida raised his face up to feel the rain evaporating, the bright heat caressing his skin.

Though he was blind, he somehow knew that in the clouds around the island a searing light was building to a white-hot intensity—growing brighter as the countdown for Bright Anvil continued to zero.

FORTY

Enika Atoll
Saturday, 5:10 a.m.

Facing into the storm, it was Mulder's turn to keep hold of Scully's arm, to be sure they wouldn't lose each other. They staggered through the blinding rain and clawing that threatened tear their small group apart.

The three fishermen led the way, pushing forward one step at a time, heads down, making their way toward the sheltered lagoon. The high coral outcropping behind the beehive bunker absorbed the brunt of the violence from across the island. Still, the wind was so heavy that it pelted them mercilessly with stinging sand and rocks.

Mulder could not see Ryan Kamida anywhere.

"Mulder, this is crazy!" Scully shouted.

"I know!" he said, but kept going.

As they worked their way along, his own doubts asserted themselves: it was absurd and illogical to go out into such a storm. "Suicidal" was more likely the term Scully would have used—but given the situation, logical alternatives were in short supply, and she must have trusted Mulder enough to follow him. She could see with her own eyes the incomprehensible disaster about to strike. He hoped he wouldn't let her down.

Miriel Bremen plodded beside them, stunned, yet willing to escape—not so ready after all to die for her cause that she would give up this last chance to getaway.

"No matter what else you believe, Mulder," Scully had to yell in his ear just to be heard, "the Bright Anvil device is going to go off in a few minutes! If we don't get far enough away, we'll be caught in that shockwave."

"I know, Scully—I know!" But his words were whisked away by the storm, and he didn't think she heard him. He turned to look at the craggy outline of the black uplift behind the blockhouse. The Bright Anvil device was out of sight in its shallow cove on the far side of the island.

The fishermen began shouting, their calls barely discernible in the ripping gale. Beyond the winds, the eerie voicelike chorus echoed, rising to a bone-jarring crescendo within the fabric of the air itself.

The rain and the gloom and the stinging sand made it difficult to see anything. Mulder couldn't locate the reinforced fishing boat where they had left it anchored. For a moment he was terrified that their only chance at escape had been swept away from the lagoon, that they were all stranded and doomed on Enika Atoll without even the uncertain protection of Bear Dooley's control blockhouse.

But a moment later he realized why the fishermen were shouting. Two of them waded out into the churning lagoon to where the winds had dragged the *Lucky Dragon* into deeper water.

The lead fisherman swung himself aboard, grabbing handholds and climbing the wet rocking hull to reach the deck. He helped his companions get aboard, and they gestured for the others to wade out to them.

Scully hesitated at the shore. "Mulder—"

"Come on in, the water's fine," he yelled and pulled her forward into the lagoon without a thought to their waterlogged shoes. "Don't be afraid to get wet! Remember, this is our vacation!"

The rain had already drenched them to the skin, and there was no sense in delaying now. Whether or not Scully believed in the supernatural danger of ghosts from the Sawtooth blast, the Bright Anvil warhead was due to detonate on the far side of the atoll. They certainly didn't have much time.

Miriel, still silent, waded beside them until they all reached the fishing boat. She scrambled onto the deck of the *Lucky Dragon* ahead of them, like a cat climbing a tree.

One fisherman ran to the deckhouse and started the engines; Mulder felt the vibrations through the boat's hull, more than he actually heard the sound. While the second fisherman ran to disengage the anchor and free the *Lucky Dragon* from its perilous mooring, the third man helped haul Mulder and Scully to safety aboard.

Before Mulder could make sure that his partner had gotten her balance, the fishing boat's powerful engines spun it about, churning up a waterspout of spray as the *Lucky Dragon* headed directly into the heart of the hurricane. Mulder grabbed the deck rail next to Scully and Miriel and held on for dear life.

Turning back to look toward the island, Mulder shouted, "Up there, Scully!" He gestured toward the crackling sky. "That's no ordinary storm!"

The clouds glowed and hissed and boiled with weird energy that made all the hairs on his arms and neck stand up. He glanced at his watch. Any moment now for Bright Anvil. Any moment now—and it would all be over, one way or another.

The boat crashed away from the atoll, threading through the rabid whitecaps that foamed around the treacherous reefs near the surface. The fisherman at the controls guided the vessel, swerving from side to side, searching for a safe passage.

Finally, the waters opened up, deeper and bluer even in the storm's gloom. The engine roared with renewed power, and the *Lucky Dragon* lurched ahead.

Mulder looked out to sea, but could find no trace of the huge Navy destroyer, the *Dallas*. He saw only a roiling froth that could have been a secondary maelstrom caused by the hurricane itself… or it might have been the sinking remnants of a massive shipwreck.

Then, with a searing flash, a small sun came up on the far side of the island. It rose hot and yellow, blasting back the hurricane for just a moment….

"It's Bright Anvil," Scully said. "Cover your eyes!"

"So, the thing worked," Miriel Bremen said in a stunned voice, just loud enough to be heard. She didn't bother to avert her gaze.

Strangely, the Bright Anvil blast seemed to act as a catalyst for that other force lurking within the hurricane clouds. With the test detonation, the eerie brightness increased a thousandfold, dropping out of the mass of thunderheads.

A brilliant ball of supernova fire plunged like a spectral blast, knotting itself into the chillingly familiar yet horrifying shape of a mushroom cloud. But the image was distorted and surreal, a seething soup of skulls and faces, screaming mouths, burned eye sockets—an unstoppable molten battering ram that swooped down on the rising blaze from Bright Anvil.

A smothering blanket of caustic fire engulfed the far-smaller test blast, crushed it, subsuming the new light in its blinding supernatural fire… and *drew* on the power. It became stronger, more animated.

"Look," Scully said, pointing toward the rapidly receding Enika shore. Terrified, the fishermen increased the power of their engines, roaring through the high whitecaps, away from the vengeful atomic ghosts… and into the typhoon.

Even from that distance, Mulder could make out the small form of a lone figure high up on the beach.

"That's Ryan," Miriel said in dismay.

The blind man was standing on top of a metal drum—the barrel of ashes that had been removed from the *Lucky Dragon*—waving his hands toward the skies in a summoning gesture. Mulder had seen similar movements before—they reminded him of a traffic controller.

Ryan Kamida was guiding the blinding apparition.

Like a living thing with a purpose, the crackling, blazing swarm of atomic victims swept over the surface of Enika Atoll. The radioactive backwash incinerated the jungle that had regrown in forty years and vaulted the high coral mound that had shielded the control blockhouse.

"Do you see it, Scully?" Mulder said in absolute awe and astonishment. *"Do you see it?"*

Growing brighter in the blaze of a chain reaction of unleashed nuclear fire, the echo mushroom cloud rushed across the island, plunging down on the sheltered side with enough force to make Mulder shield his eyes and back away. The fury increased, vaporizing coral, turning rock into lava....

As the *Lucky Dragon* continued its race into the hurricane, the vengeful blaze on the atoll reached a fever pitch—and the bone-chilling screams became more distinct in the wind. The skeletal, phantom faces blurred, swirled together, a mixture of light and shadow. Then another voice joined theirs.

Mulder thought he could recognize the voice of Ryan Kamida; his own triumphant shout joining with those of his family and his people, bound together in one primal, coalescent force—a force whose mission had now been accomplished.

The glow died away on Enika Atoll, leaving it sterile and barren, simmering with residual heat and scoured clean of all life. The *Lucky Dragon* shot onward into the fury of the storm.

FORTY-ONE

Western Pacific Ocean, Exact Location Unknown
Saturday, Late Morning

Mulder's watch had stopped, but he suspected it had more to do with the harsh treatment and drenching it had received than with any sort of paranormal phenomena. He couldn't tell what time of the day it was, other than late morning. Already the tropical heat in the typhoon's aftermath felt oppressive, pounding down on the *Lucky Dragon*.

The fishing boat looked as if it had been vandalized by a street gang. Every visible surface was scored or scraped, two front windows were smashed, a few deck rails bent, the hull scarred from scraping debris—but somehow the vessel had survived the pummeling. They had fought against the wall of the typhoon for several hellish hours, struggling farther and farther from the aftermath of Bright Anvil, until they had somehow skirted the edge of the wind wall and escaped into the blessedly clear seas beyond.

The *Lucky Dragon* had taken on a good deal of water, and the three fishermen took turns bailing out the cargo hold, though Mulder thought they worked more out of a need for something to do than because the sturdy boat was actually in danger.

At the rear of the vessel, Miriel Bremen kept to herself, brooding, like a broken doll. She had lost her eyeglasses sometime in the frantic push toward the boat, or during the whipping storm, and she blinked into the sun, unable to focus. She didn't talk much. Scully tried to comfort her, attempting to strike up a conversation, but the protester was obviously in shock, overwhelmed by what she had seen.

Sitting out on the deck in the sun, Mulder wore his rumpled suit jacket as protection against the baking rays, though the heat was nearly intolerable. He wished he had unpacked at least one of his Hawaiian shirts, his swimsuit, or—at the very least—his suntan lotion. Now they were all lost. Water still trickled off the deck and stood in briny pools reflecting the sunshine.

In a morbid moment, he considered the grim possibility that the six of them might never be rescued, that someone would eventually find a ghost ship bearing their skeletons drifting alone in the Pacific, rather like the *Mary Celeste*. The scenario had a certain creepy irony to it. It would be a fitting end to this bizarre adventure.

He pulled out his notebook and a waterlogged pen that managed to produce a trail of spotty ink after he shook it several times and scribbled on a sheet of paper. Concisely, Mulder summarized the things he had seen and outlined his hypothesis. At least would-be rescuers would find that much information, if nothing else.

If they ever managed to get back to Washington, D.C., he would type up his full report, create a detailed X-File—and in all likelihood, no one would believe him. He had gotten used to that. In this instance, however, he had numerous eyewitness accounts, pieces of evidence, radioactive bodies, not to mention a secret nuclear test. Once Brigadier General Bradoukis knew that the vengeful Enika ghosts were no longer a threat, he might be willing to stand up for Mulder's work.

Scully came up beside him in the bow and bent down to see what he was doing. She had tied her hair back, and her skin already showed the pinkish flush of sunburn. "You should keep to the shade, Scully," he said. "That's no way to get a good tan."

She squatted down next to him. "What are you writing?"

"Oh, you know," he said, "I neglected to buy a postcard on Enika for Assistant Director Skinner, and I thought this would be the next-best thing. I wouldn't want him to think we forgot about him on our tropical vacation."

She frowned. "You're still convinced this all was caused by a cluster of spectral phantoms seeking revenge for nuclear tests conducted forty years ago, aren't you?"

He looked at her curiously. "Scully, you saw what I saw."

"Mulder, I saw a bright flash in the sky. You heard Bear Dooley when all the power went out—he said that some other government must be attempting the same thing he was trying to do, only they did an air burst, using the same hurricane for cover."

"Sounds like quite a coincidence, don't you think?" Mulder asked.

"I'll believe in coincidences before I go looking for supernatural answers to every unexplained occurrence."

Mulder just shook his head, wondering why, after all the adventures they'd had together and all the evidence she had seen, Scully couldn't just accept it. But then, she didn't *want* to believe, as he did.

"Any luck with the radio yet?" he said, changing the subject.

"No, it was damaged in the storm. We haven't been able to raise anyone. The batteries are wet."

Mulder pulled out his cellular phone. "I think I'll try nine-one-one again. The storm must be dissipating by now, wherever it is."

Scully looked at him, shaking her head at his optimism. She extended a sunburned hand to indicate the endless horizon of blue waters stretched out in all directions. "Who do you expect to reach way out here?"

"Oh I don't know," he said, "maybe another atomic ghost, a Russian spy ship... maybe even the *Love Boat*. You never can tell." He punched buttons over and over, sending signal after signal. Using all the access codes he carried in his excellent memory, adding a few Scully knew, he tried every general emergency number, federal operator, and military extension they could come up with.

Finally, to his utter surprise, someone answered.

"You have reached the United States Missile Tracking and Testing Station on Kwajalein Island." The voice was gruff and robotic. "This is a restricted number. Please get off the line."

Mulder sat up quickly, almost dropping the phone overboard in his surprise. "Hello, hello?"

"I repeat, this is a restricted number—"

"This is United States Federal Agent Fox Mulder with an emergency distress call out in... out in the Western Pacific somewhere. I don't know my exact position. I think we're near the Marshall Islands—well, we *were*, anyway."

"Are you requesting assistance?" the deep voice came back. "You should not be on this channel. Please try the appropriate contact numbers."

In exasperation Mulder said, "Then send someone out here to arrest us for using your number! I'm with the Federal Bureau of Investigation, and yes, we are definitely in need of rescue. Six of us barely survived the typhoon—there may be many people injured or missing at Enika Atoll. A group of scientists as well as a Navy destroyer, the USS *Dallas*, may have sustained severe damage. There's a strong possibility of many deaths. We urgently need assistance. Please respond." He glanced up at Scully. Her eyes were bright. "Can you home in on my signal, Kwajalein?"

"We're a *tracking station*, Agent Mulder. Of course we can find you," came the answer. "We'll send a cutter out as soon as possible."

Mulder grinned broadly as Scully reached out to shake his hand in congratulation. He was already scanning the sun-bathed field of ocean, as if a rescue ship would appear any second.

He looked down at the phone in his hands. "Think I should have made that a collect call?"

FORTY-TWO

FBI Headquarters
Washington, D.C.
Tuesday, 2:06 p.m.

The FBI Headquarters building in Washington, D.C., was a concrete-and-glass monstrosity that someone had considered "modern architecture" in decades past. Because it housed the Federal Bureau of Investigation, the unattractive building had been dubbed "the Puzzle Palace."

Scratching at patches of dry skin from her peeling sunburn, Agent Dana Scully sat at her computer terminal in her small cubicle. She was relieved to be back in Washington, D.C.—for a few days, at least. She couldn't count on staying home for any length of time, and so she spent whatever free hours she could scrape together assembling her notes for submittal to the assistant director.

Going through the familiar motions, tidying up the details, usually helped her to resolve the case in her mind, to sift through the questions and line up explanations, putting any remaining uncertainties to rest.

Scully sipped another cup of coffee—cream, no sugar—enjoying the taste of fresh-brewed, the first decent cup she'd had in a good many days. She rummaged through her notes, scanned another sheet of paper, double-checked a press release, and went back to her typing.

```
    The U.S. Navy has released information that the Spru-
ance-class destroyer, the USS Dallas, sank due to the
unexpectedly severe force of the typhoon that struck
the Marshall Islands early Saturday rooming. All hands
on board were lost. According to the National weather
Service, this hurricane was one of the most unusual
such storms on record, both for its odd and unpredictable
motion, and for its unexpected intensity, particularly
within the vicinity of Enika Atoll. Meteorologists who
have analyzed satellite imagery of the storm system at
the time it struck the atoll are still unable to
explain its behavior.
    Rescue teams arriving at Enika in response to Agent
Mulder's distress call found no survivors among the
members of the Bright Anvil team. The reinforced
control blockhouse had been sheared from its foundations;
```

as the attached photographs show. No bodies were recovered, which the Navy notes is not surprising, considering
the incredible force of the storm.

She paused to stare at the glowing screen, shaking her head.

Morale at the Teller Nuclear Research Facility in
Pleasanton, California, reportedly has been shaken by
this disaster. The loss of so many employees is
completely unprecedented. The only comparable incident
in the facility's history occurred when a small aircraft
crashed en route to the Nevada Test Site in 1978.

Curiously, DOE representative Rosabeth Carrera at
the Teller Facility released an official report that
the team of scientists on Enika was conducting a
"hydrologic survey of ocean currents around the reef."
From my personal knowledge of these events, however, it
is clear that the statement is blatantly false. I
recommend that little credence be given to such explanations. I suspect more accurate details are available
in certain classified files.

After another long sip of coffee, Scully reread what she had written and was
surprised at her open skepticism over the official story. That wasn't what the
oversight committee wanted to hear. But Scully knew about Bright Anvil and
the test, no matter who wanted to cover it up. She could not report otherwise
in her writeup.

Scully paged through her notes again and continued with her report.

\\\\\\\\\\\\\\\\\\\

Assistant Director Skinner held open the door of his office. "Come in,
Agent Mulder," he said. The lights in the office had been switched off, killing
the garish fluorescent glare and letting the bright afternoon sunshine provide
all the illumination he needed.

"Thank you, sir," Mulder said and entered the room, setting his briefcase
down on the wooden desk. Framed portraits of the president and the attorney
general hung on the wall, staring down at him.

This place held unpleasant memories for him. Mulder had been called on
the carpet many times before for insisting on explanations the Bureau didn't

want to consider, for prying the lid off details that other people wished to keep hidden. Skinner had often found himself in an uncomfortable position in the middle, between a persistent Mulder and the shadowy string-pullers who refused to be identified.

Skinner closed the door behind him. He took off his glasses and polished the lenses on a handkerchief. Beads of sweat speckled his bald head. Mulder noticed that the office was quite warm.

"Air-conditioning's not working again," Skinner said, by way of a cordial opening to the conversation. "You didn't get much of a tan in your travels, Agent Mulder—first to California, then New Mexico, then out to the South Seas."

"I was on duty, sir," Mulder said. "No time for sunbathing. Not during the typhoon, at least."

Skinner looked down at the handwritten notes torn from Mulder's damp notebook. Mulder had promised to type them up later, when he got the chance, but the assistant director held the crumpled sheets of paper with a weary look on his face.

"Don't bother with a more formal report, Agent Mulder," he said. "I can't submit this to my superiors."

"Then I'll write it up for my own use," Mulder answered. "And place it in an X-File."

"That's your choice, of course," Skinner said, "but it's a waste of time."

"How can that be, sir? These are events I witnessed with my own eyes."

Skinner looked hard at him. "You realize you have no corroborating evidence for any of these explanations? Neither the Navy nor the Teller Nuclear Research Facility accepts your scenario. As usual, you've handed me a report filled with wild speculation that is proof of nothing except your superior ability to concoct supernatural explanations for events that have rational causes."

"Maybe there aren't always rational causes," Mulder said.

"Agent Scully usually manages to come up with them."

"Agent Scully has her own opinions," Mulder said, "and while I respect her entirely as my partner and as an FBI field agent, I don't always agree one hundred percent with her conclusions."

Skinner sat down, frustrated and not sure what to do with his recalcitrant agent. "And she doesn't always agree with yours either. But somehow you two manage to work together."

Mulder pushed forward in the hard wooden chair. "You must have contacted General Bradoukis at the Pentagon, sir. He can corroborate many of the events that I've described in these notes. He knows about Bright Anvil. He knows about the ghosts. He sent us out there because he feared for his own life."

Skinner fixed Mulder with a sharp gaze. The sunlit windows reflected off the lenses of his glasses. "General Bradoukis has been reassigned," he said. "He can no longer be reached for comment through the Pentagon, and his current whereabouts are classified. I believe he's participating in a new experimental test program."

"How convenient," Mulder said. "Don't you think that's a little odd, the one person officially involved in this entire business? Didn't General Bradoukis provide details when he contacted you about our assignment to the Marshall Islands?"

Skinner frowned. "I received a phone call from the Pentagon, Agent Mulder—but the man refused to give his name. He did, however, submit the proper authorization code. When the Pentagon requested that I approve your travel, I did so. I don't know any General Bradoukis."

"That's funny—he claimed he knew you," Mulder said.

"I don't know any General Bradoukis," Skinner repeated.

"Of course not, sir," Mulder said.

"And about this entire secret nuclear test, this 'Bright Anvil' you keep mentioning—I don't want to see anything about it in your official report. Aboveground nuclear weapons tests have been banned by treaty since 1963."

"I know that, and you know that," Mulder agreed. "But nobody seems to have mentioned it to the Bright Anvil team."

"I did some digging before I contacted you about our meeting this morning. I spoke directly with Ms. Rosabeth Carrera, enough to learn that there are no records of any project named Bright Anvil. Everyone I've talked to denies even the possibility of a 'fallout-free nuclear weapon' or that one was ever under development. They say it's scientifically impossible." Skinner nodded as if satisfied with this development.

"Yeah, so I've heard. And I suppose you believe that Dr. Emil Gregory, one of this country's preeminent nuclear weapons scientists, was in charge of a project to map ocean currents and temperatures around the reefs in the Marshall Islands? That's what the official story says."

"That's not my business, Agent Mulder."

Mulder stood up from his chair. "What I would like to know, sir, is exactly what happened to Miriel Bremen? We haven't seen her since she was rescued along with us. We were separated on the transport plane that brought us back to the States. Her home phone has been disconnected, and a nurse at the hospital where we were treated claims that she departed under guard with two men in military uniforms. Miriel can corroborate our story."

"Agent Mulder," Skinner said, "Dr. Miriel Bremen has agreed to assist in recreating some of the work of Dr. Emil Gregory. Since she is the only surviving link to his project, she has decided to cooperate with the Department of Defense so that his developments aren't lost."

Mulder was astonished. "She would never agree to that."

"She already has," Skinner replied.

"Can I speak to her?" Mulder said. "I'd like to hear that from her lips."

"I'm afraid that's impossible, Agent Mulder. She's been taken to a secluded think tank. They're quite anxious to get some of the work back on track, and they don't want her distracted by any unpleasant interruptions."

"In other words, she's being held against her will and coerced to work on something she vowed never to touch again."

"Like studying ocean currents? Agent Mulder, you're being paranoid again."

"Am I?" he said. "I know Miriel was facing numerous felony counts of sabotage, trespass, even suspicion of murder. I'm sure the offer of dropping all those criminal charges could be very persuasive in getting her to cooperate."

"That's not my department, Agent Mulder," Skinner said.

"Don't you even care?" he asked Skinner. He stood up and placed his hands on the edge of the assistant director's desk. He didn't know what he expected for an answer.

Skinner shrugged. "You're the only one who doesn't accept the official explanation, Agent Mulder."

Mulder reached over to retrieve his handwritten notes, knowing they would do no good if he left them there in Skinner's office.

"I guess that's always been my problem," he said, and then left.

\\\\\\\\\\\\\\\\\\\

After pacing the room and pulling her thoughts together, Scully continued her report. She sat down, stretched her fingers, and began typing again.

The events I witnessed as we departed from Enika Atoll on the fishing boat, the *Lucky Dragon*, can best be explained as the air-burst testing of another nuclear device, undertaken by a government or governments unknown. It must also be remembered that through the darkness of the hurricane, the heavy downpour, and high winds, precise details were difficult to ascertain visually.

From my personal observations, I can attest to the fact that the Bright Anvil test device did detonate at approximately the time scheduled, though I have no way of determining the magnitude of this blast or the efficacy of its supposedly fallout-free design.

However, according to reports from the rescue team, measurements of residual radioactivity on the island were listed as well within normal levels. This information has not been confirmed.

She skipped a few lines. On to the next part, the hardest part.

As to the bizarre deaths of the two other victims clearly involved in the Bright Anvil project—Dr. Emil Gregory and Department of Energy administrator Nancy Scheck—the explanation remains vague. The deaths of Scheck and Gregory might be attributable to a brief but intense nuclear accident involving unspecified equipment developed for the test program.

Spread out on her desk lay the gruesome black-and-white photographs of the victims, burned corpses contorted into black scarecrows. Neatly typed autopsy reports were tucked away in manila folders beside the photos.

It remains unclear whether any connection exists to three similar deaths caused by extreme heat and exposure to high levels of radiation—Oscar McCarron, a rancher from Alamogordo, New Mexico, and Captains Mesta and Louis inside the Minuteman III missile bunker at Vandenberg Air Force Base. The similarity of circumstances implies a relationship between these events, but the specific cause of such a powerful and deadly nuclear accident, the origin and types of any equipment involved, and how it might have been transported to such diverse places remains unexplained.

Unsatisfied, Scully looked at the words on her screen. She read them over and over again, but could think of nothing more to say. She was still not comfortable with her path of logic and her hand-waving explanations, but she decided that enough was enough.

Scully stored the document, then printed out a copy for delivery to her superiors. It was sufficient to close the file, for now.

She switched off her computer and walked out of the office.

END